Lytton Strachey
and the Search
for Modern Sexual Identity
The Last Eminent Victorian

HAWORTH Gay & Lesbian Studies
John P. De Cecco, PhD
Editor in Chief

One of the Boys: Masculinity, Homophobia, and Modern Manhood by David Plummer

Homosexual Rites of Passage: A Road to Visibility and Validation by Marie Mohler

Male Lust: Pleasure, Power, and Transformation edited by Kerwin Kay, Jill Nagle, and Baruch Gould

Tricks and Treats: Sex Workers Write About Their Clients edited by Matt Bernstein Sycamore

A Sea of Stories: The Shaping Power of Narrative in Gay and Lesbian Cultures— A Festschrift for John P. De Cecco edited by Sonya Jones

Out of the Twilight: Fathers of Gay Men Speak by Andrew R. Gottlieb

The Mentor: A Memoir of Friendship and Gay Identity by Jay Quinn

Male to Male: Sexual Feeling Across the Boundaries of Identity by Edward J. Tejirian

Straight Talk About Gays in the Workplace, Second Edition by Liz Winfeld and Susan Spielman

The Bear Book II: Further Readings in the History and Evolution of a Gay Male Subculture edited by Les Wright

Gay Men at Midlife: Age Before Beauty by Alan L. Ellis

Being Gay and Lesbian in a Catholic High School: Beyond the Uniform by Michael Maher

Finding a Lover for Life: A Gay Man's Guide to Finding a Lasting Relationship by David Price

The Man Who Was a Woman and Other Queer Tales from Hindu Lore by Devdutt Pattanaik

How Homophobia Hurts Children: Nurturing Diversity at Home, at School, and in the Community by Jean M. Baker

The Harvey Milk Institute Guide to Lesbian, Gay, Bisexual, Transgender, and Queer Internet Research edited by Alan Ellis, Liz Highleyman, Kevin Schaub, and Melissa White

Stories of Gay and Lesbian Immigration: Together Forever? by John Hart

From Drags to Riches: The Untold Story of Charles Pierce by John Wallraff

Lytton Strachey and the Search for Modern Sexual Identity: The Last Eminent Victorian by Julie Anne Taddeo

Before Stonewall: Activists for Gay and Lesbian Rights in Historical Context edited by Vern L. Bullough

Lytton Strachey
and the Search
for Modern Sexual Identity
The Last Eminent Victorian

Julie Anne Taddeo, PhD

Routledge
Taylor & Francis Group

NEW YORK AND LONDON

First Published by

Harrington Park Press®, an imprint of The Haworth Press, Inc., 10 Alice Street, Binghamton, NY 13904-1580.

Transferred to Digital Printing 2011 by Routledge
711 Third Avenue, New York, NY 10017
2 Park Square, Milton Park, Abingdon, Oxon, OX14 4RN

Copyright acknowledgments can be found on p. ix.

Cover design by Jennifer M. Gaska.

Front cover painting: Henry Lamb; 1883-1960. Portrait of Lytton Strachey, Oil on canvas; 1914. © Tate, London.

Library of Congress Cataloging-in-Publication Data

Taddeo, Julie Anne.
    Lytton Strachey and the search for modern sexual identity : the last eminent Victorian / Julie Anne Taddeo.
       p. cm.
    Includes bibliographical references and index.
    ISBN 1-56023-358-3 (alk. paper) — ISBN 1-56023-359-1 (pbk. : alk. paper)
      1. Strachey, Lytton, 1880-1932. 2. Homosexuality—Great Britain—History—20th century. 3. Authors, English—20th century—Biography. 4. Biographers—Great Britain—Biography. 5. Modernism (Literature)—Great Britain. 6. Critics—Great Britain—Biography. 7. Gay men—Great Britain—Biography. I. Title.

PR6037 .T73 Z87 2002
828' .91209—dc21

                                        2001051594

CONTENTS

ABOUT THE AUTHOR

Julie Anne Taddeo, PhD, has been teaching modern British and European history and women's studies at Temple University in Philadelphia since 1996. She has also taught at the University of Rochester and St. John Fisher College. Dr. Taddeo has published articles on Strachey, Bloomsbury, and sexuality in the *Journal of the History of Sexuality* and in the anthology *Un-Manning Modernism: Gendered Re-Readings,* and has also published an article on the mysteries of Anne Perry in *Clues.* She has presented at numerous conferences and has contributed to forthcoming anthologies on British history and women's studies. She is a member of the American Historical Association, the American Association of University Women, the New York State Association of European Historians, and the Upstate New York Women's History Organization.

Preface and Acknowledgments

This work, as with the first publications of most academics, began as the subject of my doctoral dissertation. I discovered Lytton Strachey in a graduate seminar when a colleague suggested that, since I was interested in gender, I might want to study Virginia Woolf. As the once forgotten but now overly documented female modernist, Virginia Woolf did introduce me to Strachey through a series of letters between the two Bloomsbury modernists. Immediately I discovered that it was Strachey who posed the greater challenge to feminist scholars. From a family of suffragists, a homosexual and neurasthenic, and a writer in the tradition of Oscar Wilde, Strachey seemed the perfect champion of a brand of modernism that was essentially feminist and sexually liberating. Upon a closer reading of his thousands of letters and his journals, I discovered a very different man. Caught in the transition from the old world of the Victorians to the new world of post–World War I England, Strachey believed he was hastening the demise of his "repellent ancestors." Yet, so much of his writings, both private and those intended for publication, reinforced Victorian stereotypes and definitions of class and gender. His story is simply that—his story; I make no claim that Strachey is representative of all male homosexual intellectuals, but his story can tell those of us interested in issues of masculinity, homosexuality, modernism, and cultural history about the struggles even the so-called rebels endured as they tried to create new types of art and identity. This study is not an attempt to write his biography, a project previously done in great detail and beauty by Michael Holroyd, but it does examine Strachey's life as a way to understand some of the issues concerning his generation of Cambridge and Bloomsbury colleagues, and how they battled the Victorian ideology, often without success.

Each of the chapters can almost be read as a separate essay. I examine Strachey's role at Cambridge before World War I and how he created his version of homosexuality out of the Victorian tradition of male romantic friendship. His version, though on the surface liberating and playful, eventually led to conflict and great unhappiness for

Strachey as he pursued a constraining notion of Ideal Love. The next chapters look at Strachey's relations with the British Empire, as he constructed a rich fantasy life that rested on racial and class differences, and then his friendships and professional rivalries with the women of Bloomsbury. These relationships call into question his own feminism as well as raise concerns about his marginal status as a homosexual in the post-Wildean era. Last, I try to link Strachey's life and work to the larger movement of English modernism, and how his use of sexuality, androgyny, and history defined, yet also undermined, his brand of modernism.

This project has been assisted at various stages by the kindness and generosity of several individuals. While a student at the University of Rochester, most of my primary research was funded by grants from the university and the Susan B. Anthony Institute for Women's Studies. The Bernadotte E. Schmitt Grant of the American Historical Association provided additional funding for travel and research. In England, I was helped by Sally Brown and a wonderful, efficient staff at the British Library; Jackie Cox, the curator of the Keynes's Papers at King's College, Cambridge University; and Elizabeth Inglis, curator of the Monks House Leonard Woolf Papers at University of Sussex, as well as librarians Deborah Shorley and Dorothy Sheridan. I want to acknowledge the Society of Authors as agents of the Strachey Trust for permission to cite from these papers, as well as those held by The Berg Collection of English and American Literature at the New York Public Library and the Raymond H. Taylor Collection at Princeton University. I owe a special debt of gratitude to Jeremy Crow of the Society of Authors for his assistance in locating and obtaining copyright permissions. Michael Holroyd graciously met with me and encouraged yet another study of Lytton Strachey, while Barbara Caine, whose own research on the Strachey family promises to shed further light on this very Victorian, yet also so modern, family, provided useful information on certain Strachey letters.

My advisers at Rochester, Bonnie G. Smith, Stewart Weaver, and William McGrath, provided useful commentary and criticisms, and Seth Koven at Villanova University constantly pushed me to ask new and "sexier" questions about Strachey's sexuality. Colleagues William Peniston, George Robb, and Alexandra Lord encouraged me to publish this work and engaged me in numerous discussions of male sexuality.

On a personal note, I want to acknowledge the support of my parents, Joseph and Josephine Taddeo; my sister, Laura Taddeo; cousin JoAnn D'Angelo; and good friend Karen Brankacz, who listened to drafts, attended conferences, taught me computer skills, looked up bibliographic resources, and offered encouragement and pastries. Also, my thanks to Paulo Bedaque, who for the past ten years has been my constant companion and friend, reader and critic, and, to quote Strachey, my "glimpse of heaven."

Final thanks to The Haworth Press, especially to Rebecca Browne, Amy Rentner, and Peg Marr, who answered my numerous inquiries, and to my editor Dr. John DeCecco. I am grateful to Haworth for taking an interest in my research and encouraging other new scholars in the field of sexuality, literature, and history.

COPYRIGHT ACKNOWLEDGMENTS

Some of the material in Chapter 1 was previously published as "Plato's Apostles: Edwardian Cambridge and the 'New Style of Love,'" in the *Journal of the History of Sexuality*, 8(2), pp. 196-228. Copyright 1997 by the University of Texas Press. All rights reserved.

A segment of Chapter 4 appeared as "A Modernist Romance? Lytton Strachey and the Women of Bloomsbury," in *Unmanning Modernism: Gendered Re-Readings*, pp. 133-152, edited by Elizabeth Jane Harrison and Shirley Peterson. Copyright 1997 by the University of Tennessee Press.

Unpublished writings of J.M. Keynes and G. Lowes Dickinson copyright The Provost and Scholars of King's College, Cambridge, 2002.

Quotations from correspondence between Lytton Strachey and Leonard Woolf used with permission of The Society of Authors on behalf of the Strachey Trust, as well as the Berg Collection of English and American Literature, The New York Public Library, Astor, Lenox and Tilden Foundations. Strachey-Woolf letters contained in the Leonard Woolf Papers, Special Collections, University of Sussex, reproduced with permission of the Librarian, University of Sussex.

Material from *The Diary of Virginia Woolf*, edited by Anne Olivier Bell; *The Letters of Virginia Woolf*, edited by Nigel Nicolson and Joanne Trautmann; and *Virginia Woolf: Moments of Being*, edited by Jeanne Schulkind, all published by Hogarth Press, copyright 1980, 1975, and 1976, respectively, by Quentin

Quoted material from David Garnett used with permission of A.P. Watt, Ltd., as agent for Richard Garnett.

Last, I would like to mention that I attempted, without success, to locate the copyright holders for letters quoted from the following: Gerald Shove; A.R. Ainsworth; Dadie Rylands; Harry Norton; Arthur Hobhouse; James Doggart; Bernard Swithinbank; Max Beerbohm; and Philippa, Pernel, Marjorie, and Oliver Strachey. Most of these are held by the British Library, and if anyone has information, the author would appreciate the opportunity to correct this omission.

Introduction

"I don't know whether I'm hopelessly classical or simply out-of-date."[1] On the eve of his death Lytton Strachey looked back on his literary career with regret and self-reproach. Though at the center of England's Bloomsbury Group, he envied and failed to compete with his more prolific colleagues E. M. Forster and Virginia Woolf, and none of his publications had aroused the public outcry or debate associated with those of his enemy D. H. Lawrence. By 1930, Strachey's claim to fame as the satirist of an array of such eminent Victorians as the queen and Florence Nightingale paled beside the popularity of the "so many modern writers whom so many other people like very much."[2] These unnamed writers who incited Strachey's wrath had dared to challenge his own self-appointed position as cultural innovator and rebel. Since his undergraduate days at Cambridge University, Strachey had boasted of his guiding role in England's "new age" and had tried to construct a literary and public identity that accentuated his break from his nineteenth-century ancestors. Yet, even as he denounced his heritage, Strachey maintained a peculiar allegiance to Victorianism, and his middle-age lament indicated a reluctant awareness that he had finished last in the "battle of the moderns."

The English brand of modernism to which Strachey aspired involved a prevailing sense of dislocation from the past and a commitment to the active remaking of art. The self-styled modernists believed the era of Victorianism had ended, and in its place they offered a new conception of society, art, and thought.[3] A disillusioned vision, an impending sense of crisis, a disregard for old forms, and an awakened sexual curiosity characterized Strachey's generation of artists, writers, philosophers, and activists.[4] Historians and literary critics traditionally have accepted Strachey's view of himself as a member of the intellectually and socially elite group of modernists. Paul Fussell, Noel Annan, and Paul Levy, for example, praise the writer's "feline prose" that "tore the skin off middle-class respectability," and they interpret Strachey's published biographies and flamboyant dress as deliberate parodies of the Victorian ideals of virility and manly action.[5] Strachey's biographer, Mi-

1

chael Holroyd, credits him with "smuggling deviant sexual behavior into our [British] national heritage with his subtle reassessments of Elizabethan and Victorian times." Strachey's influence especially extended over "modern behavior with his extraordinary free and tolerant lifestyle."[6]

Since the 1960s, Strachey and the Bloomsbury Group in general have incited interest among feminist and queer studies scholars, not so much for their publications and art, but for their lifestyles, which seemed to challenge Victorian convention. In her now classic 1973 study of androgyny, Carolyn Heilbrun pointed to the Bloomsbury Group as the forerunners of the sexual liberation movement of the 1960s.[7] Two decades later, queer theorists in the 1990s, having exhausted their analyses of Oscar Wilde and E. M. Forster, at last turned to Strachey, who in his capes, earrings, and heels, and with his lounging pose and comedic belittling of historical figures, seemed the very embodiment of camp. American critic Edmund Wilson described Strachey as "the high-voiced old Bloomsbury gossip gloating over the scandals of the past,"[8] and George Piggford and Christopher Reed continue to read Strachey's life and writing as part of a larger project of homosexual transgression against Victorianism.[9] Some feminist scholars since Heilbrun's study have taken a different approach to Strachey and his position in the Bloomsbury Group. Encouraged by Sandra Gilbert and Susan Gubar to "rethink" and "engender" modernism, feminist critics either see Strachey as the champion of strong women or condemn him as the patriarchal misogynist who dominated Dora Carrington and envied the success of Virginia Woolf.[10]

These varying interpretations of Bloomsbury's leader suggest that his self-fashioning as Britain's leading modernist was riddled with complications. In Strachey we see a man caught in the evolution to modernity, whose troubled sexual life was shaped by the larger historical transition away from Victorianism. Although some fans of Bloomsbury continue to stress the group's "complete freedom" from class and gender consciousness pervasive in British society in the early twentieth century,[11] a closer reading of Strachey's life and work will highlight his own struggle with Victorian mores and practices. Despite his challenge to his colleagues to "fuck, bugger, and abuse themselves to their hearts' content,"[12] he faced tremendous guilt and fear, as well as legal and social obstacles, whenever he tried to follow his own advice.

The vast bulk of Strachey's unpublished prose, poetry, and correspondence examined in the following chapters reveals a disparity between his desire to "be modern" and the actual extent of his sexual, literary, political, and social avant-gardism. Despite his determination to disassociate himself from his parents' generation, Strachey ultimately reinforced the ideas, institutions, and morals of his Victorian predecessors, whom he declared lived within a "glass case of physical and intellectual impotence."[13] At the same time that he questioned and ridiculed all things Victorian, his writings and sexual behavior depended on his battle with this ideological formulation.

Rooted in ideas of sexual, class, and racial differences, Victorianism promoted the superiority of the upper-middle-class, university-educated English man and stressed his alienation from women, the lower classes, and the "inferior" nonwhite races. The nineteenth century saw the establishment of increasingly rigid boundaries between private and public selves so that gender differences solidified into apparently natural and immutable traits. The striving competitive masculinity and a nurturant, domestic femininity became the guiding rubric within which various aspects of culture were subsumed.[14] Mary Poovey's study of mid-Victorian culture notes the "work" performed particularly by the ideology of sexual and gender differences in all areas of English life. She, similar to Michel Foucault, asserts the absence of individual choice and conscious control exerted by Victorians over their own thoughts and actions.[15] Strachey's rebellion against the Victorians was complicated by his dual position. He wrote from a position of authority, as a Cambridge-educated male from one of England's leading imperial families, but he also was a homosexual, existing on the moral and legal margins of "respectable" society. At the same time that he satirized "eminent Victorians," he longed for validation, which he received in the form of an invitation to court, as well as letters from his adoring public, and in his relations with "modern" women who nevertheless allowed him to play the role of patriarch. Victorian notions of difference often empowered Strachey, whether in his relations with those he regarded as his sexually, racially, or socially defined "others" or in his creation of a new literary form, the "psychobiography." As both a proponent and prisoner of Victorian ideology, therefore, Strachey did not represent a new "modern consciousness" but rather the final chapter of his own collection of miniportraits, *Eminent Victorians* (1918).

Between 1967 and 1969, Michael Holroyd published a two-volume biography of Lytton Strachey's life and work.[16] Holroyd described Strachey's attitude toward the Victorians as a combination of awe and repulsion, and his detailed and heavily psychoanalytical study presented Strachey's battle against an overbearing mother and his triumphs over personal and professional insecurities. Holroyd also was the first biographer to acknowledge and even document Strachey's homosexuality as well as the sexual relations of the entire Bloomsbury Group. My own analysis begins in part where Holroyd's finishes and addresses the impact of gender, class, and race on Strachey's public and private lives. Also, though Holroyd exposes Strachey's homosexuality, he fails, as Julian Symons notes, to address the division in Strachey's personality between the fascination held for him by male beauty and the desire for sexual satisfaction.[17] The ongoing battle between what Strachey called his "higher" and "lower" selves not only affected his personal relationships but his writings as well. In addition to his Cambridge and Bloomsbury compositions, Strachey's diaries and poetry offer a picture of the biographer that clearly undermines the image of sexual iconoclast he so carefully constructed for public consumption. My analysis relies most heavily on Strachey's unpublished correspondence with his family, colleagues, lovers, and fans. Letters, he believed, were "the only really satisfactory form of literature" that drew one into the world from which they had been written, and in Strachey's case, his epistles revealed a private self at odds with his public image.[18]

In presenting Strachey as the last eminent Victorian, I also reject the standard association of modernism with sexual innovation, transgression, and liberation. In her discussion of Bloomsbury, Carolyn Heilbrun, for example, identifies Strachey and his colleagues as the earliest major proponents of the "androgynous way of life." For the first time, Heilbrun argues, a group existed in which "masculinity and femininity were marvelously mixed in its members."[19] Quentin Bell, the most prolific (and biased) of the Bloomsbury chroniclers, doubts that any group had ever been "quite as radical in its approach to sexual taboos" as Strachey's.[20] The following chapters, however, question Strachey's alleged personal and artistic blurring of gender lines and explore, instead, his social and literary polarizations of men and women. Also, Strachey's troubled attempts to accept and act out his homosexuality contradict claims that the author confidently paraded his sexuality before a shocked and disapproving public. Strachey cast himself as an avant-garde writer and personality and deliberately used his homosexuality to create a new political and social identity. However, undermining the self-constructed image of androgyne, rebel, and modernist par excellence was Strachey's lingering, though often unconscious, commitment to Victorian sexuality, masculinity, and morality. The image of the upper-middle-class white Englishman held a particular fascination for Strachey, representing to him security, power, and even a refuge from himself.

A central theme of this study concerns Strachey's "crisis of identity." To several of his friends Strachey expressed his regret that "one can't now and then change sexes."[21] However, in place of the standard interpretation of Strachey as the embodiment of androgyny and the alternative to Victorian virile masculinity, I see his life as an unconscious caricature of the bourgeois Victorian woman. Until he achieved literary success at age thirty-eight, Strachey failed to escape the restrictive sphere of his parental home. Suffering from repeated bouts of unidentifiable illnesses, Strachey used his "neurasthenia" as an excuse for his financial and professional failures as well as a refuge from homosexual desire. While his sisters, Dorothy, Philippa, and Marjorie Strachey, rightfully claimed the title of "New Women" as writers, suffragettes, and educators, Lytton sought male protectors and feared the onset of adulthood and responsibility. Long before his Bloomsbury colleague Virginia Woolf coined the now famous phrase, Strachey wrote of his longing for a "room of his own," and an income to achieve the independence expected of his sex.[22]

The eventual attainment of monetary and social success, however, did not remedy Strachey's physical and psychological debilities. His postwar fame and frequent public appearances only increased his sense of inadequacy. The British press not only reviewed his books but passed comment on his looks. References to the large nose, pale complexion, and "the daddy long legs, big lips" of the "inhuman old maid of a man" agonized Strachey, since he blamed his appearance for his inability to find and hold onto love.[23] Also, though he craved success, he now wondered, "Can a popular author be a good one? It's alarming to be welcomed with open arms by Gosse, Jack Squire and *The Times.*"[24]

Scholars have virtually ignored Strachey's postwar writings, which did not achieve the critical success of his 1918 bestseller, *Eminent Victorians*. These later works (both published and unpublished) reveal to an even greater extent Strachey's conflicting commitment to both modernism and Victorianism. His writings were also therapeutic, allowing him to imagine guilt-free fantasies of sexual fulfillment and to wreak revenge upon strong-willed women who threatened the gender order. In treating what he called the "very interesting question" of sex, for example, Strachey now turned to the "modern psychology" of Freud.[25] Eager to please his younger brother James, a Freudian analyst and translator, yet unwilling to undergo psychoanalysis himself, Strachey applied Freud's theories to his literary studies of Queens Victoria and Elizabeth I. Strachey manipulated Freud's ideas about female sexuality to reinforce traditional concepts of gender while completely ignoring Freud's theories of male homosexuality. That Strachey still used the traditional form of biography in conjunction with the "new" psychology to attack female icons partially explains his growing rift with Virginia Woolf. Moreover, as a self-proclaimed "modern inquirer" and "explorer of the past," Strachey seemed to acknowledge the tension between the two worlds of Victorianism and modernism that his writings revealed.[26] Gerald Brenan believed Strachey's works placed him on the "borderline between the new and the old,"[27] a statement that also summarized how the writer lived his life, moving back and forth between his identities as bourgeois Victorian and anti-Victorian rebel.

The tension between Strachey's commitment to Victorian mores and his desire for sexual freedom influenced his concept of love between men formulated during his undergraduate career at Cambridge. In his second year at university, Strachey was elected to the secret Society of Apostles. The Brotherhood to which he now belonged constructed its own code of manliness that sanctioned all-male romantic friendships. The Apostles advocated the Neoplatonist doctrine of the Higher Sodomy, following in the tradition of such eminent Victorian champions of Greek Love as John Addington Symonds and Goldworthy Lowes Dickinson. Chapter 1 examines the philosophy of Brotherly Love and Strachey's attempts to realize its ideals in his relationships with the artists Duncan Grant and Henry Lamb, Cambridge undergraduates J. T. Sheppard and Arthur Hobhouse, and Oxford students Ralph Partridge and Roger Senhouse. These encounters promoted a commitment to a standard of masculine behavior that did not always defy the Victorian code of sexual conduct but actually upheld nineteenth-century notions of gender and class differences. Devotion to the Higher Sodomy served two major functions: it shielded the Brothers from affiliation with the newly identified, illegal, and pathological type, the "homosexual" or "invert," and also guaranteed the Apostles' status as members of an elite circle of privileged men. Strachey and his Brothers built on an already established Victorian bourgeois tradition of "manly love" to identify themselves as superior to all women and most men beneath their social and educational levels.

Election to the Apostles was for Strachey *the* defining moment of his life and therefore an appropriate starting point for my analysis. What mattered most to the young Strachey was that at Cambridge he discovered other "Greek souls" and found a justification for what he sometimes feared was a "disease" marked by "unnatural desires."[28] Within the rooms of his Brothers, Strachey savored the "ethereal atmosphere of free and audacious inquiry." Unfortunately, the Apostles' discussion and sometimes practice of Brotherly Love was overshadowed by the fate of Oscar Wilde. After Wilde's trials in 1895, growing suspicion was directed at such secret societies within the male bastion of the university.

Since the 1985 publication of Eve Sedgwick's *Between Men: English Literature and Male Homosexual Desire,* the emergence of male homosexuality at the fin de siècle has become a prominent topic in Victorian studies.[29] Still, little scholarly interest has been directed to the Edwardian and post–World War I periods in which Strachey and other young men coped with the Wildean legacy of repression. Such scholars as Jonathan Dollimore, Ed Cohen, and Alan Sinfield use the case of Oscar Wilde as a historical example of rebellious sexuality and writing. Wilde's trial dominates theoretical discussions of homosexuality since it represents a turning point—after 1895 the homosexual becomes *the* "category of sexual transgression."[30] The subject of all-male Love before Wilde's demise is another area of recent scholarly interest. However, these studies tend to concentrate on the Greek revival at Oxford, thus ignoring the Cambridge Apostles' use of Hellenism (both before and after the Wilde trials) as a discursive space in which desire between men was validated.[31] The Apostles' use of the platonic ideal of "spiritual procreancy" can be read, in a similar fashion, as a form of homosexual counterdiscourse.[32] Although Strachey engaged in a series of unsuccessful and unfulfilled love affairs at Cambridge, he did find intellectual freedom within the Society, where sex and male Love served as the weekly topics of discussion. However, this counterdiscourse also forced men such as Strachey to keep homosexuality private, to censor their published writings as well as their private letters and diaries, and to experience a crisis of confidence alleviated only by their sense of gender and class exclusivity. Furthermore, Ed Cohen reminds us that textual depictions of male Love both reproduce and resist the dominant heterosexual ideologies and practices.[33] As an Apostle, and later as a member of Bloomsbury, Strachey legitimized, not only a theory of all-male Love, but a theory of male supremacy and female inferiority that counterbalanced his role as sexual outcast.

Despite such efforts to validate all-male Love, the Wilde trials left their imprint on Strachey's generation of homosexual intellectuals. Any distinctions within the public imagination between the aesthete, the introspective weakling of the ivory tower, and the homosexual had disappeared. Any signs of "enfeebled masculinity" (which the sickly Strachey exhibited) contradicted the ideal of English manhood: dutiful, physically and morally robust, and self-sacrificing.[34] Hounded by the need for secrecy, the Edwardian Apostles, therefore, tried to distance themselves from the image of the "queer" that had emerged during Wilde's prosecution.[35] Unlike the leisured effeminate aesthete who paid for sex with lower-class boys, the Apostle invoked the "Greek view of life." Hellenism provided a justification of sexual and emotional ties between men of the same social background and offered a defense against feminizing representations of men who desired other men.[36]

Despite such a defense, Strachey was often reluctant to cross the line from spiritual to physical love. His pursuit of a spiritual, higher Love conflicted with his rich fantasy life of "lower" sexual adventure in London's East End, the Arabian desert, or the English countryside. Chapter 2 builds on the current theme in literary and gender studies of "sexual exiles" who crossed boundaries of race and class not only to find physical gratification but to escape the constraints of normative bourgeois masculinity. Similar to André Gide, Oscar Wilde, and E. M. Forster, Strachey saw "Oriental" and working-class youths as more permissive, and as likely practitioners of the "lower sodomy." Though he wrote endless essays on the spiritual joys of Brotherly Love, he found the pursuit of these sexual "others" to be a much easier and less guilt-ridden enterprise. Unlike Gide and Wilde, most of Strachey's encounters with these others were imaginary; he used his journal and private fiction to indulge his fantasies, to create a safe place for his desire. Troubled by fears of penetration and linking sex with disease and death, Strachey fashioned his own literary empire in which he reigned supreme. Though he secretly desired what he considered the "unique" mind and body of the ploughboy, boxer, and gondolier, Strachey asserted his superior control and preserved himself from the "taint" of such youths. Assuming difference as the basis of desire, Strachey perpetuated in action and fancy the very system of domestic, foreign, and sexual imperialism that he condemned in print. While these private writings clashed with Strachey's public persona as the opponent of empire, his imperialist fantasies inevitably grew out of his and his Cambridge Brothers' dual construction of the higher and lower forms of all-male Love.

Cambridge would always remain to Strachey "a complete myth . . . with all the mystery and importance of a myth," but this idealized view of the university and his relationships within its protective walls would make his encounters with other men and women quite problematic. Strachey's ascendancy within the Society and his credo of "frankness" eventually paved the way for his intellectual and sexual leadership of the Bloomsbury Group by 1908.[37] The socially privileged intellectuals of Strachey's Cambridge circle preferred the pursuit of the "greatest good" of male friendship to the company of women. Women belonged to the "phenomenal" and insignificant world outside of Cambridge and remained, even in the opinion of these moderns, an inferior sex. Strachey's friendships with Virginia Woolf, Lady Ottoline Morrell, and Dora Carrington have been misrepresented by scholars as evidence of the writer's feminist sympathies. In fact, Strachey preferred women as nurturers and nurses rather than as artistic equals and rivals. The correspondence between Strachey and Carrington, with whom he shared a country residence from 1915 to 1932, offers not a picture of two androgynous souls in perfect communion, but one that bordered on a conventional patriarchal union of male economic provider and female caretaker, hostess, and domestic drudge. Chapters 3 and 4, therefore, address Strachey's often ambiguous relationships with the women within his family and literary and social circles. These relationships strongly influenced his writings for publication. Though he boasted that he reinvented the art of biography, he did little to undermine the representations of men and women fashioned by his Victorian predecessors. Similar to Heilbrun, Barbara Fassler praises Bloomsbury's introduction of androgyny into English literature and human relations, but both scholars overlook Strachey's personal and literary obsession with gender difference.[38] In fact, his portraits of female reformers and monarchs attacked rather than applauded the assumption of power by women. He created portraits of grotesque anomalies—women who, similar to those of Bloomsbury, violated such traditional norms of femininity as sexual passivity, intellectual inferiority, and powerlessness. With the publication of Strachey's *Elizabeth and Essex* (1928), his Bloomsbury colleague Virginia Woolf saw in him not a feminist ally but a man who seemed intent on stifling female creativity. Yet, Strachey's critical representations of women also hint at his own gender insecurities. The strong woman of Bloomsbury or Buckingham Palace challenged his already shaky position of masculine authority, and it was Strachey's duty and privilege to restore her to her proper place. His biographies ultimately tell us less about his subjects than they do about his own sexual politics and his relationships with other female modernists.

Lytton Strachey lived within the swirling context of British modernism, the devastation of the Great War, and the emerging movements of feminism and psychoanalysis. The final chapter addresses Strachey's place within this literary and sexual movement. Similar to other feminist historians, I attempt to "reread" modernism, albeit a very small aspect of it. This involves not merely recovering the lost voices of female modernists but also returning to "famous" male texts, such as *Eminent Victorians,* that have become part of the canon and asking new questions about gender and sexuality. From the very start, modernism was not a unified movement even within England. Bloomsbury faced its harshest criticism from another modernist faction headed by Ezra Pound and Wyndham Lewis, and such contemporaries as Bertrand Russell and D. H. Lawrence loathed the political passivity and intellectual elitism of Strachey and his friends. For Strachey, the personal struggle to "be modern" was hampered by ideological as well as social, legal, political, and moral obstacles. He and his colleagues fashioned themselves as innovators who offered new methods of art, literature, and behavior in place of those of their parents' generation, but they too often seemed content to limit their modernism to, or equate it with, anti-Victorianism. Championing a modernist mission of antihistoricism, Strachey exerted his authority as biographer-historian to attack, ridicule, and weaken the authority of the Victorians. Afraid that his poor health and sexuality ousted him to the margins of bourgeois, manly hegemony, Strachey used satire to establish a position of power within his own new ruling class of intellectuals. Ridden with contradiction, Strachey's brand of modernism reveals a debt to Victorianism much stronger than either he or most historians have acknowledged.

As a sexually transgressive movement, modernism is itself suspect. Recent studies on the gender of modernism criticize the male-dominated club of artists and writers who created derogatory images of women as sexual predators and castrating man-haters.[39] Although Strachey was not the "typical" male modernist, who similar to Ezra Pound or D. H. Lawrence advocated an "aggressive heterosexuality," he did regard himself as a liberator, encouraging his colleagues to "talk, talk, talk" about sex, semen, and buggery.[40] The phallocentric obsession of Apostolic discourse carried over into Bloomsbury and tended to disregard sapphism as a worthy topic or practice. Even the use and practice of androgyny and bisexuality (which, for the Bloomsbury Group, were interchangeable concepts) supported rather than undermined a binary system of gender. The group's experiments in "unconventional" sexual and living arrangements (such as the cohabitation of Strachey and Carrington, and the affair between the homosexual artist Duncan Grant and the married Vanessa Bell), though intended as proof of the group's radicalism and rejection of the "hypermasculinity" of Sir Leslie Stephen's generation, often failed to challenge patriarchal norms. As did other bohemian subcultures, Bloomsbury conceived itself as a site of transgressive behavior against the bourgeois order, yet this opposition was counterbalanced by reinforcement and affirmation of male privilege and authority.[41]

Upon the death of Lytton Strachey in 1932, his younger brother, James, preserved every written record of Lytton's private and public lives. My project on Strachey began as a case study in self-fashioning. Robert Elbaz regards the self as the exclusive property of its owner—an object on which one can operate. The individual, refusing to believe identity is "absolutely fixed," controls the process of creating, writing, and acting the self.[42] Stephen Greenblatt, however, rejects self-fashioning as an autonomous process. Though individuals think they are fashioning themselves, through their manners, demeanor, adherence to outward ceremony, and speech, they are actually being fashioned by such institutions as the family, church, state, and by such categories as class, race, and gender. Individuals, Greenblatt concludes, merely "cling to the illusion" that they control the identity they create and display in their behavior and writings.[43] In the case of Strachey, he firmly believed that he controlled the process of self-fashioning. By positing the Victorian as other, he would be everything that a Victorian man was not: effeminate, frail, flamboyant, cynical, and antibourgeois.

The issue of self-fashioning is particularly relevant to our understanding of late nineteenth- and early twentieth-century culture. As Michael Adams, Robert Wohl, and others have shown, intellectuals and students across Europe experienced a "crisis of identity."[44] The repudiation of liberal ideology, rationalism, imperialism, and industrialism and the younger generation's search for a new identity were spurred on by the Great War and resulted in new artistic and literary movements, of which Bloomsbury is just one example. The members of Bloomsbury had no intention of purging themselves of their Victorian heritage through "blood and fire," as other members of the generation of 1914 did. The "new civilization" that Strachey hoped to lead would be a sexual utopia, a haven from a previous era of repression. The Bloomsbury Group, therefore, resolved their own crisis of identity by fashioning for themselves and the outraged public the image of sexual rebels, liberators, and cultural iconoclasts.

An initial comparison of Strachey's private record of his own life (his diaries and letters) with historians' and critics' evaluations of his life and work was so contradictory as to warrant a new look since Holroyd's 1967 biography. In the course of my research, I discovered that what was most important to Strachey remained curiously absent from his writings intended for publication—i.e., his sexuality. It is not my intention to offer an alternative biography of Strachey or a comprehensive study of the history of homosexuality in England. Rather, this project uses Strachey to explore, on one level, the larger relationship between homosexuality and modernism and, on another level, the more personal relationship between one upper-middle-class intellectual and his sexual self. Rereading modernism through the lens of gender uncovers the complexities of Strachey's life as well as the ambiguous sexual politics of modernism within a particular context.[45] In his attempt to fashion for himself a new sexual identity, Strachey often found himself at odds, as well as complicit, with familial, cultural, legal, and moral institutions and expectations. His experiences suggest that, contrary to the theories of late Victorian sexologists, no single "type" of homosexual person existed, but rather a multiplicity of homosexualities. His behavior, appearance, ideas, and writings about all-male Love differed from those not only of other Apostles but of men outside the Society. Although Strachey saw his homosexuality as empowering, he sometimes needed to draw from Victorian normative masculinity. Since the forging of a new sexual identity could be full of dangers for the Edwardian homosexual, Strachey often found stable ground in bourgeois ideas and institutions. Medical, legal, and political discourses of the fin de siècle posited the homosexual as a national enemy and threat to the British race, and, hence, Strachey's defense of gender, class, and race privilege seems understandable; he simply could not let all borders and definitions dissolve.[46] As Marianne DeKoven argues, the lives and texts of other male modernists also revealed such an irresolvable ambivalence. Theoretically, the modernists of Strachey's generation longed to destroy the old order, to rewrite patriarchal culture, but they still feared the loss of hegemony that such changes might entail.[47]

After leaving Cambridge, Strachey briefly played with the image of the queer and used it to symbolize his break with his family of imperial civil servants and hunters—the older Strachey men who embodied all of the required traits of Victorian manliness. Once he assumed leadership within the Bloomsbury Group, Strachey deliberately played the role of effeminate, artistic aesthete to pit himself against the acceptable norm of masculinity represented by hardy self-control and athleticism. After the success of *Eminent Victorians,* however, Strachey returned to his sober tweeds and only occasionally paraded privately in women's attire.

The various stages in Strachey's self-fashioning illustrate what Judith Butler calls the "performance" of gender. Butler defines gender as an act, a public performance of repeated gestures and stylized movements.[48] Strachey used his gender performance as a subversive strategy but occasionally drew from and rejected prevailing norms of bourgeois masculinity when it suited him. He adopted the behavior of the female hysteric and the bawdy effeminate queer, yet he also desired and hoped to be the virile Apollo of his dreams, strong, manly, and beyond physical touch. Among his circle of friends, Strachey stylized himself as a "progressive homosexual,"[49] but his gender performance collapsed when he was alone and sought refuge in his diaries. On occasion, Strachey's parody of English masculinity alienated even his Bloomsbury colleagues. E. M. Forster, for example, did not see Strachey's effeminacy as subversive, but rather as dangerous to other men-loving-men such as himself. In *Maurice,* Forster modeled the effeminate homosexual of the "Oscar Wilde sort" on Strachey. The character of Risley embodies all the worst traits of the "aesthetic push" in which Maurice finds himself plunged at Cambridge. Yet, as Strachey noted, Forster's own version of the intellectual homosexual who craves physical interaction with the more virile working-class male is equally problematic.[50]

Literary critic Perry Meisel refers to "the myth of the modern" created by the writers and artists of the postwar era and historians alike.[51] Strachey's life and work offer further evidence against the neat shift from nineteenth- to twentieth-century political, sexual, and social culture and ideas. Hence, World War I plays a minimal role in my discussion of Strachey. The disillusioned British public in 1918 welcomed Strachey's scathing commentary on hero worship and militarism. Although Bloomsbury considered politics "as exciting as a game of bridge," the group did protest the war, and Strachey's appearance before the war tribunal, seated on an air cushion, expressed his contempt for the military examiners.[52] The war, however, did not alter Strachey's views on gender or class, nor did his postwar success ease his conflict with his sexuality. The myth of the modern allowed Strachey to take his place beside the other young men who claimed to offer an alternative literary vision. More important, the myth allowed him to escape from the ugly and frail image he had of himself and to present himself to the public as its liberator from what he declared to be the repressive Victorian past.

The Strachey papers not only document a life in crisis but are crucial to historians' larger study of fin de siècle Britain and the current debate on individual agency versus the power of ideology. Recent feminist historiography has documented the difficulties confronting the Victorian and Edwardian "New Women" who strove to redefine the female sphere of activity.[53] As a cultural critic and Higher Sodomite, Strachey also hoped to move beyond his dictated sphere, to "now and then change sexes," but the Victorian prescription for bourgeois manhood hampered much of his effort. Though Strachey and his Bloomsbury colleagues announced themselves as the creators of new forms of identity, consciousness, and art, the influence of Victorian heritage survived even the onslaught of the Great War.

Chapter 1

Brotherly Love:
The Cambridge Apostles
and the Pursuit of the Higher Sodomy

During the decade before the Great War, the aspiring writer Lytton
Strachey and the economist John Maynard Keynes exchanged a series of letters in which they discussed their vision of a "new monastic
age"—a great moral upheaval led by the young men of Cambridge.
The mission confronting them would not be easily accomplished, as
Strachey noted. "Our greatest stumbling block," he wrote, "is our
horror of half-measures. We can't be content with telling the truth—
we must tell the whole truth; and the whole truth is the Devil. . . . It's
madness of us to dream of making dowagers understand that feelings
are good, when we say in the same breath that the best ones are
Sodomitical." Nevertheless, Strachey continued, "our time will come
about 100 years hence, when preparations will have been made, and
compromises come to, so that, at the publication of our letters, everyone will be, finally converted."[1] Although Strachey and Keynes only
half hoped for mass conversion to sodomy, they did expect eventual
widespread toleration for its practitioners. As staunch critics of their "repellent" Victorian ancestors, they associated their ideological devotion
to the "New Style of Love" with the birth of the modern age.[2] Strachey
and Keynes represent just two Edwardian intellectuals who claimed to
challenge the moral rigidity of their parents' generation with their own
code of sexual and masculine behavior. They transformed the definition
of "sodomy" from an illegal and sinful act to an alternative creed of manliness and transcendental love. Through their affiliation with the elite
Brotherhood of the Conversazione Society, otherwise known as the
Cambridge Apostles, these men hoped to spread the gospel of the Higher
Sodomy among other enlightened contemporaries.

Though Strachey and Keynes eventually earned fame respectively as a biographer and an economist, both men considered their primary identity as Apostles and prized this membership that expired only upon death. The Cambridge Apostles represent an important chapter in the history of sexuality and masculinity in early twentieth-century England. Keynes and Strachey regarded themselves as rebels whose devotion to Plato was part of a larger agenda—that is, their ideological opposition to Victorianism. According to fellow Apostle Leonard Woolf, "all around us there was taking place the revolt (which we ourselves in our own small way helped to start) against the Victorian morality and code of conduct."[3] Their generation renounced religion and politics, proclaimed the death of God, and declared that "love is the only reality."[4] This alleged shift in values and goals of the Society was critically observed by some of its older members. In his essay, "Portraits from Memory," Bertrand Russell recalled:

> J. M. Keynes and Lytton Strachey both belonged to the Cambridge generation about ten years junior to my own. It is surprising how great a change in the mental climate those ten years had brought. We were still Victorian; they were Edwardian. We believed in ordered progress by means of politics and free discussion; the more self-confident among us may have hoped to be leaders of the multitude, but none of us wished to be divorced from it. The generation of Keynes and Strachey . . . aimed rather at a life of retirement among fine shades and nice feelings, and conceived of the good as consisting in the passionate mutual admirations of a clique of the elite.[5]

Indeed, Strachey and Keynes preferred discussions of sex over politics and religion, but they did not, as some argue, lead a "homosexual mafia" at Cambridge. Historian and Apostle Noel Annan identifies Strachey's generation of Brothers as "a cult of homosexuals" who engaged in a "self-conscious act of defiance against the Establishment."[6] The leader of this cult, Paul Levy adds, was Lytton Strachey, who single-handedly "altered the character of the Society . . . into overt, full-blooded—almost aggressive homosexuality."[7]

A renewed look at the Apostolic code of male Love as preached and practiced by Strachey and his colleagues calls into question such interpretations. A tradition of romantic friendship already existed within the Society long before the Edwardian members refashioned it as the Higher Sodomy. The assumption that the Higher Sodomy was merely a code name for homosexuality also obscures the complex emotions and experiences that united, and sometimes divided, the Society members. The different ways in which the Brothers interpreted and followed their philosophy of manly love, whether for a lifetime (as in the case of Strachey) or simply during their undergraduate careers (as in the case of Leonard Woolf), suggest a multiplicity of identities subsumed under the category of Higher Sodomite. Furthermore, while devotion to the Higher Sodomy allowed the Brothers to experiment with a range of sexual practices and identities, it did not necessarily place them at odds with the dominant masculine culture outside the Society. At Cambridge the Brothers enjoyed the "ethereal atmosphere of free and audacious inquiry," but while they claimed to be "the priests of a new civilisation," they advocated a version of male Love that further emphasized class privilege, gender difference, and male superiority.[8] Most troubling for Strachey, however, was not the bourgeois undertones of the Higher Sodomy, but the restrictions that adherence to such a code of chaste male Love posed for him. Resurrecting Plato's *Symposium* in the early twentieth century further intensified, rather than alleviated, Strachey's guilt over his "unnatural passions."[9]

This chapter begins with a brief history of the Apostolic Brotherhood and the changing attitudes about male romantic friendships that occurred at the fin de siècle. The second half of this chapter then examines how self-proclaimed Higher Sodomite Lytton Strachey extended his pursuit of Brotherly Love outside the Cambridge circle and sought the "ideal" in such men as Henry Lamb, Ralph Partridge, and Roger Senhouse. His greatest, and most disappointing, attempt at Platonic bliss involved the artist Duncan Grant. In these relationships we see Strachey's unsuccessful bids for love and the contradictions and problems inherent to the Apostolic doctrine of male romantic friendship. In addition to Strachey's own insecurities, social, legal, and ideological constraints hindered his realization of Brotherly Love. The literary artifacts of Strachey's relationships (all unpublished during his lifetime), not only refute historians' oversimplified designation of the Apostles as "homosexual rebels," but also reveal the difficult process of overthrowing Victorianism to construct a new and liberating sexual identity.

Still in existence, the Cambridge Society of Apostles remains a secret and privileged circle of undergraduates, fellows, and dons. Posthumous publications of the Brothers' private correspondence and memoirs have enlightened nonmembers of the Society's weekly proceedings and discussions. The 1979 to 1982 revelation of Soviet infiltration also attracted the larger public's attention to the workings of the Brotherhood, but the most outstanding feature of the Society is, quite simply, the fame of its individual members.[10] Strachey's and Keynes's contemporaries included the philosophers G. E. Moore and Bertrand Russell, the soldier-poet Rupert Brooke, the Freudian psychoanalyst and translator James Strachey, and the publisher Leonard Woolf. Even middle age and notoriety did not alter the Brothers' ritualistic consumption of anchovy toast and essays behind locked doors at Cambridge. The hearth rug, or pulpit, remained a sacred space around which the Brothers continued to gather on Saturday evenings.

A highly selective election process annually increased the size of the Society. Apostles and Angels (those who "took wings," or graduated) sponsored possible candidates, or Embryos, who displayed the Apostolic attitude of "absolute candour, sincerity, and uninhibited frankness."[11] Intelligence and good looks or outstanding eccentricities also increased the likelihood of one's election. Strachey's lanky frame, high voice, and clever mind, according to Brother Desmond MacCarthy, quickly attracted the attention of the Society. Once elected, an Apostle swore the "curse," or vow of secrecy, and placed all other obligations second to those of the Brotherhood. In addition to secrecy and ritual, the Apostles invented a coded language and a schema of the world that divided "reality" (anything and anyone related to the Society) from the "phenomenal" (the non-Apostolic realm of women, "womanisers," politics, and newspapers). Though they claimed they wanted "everyone" to "be Apostolic," the Brothers believed they belonged to "a certain type, rare like all good things." The Society bolted its doors to the uninitiated, allowing only the select few to "breathe that magic air."[12]

Elected February 1, 1902, Apostle number 239 Giles Lytton Strachey, wrote in a "Private and Confidential" letter to Lady Strachey:

> My Dearest Mama, this is to say, before I am committed to oaths of secrecy, that I am now a Brother of the Society of Apostles. How I dare write the words I don't know! . . . It is a veritable brotherhood—the chief point being personal friendship between the members. The sensation is a strange one.[13]

Richard Deacon's history of the Apostles points to Strachey's election as the catalyst to the "homosexual phase in Apostolic life." This phase, Deacon notes, "blossomed in the latter part of the last century, reached hot-house proportions in the early part of this century, becoming blatantly and even ostentatiously aggressive under those two predacious pederasts" Keynes and Strachey.[14] Deacon's botanical metaphor, however, ignores the already existing philosophy of love and friendship that so appealed to the newly elected Strachey. Also, in his homophobic zeal to salvage the reputation of the "very many heterosexual members down the ages," Deacon exaggerates the influence of Strachey and Keynes over the sexual behavior of their colleagues.[15] As he assumed his position as the newest addition to the Society in 1902, Strachey prepared to learn more of Brotherly Love from the older Apostles and Angels. Aware of the prestige of the Society and unsuspiciously approving of its morals, Lady Strachey, therefore, applauded her son's nomination.

The Conversazione Society originated in 1820 with twelve founding members who borrowed their nickname, without irony, from biblical history. The Tory Evangelical undergraduates, in preparation for their futures as clergymen, used their organization as an oratorical mechanism. A founding Brother explained the mission of the Society:

> The 'Apostles' was the name we gave ourselves in secrecy, but I think it would be more becoming to describe ourselves as Apostolicans in that we were all evangelists. We were concerned to propagate and explain the gospels and in doing this honestly and sincerely to resolve all doubts concerning our respective interpretations by debating them in secret.[16]

By the next century, the Edwardian Apostles mocked the religious roots of their group yet still adhered to a sense of mission. They maintained the secrecies and ceremonial procedures, but these new Brothers prided themselves on ushering in "the death of God." Truth and Love, Strachey preached, could not coexist with the hypocrisy of Victorian Christianity.[17]

Strachey's generation of Apostles cannot be credited entirely with the diminishing religiosity of the Society. Under the influence of Alfred Tennyson and Arthur Hallam, the Brotherhood began its transition to a cult devoted to male friendship. Tennyson's brief membership ended with his resignation in 1830, precipitated by his failure to compose an essay on the subject of ghosts. With his dedication of *In Memorium* to the ghost of Hallam, or "HIM, whose name is LOVE," twenty-five years later, Tennyson returned to the Society.[18] Hallam's death only four years after his own election to the Apostles did not terminate his influence either. His 1831 prize-winning essay, "On Cicero," reminded Hallam's Brothers of "the lively sentiment between man and man" and the superiority of "this highest and purest manly love" found in the pages of Plato.[19] In his study of the letters between Hallam and Tennyson, Richard Dellamora notes that these early Apostles sought to "express desire for other men, even when such desires [were] rarely consummated in the flesh." Still, the young men were careful to "fence intense male bonding from sexual activity," but this does not mean that they were unaware of, or necessarily opposed to, the possibility of consummation.[20] The discourse of Platonic love now took its place beside such other weekly topics as utilitarianism and Christian liberalism. By the last two decades of the nineteenth century, politics and religion completely yielded to philosophy, love, and the pursuit of "the good life."

The "veritable brotherhood" of love and friendship promoted by the Victorian Apostles arose amidst the homocentric university setting of Cambridge. Similar to the public school and gentlemen's club, the Victorian university represented just one section of the broad spectrum of male homosocial territory. Within this haven from the world of women, desire between its male occupants characterized the structure of gender relations. Nineteenth-century rules of masculine behavior, according to Eve Sedgwick, even allowed for genital contact among boys or men, provided its practitioners eventually wed members of the opposite sex.[21] Upper- and middle-class men explored a range of forms and intensities of liaisons with one another without admitting culturally defined "femininity" into them as a structuring term.[22] With bachelorhood delayed sometimes until middle age, male friendships served as the central emotional factor in the lives of upper-middle-class men. The predominantly male atmosphere of Cambridge survived the policy reversal of the 1880s; dons and fellows now voluntarily rejected matrimony, preferring the company and conversation of their male colleagues and students to that of women. The proximity of Girton and Newnham Colleges for women also failed to elevate female intellectuals to the realm of "reality," and the Society, following the lead of the faculty, continued to deny admission to women. Contact with the opposite sex, other than family relations, jeopardized the "Apostolic character."

"Passing the love of women," these male romantic friendships among the Brothers also contributed to the formation of manliness.[23] Restraint defined normative masculinity, and, in principle, sexual self-control was exercised by even the Higher Sodomites at Cambridge. But John Boswell points out that when men chose such phrases as "Brotherly Love" to describe their friendships, they deliberately invested their relationships with erotic meaning. When undergraduates at Oxford or Cambridge invoked the ancient Greek image of a brotherhood, they were not simulating sibling relationships, but a form of male bonding that allowed for a range of behaviors that did not exclude same-sex desire.[24] The ambiguity of the ancient Greek model of friendship could, therefore, imply a bonding of male equals, or a spiritual, educational, and/or sexual union between two men of slightly different generations.[25]

In her study of Victorian Oxford, Linda Dowling describes a similar intellectual and sexual milieu to that found at its rival university, Cambridge. Hellenism provided male undergraduates and dons alike with a "coded" or hidden counterdiscourse that swept aside the fears of corruption and effeminacy associated with male love. Through the nineteenth-century revival of such classical Greek practices as the intense friendship and the essay society, university students stressed the intellectual procreancy and regeneration of Greek Love. Once outside the university, however, Plato's modern followers at the fin de siècle lost the "virilizing authority of the Greeks" and now fell prey to medical and legal authorities who associated male love with disease and criminality.[26] After the passage of the 1885 Labouchere Amendment, pederasty was no longer part of the warrior ideal of classical Greece, but an example of "morbidity" punishable with two years hard labor.

Despite the criminalization of homosexuality and the 1895 trials of Oscar Wilde, the Brothers at Cambridge continued to invoke Dorianism, read Walt Whitman's poetry, and engage in a cult of boy worship. Strachey's generation further intensified the Society's allegiance to the Greeks. Whereas historian Richard Jenkyns argues that university students such as Strachey used Platonism as a "screen to hide behind," Strachey's generation of Apostles quite simply saw this ancient philosophy of male friendship as a way to comprehend and explain their feelings for one another.[27] These men tried to fashion for themselves a nonmedical, nonpathological identity that erased the newly constructed boundaries between heterosexual and homosexual males. By strengthening the Society's devotion to Plato, Strachey and Keynes eschewed the claims of sexologists that inversion was perversion. Their "New Style of Love" promised to unite a select group of men and protect them from suspicion and marginalization.

Even before Strachey's and Keynes's "takeover" of the Society by 1903, the older Brothers were aware of the encroaching medical and legal challenges to their concept of romantic friendship. Victorian Apostle Goldworthy Lowes Dickinson thought male homosexuality promised "a more romantic and passionate life than others" but agreed with sexologists that it probably led to "in most cases an unhealthy, unbalanced, perhaps ultimately insane one."[28] Apostle Edward Carpenter tried to fuse sexology and Hellenism to emphasize the creative and artistic potential of homosexuality. Strachey, however, refused to accept the clinical definitions of normal and abnormal sexuality; the Higher Sodomite pursued the "love of souls." Yet, his efforts to remind his Brothers of the spirituality of their love were often futile. Even as late as 1922, his younger friends, upon reading texts on sex pathology conceded "how imperfect we all are."[29]

During the year after Oscar Wilde's trials, then sixteen-year-old Strachey first discovered Plato's *Symposium* "with a rush of mingled pleasure and pain . . . of surprise, relief, and fear to know that what I feel now was felt 2,000 years ago in glorious Greece."[30] The *Symposium* was also the new bible of the Apostles, the other "Greek souls" among whom Strachey found himself just a few years later. He and his Brothers interpreted from this and other Greek texts their own discourse of male sexuality that competed with a dominant repressive and homophobic culture.

At Cambridge the Apostles formulated the doctrine of the Higher Sodomy to distinguish themselves not only from women and men outside the university but also from other undergraduates within it. As one of the spiritual descendants of Plato, Strachey proudly accentuated his Brothers' perceived difference from the unfortunate majority. He searched the Society's ark, a "charming cedarwood chest" that stored previous essays and meeting minutes, for a roster of Higher Sodomites, and reminded his Brothers that only "US—the terribly intelligent . . . the artistic . . . the overwhelmed" attain Love.[31] Creating their own haven within the larger haven of Cambridge, the Apostles used a rhetoric of secrecy to further guarantee their elitism. Some outside observers (usually women) of the Apostles regarded this emphasis on secrecy as a possible indication of sexual deviance.[32] While such gestures as secrecy may solidify a male community, they also call attention to, and arouse anxiety over, the unstated boundaries that structure the homosocial continuum.[33] The Apostles countered these anxieties and reasserted their masculinity not by admitting but by removing women from their intellectual and physical lives. In one of his many poems in praise of the Higher Sodomy, Strachey acknowledged that the talk and behavior of the Apostles "may perplex the votaries of the other sex," but such conduct raised the Sodomites to "astounding heights."[34] The phrase "higher sodomy" itself deliberately signified the intellectual, physical, spiritual, and emotional superiority of the Apostolic man and further sanctioned the bonds of all-male friendships. This form of manly love did not encompass the dirty acts of "buggers" who lurked in subway stations and dark alleys, nor did the Higher Sodomy include the even baser practices of the reputed womanizers at Oxford. Rather, the roots of the Higher Sodomy, Strachey and his Brothers asserted, extended to ancient Greece and emulated Plato's dualistic construct of love: the sacred, nonphysical male love far exceeded the profane bodily expression of desire. Should "copulation— the act of beasts," occur, the Apostolic identity still preserved the dignity of the Brothers. After all, physical intimacy between intellectual and spiritual equals did not resemble the lust of "ordinary" men. Ultimately, the Higher Sodomy promoted not a sexual agenda but a glorification of male friendship.

Although Strachey and his Brothers at Cambridge may have looked to the *Symposium* rather than *Studies in the Psychology of Sex* for self-definition, they set for themselves a standard of behavior impossible to achieve. For Strachey, the Higher Sodomy was so invested with "the mystery and the importance of a myth"[35] that he became "oppressed by the agony of human relationships."[36] His version of the "Love of Souls" also remained quite juvenile. In his Apostle story, "The Fruit of the Tree," Strachey offered his Brothers his fantasy of a romance between "two wonderful contraries"—a shy boy and an older bully who share jam and sardines. Even though the youths are "amazingly matched" by their "opposites," the "old drawbacks, the old crudities" destroy the friendship and the promise of "something more."[37] Strachey's Apostle essays and poems constantly reveal a tension between self-liberation and self-denigration. At times he gloried in the sensual nature of the love of souls, yet in such works as "The Resignation" he begged to be "patient, virginal and proud."[38] What he feared most was that his Apostolic readers would think him "unclean."[39]

The Edwardian practitioners of the Higher Sodomy paid homage to three of their older Brothers who provided the Society with a history, philosophy, and justification of its friendships. Elected to the Society in 1866, J. E. McTaggart lectured on Hegel and, in his free time, allowed such privileged undergraduates as Strachey and Leonard Woolf to pay court in his rooms every Thursday evening. His Apostle paper "Violets or Orange Blossoms," a defense of male love, was prized and reread by future members of the Society. According to McTaggart's theory of reincarnation, male friendships developed out of a recognition of souls that had known one another in a previous existence. The communion of male souls in the perfect love of friendship constituted a heaven in need of no God. McTaggart designated Love—male love—as the Absolute.[40] Though he married in 1899, McTaggart promised the Society that his new state would neither replace nor transcend his ties to his Brothers. He refused to allow his conjugal relations to erode the "all-consuming" bonds of spiritual love.[41] In fact, his "phenomenal wife," Margaret Bird, seemed "almost Apostolic" in her fondness for metaphysical discussion and schoolboys.[42]

The most outspoken advocate and defender of male love was McTaggart's colleague Goldworthy Lowes Dickinson. This philosopher and Angel traced the classical Greek origins of both the spiritual and physical aspects of the Higher Sodomy. In an 1896 publication, Dickinson promoted the Greek view of life, oddly unaware of the similarities between the classical heritage he described and his contemporary society. Dickinson seemed smitten with the Greeks' gendered system of work and love. He praised the women of ancient Greece who nurtured the state's future soldiers and citizens but cited their shortcomings as the emotional and intellectual companions of men. Though some Greeks anticipated Tennyson's Victorian belief in the "complementarity of the sexes," even they possessed enough insight to recognize the "essential inferiority of women."[43] Determined to exclude women from the Society, Dickinson repeatedly reminded his Brothers of this "cardinal point" of innate female inequality. As objects of romantic love, women ranked far below men; in male-male love, the superior male self was duplicated instead of merely complemented. *The Greek View of Life* was also Dickinson's response to the recent Wilde trials. Passionate friendships between Greek men, Dickinson argued, were an "institution," particularly pederastic ties between youths and adults. The Apostles evoked the friendships of Achilles and Patroclus, Solon and Peisistratus, and Socrates and Alcibiades, in their pursuit of younger Embryos. As patrons or "fathers" of new brothers, the older Apostles and Angels expected devotion and affection. Whether in classical Greece or Victorian England, Dickinson insisted that the "highest reaches of emotional experience" existed in these male friendships.

Dickinson himself did not discover the "highest reaches" until his own election to the Apostles in 1890. In his memoirs, the philosopher confessed he expected, as a youth, to find love with a woman. However, his participation in the Society reaffirmed his "discovery of Greek Love as [he] had read of it in Plato."[44] Among his Brothers he joyously realized that male love "was a continuous and still existing fact," not simply an "exceptional Greek phenomenon."[45] But, in championing Plato as the new God, Dickinson came to regret the limits he placed on himself and his love. As a Cambridge don, he sought pederastic unions with such undergraduates as Roger Fry and E. M. Forster but usually feared to progress "beyond the embrace." Such actions, he believed, would "lower their love." His poetry dwelt on the "long duel" between love and desire. In his dialogue between the body and soul, the soul insists "we are bound together, that is why / what raises you, you see, may lower me." Regretfully, the body tells the soul, "So last as first, you miss the best of life / Waging with me this vain and desperate strife."[46] Even Dickinson realized that beyond the domain of Cambridge, "the city of friendship and truth," his theory of male love encountered serious moral and legal challenges. At times Dickinson internalized the phenomenal attitude regarding the Greek view of life and called himself "a man born crippled."[47] Strachey, although proud that he and his Brothers were not like "normal men," also regretted at times his own "unnatural affections."[48]

By 1903 Dickinson and McTaggart relinquished their sovereignty to the new philosophical genius of the Society, G. E. Moore. With the publication of *Principia Ethica,* Moore identified love and friendship as "the highest of human goods." Personal affection, an end in itself, "was of a completeness so great as to deserve setting this quite apart."[49] Similar to McTaggart, Moore associated copulation with women but "true love" with men. Women, like wine, belonged to "the most primitive of the so-called pleasures."[50] Though the young philosopher did not explicitly promote homosexuality, many of the undergraduate Apostles used the text as a defense of their romantic friendships. The "most self-evident goods" of "human intercourse" and "beautiful objects" surely included the pursuit of attractive young men. Upon reading the work, Strachey sent letters to several Brothers, announcing the "triumph of Truth," and to Moore he offered a "confession of faith." Grateful to Moore for rescuing Plato from "that indiscriminate heap of shattered rubbish," Strachey and Keynes pledged to instill a devotion to "Moorism" among the newcomers to the Society.[51]

Years later, Keynes admitted that the Apostles virtually ignored Moore's chapter on moral obligation. The young men were mainly interested in "states of mind," not action, achievements, or consequences. Their "undisturbed individualism" and political apathy was, for them, a protest against their parents' generation. Living only "in the present experience," the Apostles "repudiated entirely customary morals, conventions, and traditional wisdom." As Keynes explained in "My Early Beliefs," he and his Brothers were, "in the strict sense of the term, immoralists."[52]

Moore's Apostle papers, before the publication of *Principia Ethica,* did voice his belief in the merits of the Higher Sodomy. However, he was strict in his emphasis on the spiritual aspects of male friendship. In his 1894 essay "Achilles or Patroclus?" Moore argued that Brotherly Love was "the one final end of life," but he battled with the idea of copulation that "stunts or kills the capability . . . of enjoying the happiness of true love."[53] Moore recognized the difficulty in following his own philosophy and preferred at times the brand of Moorism as redefined by Strachey and Keynes. In 1899, Moore began a relationship with the Cambridge undergraduate A. R. Ainsworth, and though they lived together for several years until Ainsworth's marriage to Moore's sister, the two men carefully monitored the intensity of their friendship.[54] Lust and physical gratification, Moore insisted, would corrupt their pure bond.[55] Confronted by Strachey with the suggestion of a more physical union, Ainsworth replied that "it makes me feel smothered."[56] Having lost his young friend to a member of the opposite sex, Moore eventually followed the lead of McTaggart and wed in his middle age. As Victorian-educated gentlemen, they accommodated their philosophy to the social expectations and obligations of marriage and fatherhood. However, their lifelong membership to the Society guaranteed their continued attachment to youth and Love.

Moore's worshippers included his younger Brothers Keynes, Strachey, Woolf, and J. T. Sheppard, all of whom regarded *Principia Ethica* on par with Plato's *Symposium.* Within their privileged fraternity, they welcomed the meeting of other "Greek souls," but, curiously, devotion to Moorism led to a decline in the number of new members that the Brothers agreed to elect. Lytton Strachey's 1902 questionnaire regarding the possible election of Thoby Stephen indicates that Thoby's acknowledged beauty and "magnificence" could not compensate for his lack of understanding of Moore's philosophy. Occasionally, the strict requirements were ignored; the following elections of Arthur Hobhouse in 1905 and Rupert Brooke in 1908 proved that blond hair often did outweigh an Embryo's passion for philosophy.

Lytton Strachey and Keynes assumed their ascendancy over the Society between 1902 and 1906. Noel Annan believes the two men deliberately tried to "outrage the older generation" with their talk of the Higher Sodomy, and Bertrand Russell at the time of their leadership complained that in his own day homosexual relations among the Brothers "were unknown." Yet, Russell could not have been oblivious to the pederastic tendencies of Oscar Browning, McTaggart, or Dickinson. Still, he particularly disliked Strachey's "pose of cynical superiority," which to him was the mark of a "diseased and unnatural" person.[57] "Only a very high degree of civilisation enables a healthy person to stand him," he once told his lover, Lady Ottoline Morrell.[58] Convinced of the detrimental effects of all-male love, Russell ignored Strachey's message of the intellectual and spiritual benefits of the Higher Sodomy. Strachey's diary expressed what he saw as the essence of Sodomitical relations: "I want our intercourse to be unmarred by the weaknesses that I know are mine too often . . . let us be occupied with the cleansing aspirations of our art as much as with each other and with ourselves."[59] This constant reminder of the spiritual over the physical compelled one Brother to complain that the Apostles talked about copulation "but no one practices it!"[60]

Keynes's biographer, Robert Skidelsky, claims that for all their talk about sex, it was not really a homosexual bond but their unworldliness that united the Apostles.[61] They formed a protective coterie for those who were too shy or awkward to be comfortable in the phenomenal world. Leonard Woolf boasted that he and his Brothers were "really wonderful as failures," but his future wife put it less kindly when she described the Society members as "deficient in charm and beauty," and lacking in "physical splendour."[62] The men especially favored a state of adolescence, and the Angels of the 1890s joined the Apostles and Embryos of the 1900s in an effort to remain forever bound to the last shred of youth. As Leonard Woolf proudly declared, "We shall never 'settle down'—we shall be grey-haired undergraduates in our coffins. Is that the supremacy? After all, I believe it is."[63] The Society's bond of Brotherly Love promised its members the "prolonged innocence of boyhood."[64]

Leonard Woolf's membership in the Society was proof that Apostles could, if they so chose, distance themselves from the homosexual implications of the Higher Sodomy. Woolf had little interest in forming romantic attachments with his Brothers, but his correspondence makes it clear that he enjoyed the discussions of Brotherly Love. Unlike Russell, Woolf celebrated what he saw as Strachey's triumphant spread of sodomy throughout the university. Above all, he believed that membership in the Society offered certain men a position of superiority, and those who had felt out of place at public school now had their revenge. In his autobiography, Woolf explained that the Society was a refuge for the outsider—the scholar and intellectual who had been rejected by the "bloods" and the athletes: "But I think that we— and Lytton in particular—got a special measure of dislike from the athletes and their followers . . . and Lytton always looked very queer and had a squeaky voice."[65] Once outside Cambridge and now exposed to the phenomenal world, however, Woolf began to question the behavior of certain Brothers, including Strachey. In his letters from Ceylon, where he worked as a civil servant, Woolf boasted to Strachey of his relations with women and his growing passion for Virginia Stephen. Meanwhile, Strachey complained that Woolf "hardly referred" to his accounts of his own love affairs at Cambridge. Reminding Strachey that his behavior would surely arouse the "condemnation of Moore," Woolf went so far as to destroy a letter from Strachey that he considered too indecent.[66]

Though Strachey confessed to Woolf that he occasionally "sunk in the mud of [his] passion," he continued to write papers for the Society on the need for "restraint."[67] The tension between the spiritual and physical, or the higher and lower sodomy, became quite obvious in a number of Strachey's relationships at Cambridge. In 1902 Strachey believed he had found his ideal in another newly elected member of the Society, John T. Sheppard. Though only two years Strachey's junior, Sheppard assumed the role within this pederastic union as his "Dear Baby" and "Infant." Attracted to his friend's "intelligence, kindness, and character," Sheppard easily ignored Strachey's reputed physical unattractiveness. The almost daily correspondence between the Brothers reveals an increasing yet hesitant familiarity. When Sheppard signed one letter as "Your loving Frank," he added in a postscript, "I hesitated sometime before I wrote the last word, but it *is* appropriate, I think, and I like it, and I *have* written it."[68] In response, Strachey also rejected formality and ended his subsequent epistles with "Your loving Lytton." The two Brothers shared not only letters and Christian names but also dance lessons, holidays, embraces, strawberry-flavored kisses, and poetry. One inspired poem envisioned Sheppard as Strachey's "friend . . . brother . . . strange twin brother," with whom he longed "to fight, to leap, to run / to hunger, to embrace, to lust, to feel / each passionate moment thick upon each sense."[69] Such expressions of intimacy did not alarm those outside the Society. Sheppard's mother encouraged her son to spend more time with Strachey, certain that "it does you good only to see his face."[70]

The friendship that appeared so strong on paper and earned the approval of parents quickly dissolved under Strachey's own scrutiny. Within a year he recognized that, as a loving friend, in "flesh and spirit," Sheppard fell short of his ideal. In his "poor imagination" Strachey still loved his Brother yet could not excuse Sheppard's flaws of tardiness and "vagueness." To Strachey, "Romance," not Sheppard, was "the only thing worth living and dying for." Overwhelmed by Strachey's "visions" and "excitements," Sheppard confessed that he did not understand his Brother's definition of "platonic" and expressed "a terror of something—even the best things we have."[71] In answer to Strachey's pleas that, rather than fear him, he accept his love as a gift, Sheppard warned "You must not be carried off by fancies."[72] But, the final blow to the friendship, according to Strachey, was Sheppard's increasing interest in things "phenomenal." While Sheppard enjoyed the discussion of the Higher Sodomy, he relegated its lofty aims to his own pursuit of a future in academia and to his flirtation with Strachey's younger sister.

By 1903 Strachey concluded that, though they were Brothers, he and Sheppard ultimately belonged to "a construction of worlds so different," and they returned to formal forms of address.[73] Three years later, Strachey dared to call him "by the once familiar name" of Frank, but Sheppard, perhaps out of shame, preferred "to forget everything that happened since about the year 1900."[74] This failed relationship was alluded to in a play Strachey wrote for his Brothers in 1903, "Iphigenia in Tauris." In a previous attempt at Greek drama Strachey had celebrated the romantic love between male friends, yet in this unfinished effort, Pylades declares to Orestes, after being embraced by him, "You sicken me. You don't seem to care for any of the ordinary things . . . when you talk of something more than friendship, and I don't know what, ugh, you ought to be ashamed of yourself."[75] Strachey had added to Sheppard's letters a much stronger tone of reproach and disgust. Was he mocking Sheppard's prudishness or punishing himself for violating the rule of restraint? Despite the unhappy ending of both the fictional and actual relationships in 1903, this friendship set the pattern for most of Strachey's future loves. Although the age gap increased from two to twenty years, Strachey's objects of love all possessed physical qualities absent in himself, and in each instance, Strachey ignored the individual to pursue an abstract notion of Love. Since even his own Brothers did not understand his definition of platonic friendship, Strachey's vision of Brotherly Love was doomed to failure.

Sheppard's warning that the ideal "can only be in [Strachey's] fancies" went unheeded,[76] and Strachey soon found a replacement for his "Dear Baby" in a freshman Embryo, Arthur Hobhouse. Claiming the role of "father," Strachey offered to sponsor "Hobby's" election to the Society. Hobhouse looked "pink and delightful as embryos should," and his beauty and cleverness left Strachey entranced.[77] Unfortunately, Hobby preferred the attentions and sponsorship of Keynes, leaving Strachey, once again, with his "dead, shattered, dessicated hope of some companionship, some love."[78] In "The Two Triumphs," a poem dedicated but never delivered to Hobhouse, Strachey mournfully queried, "Why do you let him love you? Why not me? / Am I less worthy? Ah! That I am more / Is why I still must lose you, and why he / May taste the sweet fruit to the bitter core."[79] Although Keynes enjoyed Hobby's kisses and the touch of his hair, Strachey refused to acknowledge these as signs of Love. Untainted by physical expression, his own affection for the Embryo adhered faithfully to the Apostolic standard and thus represented the greater "triumph."

Having failed to achieve the ideal within his small circle at Cambridge, Strachey finally turned his attentions to those inhabitants of the unfamiliar phenomenal realm. With such little success among those trained in the philosophy and goals of Brotherly Love, Strachey wondered if he might find common Greek souls elsewhere. Rather than adapt to the "wrong world" outside the "only place" of Cambridge, Strachey attempted to introduce his new associates to the dictates of the Higher Sodomy. In this quest he was joined by Brother Keynes, but only Strachey carried his search into and beyond middle age. In seeking converts to the Greek view of life, Strachey longed to retain "the last shred of youth." Unlike those Brothers who grew old and married, Strachey remained "credulous and hopeful" that death would rescue him from such "disillusionment."[80] Strachey urged his young lovers to join him as he ran "out into the garden to pick nice sunshiny flowers and throw them into the face of the world," for soon they would be "middle-aged, married, respectable, and quite oblivious of how ridiculous they are."[81]

In early August of 1905, Lytton Strachey informed his "Brother Confessor" Keynes: "I've managed since I saw you last to catch a glimpse of Heaven. Incredible, quite—yet so it's happened. I want to go into the wilderness, or the world, and preach an infinitude of sermons on one text—'Embrace one another.' Oh yes, it's Duncan."[82] Strachey's maternal first cousin Duncan Grant had abandoned a university education to pursue an artistic career, supported by his family and numerous male admirers. Though not a Cambridge undergraduate, he befriended several Apostles, and his relations with Strachey and Keynes introduced him to the ideas and practices of the Higher Sodomy. The literary evidence of the ensuing love triangle highlights the problems that the Brothers confronted in their adherence to the code of romantic male love once outside the protective shelter of Cambridge. In converting theory into reality, they also recognized the difficulty in maintaining the fine line between spiritual and physical love.

Strachey initiated his pursuit of Grant after he left Cambridge and returned to his repressive parental London abode. Reluctantly, he began a career in journalism and lived primarily among women (his mother and three sisters). Lytton's entrance into the phenomenal world was complete, but Grant's temporary residence in the Strachey household rescued his cousin from these mundane distractions. The issue of incest briefly troubled Strachey, but he assured Keynes of his preference for the "mental" aspects of love and of his ability "to keep the physical affection in abeyance."[83] Much more than Sheppard or Hobhouse, Grant represented the Apostolic vision of masculine beauty and strength found only in Greek gods, and his face "was bold and just not rough . . . the full aquiline type, with frank blue eyes and incomparably lascivious lips."[84] He also was five years Strachey's junior and welcomed his cousin as a patron and worshipper. Above all, Grant belonged to the category Strachey defined as "true genius." As an artist he was "a colossal portent of fire and glory" and possessed all the traits Strachey lacked yet endlessly desired.[85]

From its beginning, the relationship displayed ominous imbalances. In return for his love letters, gifts of money, clothes, and books, Strachey received confessions of infidelity and long periods of silence. Both he and Grant seemed uncertain what path their love should take. During his free moments from his own phenomenal work at the India Office, Keynes sent Strachey letters of advice. While he declared "I am in love with your being in love," he warned his Brother "in the name of all that's good, don't go buggering him for buggery's sake. It would be so damned easy."[86] Keynes's warning seems to imply that Grant's exclusion from the real world of Cambridge made the artist susceptible to "degraded" physical expressions of love.

The degree of physical intimacy between Grant and Strachey remains unclear from their correspondence and the latter's journal. Strachey feared "the impediment of the flesh" and considered "the physical" as a "cruel and insurmountable barrier" to the "most cherished of our visions, and our most beautiful dreams."[87] Michael Holroyd also notes the Apostolic tendency of exaggeration in sexual matters. Infatuations rarely progressed beyond talk, and when a man "proposed," he simply extended an invitation to use Christian names; "rape" and "copulation" usually implied no more than a kiss or embrace. Leonard Woolf lightheartedly accused Strachey of "corrupting Cambridge just as Socrates corrupted Athens . . . for it seems to have completely broken out into open sodomy," but Strachey's pre-Duncan "affairs" with Apostles J. T. Sheppard and Arthur Hobhouse involved no more than sitting side by side on a sofa and embracing.[88]

Another explanation for the lack of detailed accounts of the physical relations between "loving friends" was the need for self-censorship and discretion. Keynes repeatedly warned Strachey to seal his letters properly, and Grant scolded his cousin for kissing him before their female relatives. But, more obvious to the Apostles than the lack of privacy was the absence of a language of sexual experience. Within the Society Strachey prohibited the use of slang, but the alternative medical vocabulary implied only deviance. To protect the "divinity" of male love, Strachey therefore urged the use of "certain Latin technical terms of sex" and warned that to avoid them "was a grave error, and even in mixed company, a weakness, and the use of synonyms a vulgarity." Holroyd criticizes Strachey's "undeveloped character" for his reliance on "the aid of a dead language," but the Apostle perceived that he and his Brothers had only the language of heterosexual experience from which to draw.[89] Unable adequately to describe his feelings to Grant, Strachey lamented, "I have nothing to say—except the unsayable."[90]

Alan Bray's research on the molly subculture of late seventeenth-century London describes a similar linguistic dilemma. Similar to the Apostles, the mollies converted such heterosexual terms as "chapel," "marriage," and "husband" to "new and ironic applications."[91] Bray implies a deliberately ironic use of the dominant language, but actually no other supply of words existed to describe the identities and acts of the molly or sodomite. More than a century later, the Apostles continued to grapple with this barrier to self-expression. Desmond MacCarthy noted that the Apostles "had no cut and dried rules of what a man ought and ought not to say to each other," a fact that could be both liberating and threatening for the young men.[92] Lytton's brother, James Strachey, asked the Apostles why "[w]e who are cleverer at analysis than Cicero and Montaigne . . . use 'love' to denote all feelings of a certain kind—whether towards men or women, while for a certain *other* kind we still have the word 'friendship?' "[93] Perhaps, Lytton once told Sheppard, "words when they are written are poor weak things, not much stronger or deeper when they are spoken. It is only our passions that have force, our emotions, and our desires."[94]

Imprisoned by language, Strachey resorted to the traditional essay and poetry forms to communicate his feelings for Duncan. Through his writings, many of which he shared with his Brothers, Strachey hoped to resolve his confusion on the two aspects of Love. While his poetry declared that "kisses are but accidents" and pure, spiritual love "the established infinite," Strachey battled his desire to "copulate" with Duncan.[95] Instead, he longed for "a universe of amaranthine calm, devoid of thought, forgetful of desire."[96] Standing on the hearthrug in December 1905, Strachey asked his Brothers, "Shall we take the Pledge?" and "hold under strict control the natural impetuosity of our desires?" The essay argued in favor of the Platonic view of temperance that discouraged any emotion "carried beyond a certain point" and warned against "that state of mind . . . in which the will is completely overmastered by passion." Though he confessed a desire for "the pleasures of physical expression," Strachey ultimately "pinned his faith to the flagstaff of Temperance." The idea of a superb restraint seemed to him "a wonderfully eminent one."[97]

Despite his confidence before his Brothers, Strachey soon found himself "lost among impossibles," and his letters to Grant indicate the weakening of the "superb restraint." The "heavenliest contradictions" between "the pure, the true, the secret, holy, and essential" Grant and "the body's flesh" had now become a living hell.[98] Grant's strength and beauty, Strachey conceded, were "trifles worth having," but the older cousin feared corruption of his "visions of perfect love which drown[ed] [him] in lakes of ecstacy."[99] Only to Keynes could Strachey confide that

> there are moments when it flashes upon me that it is only Duncan's body that I really care for and that it's only my mind that he cares for. . . . I sometimes find him very young; I wonder if he sometimes finds me proportionately unattractive.[100]

Unfortunately, Grant's version of his relations with Strachey remain unrecorded. Whether Strachey ever asked Grant to define his own concept of Love seems doubtful.

The departure of Grant to Paris in 1906 forced Strachey to pursue his ideal solely through letters. Before long, Grant admitted not only that he had fallen in love with Hobhouse, Strachey's and Keynes's former passion, but had proposed to his younger cousin, James Strachey, as well (in this instance, because of the familial ties, a proposal probably implied more than an exchange of Christian names). From Paris, Hobby sent written apologies to Strachey, admitting that his success with Grant was "a miscarriage of fortune because [Strachey's] feelings . . . are stronger."[101] The discovery of the Grant-Hobhouse cohabitation strengthened the bond of friendship between Strachey and Keynes. Both men envied the ease with which Grant seemed to deal with physical intimacy. The two Brothers, so self-assured on the hearth rug, confided their insecurities and self-loathings. Strachey refused to believe that anyone could be attracted to his frail body.[102] He also expressed a disdain for, or perhaps a fear of, physical intimacy. "The discomfort, the worry, and the unhealthiness" of physical love, he claimed, "are all too great."[103] Keynes, similar to Strachey, detested his physical appearance and avoided "hurling his hideous form" upon others.[104] The two god-like youths in Paris clearly preferred each other's beauty to the intellectual companionship and adoration of the London-based Apostles.

Unable, or unwilling, to compete with his new rival, Strachey retreated to his bed. Throughout his life he suffered from unidentifiable illnesses that usually struck during emotional crises. With his brother James at Cambridge, Strachey received care from his sisters, but he hid from them the secret of his depression. Keynes urged his friend to explain to Philippa Strachey the truth of his feelings for Duncan. Surely, this suffragette would comprehend the "inward and spiritual grace" of Strachey's emotions.[105] Lytton, however, insisted that a woman would only recognize "the absurdity of the whole thing"; such a subject "cannot be touched on." He not only feared that Pippa "would think [him] a hysteric" but doubted her ability to understand his love for Grant, which "passed the love of women."[106]

From the very beginning of his infatuation with Grant, Strachey predicted failure. In a more lucid moment, he recognized that in making Grant "the complete, the absolute, the adored," he placed the artist "too far above" his own reach. Correctly, he guessed that Grant "didn't dare face something he couldn't reciprocate."[107] Grant expressed no interest in attaining the ideal. To give kisses and embraces to his grateful cousin posed no problem, but exclamations of love, devotion, and commitment frightened and alienated him. To Keynes, Strachey wrote, "I don't think it occurs to him that I want so much. Oh! not copulation—but sleep and waking in his arms."[108] In one of his infrequent and unusually verbose epistles to Strachey, Grant explained that he was not searching for the "innermost secret of things"; rather, he felt an affection "on a lower level"—a wild thing, beastly and selfish.[109] Strachey desperately attempted to convince Grant, and himself, otherwise:

> I know there's a sort of passion—an animal feeling, a passion without affection which is merely bodily pleasure and doesn't count. But you have affection towards me—of that I'm convinced. When you embrace me you really do love me.[110]

Perhaps, Strachey continued, his advantages of age and literary skill simply made his feelings appear "more wonderful and dazzling" than those of Duncan. In despair, the champion of Platonic love longed "to be somehow someone else, to be able to say something." In short, Strachey wished to be a woman, so that he might embrace and kiss Grant, and "say all the things that a woman would be able to say." Ignoring the obstacle of Hobhouse, Strachey asked, "Isn't it true that if we were married it would be all right?"[111] Grant, surmising that Strachey really expected him to play Alcibiades to his cousin's Socrates, protested the attempt to "mold" him in the name of Love. Years later, the artist informed Strachey that his "searchlight of criticism" drove Grant away: "I felt distinctly, as I occasionally do, that you would go on always mentally finding fault with me until I became a second you."[112]

To Strachey's ravings that he had found and lost in Grant "a divinity, a quintessential soul," Keynes professed his disbelief that "intellectual and aesthetic pleasures and the physical and the passionate" exist "in a lump."[113] He reminded Strachey of Moore's concept of Love that inspires "an image so powerful that it often betrays [us] into arriving at it when the reality is not there." The aforesaid image of love, and not the reality of Duncan, haunted Strachey, and Keynes hoped his friend would not suffer "all the horrors and be led the whole damned dance at the beck" of an ideal.[114] Nevertheless, Keynes agreed to his Brother's request to befriend Grant and promote Strachey's cause, for by the summer of 1907 Hobhouse had abandoned the artist. With Grant's return to London, Strachey harbored fantasies of a shared residence with both his cousin and friend, but his scheme backfired. In July 1908, he learned that Grant and Keynes had fallen in love and planned to establish a household in London.

Confronted by deceit and yet another rival for Grant's love, Strachey turned to his younger brother, James, for support and sympathy. Also an Apostle, James shared the convictions of the Higher Sodomy, and his own failure to persuade Brother Rupert Brooke of the superiority of his affections made him an appropriate replacement for Brother Confessor. Lytton considered his friends' betrayal "utterly stupid and absurd, besides being incomprehensible," and he now doubted that Keynes ever understood the principles of Platonism. Writing to James, Lytton cried:

> He [Keynes] has come to me reeking with that semen, he has never thought that I should know. Oh! but there's only one thing I think—that the nature of Love has been hidden from him, that he is playing, that they are all playing, and taking themselves in.

Strachey wondered, "[I]s it a mercy or a hell that we at any rate should know what Love is?"[115] James also doubted that Keynes and

Grant were "in love" and called their "filthy condition" "merely silly." The couple, however, did regard their "condition" as Love and embarked on a "honeymoon" to Scotland. James's prediction of a brief fling crumbled as the honeymoon developed into a "marriage," based both in London and in Keynes's Cambridge residence. At Cambridge, James observed:

> The general appearance is *extraordinarily* married. I believe they're fixed . . . Perhaps I carry things rather far, but I don't believe I should mind them if they lived together quietly and alone in their suburb by the river. But why must it constantly be dragged before my nose?[116]

While he confided his misery to James, Lytton feigned a lack of jealousy and presented the grateful Keynes with a gift of books. Their subsequent correspondence, however, reveals the strained relations. Despite Grant's reminder to Strachey of the Apostolic rule that friendship is solider than any rock, the older cousin waged a slander campaign within the Society against Keynes's reputation.

The personal relations in which Strachey and his colleagues engaged have been praised by some feminist scholars for their absence of "jealousy and domination."[117] Strachey receives particular recognition for his "marvelous capability of love" and his "joyously, even mischievously open" sexuality.[118] However, Strachey's letters to Grant, as well as to his earlier loves, tell another story. Jealousy, an emotion relegated to things phenomenal, tormented him and eroded the "colossal moral superiority" that Strachey believed distinguished Apostles from other men. Lost in a mist of "damned inexplicability," Strachey begged Grant to help him decipher "what [he] felt, what [he] wanted."[119] He preferred any contact with the artist to none at all and refused to acknowledge Grant's affair with Keynes as more than a "filthy episode." Convinced that the love between Grant and Keynes was merely physical, Strachey wrote to his cousin:

> Though I like Maynard, I cannot think of him as you do, or else I suppose I should be in love with him too! The result is that I don't take your affair as seriously as you do either, and therefore imagine that you will some day or other return.[120]

Once again, according to Strachey, Keynes had achieved the physical triumph, while he claimed victory as the spiritual lover of Grant.

Contrary to Strachey's opinion, the "nature of Love" did not elude Keynes. Strachey's rival simply achieved, though briefly, physical pleasure as well as affection and intellectual companionship from the young artist. Grant's early letters to Keynes show no signs of "hardness" nor an absence of a "touch of romance" of which Strachey accused his cousin. Grant begged Keynes to stand between him and the rest of the world, and in exchange for financial and emotional support, he offered his Apostolic protector happiness in body and mind.[121] Within a year, however, Grant's penchant for flirtation and his long silences aroused Keynes's complaints of neglect. Keynes's supplications for attention resembled those of Strachey. In a typical plea, he wrote, "Dear Duncan, if I could kiss you and hold your hand I should be perfectly happy and from wanting to I am discontented and almost quite miserable."[122] He lamented the state of "widowhood" into which Grant's distance and indifference forced him, and by December 1910, the artist's expressed interest in the beautiful Adrian Stephen hastened the decline of the "marriage." As with his cousin, Grant again used his "difference" to justify what Keynes interpreted as "unkindness or want of sympathy." While Keynes clung to his fantasy of the couple sharing "a lovely cottage til the end of time," Grant confided to James Strachey that he "could no longer believe [him]self to be in love with a person who sometimes bores [him] and sometimes irritates [him], and from whom [he] can live apart without being unhappy."[123] For Keynes, Grant still expressed a passion "that is on the whole exceedingly strong," but the Apostle rejected the possibility of physical pleasure without love. Observing with delight the decline of the marriage, Strachey surmised that Keynes "was beginning to think that Duncan hasn't got much to offer him what he wants."[124] Duncan Grant had disappointed both Apostles in their quest for "the innermost secret of things."

Keynes's failure did not pave the way for Duncan's return to Strachey's arms. In fact, Grant was on the brink of committing the unforgivable sin of womanizing with his new artistic partner, Vanessa Bell. Despite this devastating setback, Strachey ignored his Brothers' advice to marry and continued his search for a new convert to his superior notion of romantic friendship. By the end of 1910 an "exquisite vision" rewarded his patience. Unschooled in the Higher Sodomy, an outsider to Bloomsbury, and a notorious womanizer, Henry Lamb posed an even greater challenge to Strachey's philosophy of Love than Sheppard, Hobhouse, or Grant. Similar to Grant, Lamb belonged to that special class which Strachey reverently associated with "true genius," the artist. Unlike Strachey's cousin, however, Lamb was, according to Holroyd, "exclusively heterosexual," with a wife and several mistresses.[125] Nevertheless, Lamb's letters to his admirer reveal not only an affection for Strachey but an ambiguous compliance with Strachey's rules of romantic male friendship.

Michael Holroyd attributes Strachey's attraction to the womanizing Lamb as a desire for "people whom he instinctively felt might use him badly."[126] However, had Strachey simply wanted passionate or physical gratification, he knew where to look, for his private correspondence indicates a knowledge of London's homosexual haunts. Rather, Strachey's self-constructed persona as a Higher Sodomite required him to seek chaste relations with those he deemed worthy of respect and whom he sensed would not threaten his dream of "spiritual" Love (unfortunately, Strachey's confidence in his ability to resist his friends' physical charms often faltered). Moreover, Strachey recognized that he had much to gain from his new association with Lamb. He now entered the bohemian Chelsea set of parties and artists that included Augustus John and Boris Anrep and altered his appearance accordingly. Strachey grew his hair long, pierced his ears, and discarded his collars for a rich purple scarf. His friend Lady Ottoline Morrell noted in her diary her reaction to Strachey's outward transformation: "They were a surprising pair as they walked the streets of London, as Lamb wore clothes of the 1860 period with a square brown hat, and Lytton a large black Carlyle felt hat and a black Italian cape."[127] The loud colors, jewelry, and long hair were part of an attempt to imitate the reputedly "virile" artists with whom he now mingled but could also have been an open declaration of his homosexuality. Rumors of an affair between Strachey and Lady Ottoline, the wife of Liberal Parliament member Philip Morrell and a patroness of the arts, added the finishing touches to this new and sexually ambiguous image. Of course, Strachey's main intention was to win Lamb's approval. The artist, according to Ottoline, "enjoyed leading Strachey forth into new fields of experience." Together they frequented pubs and mixed with what Strachey called "the lower orders."[128]

In a letter to his brother James, Lytton raved about his new friend. He described Lamb as "the most delightful companion in the world." In addition to his beauty, talent, and arrogance, Lamb's inaccessibility intensified Strachey's longing for "this angel of the devil." Strachey regarded any sign of affection from such a man as "miraculous," and his fear that the friendship might come to an end "forced [him] to cry out so."[129] Despite his exclamations of humility, Strachey frequently wavered in his willingness to accept Lamb's indifference. He complained of his friend's melancholy moods and his refusal to establish a common residence in London. Strachey's obsessive fantasy of shared domestic bliss disturbed Lamb, whose response evoked memories of Grant: "I wish I could deserve it," he wrote to Strachey, "but an odd fate always intervenes at the moments for which I design my graceful replies. . . . Meanwhile, please give me credit for a little less delusion on the quality of your feelings for me."[130] Apologizing, Strachey admitted to being "exaggerated and *maladif* in these affairs," but he told Lamb, "I think perhaps you don't realise how horribly I've suffered during the last 6 or 7 years from loneliness." His relations with Lamb offered Strachey "a gushing of new life through [his] veins."[131]

Although he appeared calm, Strachey confided to James that his affection for the moody artist "tossed him about on a sea of emotion." His neuritis resurfaced, and after a holiday with Lamb during the summer of 1912, Strachey rushed back to Ottoline's arms "an emotional, nervous, and physical wreck, ill and bruised in spirit, haunted and shocked."[132] What had destroyed the "miraculous" friendship? Lamb explained to Strachey that

> there was only one thing which enraged me seriously—the perpetual raising of the question of our relationship. I believe that it is one of the plants that are apt to wither if one keeps digging it up to look at the roots.

All the other disagreements, he continued, "were surmountable, however acute, with the aid of a proper faith in the roots." Finally, Lamb intimated that "best friends are not always best companions."[133] Instead, the artist preferred the physical attentions that he associated with companionship from Lady Ottoline.

Rejected by Lamb for his female friend, Strachey once again retreated to his familiar world of Cambridge. Having graduated to the rank of Angel, he continued to participate in Society elections and deliver his compositions on Love to his younger Brothers. Among them he hoped to reaffirm his devotion to a concept of male friendship so strongly rejected by Lamb. An experienced and bruised practitioner of the Apostolic rule of "candor," Strachey now advised his Brothers of the "disadvantages of expressing one's feelings." He certainly knew of "the uneasiness and the doubt which it may introduce into relationships." The "most unfortunate complication" between loving friends, however, was not candor but lust, and he confessed his failure to escape this weakness. Reminiscent of his earlier speech before the Society on the glory of Platonic temperance, Strachey concluded that "the *best* moment is the embrace before copulation—or after; copulation itself . . . is copulation."[134] Standing before his young audience, he recalled a kiss given to a Brother and its "singular sequel— the second kiss so inevitably desired and so inevitably bound to surpass even the wonders of the first," but, "then just in that very moment, the disappointment, the failure, the ruin, and the dust."[135] Delivering this essay before other believers in the Higher Sodomy, Strachey reminded himself that with Lamb there was no possibility of that "singular sequel."

Outside the secure haven of Cambridge and the Society, Strachey realized "the longer I live, the more plainly I perceive that I was not made for this world." He belonged, instead, "to some other solar system altogether," while Lamb preferred "to live in the present."[136] By 1914 war intervened and rescued Lamb, who excitedly volunteered as an ambulance driver, from what he considered Strachey's realm of Platonic fantasy. Strachey himself remained a prisoner of that fantasy, and even his postwar literary fame took second place to his youthful dream of Love. Having ventured into the phenomenal worlds of Bloomsbury and Chelsea, the middle-aged Strachey now extended his search for the ideal to the unfamiliar territory of Oxford. Since his undergraduate days, Strachey had led his Brothers' derision of the rival university. Oxford was a "second-rate" institution that fostered unfeeling, nonintellectual womanizers, and "the glorification of the half-and-half."[137] Years later, the famous author managed to look beyond these flaws to discover "that fair and still-unspotted page" in the "Chronicle of Age"—youth.[138]

Reginald Partridge returned to Oxford a war hero still in possession of beauty, muscular strength, and youth. He welcomed the overtures of friendship from Strachey, who assumed his familiar role of patron and repeatedly saved Partridge from financial ruin. Strachey rechristened his new friend "Ralph" and accepted invitations to read before the Oxford Essay Club. At Oxford, Strachey shared his Brothers' gospel of Love, but he primarily directed his speeches to Partridge. Addressing Partridge as "My dear one," Strachey asked him to "believe in my fondness for you." The friendship with his "dearest creature" made Strachey "curiously happy," and he sent his "fond love" to Partridge. When apart from the student, Strachey felt "rather dejected and lonely" and longed "to press [Partridge's] hand" before he went to his "solitary couch."[139] In addition to his fond love, Strachey offered Partridge "all the kisses and etceteras" that he "didn't dare to send" in the post.[140]

With Partridge, Strachey partially achieved his dream of a domestic union. Upon leaving Oxford, Ralph accepted Strachey's offer to live at his country house, chauffer his car, and maintain the grounds. However, Partridge refused to relinquish the one flaw Strachey attributed to all Oxford men. As his physical and emotional companions, Partridge preferred women and wed Lytton's housemate and caretaker, Dora Carrington. Though Strachey insisted the newlyweds remain in his home, he confessed to Carrington that the marriage left him "dreadfully helpless." Unable to attain even the brief marital bliss enjoyed by Keynes and Grant, Strachey lamented, "I am lonely and I am all too truly growing old. . . . I have never had my moon!"[141]

Three years passed before Strachey fell in love again, and for the last time. Strachey discovered in the Oxford undergraduate Roger Senhouse a passionate lover of literature as well as "a creature with a melting smile and dark grey eyes."[142] Senhouse offered the middle-aged writer what he had searched for in all his affairs. With his new companion, Strachey returned to youth, to the "prolonged innocence of boyhood," and to the comfort of the purest love found nowhere but in a mother's arms. Roger seemed "a free gift from Providence," and two years after their first meeting in 1924, he "opened the door" for Strachey to an "exquisite Paradise."[143]

Had Strachey at last reconciled the physical and spiritual sides of Love? He claimed to have found "a divine dream come true," another Greek soul with whom he shared his intellect and body. Unfortunately, his enthusiasm soon gave way to doubt. "I fear I am almost too happy when I am with you," he told Senhouse. "Oh dear, the intricacy and intensity of existence reduces me to a shadow."[144] Finally in the presence of Love, Strachey lost his will, his importance, and his soul. Senhouse willingly participated in Strachey's fantasies, playing Nero or father to Strachey's servant or child. Yet, when Strachey rented a London flat and suggested "marriage," Senhouse retreated. The determination to realize his philosophy of male love ultimately cost Strachey his "divine dream." In an effort to escape, Senhouse wrote, "Too often I have cloaked my proper feelings, and . . . I am falling into a part that is not true to my nature."[145] Senhouse confessed that with anything more than physical love, "he was quite at a loss to know how to reciprocate." Deceived by youth and Roger's charm, Strachey collapsed "in almost despair," and though he vowed to "achieve some kind of detachment about R.," he agonized over Senhouse's silences and foreign excursions with other men.[146]

Just months before his death, Strachey confided to his diary that being apart from his "beloved one" compared only to the agony of dying. A passage in the diary also suggests that Strachey at last understood the reason for his repeated failures in Love. Did Roger simply remind him of an unrequited schoolboy passion—the redheaded George Underwood of thirty-five years ago? Was he just one more in a succession of younger men designated as the ideal? "Now I think of it, there's a marked resemblance between my feelings for him [Underwood] and for R. [Roger]," Strachey wrote.

> I was older and enormously devoted and obsessed; he was very sweet and very affectionate, but what he really liked was going off somewhere with . . . the chic older boys while I was left in the lurch, ruminating and desperate. And now, after thirty-five years . . . Well, I hope I'm *slightly* more realistic.[147]

Nevertheless, Strachey continued to deny these men a voice in his fantasy. Similar to the others before him, Senhouse tried to resist the rules dictated by Strachey, who refused "to accept the fact that he [Roger] must be allowed to have his own tastes." Disappointed that these tastes were not "what [Strachey] would have wished," he recorded his final regrets for "what is unattainable."[148]

The quest for the unattainable characterized Strachey's affairs from his university days until his death. The details of these relationships represent much more than salacious chapters in the personal stories of famous men. The surviving records provide vital evidence for the historical analysis of sexuality and masculinity in early twentieth-century England. Strachey adhered to a philosophy of male friendship that not only distinguished him from "hollow women" but from the "womanisers" who "committed the unforgivable sin" of loving the inferior sex.[149] Downplaying the physical aspects of love, the Higher Sodomite also armed himself against identification with the lowly "sodomites" and "buggers" of the corrupt phenomenal world. Unlike the Apostles, the majority lacked a notion of the "nature of Love" and settled for the "filthy condition" of lust. As in the cases of Strachey and Keynes, romantic friendships often expanded to include such beautiful and talented men as Duncan Grant or Henry Lamb. To be Apostolic, however, these relations had to maintain the precarious balance between the spiritual and physical sides of Love. The advocates of the Greek view of life were not oblivious or immune to the phenomenal world. They used their Apostolic identity as a protective shield against the growing social, moral, and legal prohibitions on all-male love. Unfortunately, as Strachey repeatedly discovered, this form of self-identification did not protect the Brothers from disappointment in love.

The conflicting notions of love that appear in the correspondence between Strachey and his friends indicate a spectrum of male sexual behavior and identity. To simply label these men "homosexual" or "heterosexual" silences their voices and reveals little of their relations or the ways in which they viewed and expressed their masculinity. Strachey's generation of Apostles comprised an all-male subculture that tried to withstand the repressive power of England's sexology movement. As Plato's descendants, the Edwardian Apostles deliberately placed themselves at odds with those outside the Society, but their feelings of superiority began to disintegrate under the watchful eyes of the dominant phenomenal culture. All public displays of male-male affection seemed forbidden. Though the Apostles declared they possessed a higher morality from that binding ordinary men, they did recognize that their claim to masculinity was especially precarious. The sense of liberation that Strachey had experienced upon reading Plato's *Symposium* did not alleviate the fears that sexology and the law had created. Rumors circulated that the Apostles were "disciples of the deplorable practices of Oscar Wilde," and that the Society was a "hotbed of vice."[150] As the medical and legal professions narrowed the definition of sodomy, the Brothers, therefore, tried to expand it. To them, "sodomy" conveyed a wide range of emotions and acts, from all-male reading parties to the exchange of Christian names and embraces; sexual intercourse did not always fall within the definition of male love. They shunned such labels as "invert" and "homosexual" and the writings of Havelock Ellis and Edward Carpenter, which seemed "sordid and silly." After reading Carpenter's 1908 publication, *The Intermediate Sex*, Dickinson remarked, "[H]e believes and practices the physical very frankly. How is it that public opinion hasn't managed to get him to prison and murder him is a mystery."[151] After the war,

Strachey was especially appalled by reports of younger men at Cambridge seeking "the treatment" for homosexuality—spending two hundred pounds and four months on the analyst's couch "to wonder whether they could bear the thought of a woman's private parts."[152] He continued to return to Cambridge, as an Angel, to remind his Brothers and himself, that they still had the "greater triumph."

Identifying oneself as a Higher Sodomite, therefore, represented a form of resistance and self-affirmation. Rather than accept the marginal status of "inverts" and be lumped into a category that pathologized all forms of male-male love, the Brothers carved a space for themselves that excluded divisions between normal and abnormal men. Unfortunately, the phenomenal world and its morals constantly intruded and eroded the Apostles' more fluid concept of male love. At the very age at which Strachey discovered Plato, he witnessed the criminalization of this form of male love under the 1885 Criminal Law Amendment Act, and the "depressing" memory of Oscar Wilde's trial and rumors of ruined reputations of public school masters haunted his adulthood. Had Wilde not been convicted, Strachey believed the "history of English culture might have been quite different."[153] Yet, even Strachey avoided the company of those whose reputations were dubious. In a letter to Keynes, he described one such incident involving a suspected homosexual: "I was dreadfully afraid of his clinging to us (after your accounts) and I fear I may have been rude."[154] But Keynes simply reminded Strachey "how damned careful one has to be . . . in this respect one is so hopelessly in the hands of others."[155] Marginalized by sexology and the law or magnified by Platonism, neither discourse proved sufficient to encompass the complicated relationships (many of which were unmarked by the physical) among the Brothers.

The romantic relations between the men discussed in this chapter not only challenged the neat medical and legal distinctions between "normal" heterosexual and "abnormal" homosexual men but also threatened some of their contemporaries' concepts of masculinity. One of Strachey's most outspoken critics of his own day was the controversial writer D. H. Lawrence. Lawrence despised the entire Society of Brothers and the Bloomsbury Group but especially considered Strachey and Keynes as "the prevalence of evil." He hoped to rescue his friend Bertrand Russell from the younger generation of Apostles whom, he believed, had introduced to Cambridge the "insidious disease" of sodomy.[156] Russell's letter to Lady Ottoline attests to the success of Lawrence's mission: "You had nearly made me believe there is no great harm in it, but I have reverted, and all the examples I know confirm me in thinking it sterilizing."[157] Russell, so actively involved in political and social movements, feared that his Brothers' devotion to a cult of male love placed them too far above the phenomenal world. He defined "manly" behavior in terms of action and blamed the Edwardian Apostles for their neglect of duty. Lawrence, whose novels of sexual passion assigned no place to an intellectualized version of male friendship, also saw the Brothers not as men but as "beetles." For Lawrence, sexual liberation and the "phallic regeneration" of England did not allow for desire between men, even when such desire, according to the Brothers, comprised the "love of souls."[158] Strachey sensed Lawrence's contempt. At a party he "noticed for a second a look of intense disgust and hatred flash in his [Lawrence's] face—caused by—ah! whom?"[159] Stressing his own class superiority, Strachey was able to laugh at Lawrence's "obsession with moralizing, to say nothing of a barbaric anti-civilisation outlook which I disapprove of."[160]

Within the Society, Strachey faced severe condemnation, not only from older members such as Russell, but also from younger ones such as Rupert Brooke. Brooke recognized the prestige of the Society but tried to distance himself from what he perceived as its taint of effeminacy. Strachey feared this hostile Embryo as "a dangerous unknown entity" and tried to prevent Brooke's election to the Society in 1908. After several failed attempts to befriend Brooke, Strachey preferred to tease him about football matches and finally wrote him off as a "dim prig."[161] For Brooke, simply to be thin and sickly like Strachey was to be homosexual. In his war sonnet, "Peace" (1914), Brooke denounced his Brothers as "half-men" with their "sick hearts" and "dirty songs." Disgusted by what he saw as their lack of virility, Brooke exaggerated the behavior he witnessed at Cambridge. Still, even Keynes and Strachey were careful to stay within certain bounds of acceptable masculinity. When either man attempted cross-dressing, for example, they did so not at Society meetings but behind closed doors with their female friends. Not only Brooke regarded Strachey's lounging style and high-pitched voice as suspect; Apostle E. M. Forster, upon meeting Strachey in 1902, imagined the "risk" of "knowing a person with a voice like that."[162]

Such groups as the Apostles can be read, according to Rita Felski, as a heroic protest against bourgeois masculine culture or, more likely, as an expression of disdain for anyone who is not part of the same bohemian elite.[163] Though Strachey and Keynes spoke of giving the world a "great moral upheaval," they did not, as they believed, promote a "radical" or altogether new philosophy. The practitioners of the "New Style of Love" looked to the past for a pattern of action and ultimately refashioned a "glorious Greece" in the Victorian image. Their updated version of Greek Love, "the greatest of all goods," reinforced the nineteenth-century concept of innate difference between the sexes and necessitated the separation of men's and women's spheres of activity. Devotion to the Greek view of life, which grew out of the Victorian revival of classical education, ironically condoned the class and gender system Strachey had declared "repellent."[164] As Peter Gay has shown, classical culture was remote enough to be the special province of those who could master difficult dead languages, yet close enough to give pleasure and supply models.[165] While Strachey may have failed at football, he did excel at the "masculine" and upper-class subjects of Greek literature and male friendship. Strachey's generation of Apostles looked to the Greeks for legitimacy, rather than to the emerging medical and legal discourses, but as the following chapter will show, the Higher Sodomy was rarely transgressive on the social and political levels or sexually liberating on the personal one. Furthermore, the Higher Sodomy rested on Victorian notions of race and resulted in a form of sexual imperialism. The dualism between spiritual love and physical passion compelled many Brothers to journey to the slums of London or abroad for sexual gratification. By making a distinction between the higher and the lower forms of sodomy, the Apostles set for themselves a standard of sexual behavior that they did not always find easy or desirable to achieve. Looking back, Keynes criticized the Apostolic view for its "thinness—not only of judgment, but also of feeling." The ideal, he said, "left out altogether certain and powerful and valuable springs of feeling."[166] In other words, emotions and bodies disrupted the idea of pure love.

The opposite sex particularly suffered the scorn of the Higher Sodomites. Intellectually, physically, and emotionally inferior, women failed to offer the Apostles the level of friendship derived from ancient Greece. Keynes confessed his hatred for the "stupid, ugly and repellent" female mind, and Strachey preferred his well-educated sisters in the roles of domestic caretakers and nurturers.[167] Mothers and sisters merited respect, but as confidantes and companions, they ranked far below men. Barred from the "real" world, women lacked an understanding of the male pleasures of conversation, friendship, and physical and spiritual love. Belief in the Higher Sodomy, however, did not prevent Apostles from marrying the inferior female other. Twice rejected by Grant, Strachey proposed marriage to Virginia Stephen, driven by "the horror of his present wobble and the imagination of married peace."[168] His Brothers McTaggart, Moore, Keynes, and James Strachey all wed, and even Lytton eventually settled into domestic intimacy with Dora Carrington. Despite these female and phenomenal distractions of their advancing years, the Apostles periodically retreated to Cambridge. The return to "paradise," whether to deliver essays or sponsor Embryos, reaffirmed their Apostolic identity, youth, and "colossal moral superiority."

At one point during Strachey's painfully unsuccessful pursuit of Duncan Grant, Keynes noted with amazement that the two Brothers never fell in love with each other. After all, they were intellectual equals and champions of Platonism. The philosophy of Brotherly Love, however, rested on difference, and the Higher Sodomite essentially defined himself in relation to the other. Though they shared Strachey's social background, his selected ideals represented the attributes he both lacked and coveted. Grant and Lamb possessed the creative and "untrained" mind of the artist, while Sheppard, Hobhouse, Partridge, and Senhouse dangled youth, strength, and beauty before Strachey's eyes. Strachey assumed that these youths, with their different bodies, minds, and attitudes, awaited his admiring yet controlling guidance. As he attempted to realize his theory of male love, Strachey never considered its oppressive aspects. He expected each designated ideal to fulfill a vision of Love discussed at Saturday evening meetings, and he repeatedly ignored his friends' refusals to become "a second you." Possibly, Grant and Senhouse described their brand of love as beastly, wild, and "lower" to defend themselves from the "visions of ecstacy" in which Strachey longed to drown them. Even the womanizers with whom he fell in love preferred the possibility of the physical rather than succumbing to Strachey's Platonic fantasy of spiritual oneness.

The extension of the Higher Sodomy beyond the rooms of the Conversazione Society revealed the Brothers' need to distinguish themselves from the non-Apostolic man and woman. Outside of Cambridge existed the "limbo of unintimacy" in which the vast mass of "individuals so devoid of colour" dwelled.[169] Strachey's Greek soul raised him above these "pale essential beings" who chose the basest form of physical love over manly intellectual and spiritual companionship. However, the self-styled Platonist occasionally discovered, though briefly, worthy objects of his pederastic devotion. Unfortunately, the process of idealization, so central to the Higher Sodomy, inevitably wrought disappointment, and the aging Strachey finally conceded that "one's love seems to be sometimes so far above oneself, one despairs."[170] The infidelity of Grant and Senhouse and the womanizing tastes of Lamb and Partridge ultimately proved the superior triumph of the proponents of the Greek view of life. Until the rest of the world was converted, the Apostolic seekers of the ideal would continue to "suffer in eminent silence til the day after tomorrow."[171]

Chapter 2

Ploughboys, Postboys, and Arabian Nights: Lytton Strachey Explores the Sexual Empire

In one of his many letters to his fellow Apostle John Maynard Keynes, Lytton Strachey once referred to the endless possibilities for sexual fulfillment that surrounded them: "One's amours are very like the British Empire—all over the shop, in every sort of unexpected ridiculous corner. One plants one's penis on so many peculiar spots!"[1] The so-called "lower orders" and "black races" that lived within the borders of England and its empire surely existed for their amusement. Strachey's boast seems to contradict his Apostolic declarations of sexual restraint as well as the reputation he later established for himself with his 1918 bestseller, *Eminent Victorians*. While he publicly denounced the political and financial costs of imperialism, he privately enjoyed its erotic opportunities.[2] As a homosexual, however, Strachey did occupy a less secure position within the homeland than most upper-middle-class men, and his path to the empire often was strewn more with guilt than pleasure. This chapter examines his attempts to reconcile the real and phenomenal, or the higher and lower, forms of love through the construction of his very own sexual empire.

The story of the wealthy European male who planted his penis in foreign terrain has been well documented in recent historical and literary studies. Equating male travel with a "spermatic journey," Eric Leed describes how European men used their foreign vacations to fulfill "primal needs" with exotic partners.[3] According to Jeffrey Weeks, the world of fleeting contacts, casual sex, and the excitement of meeting other people from another class or race was inherent to the upper-middle-class male ethos.[4] In the nineteenth century, the Orient (broadly defined to encompass India, Asia, and Africa) especially represented a space in which Europeans expected to find a different type of sexuality unobtainable at home. As Edward Said notes, through travel and literature, the West observed the East, reduced it to clichés and stereotypes, and engaged in a thorough, guilt-free penetration of its secrets.[5] More "primitive" and "natural" cultures could be found closer to home, as well, in the slums or in the Mediterranean. In *The Seduction of the Mediterranean,* Robert Aldrich traces the homosexual's journey from northern to southern Europe—a regression from civilization to a more "natural" and "free" state.[6] Darker complexions and poverty signified to the Victorian imagination not only racial inferiority but also savagery and sensuality.[7] Desire for the "other" provided the Westerner with an escape from "drab bourgeois life" and entailed a liberating loss of inhibition.[8]

For the upper-middle-class homosexual at the fin de siècle, the "journey to sex"[9] was further necessitated by the threat of public exposure and incarceration. Such late Victorian writers as John Addington Symonds, Oscar Wilde, and Andre Gide traveled to Venice or Algiers to escape the panoptical gaze of legal and medical authorities who had designated same-sex desire as illicit, pathological, and illegal.[10] As Stephen Adams points out, in the nineteenth century, "going away" was the more likely starting point than "coming out" in the homosexual's assertion of his identity.[11] These "sexual exiles" crossed boundaries of class and race not only to find physical gratification but to free themselves from the constraints of bourgeois masculinity; escape into the realm of the other promised an "erasure of the self."[12]

The notion of homosexuality as a strategy of transgression and liberation, however, is severely limited, as a discussion of Strachey's case will illustrate. Richard Sennett's theory of containment contends that transgression ultimately involves defiance based on dependence—i.e., a rebellion not against authority but within it.[13] For such men as Wilde and Strachey who linked desire with race and class differences, transgression became a form of imperialism. The upper-middle-class homosexual did not necessarily "lose" himself within the realm of the other but rather required that realm to reaffirm his own class identity and position of superiority.[14] Although sexual colonialism may seem exploitative, it is also indicative of the fragility of masculinity at the psychic level.[15] Designating the Indian, black, Italian, and laborer as "erotic spectacle" and the embodiment of social and sexual inferiority, the wealthy homosexual protected himself from becoming what Kaja Silverman calls a "marginal male subjectivity."[16]

At various stages in his career, Strachey played with different sexual identities, switching back and forth between bourgeois masculinity and a more effeminate type of behavior that athletic observers such as Rupert Brooke and George Mallory called "queer." Whether he was shooting at stags and wearing tweed suits to please his family and reading public or donning the high heels and scarves of his female Bloomsbury friends, Strachey frequently blurred the boundaries between these two supposedly separate identities. Reluctant to accept the confining label of "homosexual," Strachey sought idealized unions with younger men of his own class, while displacing his desire for them onto foreign and working-class youths. Though he poked fun at normative masculinity in his literary constructions of imperial sexuality, Strachey's model of male-male love relied on differences of age, class, and race and was rarely guilt free. The letters and stories examined in this chapter (most of which were not intended for publication) highlight some of the problems that confronted Strachey as he sought to express and enjoy male desire during a still very repressive era. Ultimately, he found his own spermatic journey littered with legal, social, and personal obstacles.

Much of the focus in queer studies has been devoted to Victorian bourgeois male intellectuals who viewed foreigners through the "lens of exoticism" and inextricably linked their sexual identity and behavior to the other. In the post-Wildean years, all homoerotic desires and acts were forbidden and suspect, thus making the Orient, Mediterranean, or London slums even more inviting. Strachey's relationship to the other, however, was much more ambivalent and complex. Until his death in 1932, he continued to prefer what his colleague E. M. Forster came to consider an outdated and constraining version of Neoplatonism, resorting to imperialist fantasies and acts to preserve the "inward and spiritual grace" of male love between social equals. Although his experiences may not have been representative of all upper-class homosexuals, Strachey's self-immersion into his private empire suggests the limited options for those who aspired to be Plato's descendants in early twentieth-century England. Frustrated over his repeated failures to find his ideal in the world outside his fiction, Strachey despaired that "my love's far larger than the universe, yet lies forever coffined in my verse."[17]

In his writings Strachey replicated (perhaps unconsciously) imperialist discourse, treating class and race as interchangeable, to create a male other onto whom he projected what he sometimes called his own "unnatural desires."[18] He sexualized and bestialized the other and desired the very traits that defined the other as inferior. Within the borders of his literary paradise, Strachey found freedom from the watchful eyes of family and police, and from his own insecurities and fears about the body. At times, Strachey moved beyond this imaginative space and crossed over into the world of the exotic other, but disillusionment, disgust, and fear colored his descriptions of these encounters. The unpublished page, therefore, seemed to offer the safest arena in which to acknowledge and articulate desire. Referring to his diary, Strachey wrote, "I hope it will fulfil the office of safety-valve to my morbidity."[19]

Strachey attributed his retreat to fantasy to the "restriction" and "oppression" of his upbringing. In his essay "69 Lancaster Gate," he described for his Bloomsbury colleagues the quintessentially Victorian home of his youth. Though a descendant of "the aristocratic tradition of the eighteenth century," Strachey was born in 1880 into "the middle-class professional world of the Victorians in which the old forms still lingered." Despite his family's background of wealth and titles, Strachey deliberately emphasized and exaggerated its new bourgeois status, the stifling dinners, and his parents' overbearing presence to magnify his own eventual rebellion. The conclusion of the essay alludes to the association Strachey made between his sexual desires and his escape from "the weight of the circumambient air" of Lancaster Gate. At night when he imagined the naked "slim body of a youth of nineteen" beside him in bed, he at last "threw off that weight, [his] spirit leaping into freedom and beatitude." Curiously, when that form beside him was not an illusion, but rather a fair-haired youth of his own class (his cousin Duncan Grant), he wondered "why it was that I did not want—not in the very least—what the opportunity so perfectly offered."[20]

The Strachey who read this essay before his Bloomsbury audience in 1922 ridiculed his bourgeois childhood, but throughout his life he tried desperately to fit in at 69 Lancaster Gate. Unlike his older brothers who followed their father's career path into colonial civil service, Lytton, diagnosed a neurasthenic, seemed destined for the sickbed. Since, as he told Keynes, the subject of his homosexuality "cannot be even touched on," his family correspondence from Cambridge, where he hung Sir Richard Strachey's portrait, was filled with news of flirtations with attractive women and the occasional stag hunt. He envied his sisters, Philippa and Pernel, for their radical activity as suffragists, and Dorothy, whose marriage to the French artist Simon Bussy "shook the foundations" of the family home.[21] Yet his own acts of rebellion—pierced ears, velvet cloaks, purple scarves—had to be hidden from his mother, "her Ladyship." Only at Bloomsbury's private parties, in the enclosed rooms at Cambridge, and in his writings did Strachey feel free to escape the restrictive norms of masculinity embodied by the older Strachey men.

Nevertheless, the Orientalist tone that would come to dominate Strachey's "liberating" fantasies was both an affirmation and by-product of his birthright. The eleventh child of Lieutenant General Sir Richard Strachey and Jane Maria Grant, Lytton remembered a childhood filled with tales of ancestral service to Victoria's empire. And, as the godson of the First Earl of Lytton, Viceroy of India, Lytton Strachey seemed destined for his own career as a colonial civil servant. To that end, Lady Strachey supervised her son's early education, the fruits of which included watercolors of imagined Arabian deserts, camels, and Asian men, and a nursery "National Song" that urged children to "Live for England's Glory, Die for England's Gain!"[22] She also compiled a required reading list for young Lytton that combined Goethe and Virgil with Kipling and the *Lives of Indian Officers.* Unlike his older brothers who acquired their knowledge of India firsthand, Lytton breathed the Eastern air of his mother's memories. India was for her a "stage-play reminiscent of the *Arabian Nights,* but, she added, the country's "deceitful and cunning natives" had to be "judged by a different standard."[23] The image of a dark and barbaric race, in which Indians and Arabs remained indistinguishable, shaped Strachey's perception of the nameless masses ruled by his parents' generation.

Strachey's indoctrination in the merits of colonial rule and its professional benefits continued throughout his public school years. Similar to the Strachey family, the late Victorian school disseminated and celebrated British imperialism.[24] The public school also contributed to the process of "Englishness," or the construction of a national male identity based on gender, race, and class exclusivity.[25] The young boys of the public schools learned not only the elite dead languages of Greek and Latin but also the ideals of service, habits of authority, and feelings of superiority.[26] Unfortunately, Strachey's persistent ill health interfered with his headmaster's plans to foster within this general's son the necessary traits of athleticism, leadership, and patriotism. Lady Strachey, therefore, took it upon herself to supplement Lytton's diet with beef teas and his formal education with a partial tour of the empire. While on a six-month recuperative cruise in 1893, Strachey passed the days improving his geography and English composition as well as his appreciation for the home country's possessions. For the teenage boy, the voyage "was like some beautiful dream," enhanced with "picturesque Arabs, camel rides, magical beauty, thrilling adventures, and marvellous carnivals." Strachey's travel log not only echoed the memories of his mother but confirmed his own view of the strange races he encountered as "unique" but "not so nice."[27]

During the cruise Strachey crafted one of his first tales of the Orient. "An Adventure in the Night" applauds the bravery of the English colonial servant who slays tigers and commands the natives all in a day's work.[28] Confined to bed with intestinal problems, Strachey concocted for himself a fearless and strong alter ego, a man more similar to his father than himself. Lytton patterned his sketch of the conquering hero and obedient beasts on other stories of the empire he had read at home. According to Satya Mohanty, such children's fiction as Kipling's *Kim* helped to fashion the imperial self from within, simultaneously shaping and articulating colonialist desires.[29] Though not laden with sexual overtones, Strachey's own story indicated an early awareness of the alleged dangers of the Orient, as well as the sharp racial and class distinctions between the ruler and the ruled. A hazardous and threatening environment, the Eastern landscape in Strachey's adult fiction would come to harbor passions that needed to be tamed and controlled.

This attitude toward the Orient as a vast region outside the confines of "civilization"—a region to be explored, enjoyed, and mastered—carried over into Strachey's university writings. Similar to Oxford, Cambridge University sent forth hundreds of young men prepared for the India Civil Service Exam, including Strachey's closest friends, J. M. Keynes and Leonard Woolf. At Cambridge, Strachey further articulated his theories on the advantages of the empire. In an essay titled "Shall We Be Missionaries?" he presented two opposing views of imperialism: one as an excuse for vandalism and murder and the other as a necessity for the protection and development of England's dependencies. The essay regretfully acknowledged that men such as Sir Richard Strachey served the empire as "merely policemen and railway makers, and benevolent merchants." Disappointed that the British Empire "cannot be properly compared to the Roman empire,"

Strachey concluded that Victoria's rule at least prevented "a state of things only less tolerable than barbarism."[30] Strachey also paid homage to the efforts of the imperial administrator, selecting his family's hero, Warren Hastings, as the subject of his senior thesis. Declaring Hastings the "one great figure of his time," Strachey attributed the salvation of India, "and with India the Empire," to the practical statesmanship of the eighteenth-century imperialist.[31]

Despite his written testimonies to the necessity of the empire, Strachey had no intention of leaving behind the "comforts of civilisation" to become "a good public servant."[32] He performed so poorly at his interviews with the board of education that he permanently shattered Lady Strachey's ambitions for his career as a civil servant. Strachey's biographer, Michael Holroyd, insists that the Cambridge graduate deliberately sabotaged his future as an act of rebellion against his mother.[33] This rebellion, however, only guaranteed his prolonged residency at Lancaster Gate, now dominated by the Strachey women, who provided their brother with "a little rest, a little home life, a little comfort."[34]

After breaking with family tradition, Strachey tried to convince his friends to follow his lead in escaping "the horror of the solitude and the wretchedness of every single creature out there."[35] The real evils of colonial service, he argued, lay in the "degrading influences of those years and years away from civilisation."[36] In his letters to his young Oxford friend Bernard Swithinbank, Strachey recalled his vicarious experience of imperial duty: "I've seen my brothers and what's happened to them, and it's sickening to think of!" Rather than go to Burma where he would "be a great man and rule the blacks," Swithinbank should imitate Strachey's example and enjoy his "chance of being well-off and comfortable among the decent things of life."[37]

Once outside the haven of the university, the Apostles' successful avoidance of such lower "phenomenal" distractions as lust and wealth proved almost impossible. Strachey doubted whether any but "exceptional Apostolic persons ought to have anything to do with it [the phenomenal world]." Even his hero, Hastings, did not escape criticism, since his decision to go to India had cost the world "a great Greek scholar." As for himself, Strachey announced that he was "going the whole hog," renouncing ambition, "useful" professions, and contact with "the working man."[38] Much to his dismay, most of Strachey's Cambridge colleagues refused to disassociate themselves from phenomenal concerns, and upon graduation, many Brothers chose the secure path of civil service. Once away from England, the young colonial agents reported to Strachey of their discovery of the sexual novelties of the imperial world. At Cambridge the Brothers had found literary treatments of homosexuality in their Greek texts, but the Orient was where it was practiced in the present day.[39] Not only did these young men assume that they would be free of all social, moral, and legal inhibitions, but that the natives would gladly indulge their sexual whims.[40]

Strachey's vision of the empire as an arena of seductiveness and corruption seemed confirmed by the reports of his friends abroad. In his letters from Ceylon, where he "ruled the blacks" as a civil servant from 1904 to 1911, Leonard Woolf told Strachey of the "sheer desperation of life."[41] Woolf described his own "degraded debauches [with] half-caste whores," as well as the "apparent rampantness of sodomy" among the natives. Strachey received this news with a mixture of envy and disgust. He reminded Woolf of the Apostolic creed of restraint and urged him to return at once to the security of Cambridge. Woolf, however, accused Strachey of a neglect of "duty": "I have never said that to rule niggers in Ceylon with a zest . . . and have a 'jolly good time' is Apostolic, but such a 'condition' is happier than that of a decaying querulous Apostle with nothing but memories and desires."[42] Ignoring this reproach and the lure of the "extraordinarily beautiful" male bodies in Ceylon, Strachey still insisted that no pleasures alleviated the great pain of life outside of England.

While other Apostles served the empire, Strachey proudly distinguished himself from these colonial agents. Even his older brother Oliver Strachey, also employed in imperial service, had warned that in India he would find "nobody who has ever read a book, or looked at a picture, or heard a particle of music, or ever thought, or even spoken to anybody who has ever thought."[43] Small wonder that Lytton declined an invitation to India in 1906, though his brother Oliver suggested that such a visit promised a journalist "an immediate capacity to write with intimate and first-hand knowledge on all questions of the East."[44] Such firsthand knowledge was not, however, a prerequisite for Strachey's membership to the Oriental Club in 1922. Though not an Anglo-Indian by birth or service, Strachey took his place among retired civil servants and military officers who gathered at this West End sturdy fortress of Anglo-Indian solidarity.[45] Announcing his membership to Virginia Woolf, Strachey wrote, "Do you know that I have joined the Oriental Club? . . . One becomes 65, with an income of 5000 a year, directly one enters it.

Just the place for me, you see. Excellent claret, too."[46] As "public schools of adults," such clubs asserted the racial and class superiority of their members.[47] When he did venture abroad, Strachey longed to return to the comforts of his club. Similar to the British Museum, the club represented to him "ordinary life, freedom, and civilization"—in short, the very antithesis of the Orient.[48]

Contented to remain an armchair Orientalist, Strachey relied on his imagination and the reports of friends to compose his tales of the East. His vision of the world outside of England was no different from that of most middle- and upper-class tourists and colonial servants. In particular, Strachey adopted the association of the Orient with sexual escapism. The Victorian clichés of the East—sodomitic princes, ointments, harems, slaves—and the stereotypically lustful and deceitful "blacks" repeatedly appear in Strachey's private fiction of Oriental sex. In his stories he attired foreigners in silk robes and then unveiled the mysteries that he hoped lurked beneath them. He did not need to don this attire himself, as did his countrymen Sir Richard Burton and T. E. Lawrence. Without physically journeying to the parts of the "Sotadic Zone" in which, according to Burton, "*le vice*" prevailed, Strachey easily envisioned the "unspeakable" practices of a "race born of pederasts."[49] Reading Leonard Woolf's letters, Strachey conjured up images of crimes of passion committed by black catamites and respectable white men. He was certain that lascivious male natives ran naked and wild, inciting their English rulers to lose control.[50]

Well versed in the nineteenth-century cult of the exotic East, Strachey assumed that to submit to the "black's" embrace was to pass from a world of civilized values to one of primitive and self-destructive passion.[51] In Strachey's case, he protected his already fragile masculinity by maintaining a physical and literary distance from the East. The Orient provided a malleable territory for literary experimentation, while his own reluctance to venture outside the Western world kept his fantasy of imperial sex in tact.

Strachey's friends expressed surprise at his reluctance to actually visit the erotic sites of which he wrote. His cousin, the artist Duncan Grant, convinced Strachey that the world of his imagination was not unlike the reality. Describing a visit to Senegal, Grant declared that "the camels, the cries, the colours, the mysteries, the beauties" were the *Arabian Nights* reincarnate.[52] Receiving postcards on which appeared turbanned, half-naked, dark-skinned youths, Strachey ignored his friends' pleas to "Come out East."[53] Though he may have wished he were there, Strachey declined the invitations, responding that "the thought of pure lust is unpleasant to me."[54] Thirty years after his boyhood cruise, the forty-three-year-old Strachey finally traveled beyond the borders of "civilisation." During a visit to Algeria he observed that "the Arabs in this country place seem to me most romantic in their white head-dresses—but oh! so unapproachable." Beneath their "romantic" guise, all Arabs, Strachey concluded, were "undoubtedly dangerous."[55] Illness, which always accompanied Strachey on his travels, facilitated his resistance to the Arabs' exotic charms. Indeed, Strachey used his sickness as a strategy of protection from his "lower" desires. To justify his avoidance of temptation, he explained to his friends, "My tastes are not at all in the direction of blacks. . . . The more black they are, the more I dislike them."[56]

Strachey primarily approached the East not as an active participant but as a curious and admiring observer. Most of his adult fictional depictions of the East remained unpublished in his lifetime and were intended as entertainment for his Cambridge and Bloomsbury colleagues. Strachey's stories specularized[57] the inhabitants of the Orient and designated the "black" as the essence of social and sexual marginality. Unspecified Arab countries provided a convenient setting for the exploration of the theme of homosexuality, as practiced by both the natives and the visiting white men. Idealizing the Orient as a homosexual "promised land," Strachey further strengthened the artificial sexual polarity between the Western and non-Western worlds.

In her study "The Chic of Araby," Marjorie Garber identifies the Orient as an "intermediate zone"—a place where pederasty, homosexuality, and transsexualism were perceived by Westerners as viable options.[58] Strachey's fiction of sexual escapism frequently applied such techniques as transvestism and mistaken identity. Written solely for the eyes and ears of the Apostles, "An Arabian Night" described the persistent love of a king for a common shepherd. Despite the king's promises of jewels and wealth, the youth preferred the "sinewy limbs and brawny body" of the local blacksmith. To win the attentions of the boy, the monarch ordered his arrest and then, disguised as another prisoner, aided in the shepherd's escape from jail. At night, the king finally removed his cloak, revealing his "goodly proportions, noble to look upon, with a mighty body and long limbs." Unable to resist such a "manly form," the shepherd at last acknowledged his love for the king and returned with him to his palace and bed.[59]

Literary critic Paul Levy calls "An Arabian Night" Strachey's vision of a homosexual utopia. The exotic background, Levy notes, provided not only "color and romance" but a locale where the prejudices of Strachey's own society could be suspended.[60] Levy ignores, however, the Orientalist assumptions that form the foundation of Strachey's sexual paradise. In making the "deviant" and illegal desire of England the norm of Arabia, Strachey perpetuated the notion that the "lower sodomy" *was* rampant among the "darker races." Also, the unresolved class and age antagonisms between the monarch and the shepherd remained crucial to the men's union. As he lay in his "bed of state," the king introduced the shepherd, now adorned with a silken turban and golden ornaments, to the rest of his envious court. As the third-person narrator of this tale of lust, Strachey unveiled and unleashed the passion that he believed raged beneath the clothes of these dark men.

When the Englishman did appear in Strachey's fiction of exotic lust, he usually served as an object of pity. Struggling with his passion for men and persecuted by his country's legal code, the Western gentleman sought refuge in the Orient. In "A Curious Manuscript Discovered in Morocco, and Now Printed for the First Time," Strachey detailed the tribulations of a former university don. Having dared to love another man, the English don was driven from his home and propelled toward that "barbarous country" of the story's title. Once there, he wondered, "[S]upposing I had committed every one of these 'immoral' acts, are you quite sure that you are right to bundle me off to Morocco?" While the dark continent, or "home of savages," freed him from the legal and moral barriers to his love, the sacrifice of "civilisation" and the hordes of "coloured men" lessened the joys of his newfound liberty. Condemned for "copulating in a somewhat unusual manner," the don now lived among "savages unacquainted with the classics," whose chief amusement "is to roast their enemies in front of the kitchen fire."[61]

The dilemma between sexual liberation and cultural deprivation also summarized the theme of Strachey's unfinished typescript "The Intermediaries, or Marriage a la Mode." Bequeathed a set of "strange papers" from a former university friend and colonial colleague, the narrator could not escape the documents' "queer effect." Reading the papers "out there, in that wide flat broiling dazzling desert, among those gibbering savages and those stagnant lagoons," he discovered the tragic secret of his deceased friend. Upon his return to England, the narrator immediately shared the horrific papers with another Englishman, but before handing over the mysterious legacy, he warned:

> Think of the lagoons as you read the things, and remember that they were type-written out there, five thousand miles from Cambridge, by a typewriter which reigned supreme over half a continent . . . a mysterious image of Europe, of civilisation, of home.[62]

Leonard Woolf's description of the "sheer desperation of life" that dominated the region "out there" strongly shaped Strachey's tale of the consequences of leaving behind the university, intellectual male company, and the higher Love of the Greeks. The image of the typewriter ensured the superiority of the dead friend, the narrator, and Strachey over the savages who somehow lured white men to commit unspeakable sins of the flesh. Strachey's story is also reminiscent of the Victorian imperialist writings of H. Rider Haggard. In *She*, the homoerotic longings of Cambridge bachelor don Ludwig Horace Holly for his beautiful but dying friend, John Vincey, compel him to accept the mysterious chest of papers that eventually leads him to the "measureless desolation" of Africa, all the while "longing for my comfortable rooms at Cambridge."[63]

Strachey's private stories contrasted significantly with his diaries' accounts of his own sexual practices and desires. In fact, such desires and explicit references to his sexual behavior remain absent from his journals, which instead chronicle his battles with his career and health. He had idealized Cambridge and its inhabitants, so that any discussion of male desire would have to take place in the realm of the make-believe. When he met athlete George Mallory in 1909, Strachey described him at length to his friend Clive Bell, relying on Oriental references to capture his sexual allure. Mallory had "the refinement and delicacy of a Chinese print . . . yes, he has Chinese eyes," and his beauty "plunged [Strachey] up to the eyes in all the spices of Arabia." Unfortunately (or perhaps fortunately, given Strachey's fear of sexual reciprocation and his "uneasy" health), Mallory's foreignness was tempered by his "Englishness"—his plan to be a schoolmaster and his unremarkable intelligence.[64]

Strachey also faced moments when writing about the other became playing the other. Strachey occasionally wrote Oriental-themed plays for his colleagues to perform at parties and, in one instance, for a women's suffrage benefit sponsored by the Strachey sisters. A strange choice, the play "A Son of Heaven" depicted the Chinese imperial court at the time of the Boxer Rebellion but also resembled life at 69 Lancaster Gate—with an overbearing Empress Dowager, her weakling son, and a troup of eunuchs.[65]

This use of camp Orientalism, as George Piggford notes, was typical of Bloomsbury. Strachey enjoyed dressing in silk garments, looking, in Virginia Woolf's words, like an "oriental potentate," while the young Virginia Stephen and her brother Adrian had once disguised themselves as Abyssinian royalty, in turbans, caftans, and blackened faces, as part of the Dreadnought Hoax.[66] Piggford insists these acts deliberately parodied Victorian sexuality and colonialism, but even Bloomsbury's most radical members often spoke as colonizers, representing the dominant structures of power.[67] Keynes and Strachey, for example, were determined to keep blacks out of the Society of Apostles, though they jokingly fantasized about finding them in their beds at night, and at Gordon Square, members of the Bloomsbury Group discussed such pressing issues as the need to sterilize blacks in England.

Although most of Strachey's accounts of male passion among the savages were for private audiences, homoeroticism did spill over into his published biographical studies. In writing the history of General Gordon (Part IV of *Eminent Victorians*), Strachey attributed to the colonial soldier the very desires that he secretly harbored toward the mysterious races. Similar to Strachey, Gordon's "soul revolted against dinner parties and stiff shirts," and the presence of "especially fashionable ladies filled him with uneasiness."[68] According to Strachey's account, Gordon "was particularly fond of boys" and encouraged the ragged street Arabs and rough sailor lads to crowd about him. Welcoming these youths into his home, Gordon offered them lessons, advice, and employment to prepare them "as they went out into the world." This portrait of the general presented Gordon's paternal and loving interest in the "coloured boys" of Khartoum as his most admirable character trait. In this world away from England, Gordon discovered the "glamour and mystery of the whole strange scene." He relished the "dark-faced populace, the soldiers," and, most of all, the "re-awakened consciousness of power." This discovery "seized upon, engulfed, and worked new transformations," not only upon Gordon, but upon his biographer as well.[69] Outside Strachey's London bedsit and small circle of friends existed a wealth of dangerous and tempting attractions, pursued and dominated by men much braver than himself. To Strachey, Gordon seemed a hero on par with Warren Hastings. Though he disliked Gordon's warmongering, he envied his accessibility to foreign youths.

Fortunately for Strachey, the sexually curious did not have to travel as far as Khartoum to discover potential objects of desire. In particular, the nearby territory of southern Europe was home to a less threatening and slightly more familiar "other," but one that gave imaginary satisfaction, nonetheless. In the Mediterranean countries, the mysteries of race and class merged in the tanned skin and muscular physiques of the guides and waiters who serviced the wealthy male tourists. Venetian gondoliers frequently appeared in the travel accounts of such Victorians as John Addington Symonds, whose tubercular frame sharply contrasted with the "powerful and radiant manhood" of the working class.[70] Italy, the home of "Botticelli's art and naked youths," also beckoned to Strachey.[71] Simply reading Duncan Grant's descriptions of the bathing "gilded youth" made Lytton "mad with envy and desire."[72] Travel to southern Europe was a natural complement to British education and culture. Conversant with classical culture and its "naughty bits," male university graduates went south in search of ruins, Renaissance art, sun, and boys; the south was, in short, a site of athleticism, mysticism, and decadence.[73] Yet, as Richard Dellamora notes, representations of the Mediterranean failed to "suture the difference between material and imaginary reality." Although these excursions provided the opportunity for imagining a "better love," this erotic fantasy was usually marked by class and ethnic snobbery.[74]

In 1913 Strachey embarked on his own grand tour of the Mediterranean, already prepared to encounter the beauties of that "perfect place." E. M. Forster had recommended the Mediterranean as an inexpensive and warm vacation spot that also offered "other advantages," so that Strachey knew where to find cheap "bed and boy."[75] Weakened by his initial attempts to write his *Victorian Silhouettes* (later published as *Eminent Victorians*), Strachey hoped to regain his physical strength and seek "adventure." (He apparently missed the ironic contrast of his own Mediterranean fantasy with his literary satire of Victorian bourgeois culture and imperialism.) He spent his Neapolitan evenings in the company of English majors and their wives and listened to

Italian love songs, but during the day he embarked on excursions into a town "packed with wonders." Writing to Lady Ottoline Morrell, Strachey conjured up images of the Italian past: "What a life it must have been . . . Some wonderful slave boy would come out from under the shady rooms and pick you some irises and then drift off to the baths as the sun was setting." He particularly longed to experience those now distant nights, for "what nights those must have been!"[76]

Unfortunately, ethnocentrism and cultural arrogance coexisted with the traveler's admiration, enjoyment, and idolization of the south. These pilgrimages to find culture and boys often were tainted by bad service, strange smells, and crowds. Strachey was not immune to these drawbacks, especially the "foreign bad weather," and spent much of his visit to Italy sick in bed. In Naples, he recovered, and found himself in "a whirl of ecstacy . . . my hands shake so with excitement" that he feared his snapshots were "no doubt all failures."[77] He visited Pompeii, but found that Forster had quite misrepresented it, and his uncomfortable lodgings ruined the pleasure of the other sights.

In Rome, Strachey reminisced about Cambridge and tried to feel at home among the architectural wonders. Those very comforts he ridiculed as "English" and bourgeois became attractive in this foreign setting. Reading the *Daily Mail* in English tea shops, he partially succeeded in domesticating the foreign, making it familiar and safe, as he admired the youths from his café table. Yet, any plan he may have had to rediscover the Platonic culture discussed at Apostolic meetings was bound to fail in this setting. The beauty of the Mediterranean youths could not compensate for the overall primitiveness of the place. In another letter to Lady Ottoline, Strachey lamented, "I haven't spoken one word to an intelligent human being for a month, and I'm beginning to feel it."[78]

In later visits to Italy, Strachey, now a successful writer, avoided this pitfall by bringing with him young male traveling companions. University-educated and handsome, Sebastian Sprott accompanied Strachey to Venice in 1922, where they found a "sublime" gondolier. Upon his return the following year, Strachey rejoiced that Francesco appeared "exactly the same as ever." Attired in his white pants, large black hat, and unbuttoned blouse, Francesco was just one of many sites to be enjoyed by the traveling pleasure seeker. The youth's beauty, however, did not raise him above the level of a "splendid animal." As Strachey rowed beside his young Cambridge companion, he noted that Sprott's collarless shirt tarnished his "ultra respectable" appearance, making him too similar to Francesco. Even on the canals of Venice, Strachey adhered to the class distinctions that separated the tourist from the "degraded gondolier."[79] During this trip, Strachey sensed that Sprott's "sentimentality is not directed toward me," but rather than look longingly at the gondolier, Strachey fantasized about another young Englishman, Ralph Partridge, at home and courting Strachey's housemate, Dora Carrington. Writing from Venice, Strachey told Ralph, "I hug you a hundred times and bite your ears. Don't you still realise what I feel for you? How profoundly I love you?" Strachey would not allow himself to enjoy fully the exotic Mediterranean and instead wished for the unattainable pleasures of home—a higher Love that he knew would remain untainted but also unrequited.[80]

In 1926 Strachey returned yet again to Italy with his last lover, Roger Senhouse, hoping that in Italy he would appear less aged and unattractive to his much younger companion. "I believe the breezes of the Channel and the sunlight of Rome will set me up completely."[81] They visited the Colloseum, drank Chianti under trees, and lodged in luxurious hotels. At last, Strachey was able to announce, "everything has equalled my wildest hopes." Rather than pay for sex with the local boys, he used the Mediterranean to seduce Senhouse, finally, he believed, enjoying the higher and lower sodomy with his ideal. This storybook setting, unfortunately, only temporarily eased the tensions caused by Senhouse's infidelities and his confessed inability to reciprocate "anything more than physical love."[82]

While Strachey stretched the literary and geographic borders of the sexually exotic to encompass southern Europe as well as the broadly defined Orient, he carefully excluded those regions he regarded as too similar to his home country. Visiting the spas in Stockholm, Strachey noted that "nearly everyone's good-looking," but he regretted that "there's a chastity about the type" that he found "mortifying."[83] The physical proximity of bath attendants failed to "agitate" Strachey, "in spite of the singular intimacies of their operations."[84] Even the Germans, whose "face and form" were "miraculously beautiful," did not arouse Strachey's desire. Sharing an imperial history, these white-skinned beauties too closely resembled Strachey's ideal of the English man's "astonishing form, molded sinuosity, divine strength, and colour, and firmness of flow."[85] For Strachey, it was not so much the body itself as the representation of the body that constituted erotic spectacle.[86]

Equating "blackness" with the male bodies of India, Africa, the Mediterranean, and the London slums, he ensured that difference, not sameness, formed the basis of his lower desires.[87]

As Strachey's own limited travels indicate, the English man of privilege did not have far to go to discover the other. The embodiment of an alien sexuality already resided within Strachey's own city. Previous generations of social scientists, moralists, and reformers had identified the "other nation" of the poor and working-class masses of London, who comprised not only a separate class but a race as well. To the nineteenth-century bourgeois reader and observer, the city represented the locus of fear, disgust, and fascination.[88] Strachey, too, saw the threat and lure of the "dangerous classes," not, as Henry Mayhew described, in their predilection for crime, but rather in what he perceived as their "debased" enjoyment of the lower sodomy. Similar to the black of the non-Western world, the English male commoner possessed a savage, sensual nature; he belonged to the category of half-man–half-child and simultaneously aroused desire and disgust.[89]

Certainly, Strachey never expected to find companionship and "real" love among the so-called "filth-packet" of the general population. He preferred to avoid "the squalor, the filth, the desolation" of the city, which he said stank and was overrun with "dirty 'furriners.'"[90] However, the lure of "outcast London" eventually triumphed over Strachey's objections, and he became what Judith Walkowitz calls an "urban explorer."[91] He crossed the geographically and class-divided city, transgressing boundaries by imagined and real illicit acts of sex. As in the cases of such other upper-class urban explorers as "Walter," Arthur Munby, and Wilde, the "socially peripheral" became symbolically central to Strachey; the "low-Other" of the East End formed a primary eroticized constituent of his fantasy life.[92] Guilt and self-loathing, however, often interfered with Strachey's enjoyment of the city and reduced him to the frustrating practice of fleeting glances. Unlike Keynes, who kept count of his sexual encounters in an engagement diary, Strachey regarded such documentation of desire as "inordinately filthy." Hearing of Keynes's "statistics," Strachey felt "as if [he] was walking in a drain."[93] Strachey's own diaries omitted such details, but his correspondence and essays directed to his Bloomsbury colleagues exaggerated his "adventures" among the working classes.

Strachey's introduction to the lower orders of the East End finally occurred during his unsuccessful courtship of the artist Henry Lamb.

His earlier forays into the slums of Liverpool, while a teenage student secretly reading Plato, had resulted in terror and flight. The crowds of people "gave [him] the shivers," but Strachey was more troubled by the reminders of his own physicality. Seeing his reflection in shop windows while avoiding eye contact with others, Strachey was "agonised by thoughts of [his] appearance. Of course it is hideous."[94] Years later, Lamb helped Strachey learn to use the city to overcome some of his insecurities. He drew Strachey away from his elite Cambridge and Bloomsbury circles and inducted him into the "Bohemian set" of cafés and pubs frequented by London's working class. Lady Ottoline Morrell (Lamb's lover at the time) recalled how the two men "would sit in pubs and mix with 'the lower orders,' as Strachey called them, picking up strange friends."[95] Strachey flirted with youths while Lamb looked for "exquisite figures" to paint. Though a self-proclaimed womanizer, the artist titillated Strachey with stories of male beauties who disrobed for money, and Strachey envied such accessibility to these bodies.

It was Lamb who presented Strachey with a Kodak camera for his Italian holidays, to snap shots of "old buildings and young boys."[96] It was also while he slummed with Lamb that Strachey began his own transformation, exchanging his tweeds for corduroy suits, red ties, purple scarves, and earrings. So different from the military and civil service dress of his male relatives, Strachey's new wardrobe violently upset some observers when he appeared at the Savile Club. When a club member asked, "But why should he dress like that?" Max Beerbohm responded, "Hang it all, why *shouldn't* he dress like that?"[97] Bragging that he now looked like a "French decadent poet," Strachey sensed that those who "eyed me with the greatest severity" perceived his style of dress as decidedly unmanly.[98] This makeover, however, was kept a secret from his mother, who still financially supported Strachey. Curiously, after the success of *Eminent Victorians,* the now independent author returned to his sober tweeds. More than ever in the public eye, Strachey carefully manipulated elements of the dominant masculinity when necessary, always prepared to shed them at private Bloomsbury parties.

The war, which fueled Strachey's literary career, eventually interrupted his pursuit of Lamb. The artist exchanged his paintbrush for a job as a dresser in a London war hospital where he discovered even more "heavenly visions." In the military hospital ward, Lamb, unbelievably, saw "no depressing spectacles of grave illness." Instead, he savored "glimpses of nice torsos during washing times," and he guessed that Strachey "could imagine the pleasure" he enjoyed.[99] Displayed on canvass or described within these letters, the young men and their nice torsos also existed for Strachey's gaze and amusement.

While "delectable visions" of soldiers posed welcome interruptions in Strachey's work, actual contact with men of the lower orders sometimes proved threatening to his masculinity and class privilege. Describing to Lady Ottoline Morrell his own military physical, Strachey commented:

> It was queer finding myself with four members of the lower classes—two of them simply roughs out of the streets, filthy, dirty—crammed behind a screen in the corner of a room, and told to undress. For a few moments I realised what it was like to *be* one of the lower classes. The appalling indignity of it! To come out after it was all over, and find myself being called "Sir" by policemen and ticket collectors was a distinct satisfaction.[100]

This incident can be read in more than one way. The removal of clothes had not only blurred class distinctions but also erased the poorer men's desirability. As the differences (visibly signified by clothes) between the men decreased, Strachey's anxiety increased. Boundaries needed to be preserved to maintain erotic desire. Or, perhaps this encounter shattered Strachey's fantasy of a democracy of a world out of clothes. It was not their clothes that emphasized differences of class, but their naked bodies—unwashed and not as well fed as Strachey's. Further, Strachey's fear of contagion reinforced the inequality of their situations and turned desire into repulsion. In another letter to Vanessa Bell, Strachey compared wartime London to "a sticky spider's web. My wings are caught and I flutter and flutter in vain."[101]

Strachey's responses to the men of the lower orders ranged from admiration to contempt. Overall, the charm of these men, he declared, derived from their faces, which were "as little intellectualized as their hands."[102] Separated from the "colourless masses," the laboring man in a rural setting elicited the most praise from Strachey. Spotting "two admirable mechanics" at the Express Dairy, Strachey asked his brother James, "Why cannot we live and die with such as those?" Though not beautiful, the mechanics "were sensible and gay" and "neither treacherous nor affected."[103] He congratulated Keynes for his "flirtations" with shepherds and young farmers in the North Downs and envied Grant's "twilight adventures with ploughboys" in Bristol.[104] When his housemate Dora Carrington informed him that their male farm laborers spent their afternoons copulating in the barn, Strachey attributed their behavior to the moral freedom of the rural landscape.

When Strachey at last befriended one of the countryside's "unaffected creatures," he assumed the patriarchal lead. During the last two years of World War I, Strachey corresponded with a young ploughboy, Ted Roussell, whom he met while on holiday in Chichester. Holroyd refers to the relationship as a "trivial romantic affair [of] little lasting significance."[105] Yet, of Strachey's hundreds of correspondents, Roussell was the only member of the lower classes to elicit such epistolary interest. Their letters reveal Strachey's class-defined notions of love and pleasure as well as Roussell's own careful manipulation of his new friend.

Historian Peter Bailey's study of Victorian working-class culture suggests how a working man played at certain roles, meeting the expectations of his social betters without completely capitulating to the arrangement in which he found himself.[106] Roussell's choice of words seemed to confirm the class barrier separating "Ned" from his "dear Sir," but the context of these letters was so apparently an undressing of class difference that he had to be careful not to threaten Strachey's position of power. (Roussell's family played along with this game, writing to Strachey to inform him of the youth's death from wounds and thanking him for his interest in Ted's welfare.) In his letters before entering the military, Roussell described the physical labor he performed on the farm ("I am still ploughing as hard as ever") and encouraged Strachey to return soon to Chichester, for "my ears are getting fit for you to come down and pull them again." In another letter, Roussell enclosed a photo of himself in uniform, and the ploughboy's misspelled accounts of military life complained of food rations and low wages. In response to such remarks as "I only get three shillings a week—I don't think it is a very big lot—do you?" Roussell received gifts of clothing, cigarettes, chocolates, and even a wristwatch from his "dear Sir."[107]

Referring to Roussell as his "donkey," Strachey playfully equated him with the other beasts of the countryside (and perhaps hinted at Ted's physical endowments), and the social barrier that divided the men both propelled and hindered Strachey's desire for the ploughboy. When Strachey read E. M. Forster's 1914 draft of *Maurice,* he criticized the relationship between Cambridge-educated Maurice Hall and the gamekeeper, Alec Scudder. Based on "curiosity and lust," such a union, Strachey insisted, "would only last six weeks."[108] Could someone such as Ted then possibly take the place of the ideal that Strachey longed for since his Cambridge days? The youth's sudden death in 1918 resolved this dilemma, thwarting any imagined or real promise of sexual fulfillment.

The occurrence of war intensified Strachey's awareness of other men of Ted's class. He spent many afternoons walking about the city streets or riding the subway, admiring "very nice red-cheeked black-haired youth[s] of the lower classes," but seldom did he engage in the "pretty courageous" act of talking to his fellow subway travellers.[109] Everywhere he turned, Strachey saw uniformed young men in trains and on the streets of London. In an untitled poem to Virginia Woolf, Strachey described how he went "searching with subtle glance the moving crowd / for some new beauty—sweet, or quaint, or proud." More than once, he told Woolf, he "found [himself] a traveller o'er enchanted ground," in which he discovered "visions delectable, and colours rare / and sweet strange looks, and smiles, and marvellous hair." But, though he longed to "sip ecstacy," Strachey lamented that "each barren minute has withheld its prize / beauty has sulked, and joy has hid its prize."[110]

As he wrote *Eminent Victorians,* visions of sailor lads disturbed his intellectual efforts.[111] Disappointed that he would never meet the young men who lay dying in trenches, he pursued on paper his newly aroused interest in these lads. His literary efforts, however, were not necessarily any more gratifying than his actual participation in the city's culture of fleeting glances. His letters refer to so many instances of sailors disappearing down train platforms, "with a lock of hair bobbing on his forehead. . . . But the train rushed on."[112] Those moments on the streets and stations in which he escaped entrapment by his own desire, or the police, also shaped his fantasies of missed opportunities with boys in uniform.

In an essay written for his Bloomsbury colleagues, Strachey recounted the events and emotions in "Monday June 26 1916."[113] At the country residence of Duncan Grant and Vanessa Bell, the war seemed a distant event, intruding only through newspaper reports on the deaths of more "divine creatures." During his visit at his friends' cottage, Strachey encountered a "vision" of a young postman with fair hair and a lovely country complexion. The young man smiled and uttered, "Good evening, Sir," and at once Strachey was smitten.[114] Though the youth's nose "looked stupid," Strachey had "no doubt that he was nice," and thoughts of "the delicious down on his cheek" disrupted Strachey's writing.[115] In the midst of this fantasy, Strachey was hit with a delightful dilemma. Reading the paper, he saw the charming face of a boxer, Jimmy Wilde, staring at him and enticing him to leave the postboy and rush back to London. Throughout the day Strachey dreamed of the boxer, "half-naked with bruised ears . . . or dressed, in a fascinating tweed suit, rather too big for him, staying with me for a week-end at my cottage."[116] Duncan Grant perceived the essence of Jimmy's appeal and told his guest, "It's only because he hasn't got a collar on. If his neck was covered, he'd probably look like anyone else."[117] Finally, Strachey decided to try his luck with just the postboy, and the next day he rehearsed their meeting, shared cigarette, and conversation. As the bicycle approached, however, Strachey saw a different postman, older and unattractive, and he decided that it was "just his luck" that the boy was probably now in military uniform.

Strachey's disappointment was more ambiguous than his essay suggested. As he experienced the events and emotions of Monday, June 26, 1916, his real or "higher" affections were actually directed toward another houseguest, David Garnett. Standing beside Garnett in the garden, Strachey felt "nervous, almost neurasthenic" and longed to throw himself onto Garnett as if he were a "feather-bed." But, as Strachey confided to his journal, "the more [he] longed to expand, the more [he] hated the thought of it. It would be disgusting and ridiculous—it was out of the question."[118] Instead, Strachey projected his desire elsewhere and concluded that "there are so many possibilities in the world," that he "shouldn't have been much surprised if something extraordinary had happened almost at once."[119] The boxers and postboys made up only a small portion of those "possibilities" from which a man of Strachey's class could, if he chose or dared to, seek "adventure."

Unlike the virile, collarless boxer and the pink-cheeked postboy, most males of the lower orders symbolized to Strachey filth, evil, and risk. The gentleman who dared to commit the lower sodomy knew of specific locations where fulfillment awaited him. Strachey's correspondence with Keynes hints at their familiarity with the boys at the Trocadero, the waiters in certain cafés, and the chance encounters in subway stations. Apostle Walter Lamb informed his Brother Strachey of the "fresh-coloured boys" at the Imperial Hotel "who brush you down and who, if rather small, are very attractive."[120] Excited by "all the painted boys" on the London streets, Strachey "felt quite rakish" as he winked at the "pretty boys."[121] He even composed verses that asked, "Who is the foolish person that supposes / that man cannot be happy at a park? / For sure it is that one need not be Moses / To find divinity in the nearest bush."[122] But, "divinity," or the ideal of male Love, existed only at Cambridge. In the city Strachey merely found "little boys [who formed] a sort of sodomitic avenue" and who "were distinctly disappointing."[123]

Nevertheless, Strachey continued to hope for an "adventure," and one night he glimpsed "two such divine boy lovers—oh! embracing and then parting, and then after all going on together." Watching the youths, Strachey "longed to give them something—a kiss or a box of chocolates," but as he approached the couple, he "found out of course that they were hideous" and he "didn't take very much more interest in the matter."[124] Viewing the other from afar, from a literal and class distance, Strachey protected his fantasy, but face to face, the laborer or common bugger became "evil-looking" and "decidedly shady." Such men, he concluded, "looked as if they belonged to some different species."[125]

Of course, a practical consideration also triggered Strachey's critical responses toward the "temptations of the corner." In another letter to Keynes, he described a "narrow shave on the tube" in which a "languishing beauty in khaki" stared at him with "drooping eyes . . . in the most marked manner." Finally, after much eye contact, Strachey decided not to follow the stranger, "partly the result of [Keynes's] admonishments."[126] Most likely, Keynes had warned Strachey of the possible threat of blackmail. The Brothers undoubtedly were conscious always of the 1885 Labouchere Amendment, dubbed "the Blackmailer's Charter," which declared illegal any public or private male "acts of gross indecency with another male person."[127] While Strachey discovered Platonic love as a teen, he witnessed the demise of Oscar Wilde, proof that even popular authors had to maintain a clear line between passionate friendships and "indecent acts." Strachey both ridiculed and pitied elderly Cambridge dons such as Oscar Browning, whose rumored affairs with golf caddies tainted his professional life—"that he should be reduced to that! most, most sad."[128] Despite attempts at humor, Strachey also knew that during the early years of World War I, as he researched *Eminent Victorians* and surveyed the city's "delights," the British government took a more than usual interest in writings on male love and used the charge of homosexuality to blacken names and reputations.[129]

Just as powerful as the legal obstacles was Strachey's perception of these youths as members of an alien, immoral race—simultaneously attractive and repulsive. Walking along "sodomitic avenues" reminded Strachey just how precarious his position of authority over his private empire was. At times, he feared that the crossing of class and racial boundaries to attain physical gratification would somehow contaminate him and transfuse the boys' lower desires through his veins. Oscar Wilde had described his own sexual liaisons with working-class boys, who were "all body and no soul," as "feasting with panthers."[130] Strachey, too, sensed the danger that the other would consume him. At such moments when his passion threatened to undermine his code of chaste male Love, he turned to Victorianism and the stereotypes of race and class, of East and West, for reinforcement and comfort. Even in those rarely documented instances in which he dared to commit the lower sodomy, Strachey protected his claim to bourgeois masculinity, to Englishness, to supremacy, or he tried another strategy, in which he asked his upper-class lover to come to him in costume, usually in a uniform, or he would take on the role of valet. These fantasies created the illusion of crossing class boundaries, and when playing the servant, Strachey relished the brief moment of debasement in which he would "have no will of one's own, no importance, no responsibility . . . how very satisfying."[131]

Aside from its dangers, the other of Strachey's empire remained vital to a concept of all-male Love that associated the real (spiritual) with upper-class intellectuals and the phenomenal (physical) with the masses. Unlike sex reformer Edward Carpenter who hoped for a blending of the social strata through "masculine love," Strachey had no dream of a union that would permanently erode class or racial barriers.[132] When Strachey imagined the object of "real" love, he saw what Eve Sedgwick has called the generic figure of a slim, gold-haired thing.[133] In Strachey's eyes, only Apostles such as Arthur Hobhouse and Rupert Brooke were "Apollos" and "angels" with a sexuality and sensibility that belonged solely to a narrowly defined English type and class. Should such a sample of perfection actually arouse his passion, Strachey insisted he would triumph over that "baser" form of love. Indeed, the censorship of desire appears far more frequently in his writings than its fulfillment.

In a short story written for Dora Carrington, Strachey told the tragedy of the Springalt page. Tormented by his attraction to a golden-haired page, the knight, "Sir Giles" (Giles was Strachey's given name) kills the youth and himself.[134] Carrington teasingly suggested that it might be easier for Strachey to imagine himself lying "nightly with his arms about the blacksmith's boy" instead.[135] Strachey's textual moments were indeed necessary, allowing him to experience a diversity of desire and engage in a variety of homoerotic behaviors that, as a Higher Sodomite, he often denied himself. When he dreamed of "those imagined faces and forms . . . that wealth of wild desires,"[136] he looked beyond the gates of Cambridge, to the Orient, the Mediterranean, or the East End. The existence of his imaginary empire made possible at last the happy union of love and desire.

Strachey's excursions into the empire illuminate not only a personal and psychological dilemma but also some of the social and legal dangers that confronted the upper-middle-class homosexual in early twentieth-century England. After 1885, those men who longed to explore the physical aspect of all-male love now certainly risked public humiliation or even incarceration. Even the Apostles' Saturday night deliberations about the nobility of male love were potentially liable to prosecution.[137] Imperial excursions in search of sexual freedom had long been the privilege of the upper-class heterosexual male, and the homosexual also discovered that many dark or poor youths were willing to offer sexual favors at an affordable price.[138] Strachey, Keynes, and Forster were only a few who followed the paths of their Victorian predecessors to regions laden with opportunity and devoid of restrictions.

Despite his pledged commitment to the Higher Sodomy, Strachey grew increasingly aware of the limitations of a chaste, spiritualized doctrine of male Love. Within his literary haven, he could safely penetrate the mysteries of the empire, and of that separate nation of working-class males within his own country. However, in his literary and social relations with the other, Strachey created a trap for himself. Forster's character Risley (modeled on Strachey) exclaims in *Maurice* that "words are deeds," and perhaps writing and sharing his textual depictions of desire with his fellow Bloomsbury colleagues and Apostles brought Strachey some degree of pleasure. Approximating desire by controlling distances, Strachey's technique unfortunately left his "higher love" for the younger men of his own class frequently unfulfilled. In his introduction to George Rylands' *Words and Poetry,* Strachey referred to the joys of writing: "We are lured down fascinating avenues . . . we ask questions and all is made clear by some cunningly chosen bunch that is put into our hands, full of expectant fragrances." Attracted to the book's young Cambridge author, Strachey could very well have been describing his own search for love. He concluded the introduction with a hint at the dangers and limits of writing (and love): "It is really a case of Frankenstein and his monster. These things that we have made are as alive as we are; and we have become their slaves."[139]

A teenage Strachey once lamented after wandering the streets, alone in the crowd, "the truth is I want *companionship*."[140] As he grew older, this search for a companion often entailed paying Cambridge students to travel with him or scanning parks and subways for pink-cheeked youths. Just as his imaginary kings seduced boys with gifts, Strachey managed to turn slumming with Henry Lamb into an artistic endeavor and correspondence with a farmboy into a charitable deed. Whether in his campy velvet or conservative tweed suit, Strachey was constantly playing a role and constantly traveling literal and imaginary distances, searching for, but often not achieving, his fantasy of Love.

When Strachey wrote about imperial sex, he was not simply seeking erotic thrills or trying to titillate his Bloomsbury colleagues, nor was he "joyously" celebrating his homosexuality, as some Bloomsbury scholars posit. His private sexual empire was, instead, part of a larger search for a space in which desire could be enjoyed without punishment. To "plant his penis in so many peculiar spots" required Strachey to create a fictional realm of Arabian pages, English postboys, and Mediterranean gondoliers who allowed him to experiment with the lower sodomy without penalty. In these stories of his real and imagined encounters, Strachey played various roles: the patriarchal benefactor, the liberated homosexual abroad, or the curious observer and crusader against vice. In *Maurice,* E. M. Forster imagined the greenwood as a retreat from civilization, science, and the law. Unable to publish his novel for six decades, Forster lamented that even in 1961 there was "no forest or fell to escape to, no cave in which to curl up, no deserted valley for those who wish neither to reform nor corrupt society but to be left alone."[141] Forster understood Strachey's need to keep his desires "coffined" in his verse. Just as Sir Richard Burton had restricted *"le vice"* to a "Sotadic Zone," Strachey tried to limit the lower pleasure to the unpublished page. Within that space he could remain supreme, untainted, and eminently Victorian.

Chapter 3

Mothers, Monarchs, and Monsters: Strachey and the Phenomenal Sex

"And what about the ladies? Don't they *ever* figure in your world?"[1] In his query to Strachey, the younger Cambridge Brother Gerald Shove intimated that the Apostolic division between the "real" and "phenomenal" worlds, and hence between genders, was perhaps impossible to maintain. The Society preached that women upset the neat dichotomy of love and lust and served no intellectual or sexual use to either the lower or Higher Sodomite. Yet, women undeniably had figured in Strachey's world: as providers of motherly love, as subjects of historical analysis, and even as occasional romantic interests. While Strachey repeatedly told his Brothers to avoid the company of the opposite sex, he always lived, aside from his school years, among women and remained dependent on them for domestic and emotional comfort. His published writings often centered on the lives of such famous women as Florence Nightingale and Queens Elizabeth I and Victoria. The only women truly worthy of regard were those who ignored or repressed their "feminine natures" to achieve the power traditionally reserved for men. Bloomsbury was further proof that in Strachey's own day women excelled as writers and artists. For the men of Cambridge, schooled in theories of masculine superiority and male romantic friendship, Bloomsbury represented the first opportunity for serious physical and intellectual interaction with the phenomenal sex. Such examples of female accomplishment, however, did not altogether destabilize the Victorian conceptions of sexuality that Strachey embraced.

This chapter challenges the claims of scholars who have heralded Bloomsbury as both a feminist experiment and the "first actual example of the androgynous spirit in practice."[2] The Victorian definitions of "masculine" and "feminine" continued to shape Strachey's own behavior as well as his personal and literary treatment of the opposite sex. However, simply to label Strachey a misogynist or patriarch obscures the complexity of his relationships with women and of his work. The assumed pose of superiority actually concealed a fear of women who threatened his credo of male genius. His literary portraits transformed strong women not into androgynous heroines but into grotesque male pretenders, while his friendships with the women of Bloomsbury revealed his search for the perfect wife—chaste, angelic, domestic, and adoring.

As the most vocal male voice of the Bloomsbury Group, Strachey regarded his female colleagues with a mixture of admiration, envy, and hostility. His relations with women suggest a "crisis of masculinity" most manifest in his need to regain a position of power and authority allotted to other men of his class. Also, Strachey's encounters with female members of the Bloomsbury Group, particularly his professional rivalry with Virginia Woolf and his living arrangement with Dora Carrington, illuminate the lingering Victorian definitions of gender that complicated the modernist sexual experiment.

In one of Strachey's essays delivered before his fellow Bloomsbury members, he recalled the first three decades of his life at "69 Lancaster Gate." The essay offered a picture of the "middle-class professional world of the Victorians, in which the old forms still lingered."[3] Within that first home Strachey acquired "the solid bourgeois qualities [that] were interpenetrated by intellectualism and eccentricity."[4] In particular, Strachey described the household's female head, who shaped young Lytton's future interactions and expectations of the opposite sex. Dressed in her sweeping black satin, Lady Jane Strachey oversaw "a multitude of outside interests, a large correspondence, and a curiously elaborate system of household accounts," while she also pursued her own passion for Elizabethan drama and the Women's Progressive Movement.[5] Meanwhile, her husband, Sir Richard Strachey, remained a shadowy figure in Lytton's life. After his retirement from the India Civil Service, Sir Richard devoted his days to meteorology, geography, and botany, and his evenings to the reading of novels; he had little time to spare even for family meals. Though Lytton's recollections of his father include only a few shared outings to the Crystal Palace and the Royal Naval Exhibition, he did insist on hanging Sir Richard's portrait in his room at Cambridge.

The responsibility of Lytton's education fell to Lady Strachey. She supervised her son's daily compositions of poetry and playlets, as well as his painting, acting, and literary debates, and supplemented his education with French lessons at Mademoiselle Marie Souvestre's local school for girls. Even Strachey's sporadic diary keeping began at his mother's urging, and she expected him to share his entries with her. Her own diary entry for March 22, 1886, records with pride that when six-year-old Lytton spelled out Macaulay's Lays—"And how can men die better than facing fearful odds for the ashes of their fathers and the temples of their Gods"—he added, after a pause of reflection, "for their mothers."[6] Always conscious of the intellectual debt he owed his mother, the older Strachey sent her copies of his work with requests for her comments. On his thirty-sixth birthday, as he wrote *Eminent Victorians,* Lytton informed Lady Strachey, "I know now where my path lies. . . . If I ever *do* do anything worth doing, I'm sure it will be owing to you much more than to anyone else."[7]

In addition to his educational development, Strachey's health was of primary concern to his mother. She arranged long recuperative holidays for her son and sent her daughters to nurse him at college and university. "The fact is," she told her daughter Pippa, that even at age twenty Lytton still "does not manage himself properly when there is nobody to look after him and rout him out, and feed him with milk."[8] The surviving letters between mother and son contain health news flashes interspersed with discussions of literature. Lady Strachey often acted as confidante to Lytton before he took his place among his Brothers at Cambridge. He even violated the Society's code of secrecy by notifying his mother of his election to the Apostles and describing the rituals of induction.

Despite these intimacies, the relations between Lytton and Lady Strachey were marked with tension. The illnesses that demanded her frequent attention were also part of Strachey's strategy of escape. He welcomed the doctors' orders for extended holidays away from "the weight of the circumbient air" he breathed at Lancaster Gate.[9] And, despite her supervision of his education and career, Lady Strachey was disappointed in Lytton's choice of Cambridge and journalism over Oxford and civil service. The young boy who cried "Oh Mama, dear Mama / How good you are / You smile from morn till night / And whenever you speak and wherever you are / Everything seems like a heavenly star," grew into a man who continued to regard his mother as an object of worship, fear, and criticism.[10] When Strachey pierced his ears to please his new friend Henry Lamb, he begged his brother James to "keep it *very* dark, as her ladyship would certainly have a fit if she heard of it."[11]

Though confident among other Higher Sodomites and disdainful of "womanisers," in his mother's presence, Strachey knew he had to keep his sexuality concealed. When abroad, he sent postcards to "Dearest Mama" in which he noted his searches for "good-looking women," though he mainly described "the shops, the wine, and the food."[12]

Keynes sympathized with this need for deception, recalling a "dreadful conversation" with his own mother and sister about marriage, during which he "practically had to admit to them what [he] was! How much they grasped [he didn't] know."[13] Strachey maintained a facade for the benefit of his aging mother as well as to ensure her continued financial support and approval. Observing the dynamics of his friend's relationship with his mother, which seemed to focus on intellectual matters and ignore emotional ones, Keynes believed Lady Strachey was "incapable of understanding any of her children." "How terrible," Strachey agreed, "to love so much and know so little."[14]

Strachey's own reverence for his mother was tempered with an urge to ridicule and distort maternal excessiveness. The figure of the mother rarely appears in Strachey's fiction, but when she does, she is either "unconscious" (that is, ignorant of her son's romantic interests), or she is an overbearing, domineering woman who prefers politics to domesticity. Mrs. Wilbraham of the short story "Something Wrong" cannot comprehend the friendship between her son Archie and Mr. Ravenscroft. Each time she encountered them in the dining room she sensed "that there was something wrong—something very wrong indeed," and wondered if "perhaps it was worse than quarrelling, but she couldn't think what." Immediately following her exit, "something wrong, something very wrong indeed" occurred, and the two men were locked in each other's arms.[15] Mrs. Wilbraham resembles the other mothers in Strachey's Apostle stories who either deliberately or unknowingly ignore the activities of their sodomitic sons and womanizing husbands. These fictional representations resemble the mothers of Strachey and Duncan Grant who warned their sons, before leaving for excursions to Paris, to avoid prostitutes, oblivious to the fact that the cousins had shared the same bed under their own roofs!

In his play *A Son of Heaven* (discussed in the previous chapter), Strachey created another woman who defied all traditional ideals of motherhood and femininity. Strachey's picture of the Chinese imperial court at the time of the Boxer Rebellion centers on the Empress Dowager who has usurped power from her son and commands a troup of eunuchs.[16] Vain, power-hungry, and murderous, the Empress Dowager proclaims, "Whoever dares to say I'm a woman, I'll have them cut in pieces. I'm a man, a man, a man." Her young son, however, cannot say the same for himself. In him, Strachey drew a pathetic, weak, hesitant, and loving son, appalled at the cruelty of the real world and, above all, of his own mother. In such instances, Strachey used his fiction to reconcile his contradictory emotions for his mother, whom he both thanked for setting him on the path of success and secretly blamed for his prolonged dependence and insecurity.

Whether or not Strachey compared his mother to the castrating villainess of his play, he did lament his inability to escape her presence. Lady Strachey also tried to influence her son's writing career, and mother and son clashed over his decision to write the life of Queen Victoria. In defending the queen, Lady Strachey also defended an entire set of values, and perhaps her own position as a Victorian mother whose son clearly was rebelling against her:

> I don't much fancy you taking up Queen Victoria to deal with. . . . She no doubt lays herself open to drastic treatment which is one reason I think it better left alone. She could not help being stupid, but she tried to do her duty. . . . She has won a place in public affection and a reputation in our history which it would be highly unpopular, and I think not quite fair, to attempt to bring down.[17]

Despite her entreaty, Strachey went to the British Museum "to try to dig up scandals" about the queen.

Fortunately, life with Lady Strachey was eased by the presence of Lytton's sisters. To some extent, Strachey regarded his sisters simply as younger versions of his mother, and he expected no other man to come between them and his needs. His sisters seemed to accept these terms without complaint. To Pippa, Lytton was "the sweet angel of [her] heart," and to Marjorie, her "Dear Husband."[18] As "New Women" of the early twentieth century, Marjorie, Pernel, and Philippa Strachey eschewed marriage to pursue higher education, professional employment, and service to the cause of suffrage. In the absence of husbands, they offered their lifelong maternal and wifely devotion to their brother's health and comfort. Lytton especially relied on his sisters during troubled times with his male lovers. In April 1906, following a row with Duncan Grant, he begged Pippa to come at once to Paris to accompany him on his return voyage to London, though he blamed ill health, not un-requited love, for his condition.[19] Marjorie, though upset that she and Lytton appeared "to be drifting apart," continued to agonize over his "attacks," which left him "very weak and gloomy and unable to cope with life."[20] Either Lady Strachey or her daughters were sent on nursing missions to Strachey's boarding schools, but when at Cambridge, his health miraculously did not suffer. Reporting home, Strachey announced, "I am flourishing and I am sure Cambridge suits me." While he vacationed with his Brothers in the country, Lytton wrote to Pippa, "I intend . . . to have a shot at a stag . . . before I come away."[21] The manly pursuits with his Society friends sharply contrasted his sickbed regimen at 69 Lancaster Gate.

Since the return to his parents' household usually was accompa-nied by some "attack," Strachey demanded that his sisters create a soothing atmosphere there. Before coming down from Cambridge, he told Pippa to wallpaper his room and conceded, "So far as I can see there's no probability of my leaving permanently, so that I think it had better be done."[22] Eager to please her "husband," Pippa acquiesced. She and her brother, she reminded him, shared a bond that was like a hug— "a mystical sign without any beginning or end and means everything and nothing."[23] Any arguments between them left Pippa "shattered" and threatened the stability of what she called their "love affair."[24] In a letter to Lytton, she confided, "If I feel ill there are only two people that I can bear to think of being with and those are you and Pernel. . . . For such a long time I loved you so happily and always I love you so much."[25] For his part, Lytton insisted that he "never felt the slightest doubt about [their] fundamental affection, or that it had altered." Without his sister, his life "would have been impossible."[26]

As in other Victorian sibling relationships, Strachey and his unwed sisters exchanged spousal terms of endearment to express their shared loyalty and cohesion.[27] However, jealousy and rivalry frequently dis-turbed the marital harmony the siblings tried to achieve. Throughout their childhood and early adulthood, the women outshone their brother intellectually, physically, and politically. At the Meteorological Council Sir Richard boasted of his daughters' "prowess" as "the old boys listened aghast" and murmured, "Oh yes, but everyone knows the Strachey daughters!!!"[28]

Lytton had bragged to his fellow Apostles that he hoped to shock his elders in some way, but it was his sister Dorothy who first upset the calm of 69 Lancaster Gate in 1903 with her marriage to the "unconnected," penurious, and foreign painter Simon Bussey. The wedding, which took place without the benefit of a church blessing, revealed the "extraordinary courage" of Lytton's elder sister and left his parents' home "shaken to its foundations."[29] Dorothy's career would cross frequently with her brother's. She often translated his works for French publishers, but, more important, she went on to translate the writings of André Gide and fall in love with him (mirroring Dora Carrington's unrequited love for Strachey). A homosexual, as was her younger brother, Gide dealt with sexual themes much more boldly and explicitly than Strachey, yet despite Dorothy's familiarity with all-male love, her copious letters to and from Lytton are glaringly devoid of references to sexual matters. In her private writings, she too dabbled in the theme of homosexual desire. Her short novel *Olivia* dealt with romantic friendships and lesbian desire at a girls' boarding school, similar to Lytton's unpublished tales of male desire at the elite public schools. Although they corresponded about their favorite novels, the siblings never addressed this shared literary and personal interest.[30]

Meanwhile, Strachey's younger sisters proved that a university education was no longer the sole privilege of men. Strachey even witnessed Pernel's rise to principal of Newnham College. Pernel's accomplishment, however, paled by comparison to Strachey's postwar literary success, and even her familial connection failed to entice Lytton Strachey, famous author, to guest lecture. Asking him to read a paper to "some of the young ladies" at Newnham, she hastily added, "I can't at all think you could feel any wish to do such a thing . . . so don't do anything that you dislike."[31]

Although Strachey loathed the all-female atmosphere of Newnham, he distinguished his sisters from the other "unpleasant young ladies." He even introduced them to his fellow Apostles and encouraged the Brothers to escort the women to London dances. Strachey amusedly observed what he assumed was a romantic attraction between Pippa and his philosophical mentor, G. E. Moore, and agreed with Keynes that the almost middle-aged don was a worthy match for the intelligent suffragette. "Moore came to tea yesterday," Lytton gossiped to his Brother, "and Pippa, as usual, pronounced him perfect—Well! I wonder if it'll ever come off."[32] Although Strachey's efforts at matchmaking failed, he was relieved to remain Pippa's "dear Husband." Other matches were more successful. The Apostle A. R.

Ainsworth terminated his domestic union with G. E. Moore to marry the latter's younger sister.

For those members of the Society who insisted on physical unions with the opposite sex, marriage to one another's sisters seemed the least threatening solution and even increased the bond of loyalty and devotion between the Brothers. The almost incestuous nature of the relationships ensured the exclusivity and elitism of the Society and prevented excessive and unnecessary contact with phenomenal strangers. These relations fit within René Girard's schema of the erotic triangle.[33] The bond between two Apostles held stronger than their affection for a particular woman, yet that woman represented a vital link between the Brothers. While courting Virginia Stephen, Leonard Woolf wondered if he loved her because he was in love with the Goth (her brother Thoby) and if Clive Bell loved the Goth because he was in love with Vanessa Stephen![34]

Whereas male suitors (even Apostolic ones) did not distract the Strachey sisters from their filial responsibilities, their dedication to the female emancipation movement did. Despite their concern for Lytton's comfort, they rejected, on the whole, the confines of the private sphere of marriage and domesticity. The Strachey women, Sir Osbert Sitwell observed, "were of a type different from that to be seen elsewhere." Although "something of the Victorian past clung to them still, they were more advanced than their sisters both in view and intelligence."[35] Marriage, Pernel declared, was "very unpleasant" and made her "feel quite ill," chiefly owing to "the mere boredom which is vast."[36] Upon reading "the most impudent article," "Women and Culture," in *The Spectator* (on whose staff Lytton was employed), Pernel released "frenzied screams of passion." That an essentialist view of womanhood should still prevail in 1900 seemed to her "pompous folly and crass ignorance."[37] To Lytton, however, the unnamed essayist's opinion that women were meant by nature to be wives and mothers had some legitimacy. He hoped that his sisters, though reluctant to fall prey to the "boredom" of marriage, would not ignore their duty toward him.

Following the lead of Lady Strachey, Philippa, Marjorie, and Pernel participated in the prewar suffrage movement. They aligned themselves with the moderate Millicent Garrett Fawcett rather than the militant Pankhursts. As the secretary for the London Society for Women's Suffrage, Philippa Strachey used the clout of her surname to win police protection and cooperation for the Society's marches.

The Grand Demonstration for suffrage in 1907 aroused little attention from the secretary's brother, however, and Lytton conveniently
left town for the day. Marjorie criticized this lack of political involvement, a charge he resented but did not deny. To his cousin Duncan
Grant, Strachey explained, "M. thinks that I'm neglecting my duty as
a citizen because I don't address public meetings and box with policemen. What a filthy mess of garbage politics in England are!"[38]

As his sisters planned the march, Strachey researched his essay on
Lady Mary Wortley Montagu, a woman whose courage he admired:
"She never gave in to anything or anybody and died fighting. Great
Lady Mary!"[39] He failed to note the irony of his own disregard for his
sisters' despair over yet another unsuccessful suffrage bill in May 1907.
With calm restored at home, he expressed relief that "suffragism has
simmered down into its normal state of vague agitation," and he "wonder[ed] how long it will take the Ladies to grasp the obvious fact that the
only way out of all their difficulties is universal buggery."[40] Strachey did
appease his sisters by joining the Men's League for the Promotion of
Female Suffrage, but he confided to James, "Now I doubt the whole
thing. . . . I believe the ladies will try to forbid prostitution, and will they
stop there?"[41] His fears were not wholly unfounded; it was, after all, the
efforts of feminist Purity Crusaders in the 1880s that culminated in the
passage of the Criminal Law Amendment Act of 1885. Feminism and
moral reform, in Strachey's eyes, acted in unison to make the public and
the courts too keen to punish all varieties of "male vice."

The increased emergence of such women as the Strachey sisters in
the public sphere of higher education, art, politics, and social life in
pre–World War I England did elicit critical comments from the men
of Cambridge. The Apostles' doctrine of male superiority and homosocial bonding afforded no recognition of the intellectual capabilities
of the women at Girton and Newnham. The Cambridge don and
Apostle G. L. Dickinson had prevented what he deemed a possible
sexual revolution by vetoing the admission of these women into the
Society. Meanwhile, the younger Brothers ostracized self-acknowl-
edged "womanisers" whose association with the opposite sex violated the Platonic philosophy of the elite fraternity. Every Apostle
was reminded to shun the "horrible example" of men "whose achievements with women are epic."[42]

Despite these efforts, the Society could no longer ignore the diminishing distinctions between the two sexes. The presence of women at

Cambridge threatened to shatter the neat separation of the real from the phenomenal. Furthermore, female undergraduates did not always occupy a separate space at Cambridge. Male lecturers at King's and Trinity Colleges also taught at the women's colleges, while female students attended men's lectures. Even the Tripos Honors degree examinations were distributed to these women.[43]

Strachey and his friends remained critical of these limited advances in female higher education. During his teaching career at Cambridge before the war, Keynes despaired over his female students. "The nervous irritation caused by two hours' contact with them is *intense*. I seem to hate every movement of their minds," he wrote to Duncan Grant. "The minds of the men, even when they themselves are stupid and ugly, never appear to me so repellent."[44] Strachey sympathized with his friend's dilemma but explained that women were "incapable of struggling against their fate."[45]

Unfortunately, knowledge of classical literature and history was no longer the sole domain of men. Even Virginia Stephen, who did not have the advantage of a formal higher education, studied Greek with Clara, the sister of Walter Pater, and dared to read G. E. Moore's *Principia Ethica*. According to Walter Ong, until the late nineteenth century, classical study functioned as the crucial step in gender demarcation. Access to a privileged language (what Ong calls a *patrius sermo* or "father speech") as opposed to the ordinary language (*materna lingua* or "mother tongue") defined male intellectual hegemony. With the entrance of women into universities, this male monopoly over the classics was broken, and the teaching of Latin and Greek as part of the standard male curriculum began to die out.[46] Though the "higher literacy" entered the female curriculum, the doctrine and practices of the Higher Sodomy at least remained the sacred terrain of a small circle of upper-class men. The Cambridge Society preserved its pseudoreligious rituals, coded language, double-locked doors, and secrecy to guarantee its members' separation from women.

Although women were barred from the private meetings of the Apostles, they were not absent as a topic of debate. Michael Holroyd asserts that the political and sexual radicalism of Strachey and his Brothers surfaced in the discussions and private papers of the Society. The Apostles' views on the "hollow" sex, however, reveal a radicalism tempered with lingering Victorian notions of gender. In his unpublished attempts at fiction that he shared with his Brothers, Strachey presented female characters who were foolish, deceitful, fickle, and babbling. On a loose sheet of notepaper he scribbled, "Women— superficiality pedantry conventionality lack of imagination narrowness."[47] The Brothers debated the pros and cons of marriage and proposed universal buggery as a solution to the "woman question."

While the only "real affair of the heart" existed between two socially and intellectually equal males, many men did force themselves into conjugal relations with the opposite sex. Several of Strachey's Apostle papers were devoted to the theme of a "phenomenal marriage." His essay "Does Absence Make the Heart Grow Fonder?" denied the possibility of "the marriage of true minds" between a man and woman. Unlike the Apostolic union, the "disadvantages of marriage are overwhelming." Boredom and lust defined such a union, and by far the "commonest condition in which married people spend their lives is . . . the condition of the vegetable or the cow." The minds of a man and a woman were so removed from each other and their experiences of life so different that when the two joined as husband and wife their evening conversations would be filled with "the wretched trivialities of the passing days." Strachey generously conceded that the wife was not solely to blame for quarrels that "seem to be caused by the imperfections incident to even the Apostolic human nature." On the whole, though, Apostles possessed a "refined and sensitive temperament—the temperament, that is to say, which the best persons nowadays seem generally to have." Women lacked such a temperament, and, with time, they usually lost the allure of their physical charms. Contrary to the friendships between Brothers that endured the test of time, the embraces of a married pair "must either dwindle into a mechanical contortion or be sullied year by year in a greater degree with the evil of pure lust."[48]

What would happen to the Society if a member married? Would the Apostle's unavoidable intimacy with things phenomenal destroy him and his Brothers? Another of Strachey's essays warned his friends that even the wife of an Apostle must remain ignorant of the Society's proceedings. Regarding his relations with his own hypothetical wife, he asked his listeners, "What I want to know is by what possible means am I to make that lady understand the particular value I put on the Society?" Would a wife comprehend that the Apostles "are the only people who exist?" Strachey worried that he would be "totally unable to explain the Society" to his "hypothetical and phenomenal wife." Only in the unlikely event that this wife "could recognise . . . its immense value . . . if she could feel it," then, he decided, she "ought to be elected." Such a woman who was "apostolic," however, simply did not exist.[49]

Absent from the Apostolic readings were any explicit references to female sexuality. Strachey and his friends either ignored this aspect of women or imagined the female body as something degraded and grotesque. They saw beauty only in the male physique and mind and declared "anything is better than being a woman."[50] Curiously, Strachey's dictum to avoid slang and "coarse language" when discussing male sexuality did not apply to the topic of women. In fact, he specifically selected such words as "pussy" and "cunt" to imply the vulgarity of the female body. Even his respect for motherhood did not rule out revulsion over its physiology. Strachey sighed with relief: "How glad I am that I'm not a female! How fearful to have children! How dreadful to have to go about with an enormous living ventre."[51] Needless to say, he avoided contact with pregnant women, whose bodies called to mind "a great pot with a child in it."[52] Strachey did recognize, however, that a man's disavowal of the world of women and children often led to personally catastrophic results. Lamenting his fate, one of Strachey's fictional English gentlemen is banished to a foreign land "because a certain part of [his] body penetrated A's about eight inches from the point where if it had been B's it might have penetrated with absolute impunity."[53] His questionable knowledge of female anatomy aside, Strachey understood that only certain types of penetration were acceptable.

Though Strachey's female characters usually accept the possibility of all-male love, he and his Brothers were less willing to champion the cause of sapphism. Unlike the pure love between Brothers, they considered the passionate friendships of women as debased as male buggery and womanizing. As a spiritual, cultural, and sexual model, Sappho ranked far beneath Plato. After his introduction to a sapphist whose hobby involved photographing beautiful girls, Strachey commented, "I can imagine her sort of selfish adoration of these maidens only too well."[54] Marjorie Strachey's proposal to "copulate with some woman or other" elicited her brothers' disgust. "I do hate women," James wrote to Lytton, "they manage to make everything seem indecent."[55] Keynes was surprised that the Strachey siblings talked about sapphism, but even more shocking to him was that James and Marjorie "very madly" discussed sodomy.[56] Surely, women had no business offering their opinion on this sacred subject. Despite their education and mingling among the Society members, the Strachey sisters were "unconscious" and incapable of understanding the "inward spiritual grace" that defined Brotherly Love.[57]

In a series of letters to Strachey, Keynes reported his conversations with a Miss Sheepshanks on "the subject of female loves." Miss Sheepshanks apparently believed that the inability of sapphists "to copulate" harmed the nerves and health of these women "who receive no relief to their tension."[58] Unlike Keynes, Strachey was less receptive toward her theory, though he was "amused a good deal—but really, it won't do." He did agree that "Sapphic relations" in comparison to Sodomitic ones, were "worse" for women "who are fools when young and of course the fact of it's not being properly recognized adds to the horror."[59] His comment suggests envy rather than contempt for these women; ignored by the legal code that punished male deviance, female inverts or sapphists had more freedom within the phenomenal realm of Victorian and Edwardian morality. Though not illegal, female loves, according to Strachey, assumed the form of "general hysteria."[60]

Strachey's Brothers shared his resentment toward the unequal treatment of male and female passionate friendships and inversion. "Your cousin Marjorie," Keynes wrote to Duncan Grant, "seems to Sapphise rather openly with Ray [Oliver Strachey's second wife], but these females always behave as if they had nothing to conceal."[61] At least the Higher Sodomy had its limits, which fortunately were respected at Cambridge. At Oxford, however, Keynes insisted there were those who were so inverted they wished they were women; such men could be described only as sapphists! Among the Brothers "sapphist" became a term of derision, and the subject of female loves a source of humor.

Just as copulation between women sullied the name of Love, so did physical intimacy between men and women. The company of women, however, promised certain benefits that even the Brothers could not offer one another. Surrounded by his sisters and aunts, Strachey mused, "sun, flowers, . . . and comparative comfort . . . I think it may save me."[62] Eventually, the Brothers agreed, most men, including themselves, "settled down" with women. Cambridge, of course, provided a homosocial bastion and weekend resort to which its graduates returned for contact with their intellectual and spiritual peers. The departure from the university signaled to most men of Strachey's social class the inevitable sequence of a profession and marriage. His fellow Higher Sodomite

Walter Lamb asked Strachey, "Shall we all be married some day?" and decided that Strachey "was about ready for it."[63] Strachey told Lamb and the other Brothers that at twenty-five he still knew very few women with whom he had anything approaching intimacy, and he added, "I must confess that I have never been in love with one."[64]

Once his friends became involved in such phenomenal pursuits as civil service, they seemed to Strachey to acquire an interest in the opposite sex. In response to Leonard Woolf's tales of adventure among the "half-caste whores" and even white English ladies in Ceylon, Strachey wrote to him of his own occasional flirtations. Women, however, remained to him "strange creatures." Confiding to Woolf, he wrote, "For me, I dribble on among ladies, whom I cannot fall in love with. One of them is beautiful, young, charming. Oughtn't I to be in love with her?"[65] With the young woman, Strachey followed the formula for romance: "We go for walks together, read each other sonnets, sit out together at night among moon, stars, and the whole romantic paraphernalia." Once again, he asked Woolf, "Oughtn't I to be in love? We talk about it. Oughtn't I? It's my disease, I'm afraid, not to be."[66] Outside the reassuring atmosphere of Cambridge even Strachey doubted the superiority of all-male love, and on such rare occasions lamented his lack of attraction to women as a "disease." He envied Woolf's ability to balance his identity as a Higher Sodomite with that of the womanizer; he not only kept his passion for Duncan Grant a secret from Woolf but exaggerated his own exploits with the opposite sex.

The failed flirtation between Strachey and the anonymous lady of his letters recalled an earlier friendship with a member of the phenomenal sex. While visiting his aunt during the spring of 1906, Strachey met Miss Edgerton, "a pretty terrific female," but much older than himself—"38 wishing to be 28." The "damned intimate atmosphere" made him "a little nervous," but he decided that he "felt absolutely indifferent—almost cruel—and yet just excited because of the intimate vision of another mind." He was surprised that with this particular woman he achieved a brief "affair of the mind."[67] Surrounded by his family and other women gathered by his aunt as potential love interests, Strachey performed the charade expected of him. Writing to Duncan Grant, the real object of his love at the time, he confided, "I feel a little guilty because I *know* that I could never become intimate with her, or want to become intimate, or want her to become intimate with me. . . . It's too unkind, isn't it?"[68]

The Brothers who romanced and even married women described these relations as "always degraded." Leonard Woolf argued that "after all, 99/100ths of it is always the desire to copulate, otherwise it is only the shadow of itself and a particular desire to copulate seems to me no less degraded than a general."[69] How then did these men reconcile their devotion to the Higher Sodomy with a lower form of love for the opposite sex?

Physical intimacy with women actually protected some of the Brothers from corrupting their own unions with each other. Women provided an alternative or "safety valve" whenever passion threatened to bring Brotherly Love to a "lower" level. Rupert Brooke, for example, championed the Higher Sodomy at the Apostles' weekly meetings but reacted with horror when James Strachey attempted "copulation" (he embraced Brooke in his bedroom). Surprised by the rejection, James told Duncan Grant:

> Oh God! He's in love with a woman. Why did we think him a Sodomite? . . . . Don't you see now *why* he's kept everything so infernally dark? He's ashamed—because it's a woman. Heavens! I've written it down at last. And I'm in fits of laughter.[70]

The pink-cheeked, athletic blond "Apollo" disappointed Lytton, as well, who received the news of Brooke's womanizing with disgust. James's renewed attempts at a physical, or "lower" union with Brooke resulted in more angry refusals, until James admitted:

> I found out something about him which *did* make me despair. He's a *real* womaniser. And there can be no doubt that he *hates* the physical part of my feelings *instinctively* . . . just as I should hate to be touched by a woman.

James asked Grant, "Do you blame him for being normal?"[71] Fortunately, Brooke's girlfriend Noel Olivier provided a release for the sexual tension that existed between the two Brothers. James's passion for Brooke subsided once he seduced Olivier, and neither surprised nor upset over his friend's actions, Brooke resumed his "higher" friendship with Strachey.[72]

The story of this triangle circulated throughout the Society, and all of its members seemed to understand that the choice to be "normal" implied involvement in inferior, phenomenal relations with women. An Apostle resorted to womanizing, they argued, to avoid debasing his love for another Brother. And, though they boasted of "lower" flirtations with strange boys, the Brothers described intimacies with women in the barest of details, almost in code. While abroad in 1913, Keynes wrote to Grant that in Cairo he "had a w–m–n."[73]

Strachey's relations with women revealed his own need to escape the passion that repeatedly ate away at his theoretical and unattainable notion of the ideal. His introduction to the Stephen sisters awoke him to the possibility of females as worthy intellectual and sometimes romantic companions. At first, he regarded Virginia and Vanessa Stephen as mere extensions of their brother Thoby—the blond Apollo known at Cambridge as "the Goth." After Thoby's sudden death in 1906, the sisters became the main attraction at the Gordon Square residence. With their younger brother Adrian, they organized Thursday evening "at homes" at which Thoby's Apostolic friends gathered for whiskey, cocoa, buns, and conversation. The reputed beauty of the Stephen women did not go unnoticed by Strachey and his friends, who competed for the sisters' attention and flooded them with marriage proposals. Within the cloistered chambers of the Society, all women suffered the accusation of being "merely played upon" and "not introspective," but outside Cambridge the female-dominated household of Bloomsbury seemed to prove the exception to the rule. For the first time, Strachey discussed the philosophy of Moore in the presence of the opposite sex, while Vanessa told bawdy jokes and Virginia quietly listened.

In 1906 Strachey and Virginia Stephen formally agreed to correspond, and the subsequent letters expressed not only a shared passion for literature but also an intense hostility toward their parents' generation. Soon after their first letters, they began to address each other by their Christian names (a stage in Apostolic relations referred to as a "proposal"). To his surprise, Virginia "seem[ed] to be a woman of sound and solid common sense."[74] Despite this praise of the woman who read Plato and Moore, Strachey primarily used his letters to complain of his dim career prospects and "blank" future. Unlike himself, Strachey assumed, Virginia did not "find much difficulty [to] see life steadily and see it whole"; he wondered "is it because you *are* a virgin?"[75] When she failed to match the frequency of his correspondence, Strachey blamed Virginia for falling prey to "the inconsistency of [her] sex."[76] In his letters, Strachey also posed as an interested suitor, flirting with Virginia and inviting her to "go off to the Farol Islands" with him. What began as a jest became a serious marriage proposal in 1909, following Grant's final rejection of Strachey. Explaining his motivation to his brother James, Lytton wrote:

> In my efforts to escape, I had a decided reverse. . . . I proposed to Virginia and was accepted. It was an awkward moment as you may imagine, especially as I realised, the very minute it was happening, that the whole thing was repulsive to me.

Breathing a sigh of relief when Virginia later admitted she was not in love with him, Strachey "was able to manage a fairly honourable retreat." After some consideration, he concluded that "the story is really rather amusing and singular" but reminded James that he "need hardly mention the immense secrecy of the affair."[77]

The timing of the proposal not only coincided with Grant's "betrayal," but also with Leonard Woolf's own plan to ask Virginia to be his wife. Woolf had hesitated because he was still so far from England, and "the ghastly complications" of virginity and marriage "altogether appalled" him. Marriage to Thoby's sister, however, seemed his only hope "if [he was] ever to be saved" from his "degraded debauches."[78] Detailing his future plans with Virginia, Woolf concluded, "It is undoubtedly the only way to happiness, to anything settled" and would save him from the "appalling alternatives [of] violent pleasures [and] the depths of depression."[79] As did Strachey, he assumed Virginia's name promised a purity rarely offered by "modern" women. Shortly after receiving this letter, Strachey informed his Brother that he had "beat him to the punch" but miraculously escaped without even the horror of a kiss, but, Strachey added, he regretted that he could not force himself to marry Virginia: "I could have done it and could . . . have dominated and soared and at last made her completely mine."[80] Devoid of an apology, the letter then urged Woolf to propose since he "*would* be great enough and have the immense advantage of physical desire."[81] Strachey's own proposal was not only a confused prescription for recovery from his "divorce" from Grant but also a ploy to compete with and annoy Woolf, who had suggested that Strachey outgrow his commitment to the love of men. Once the "awkward moment" of the proposal had passed, Lytton and Virginia promised to remain friends. "The important thing," he wrote to her, "is that we should like each other, and we can neither of us have any doubt that we do."[82]

Perhaps her own fears of Strachey's need to "dominate and soar" compelled Virginia Stephen to call off the proposal. Years later, she confided to her diary her relief that she had not entered into a "bloodless alliance" with Strachey: "Had I married Lytton I should never have written anything. . . . He checks and inhibits in the most curious way."[83] This passage curiously echoes her thoughts about her father on what would have been Sir Leslie Stephen's ninety-sixth birthday: "His life would have entirely ended mine . . . no writing, no books; inconceivable."[84] She apparently sensed Strachey's patriarchal potential and preferred to disarm him of this power by regarding him as a "female friend."[85]

With the obstacle of romance removed, the two founders of the Bloomsbury Group of 46 Gordon Square embarked on a primarily intellectual relationship. Years before either of his Bloomsbury colleagues became famous, Clive Bell commented to Strachey, "Somehow I can't help feeling that both you and Virginia have something so like genius as to make life wildly exciting for your friends."[86] The relations between the two writers, though, gradually became riddled with jealousy—a violation of Bloomsbury's own prohibition against competition. While he yearned to break free from his journalistic career, Strachey tried to express enthusiasm over his friend's published and "very, very Unvictorian" novels.[87] Virginia, in particular, frequently noted their very different and gendered opportunities. Reading his poetry, she declared, "I want a fire and an armchair, silence, and hours of solitude. You enjoy all those things in your island." Meanwhile, her afternoons were wasted in the company of old women "who spoil my life."[88] Strachey, she assumed, excelled in poetry, criticism, belles lettres, and fiction, while "a painstaking woman who wishes to treat of life as she finds it, and to give voice to some of the perplexities of her sex, in plain English, has no chance at all."[89] Envy turned into anger when Virginia considered the elite Cambridge circle to which Strachey, her brother, and her husband belonged. She found it difficult to write to him while he visited his alma mater. "It's all Cambridge—that detestable place, and the ap–s–les are so unreal, and their loves are so unreal. . . . When I think of it, I vomit—that's all—a green vomit, which gets into the ink and blisters the paper."[90] Though Strachey enjoyed a dual membership in the Society and Bloomsbury, a barrier between the two groups existed that even this woman "of good sense" could never cross. Excluded from the Apostolic "real world," she, to Strachey's surprise, refused to accept that privileged domain as superior.

As the other original female member of Bloomsbury, Vanessa Stephen represented more of a romantic than literary rival. After the failed marriage proposal to Virginia, Strachey directed his attentions toward her younger sister, and their intimacy was noted by relatives who declared the two to be in love. Regarding such a prospect, Strachey "roared with laughter" and "said that it certainly would be the proper thing." To Keynes, he confided, "I think she thinks really I am, and I feel I ought to be. But what is one to do?"[91] He even tried to explain to Vanessa that his real affections were directed toward Duncan Grant, but she did not "see the real jar of the whole thing" or "take in the . . . confusion of [Strachey's] states."[92]

Vanessa's understanding seemed more acute than Strachey realized or was willing to recognize. To win his confidence, she downplayed what he perceived as her "feminine" traits. In her letters she commented on the pleasures of breathing in cigar smoke and bragged that she "felt [herself] becoming very like a male."[93] For costume parties she dressed in the attire of young men, flirting with Lytton, who admitted that the outfits made him "pretty well gone under." Regarding one occasion, he told James that "it was curious, decidedly. All I can say is that I had *not* had her when Oliver came in and we had to join the others."[94] At other times, she teased him with dreams in which Lytton was arrested in police raids of male brothels, and she even dared to request details of the "beauties" at Cambridge. Their prolonged flirtation displeased Vanessa's husband, Clive Bell, whom Strachey assured, "You haven't any reason for alarm." Still, he would not give Vanessa up entirely. "What I do want," Strachey explained to Bell, "and even hope for, is a continuance and increase of her friendship, and all those sympathetic satisfactions which I seem to perceive that she can give me. Is that too much?" Strachey regretted that "there are so few possible women that it would be a blow to be cut off there."[95]

Eventually Vanessa's extramarital affair with Duncan Grant caused her expulsion from the category of worthy females. Resentment toward this competitor for his cousin's love increased after the birth of the couple's daughter. Visiting the new family on their farm in 1916, Strachey was struck by Vanessa's "dumb animality [which] came out more unmistakably that [he'd] ever known!" In his journal, he asked, "Was it their married state that oppressed me? But then—*were* they married? Perhaps it was their *un*married state."[96] When Grant had rejected his proposal of marriage and chose to live with Keynes instead, Strachey had been devastated. Now he was further confused as to why Grant preferred this woman to either of the Brothers. He accused Vanessa of refusing him a moment alone with Grant. Yet, he also seemed eager to recapture the intimacy he once briefly shared with her:

> I saw that the time had come to face Vanessa. . . . Was she plain or beautiful? I could not decide. . . . How well I knew her!—And how little—how very little. . . . If I could only have flung myself into her arms! But I knew so well what would happen—her smile—her half-bewilderment, half-infinitely sensible acceptance—and her odd relapse.[97]

Instead, Strachey walked about uncomfortably, annoyed that in the midst of all this domesticity, he was not the center of attention. In particular, he loathed her children, who "pull[ed] him to picces" and terrified him.[98] Vanessa, he believed, stood in the way of his love for Grant and posed an obstacle that he could not overcome. She offered domestic bliss and children, which, for the moment, Grant apparently preferred to Strachey's monologues on the beauty of the Higher Sodomy.

Bored, or perhaps threatened, by his female Bloomsbury colleagues, Strachey entered into the socially and sexually mixed salon of Lady Ottoline Morrell. The wife of Liberal Parliament member Philip Morrell, Ottoline cultivated a large gathering of artists, writers, politicians, and socialites at her homes in Bedford Square and Garsington. She belonged to that breed of imperious, overruling women such as Florence Nightingale, Queen Victoria, the Empress Dowager, and Lady Strachey—all of whom Strachey both loved and hated. Strachey was attracted to what he regarded as Ottoline's "masculine" qualities as well as her "motherly instincts" and "such mysteries!"[99]

Ottoline acted not only as confidante during the years following the Duncan Grant "fiasco" but also as a link to Strachey's next designated ideal, Henry Lamb. He first noticed Ottoline at "a dim evening party full of virgins" when he "suddenly looked up and saw her entering with Henry." Reporting the incident to James Strachey, Lytton said he "was never so astonished" and did not know with whom he was most in love."[100] Competing with Lamb, he tried to achieve a physical union with the "splendid, magnificent, and sublime" Ottoline, and the two were once seen embracing and kissing so fiercely that blood trickled from Strachey's lips.[101] Though his diary recorded that he "failed to make progress with O.", Strachey actually was more determined to gain a "miraculous closeness" with Lamb. Similar to Strachey's other female acquaintances, Ottoline performed a maternal function in Strachey's life. She sympathetically listened to his dreams to "bound forward and triumph"; she confided to Lamb "I have him [Strachey] very much on my mind and wish I could do *something* for him."[102]

On several occasions Strachey fled London for emotional and physical recuperative visits at Ottoline's country home. When he at last realized that Lamb was neither a lower nor Higher Sodomite, he wired to Ottoline, "Shall arrive tomorrow . . . in need of your *corragio* as well as my own."[103] Immediately, Ottoline opened her home and arms to him, the latter into which he fell, "bruised in spirit, haunted, and shocked."[104] Though in his midthirties, Lytton seemed to Ottoline still a boy—"so well and full of fun and life and youth, adorable," but also "a solitary figure . . . seeking rather timidly and nervously for human adventures."[105]

One such "adventure" that Ottoline facilitated was Strachey's desire to "change sexes" now and then. Holroyd compares the friends' cross-dressing behavior to "a couple of high-spirited teen-age girls . . . all giggling and high heels and titillating gossip."[106] While Holroyd's description is curiously tainted by his own notions of "feminine" conduct, he relies on Ottoline's depiction of Strachey as a combination of "rigid intellectual breeding and manners" with "feminine, nervous hysterical" behavior.[107] Ottoline allowed Strachey to express what he saw as his dual nature, even to wear her shoes and cry over unrequited love affairs.

Despite these constant attentions, Strachey soon changed his opinion of Ottoline. News of her sexual affairs and sapphist experiments aroused his hostility, and in his letters to his Bloomsbury colleagues, Strachey spread rumors about Ottoline. Her sexuality undermined her worthiness as Strachey's confidante and nurturer and deviated from the "miraculous" Love that Strachey sought with his own sex. The "magnificent" and "sublime" woman who pursued her own lower sexual interests became a "syphilitic," "hag," and "fearful Jezebel."[108]

Ottoline provided comfort and encouragement to Strachey during the years before he achieved the fame for which he hungered, but his need for female consolation remained even after his postwar literary successes. Strachey loved the "confiding way" of certain women, and he also wanted a home and someone to fulfill his "occasional wish for a wife." At thirty-five, Strachey decided he "needed a respite from the uncertainty of his bachelor life."[109] To write and pursue love he required freedom from the trivialities of daily existence and supposed "a wife would settle such affairs for [him]." He asked James, "Is this a fearful muddle? It's too sickening to be trammeled up in these wretched material circumstances to the extent I am." What he desired was "a little rest!—a little home life, and comfort, and some soothing woman!"[110]

Such a "soothing woman" appeared at a party hosted by the Bells in the autumn of 1915. Dora Carrington belonged to the younger generation of New Women who, similar to the Strachey sisters, ardently supported female emancipation but rejected the celibate lifestyle of the Newnham graduates. Carrington had fled her provincial middle-class home and a domineering mother whom she said imprisoned her "in a bird cage." In London, she had immersed herself in the predominantly male circle at the Slade School of Art and deliberately fashioned her appearance and personality to remove signs of what she considered her "loathsome femininity." Disappointed that her parents christened her with "a sentimental lower-class English name," she became known to friends and colleagues simply as "Carrington."[111] Her athletically boyish figure and Florentine pageboy hairdo attracted the admiring glances and advances of both sexes. She insisted on the artist's need to stay single—that absorption in the lives of a husband and children degraded women; in short, marriage, she believed, was the death of a female artist.[112]

The events surrounding her introduction to Strachey altered the next sixteen years of their lives and formed part of the Bloomsbury lore. According to Carrington, "that horrid old man with a beard" surprised her in the woods and kissed her. Armed with a pair of scissors, she sought revenge the next morning on the sleeping man's beard, but as soon as her victim opened his eyes, she declared herself hypnotized and hopelessly in love (thus saving Strachey's famous beard).[113] But, what sort of "love affair" was this to be? Another Slade student warned Carrington against pursuing a relationship with Strachey; spelling out "H-O-M-O-S-E-X-U-A-L" as her explanation, she was dumbfounded when Carrington asked, "What's that?"[114] For Strachey's part, he was attracted not only to her youth and boyishness but also to her eagerness to submit her will completely to his and place him at the center of her life. Despite her eventual marriage and subsequent love affairs, Carrington always put Lytton's health, comfort, and work before her own. Shortly after his death in 1932, she wrote to Philippa Strachey:

> I wanted to tell you that you must *never* thank me for looking after Lytton—I know some people thought he was selfish, but it was I who was spoilt. He read to me every evening after dinner, he taught me all the values I have in life on our walks; he shared everything with me, all his thoughts and flaws and happinesses. Nobody will ever know how kind Lytton was to me, a Father, and a complete friend. I was his debtor.[115]

Carrington's own description of their long union is a far cry from the androgynous marriage hailed by Carolyn Heilbrun.[116] Neither partner considered Carrington the intellectual equal of Strachey. Indeed, she constantly reminded them of this gulf and wrote letters to Lytton "with a censor inside."[117] Though they alternated roles, at all times Strachey and Carrington maintained a polarized relationship; Strachey was patriarch, husband, father, "*chére grand-père,*" and uncle, but also the son nurtured by his ever-attentive "Mopsa."

In one of his early letters to Carrington, Strachey referred to Rimbaud's imaginary seven-year-old poet—the shy boy, overprotected by his mother, and lonely.[118] Though almost thirty years his senior, Strachey understood that boy; indeed, he *was* that boy. Increasingly dissatisfied with his dependence on his mother and with his claustrophobic bedsit, he finally obtained a loan from some Apostles and proposed an experiment. He would rent a home in the country, and Carrington would join him as his companion and caretaker. Writing to the Bells, he described the new arrangement: "it appears on the whole a reasonable project. I shouldn't be able to face it alone; female companionship I think may make it tolerable, though certainly by no means romantic. I am under no illusions."[119] Eager to replace Lady Strachey as Lytton's protector, Carrington readily agreed to the scheme.

At their new home, "Tidmarsh" and then at "Ham Spray," Carrington and Strachey carefully divided the household chores and responsibilities: Carrington painted the rooms, supervised servants, canned vegetables, and cooked special meals while Strachey paid the bills.

Describing the domestic scene in its early stages, Strachey told Virginia Woolf:

> My female companion keeps herself warm by unpacking, painting, pruning the creepers, knocking in nails, etc.—Ah dearie me, dearie me. I am nodding over the fire, and she's sewing an edge to the carpet. Ah, *la vie!* It grows more remarkable every minute.[120]

Taking on the additional role of Strachey's nursemaid, Carrington provided eucalyptus oil and hot water bottles for his numerous colds. While begging for news of his "adventures" at Cambridge, she, in the same breath, reminded him to change his socks and promised him shortbread and oatcakes upon his return home. Signing her letters as "Your Chambermaid," Carrington promised to remove all unnecessary details of Strachey's daily life but made these details the essence of her own.

Before they settled into the routine of domestic bliss, Carrington and Strachey attempted a physical union. After all, they lived in such close proximity and admitted an attraction to each other, so that "the next step" seemed inevitable. Despite previous flirtations with several male Slade students, Carrington had avoided intercourse, an act she said that "made [her] inside feel ashamed, unclean."[121] While her "virginity complex" provided fodder for Bloomsbury gossip and ridicule, Carrington now offered her body to Strachey without hesitation. Her diary, however, recorded her grief over the failed attempts at consummation. Though he wanted her near, Strachey "could not keep her as a mistress." Following a long discussion, Carrington told her diary:

> He sat on the floor with me, and clasped my hands in his and let me kiss his mouth, all enmeshed in the brittle beard, and my inside was as heavy as lead, as I knew how miserable it was going to be.[122]

Consoling her, Strachey insisted that there were "a great deal of a great many kinds of love," but Carrington understood that within Strachey's hierarchy of relations, those between men reigned supreme.[123] She regretted that she was not a youth who could "give [him] that peculiar extacy [sic]."[124] That she easily accepted this secondary place within his affections seems doubtful. Carrington's frequent pleas for love were mixed with regrets of "having confessed to you that I care so much."[125] Years later, she continued to cry over "a savage cynical fate which had made it impossible for my love ever to be used by you."[126] After Strachey's death, and shortly before her own suicide, she wrote in her diary that her studio mirrored her own existence: "untidy, disorganized, and incomplete."[127] At their cottage she had tried to create a "virgin island" based on their pure love for each other, but "the outer world" (Strachey's success and his hordes of young men) kept intruding on their paradise.[128]

In the presence of Carrington, Strachey felt safe, young, and loved. To augment the attractions of home, Carrington transformed their cottage into a "perfect Paradise." She hoped to keep Strachey with her at all times by converting the country residence into an extension of Cambridge. Tidmarsh and Ham Spray houses were havens for the younger Apostles who praised her food and Strachey's conversation. One such visitor told Strachey that Carrington recalled to him "the days of childhood as vividly as though [he] were still traversing them," and the Cambridge student Sebastian Sprott thanked Carrington for the "happiness" he discovered at Ham Spray.[129] Away from home, Strachey admitted that he "felt lost in [Carrington's] absence. Without this retiring place, [he] should have undoubtedly perished many times ere now."[130] She mothered all of Strachey's friends but never passed judgment, quietly agreeing to "go off somewhere" when Strachey arranged tête-à-têtes.[131] Still, as her diary reveals, she often felt left out by all the young men who never glanced her way, and hearing their laughter in the bedrooms, she "minded [her] virginal integrity and loneliness." Other times, she forced herself to "make other attachments" because, she wrote, Strachey disliked her dependence on him.[132]

In addition to arranging parties of young men, Carrington volunteered her beauty as a lure so that Strachey could admire her male pursuers. With her first lover, the artist Mark Gertler, Strachey flirted and shared books, and he acted as go-between during the couple's incessant arguments. In love with Carrington's next admirer, war veteran and Oxford graduate Reginald Partridge (whom Strachey renamed "Ralph"), Strachey actively campaigned for the couple's formal marriage. However, Strachey insisted that the ceremony, which occurred in 1921, should not upset the smooth management of the household; Ralph became a welcome addition, as gardener, chauffeur, and object of beauty. Before agreeing to the wedding, Carrington agonized over her decision. "The real difficulty," she told Strachey, "is he likes me always to be with him and sometimes I prefer this life here. . . . You are too good—so charming that I'd like to serve you all my life."[133] Obviously aware that marriage might force Carrington to change the focus of her allegiance and servitude, Strachey hesitated: "My dear, don't let us do anything which will make that other than it is! Do you know how much I love you?"[134] Perhaps Partridge's assurance that he did not "believe it will really upset the equilibrium of the menage" won the final blessing of Strachey, who then paid for the couple's Italian honeymoon.[135]

The groom's assumption, however, that the marriage bond would be in his favor proved incorrect. Carrington continued to regard Strachey as her "Lord and Master," and to him, not Partridge, she made a Valentine promise that her "heart would in that sweet bondage die [rather than try] to gain its Liberty."[136] Jealousy also disrupted the marital harmony, as the growing closeness between Strachey and Partridge threatened Carrington's monopoly over her master's affection. In a "fearful nightmare" she envisioned that the two men, "for some mysterious reason or other, made off together—without saying goodbye—forever!"[137] Early in her marriage, Carrington confided to a friend that her love for Lytton far exceeded her feelings for Ralph: "He [Strachey] might have made me his boot-black or taken me to Siberia, and I would have given up every friend I had to be with him."[138]

Strachey reaped the most benefits from what he called their "triangular life."[139] His letters to Carrington always expressed his eagerness to return to his "family and all the comforts" of home. The security of the triangle, however, unstable from its inception, collapsed under the strain of marital infidelities and Carrington's obsession with creating a "Paradise" for her "God." By 1926, Ralph was living with Frances Marshall in London and visiting Ham Spray house on weekends. The end of her marriage did not upset Carrington as much as the possibility of parting from Strachey. It was she who proposed the weekend marriage, afraid that Strachey would lose interest in her if Ralph left permanently. She even wrote to Frances, begging her to be "a little generous," since the "happiness of my relation with Lytton ironically is so bound up with Ralph, that that will be wrecked."[140] After ten years together, Carrington really had no cause for alarm. In Ralph's absence, life at Ham Spray continued as usual, but Strachey's dependence on Carrington began to equal her own. As she became involved sexually with other men and women, he regretted her absences from home and seemed envious of her increasing sexual activities as his own declined. While in Spain, Carrington received a letter in which Strachey complained, "I am feeling rather lost and lonely and miss you a great deal," but he hastily added, "Stay as long as you can if you're enjoying yourself." Even in the company of his younger Brothers, Strachey missed the "heavenly" presence of Carrington and "thought of [her] constantly."[141]

With Carrington, Strachey achieved his closest bond with a member of the phenomenal sex. She was his mother, wife, servant, pupil, and confidante, and he even once admitted to James that he regretted never marrying Carrington. No secrets existed between them. In addition to their letters, they exchanged diaries, since, according to Carrington, "it makes life so much more full to have another person's adventures and thoughts to enjoy."[142] At times she worried that Strachey was only a visitor and she his employee, but she refused his offer of a pension.[143] Aware that Carrington pushed aside her artistic career to tend house, Strachey proposed the pension in gratitude for "putting up with [his] befogged melancholies and helping [him] to face life."[144]

In her biography of Carrington, Gretchen Gerzina asks the obvious question: Did life with Lytton cause Carrington to channel her talents into housekeeping and decoration rather than painting? Gerzina seems untroubled that Carrington "made love the center of her life" as she destroyed her own canvasses and painting tiles.[145] More important than money, Carrington explained (and convinced herself to believe), were the "vistas" that Strachey made for her. "Think of dying without knowing Donne and Hero and Leander," she cried. He gave her required reading lists and "a standard of sensible behavior which makes it much easier to be reasonable."[146] She compared their relationship to that of the Wordsworths at Windemere—"for the way they sowed broad beans and she darned socks and he read Shakespeare to her."[147]

Having obtained financial independence late in life, Strachey advised Carrington to pursue her painting seriously. He built her a studio and warned her that unless she showed and sold her work, she would never "stand on [her] own legs."[148] Ignoring his urgings, she not only remained economically dependent on Strachey but ensured his reliance on her for his daily comfort. Carrington insisted that he treat her as a penwiper with "Use Me" embroidered in green on the cover, and she told Strachey, "That's what I would like you to remember—that I am always your penwiper."[149] She even hoped that she and Strachey might die at "exactly the same moment—it would be alright."[150] To achieve that wish, she committed suicide shortly after Strachey's death in 1932. In her diary, Virginia Woolf blamed Lytton for Carrington's death: "I sometimes dislike him for it. He absorbed her, made her kill herself."[151] His power over her reached beyond his grave, it seemed. Critic Maureen Connett offers another explanation for Carrington's suicide. After Lytton's death, Carrington suddenly realized that she had given her life to him instead of following her vocation as a painter.[152] Carrington's own final diary entry best explains the reason for her suicide: "He first deceased, she for a little tried / to live without him, liked it not and died."[153]

Carrington and Strachey began their living arrangement as an experiment. The Bloomsbury members perceived themselves as architects of a new social and sexual order. But, as Ruth Brandon argues in *The New Women and the Old Men,* the irony of modernity was the traditional form it assumed.[154] The artist and the writer told their colleagues that more than financial considerations motivated their intimate but chaste "marriage." Initially, both Carrington and Strachey hid the "menage" from their mothers, who disapproved of the cohabitation of the unmarried pair, but rapidly the "experiment" developed into a more Victorian-like arrangement. Aware of Strachey's expectations of women, Carrington willingly gave up her artistic ambitions to become his "penwiper."

According to Holroyd, Carrington suffered from a "virginity complex" before her marriage to Partridge, and afterward she engaged in predominantly lesbian relations.[155] Holroyd assumes a psychological imbalance rather than deliberate posturing as the source of Carrington's sexual behavior. In Carrington's mind, she remained pure for her true husband, Strachey. Unlike Vanessa and Ottoline, she did not disappoint him by placing her affairs above her duties to the sickly writer and, through birth control and abortion, guaranteed that no children ever upset the peace and quiet of the "Perfect Paradise" she cultivated. By the age of thirty, Carrington decided that she at last "felt . . . at peace with [her] lower self," and she abandoned makeup to create an appearance more suitable to her housebound life. "It was as though," observed one visitor to Ham Spray, "she had been worn to the bone by life and love."[156]

What compelled such "new women" to subordinate their lives to the demands and convenience of men? Brandon argues that underlying women's quest for modernity was an overwhelming sense of guilt. Even the most advanced of thinkers refused to believe that women did not find their "deepest satisfaction" in family priorities.[157] According to Elaine Showalter, one of Virginia Woolf's break-downs followed Leonard's "decision" against children in their marriage. While her male colleagues incessantly commented on her sister Vanessa's fertility, Virginia was led to feel that, despite her own literary achieve-ments, she had renounced a primary female role and destroyed her hus-band's opportunity to be a father.[158] And Carrington, tormented by her "beastly femininity," nevertheless sought solace from her "moods" of depression in pickling, sewing, and tending Lytton's colds, rather than in her art. In addition, Carrington's professional insecurities were fueled by her Bloomsbury colleagues. Roger Fry's "suggestion" that she give up her ambition of becoming a "serious artist" and turn to decorative art helped dissuade Carrington from exhibiting her paintings.[159]

The Strachey-Carrington "menage" raises the equally significant and troubling question of why self-styled "new men" accepted this female subservience? Despite their claims to unconventionality, nei-ther Carrington nor Strachey seemed capable of escaping Victorian gender codes that polarized the sexes and legitimized an attendant set of differences. The Apostolic definitions of masculinity and feminin-ity that Strachey embraced at Cambridge and later applied to his rela-tions with women were further extensions of these codes. Not even the odd women he encountered—the Stephen sisters, Lady Ottoline, or Carrington—succeeded in upsetting this gender system. Perhaps, then, as Sandra Gilbert and Susan Gubar argue, the rise of the New Woman was not matched by the coming of a New Man at all.[160] (Or, the very emergence of a New Woman needs to be reevaluated by femi-nist scholars, as well.) Strachey, whether bedridden like an "old maid"[161] or flamboyantly attired in yellow and purple velvet, seemed to challenge the boundaries of acceptable masculinity. However, in the end, he still harbored a desire for, not a release from, many aspects of traditional manliness. Such manliness required that he seduce and subdue insubor-dinate women whose intellect and talent matched his own.

In the company of women Strachey longed for what he called an "immaculate" bond reminiscent of the days when he "rushed head-long to [his] mother and clasped her and kissed her with all [his] strength." Long after leaving university, Strachey continued his search for that "ecstasy" of childhood, and with the women of Bloomsbury he attempted to "again love as much as that."[162] Some of his female colleagues, however, challenged Strachey's neat dichotomy of the real and the phenomenal and forced him to question his gendered concept of love that excluded them from the higher emotional and intellectual life. Carrington especially attracted Strachey. Her need to shock her elders, her relentless self-hatred, and her search for ideal love uncomplicated by sex made her his mirror image. Together this odd couple would renounce the conventional marriage and household of their parents' generation; they would openly discuss all matters, engage in an array of relationships, and their lives and art would reflect their "modern consciousness." Yet, even for these Bloomsbury members, inherited notions of gender interfered with their claims to modernity and their attempts to put theory into practice. The retreat to the countryside may have saved them from the probing eyes of critics, enemies, and family, but how were they to transcend gender, to create an apatriarchal space?

Chapter 4

Modernism and Strachey's Flight to Patriarchy

Reminiscing about the youthful days of Bloomsbury, Leonard Woolf declared:

> We were not part of a negative movement of destruction against the past. We were out to construct something new. We were in the van of the builders of a new society which should be free, rational, civilized, and pursuing truth and beauty. It was all tremendously exhilarating.[1]

The word so frequently on the lips of the Bloomsbury writers, artists, and intellectuals was indeed "new." While their critics accused them of being either immoral anarchists or elitist, apolitical exiles from the "real" world, they called themselves "modern" and announced their intention to usher in a "new age." As they engaged in parlor room "sex talk," practiced their "new style of love," or exhibited paintings that shocked the British public, the Bloomsbury members strove to be as unlike their Victorian ancestors as possible.

By far the most vocal critic of their parents' generation was Lytton Strachey. Yet, too often Strachey lost sight of the mission described by his colleague Leonard Woolf, and the construction of something new often took second place to a negative movement of destruction against the past. In Strachey's vocabulary, "modern" signified "anti-Victorian." His obsession with the past fueled his crusade against the heroes, values, and institutions of the nineteenth century and ultimately indicated the limitations of his literary and personal rebellion.

Most historical and literary treatments of modernism adopt Bloomsbury's perception of fin de siècle Britain as a period of extensive social, cultural, and ideological change.[2] The breakdown of liberal politics and the end of sexual repression equally signified the passing of the

Victorian order. For Strachey, modernist discourses empowered him to confront and rewrite the past. Constructing himself as a modernist, Strachey not only promoted his own reputation and work but also helped create the still prevalent image of the Victorians as repressive and prudish. Eager to condemn and blame those who marginalized his homosexuality, he targeted "eminent Victorians" as his nemesis.

Literary critic Peter Stallybrass insists that it is impossible to define "the modern" as if it had a single referent. When viewed from the standpoint of feminist theory and politics, the meanings and values of the modern vary.[3] To define someone such as Strachey as modern inevitably communicates a value judgment as praiseworthy, as Strachey's ironic use of "Victorian" is derogatory. Sweeping evaluations of modernism as either a liberating or repressive movement break down once individuals and contexts are examined, and a reevaluation of Strachey's life and art highlights the contradictions and ambiguities of modernism. His attempts to fashion a new identity for himself and to write a new type of history reveal the problems involved in breaking free of tradition, as well as the lingering Victorian gender and class hierarchies that defined avant-garde subcultures in the twentieth century.

Bloomsbury comprised only a portion of the intellectual elite that claimed to renounce Victorian culture and morality. Bloomsbury's humanism and liberal pacifism, as well as its comfortable lodgings near the British Museum, clashed with the antiromanticism, authoritarian politics, and poverty of rivals Wyndham Lewis, James Joyce, and T. S. Eliot. In his study of Bloomsbury, Ulysses D'Aquila considers such contrasts as evidence against a unified modernist movement. Within England thrived several modernisms that embraced an array of doctrines, including impressionism, imagism, vorticism, and classicism. Meanwhile, the continent had its own variety of experiments that included futurism, dadaism, cubism, and surrealism.[4]

The defining trait of modernism that seemed to link all of these movements was the intellectual's sense of discontinuity between the traditional past and the uncertain present. The search for a new voice, the sense of impending crisis, the retreat from narrative history and literature, and the new devotion to form over content—all of these signaled the modernist urge, as expressed by Wyndham Lewis, to "get clean out of history."[5] After attending Roger Fry's postimpressionist exhibit at the Grafton Gallery, Virginia Woolf observed that in 1910, "human character changed."[6] The line of history had broken, taking with it the Victorians' self-confidence and belief in determinism. According to Strachey, this self-confidence was really nothing more than the Victorians' refusal to face any fundamental question fairly—either about people or God; this was not cowardice, he added, but "simply the result of an innate incapacity for penetration."[7] In his preface to *Eminent Victorians,* Strachey announced his own capacity for "penetration," implying much more than his skills as a biographer: "he [the biographer] must attack his subject in unexpected places; he will fall upon the flank or the rear; he will shoot a sudden, revealing searchlight into obscure recesses." For Strachey, modernism was a commitment to ceaseless change, the uncovering of hideous truths, and sexual liberation. He encouraged his fellow Bloomsbury colleagues to use their art and literature as well as their bodies as agents of revolt against their Victorian past.

The anti-Victorianism championed by Strachey has been challenged in recent years by some literary critics. Perry Meisel and Ulysses D'Aquila, for example, see a strong link between the Victorian culture and its most vocal challengers. The self-consciousness of the modernists represented only a "will to modernity."[8] Members of Bloomsbury declared that they were "sharply cut off from our predecessors. . . . Everyday we find ourselves doing, saying, or thinking things that would have been impossible to our fathers."[9] This dogma of self-sufficiency empowered Strachey and his colleagues as they sought a place outside the very tradition that enabled them. The members of Bloomsbury did not delude themselves completely with their own image of modernity. Roger Fry confessed that he and his friends were "the last of the Victorians."[10] Their struggle with the not so distant past was the core of their art.

Edward Said describes the modernist dependency on Victorianism as a shift in cultural authority from filiation to affiliation. Modernists rejected the cultural inheritance of their parents (filiation) to produce alternate systems of relationships, values, and beliefs and created their own associations and communities (affiliation). Raymond Mortimer, in his joint review of Strachey's *Elizabeth and Essex* and Woolf's *Orlando,* aptly noted that "the weapons they have turned on the Victorians were forged in Victorian homes."[11] In reauthorizing themselves, however, the modernists adhered to a concept of authority that brought with it its own hierarchies, canons, and exclusiveness.[12]

Modernists such as the Bloomsbury members saw themselves as a special caste, on the margins of society, yet scornful of "respectability" and professing faith in the self-sufficiency of art. Virginia Woolf described Bloomsbury's gathering place at Gordon Square as a lion's den, "full of fascination and mystery," its members all "superior and roaring at each other."[13] During its early days, Bloomsbury remained convinced that anyone over the age of twenty-five was "hopeless," and without the capacity to feel or distinguish truth from falsehood. Despite its claims, the group failed to conceive an alternative idea of a whole society, appealing instead to the "supreme value of the civilized individual."[14] It was not just any civilized individual whom the group exalted, but the male individual in particular. The Apostles who went on to form the core of Bloomsbury continued to promote class privilege and a gender hierarchy based on male genius, and, strangely enough, the women of the group cooperated in this replication of Victorian gender roles.

Most of the traits assigned by scholars to modernism—a sense of crisis, the break with the past, despair, and elitism—hardly seem the sole domain of this particular movement at the fin de siècle. The modern intellectual, however, did view the creative genius from a new perspective. Modernists shattered the traditional British conviction that each individual has a substantial inner core of self, a stable ego. Unitary selfhood was pronounced a pose. Wyndham Lewis asked, "Why try and give the impression of a consistent and individual personality?" and he recommended, "Never fall into the vulgarity of being or assuming yourself to be one ego."[15] Strachey's psychobiographies belonged to this deconstructive movement. The modern biographer, he claimed, probed his subjects' "inner selves" protected by their public masks. Virginia Woolf's stream of consciousness meanwhile tried to express a "scattered and various selfhood."[16] In *Orlando,* Woolf, as did Strachey, played with the idea that biography necessitates an objective viewpoint and that the subjects of biography are stable identities. The multiplicity of self was a modernist discovery that entailed a continuous process of construction and destruction.[17]

While modernist writing broke down boundaries of ego/self, it also broke out of the narrow rules of narrative. Urging her new friend to try his hand at novels, Virginia Stephen wrote to Strachey in 1908, "plots don't matter, and as for passion and style and immorality, what more do you want?"[18] Strachey turned instead to biography and rejected the event-centered method of Victorian historiography. In his psychobiographies, he offered his readers a probing of the "inner dynamics" of best-loved British heroes and heroines. The preface of *Eminent Victorians* can be read as Strachey's modernist manifesto. Allegedly quoting "the great Master," Voltaire, Strachey proclaimed: "*Je n'impose rien, je ne propose rien, j'expose.*"[19] No longer was it the biographer's task to compliment and commemorate the dead with two thick volumes of ill-digested material. Instead, Strachey insisted, "it is [the biographer's] business to lay bare the facts of the case . . . dispassionately, impartially, and without ulterior intentions."[20] To Strachey, the past was "the only thing we have which is not tinged with cruelty and bitterness. It is irrevocable, and its good and evil are fixed and done with." His duty as a historian was to look at this past "dispassionately, as if it were a work of art."[21]

Did Strachey dispassionately recount the irrevocable past? To his reading public Strachey set himself up as a new kind of authority— one who could separate reality from what he called "the sham of the Victorians." The text that followed Strachey's preface, however, was more ironic than its author had intended. Strachey's refashioning in *Eminent Victorians* relied very little on the objectivity that he claimed was required of a modern biographer. In fact, he slips from his stated position of objective biographer when he promises in his preface to tell the lives of Cardinal Manning, Florence Nightingale, Thomas Arnold, and General Gordon "as *he* understands them" (my emphasis).[22] Criticized for numerous errors of fact, the biographies actually read as fiction, or the past sifted through Strachey's filter of satire and hatred. Henry Lamb asked Strachey if he was "always going to make such ludicrous mannequins" of his subjects. Instead of exposing only "foibles," Lamb urged Strachey to "develop what you do respect in people."[23] Strachey used these foibles to knock the Victorians off their pedestals, to secure for himself the same position of authority for which he accused and resented his moralizing ancestors. Writing to Virginia Woolf in 1912, Strachey prophesied that in fifty years, Thackeray, Meredith, and all the other "mouthing bungling hypocrites would be relics."[24] The rapid slip of *Eminent Victorians* from best-seller status to obscurity suggests that Strachey was the real victim of history, forgotten by most scholars until his rediscovery in the late 1960s—and not for his literary accomplishments, but for his sexuality.

One of the reasons that *Eminent Victorians* was so easily forgotten, according to historian John Halperin, is that Strachey's book is, quite simply, "bad history." Irresponsible and malicious, Strachey, Halperin charges, invented facts (such as Matthew Arnold's unusually short legs) and focused more on personality than on the outside forces that shape personality.[25] It was as a biographer that Strachey hoped to attack the past and make his mark as a modern writer. Critics such as Richard Altick readily acknowledge the "Stracheyan Revolution" in biography.[26] With *Eminent Victorians,* Strachey heralded a new age of this literary form and turned biography into an art. Dismantling the old notion that a biographer merely assembles facts, Strachey interpreted, speculated, probed the psyche of his subject, and mingled the narrative voice with the subject's "inner life." The traditional biographer, according to André Maurois, described a mask and refused to look behind it, but the "new biography" refused to emulate the hero worship, idealism, and hypocrisy of the Victorians.[27] Virginia Woolf (whose father, Sir Leslie Stephen, epitomized the Victorian biographer) believed that, as an artist, the new biographer, above all, rejected filiality and therefore savored the victory of the last word.[28] Strachey's mission of "statue-toppling," however, tended to result in caricatures of his subjects and deliberate historical errors. Responding to such criticism, Strachey explained his concept of "objectivity" in his 1928 essay on Gibbon: "History is not the accumulation of facts, but the relation of them." For Strachey, the writing of history was like the making of an omelette: every historian used butter, eggs, salt, and herbs, but the omelette varied according to who mixed these ingredients.[29]

Strachey's "disingenuous streak" was the essence of his modern writing. The modern biographer now relied on creativity and altered the relationship of the reader to the biographer from trust to wary skepticism[30]—and skepticism prevailed during the early twentieth century. Paul Fussell suggests that *Eminent Victorians* appealed to the wartime generation because it reflected the irony that had become the "one dominating form of modern understanding."[31] As he listened to Strachey read from *Eminent Victorians,* David Garnett soon realized "that Lytton's essays were designed to undermine the foundations on which the age that brought the war had been built."[32] Garnett credited Strachey with challenging not only literary but political and social foundations as well.

For Strachey, World War I provided an opportunity for both literary experimentation and personal liberation. He at last moved out of his mother's home and began to work earnestly on a series of "silhouettes" of prominent Victorians. His subjects, he told Virginia Woolf, were representative of an era that bred "mouthing bungling hypocrites."[33] On the eve of the Great War, England seemed idyllic and romantic. The Bloomsbury members remained oblivious to heated parliamentary debates on Irish Home Rule, the militant activities of Mrs. Pankhurst and the suffragettes, and violent Labour strikes. Strachey and his circle continued to enjoy the pleasures of the West End, the arrival of the Russian Ballet, and the exhibitions of the Omega Workshop. On August 4, 1914, while cheering crowds gathered outside Buckingham Palace or rushed to recruiting offices, the Bloomsbury Group made plans to retreat to their country homes. However, the war at last forced Strachey to enter the phenomenal world, not only as a writer and social critic, but as a political voice against militarism.

By mid-December of 1914, British troops had been on the continent for five months and the shocking numbers of casualties shattered the hope that the war "would be over by Christmas." On the nineteenth of December, *The New Statesman* published Strachey's article describing the "tragedies of whole lives and the long fatalities of human relationships." The article was not about the war but rather a review of Thomas Hardy's poems.[34] According to Fussell, even Strachey's literary reviews had become a form of "subtle strategy" against the government. The journalist's language in the review hinted at his animosity toward the complete desolation caused by the war.[35] The impact of the war on language is also clear in Strachey's preface to *Eminent Victorians,* in which he urges other biographers and historians to use the "indirect" method, to "attack his subject in unexpected places."

For Strachey, the war had reversed the idea of progress and destroyed the "civilization, order, and beauty" that the Apostles and Bloomsbury members had long championed. In his private writings, Strachey expressed contempt for his younger Cambridge Brother Rupert Brooke, who declared the war a liberation from "a world grown old and cold and weary" and corrupted by "half-men."[36] Strachey knew at whom Brooke's criticism was directed and responded to this in his Apostle story "Sennacherib and Rupert Brooke." In the story, the fictional Brooke describes all wars as justifiable and admirable, an opinion that Strachey challenged before the War Committee.[37] Unlike Brooke, Strachey opposed "the whole system by which it is sought to settle international disputes by force."[38]

Strachey told his brother James that he and his Cambridge friends were "all far too weak physically to be of any use at all," but he was not untroubled by the question of military service.[39] He lamented the horror of the sacrificed young men whose bodies he loved, dying in the mud and filth of the trenches. His contempt for the war forced him to alter his writing of the Victorian silhouettes; he now had a clear idea in his mind and focused on the Victorian pretensions and false ideologies that he believed led British civilization to the present war. Even before the 1918 publication of *Eminent Victorians,* Strachey engaged in other activities that indicated his confrontation with the phenomenal realm. He knit mufflers for "our soldier and sailor lads," worked for the No Conscription Fellowship, distributed propaganda for the National Council for Civil Liberties, and registered as a conscientious objector after the passage of the Military Service Bill in January 1916. This act imposed compulsory service for the first time in Britain and outraged Strachey, who declared he was "willing to go to prison rather than do even clerical work for the war."[40] Meanwhile, other conscientious objectors, David Garnett and Duncan Grant, were ordered to grow crops for the government or face imprisonment. Regarding such activities now performed by his artistic friends, Strachey declared, "I cannot see the use of intellectual persons doing this."[41]

In the midst of patriotic frenzies on the home front, conscientious objectors such as the Stracheys, Duncan Grant, and Adrian Stephen comprised a minority that faced the threats of work camps, prison, or mob beatings, while other male modernists vocally embraced the war. The vorticists Pound and Lewis, for example, "blasted" the "soft" men of Bloomsbury while they embraced the virility of modern warfare. In 1916 Strachey made his own statement before the Hampstead Advisory Committee. Suffering from piles, he inflated an air cushion and, once seated, told the committee that "before the war, [he was] occupied with literary and speculative matters." However, the war "forced upon [his] attention . . . the supreme importance of international questions." His opinions in general had "been for many years strongly critical of the whole structure of society." The committee, not surprisingly, rejected Strachey's statement and ordered him to submit to a physical examination (which he failed). Curiously, Strachey did not completely distance himself from his Victorian ancestors, whom he blamed for the war. Seated among several unclad youths destined for the trenches, Strachey sighed, "I am the civilization they are dying for."[42]

Eminent Victorians was the first explosive postwar book. The social climate of 1918 favored Strachey's distaste for violence and extremism. According to Cyril Connolly, Strachey had "struck the note of ridicule which the whole war-weary generation wanted to hear."[43] No idols remained and Strachey offered no hope. The war undermined the tradition of heroism, and the faith in progress gave way to 'Stracheyesque' cynicism and despair. The hypermasculinity of Arnold, the ambition of Manning, the militarism of Gordon, and the despotism of Nightingale came to symbolize all that was wrong with the nation before 1914.

Eminent Victorians established Strachey's reputation as a leading popular author, but by 1923, with the publication of *Queen Victoria,* he was referred to by critics as a "would-be-writer." Strachey had worked for three years on Victoria's biography, which, similar to *Eminent Victorians,* was intended as an indictment of an entire age. However, his mission (both personal and literary) to tarnish a past that by the 1920s had become already too remote for most readers cost him the public and critical acclaim he craved. Furthermore, although the war had served as an impetus to Strachey's career, the author's insecurities regarding his sexuality continued to dominate his unpublished work, and it is Strachey's sexuality, rather than his literary achievements, that contemporary scholars use to discuss his position within British modernism.

This chapter, as part of the current feminist project of rethinking and "engendering" modernism, evaluates Strachey's attempts at personal and literary sexual liberation. Feminist critics of modernism tend either to emphasize the misogyny of writers such as Joyce and Lawrence or to read the homosexuality of such Bloomsbury members as Forster and Strachey as the essence of modernity itself. The relationship between Bloomsbury's androgyny, homosexuality, and modernism especially merits rethinking. During the fin de siècle, sexuality emerged as a powerful symbol in the culture of the avant-garde, with "perversion" assuming both aesthetic and political functions. Contemporary cultural criticism has continued this trend in treating homosexuality and transgression as interchangeable categories beyond the boundaries of everyday social and sexual norms. The ways in which Strachey constructed his own persona, simultaneously playing with images of deviance, effeminacy, and normative masculinity, also impacted his writing of biography and underscored how he moved between the two poles of modernity and Victorianism. He seemed drawn to historical figures, primarily women, who, similar to him, violated gender boundaries either deliberately or unconsciously. Yet, Strachey did not treat these women as heroic figures, but as monstrous caricatures of femininity. His biographies, which can be read as composites of the Bloomsbury women, ultimately tell us less about his historical subjects than they do about his own sexual politics and his relationships with the female modernists closest to him. Strachey's use of gender in his private relationships and published works upheld traditional notions of masculinity and femininity at the same time that he tried to undermine them in his public displays of dandyism.

At the center of both the Apostles and the Bloomsbury Group, Strachey fostered an atmosphere that necessitated a constant stream of "sex talk" and "outrageous" gender performances that included cross-dressing, nudity at parties, and bisexual love affairs. In 1906 Virginia Stephen welcomed this new openness as a release from what she called the "cage" of her Victorian upbringing. Strachey, who once confided that he feared (or hoped?) that his own biography would "present a slightly shocking spectacle," obviously intended his sexual behavior to be read as avant-garde.[44] For Strachey, though, his own advice regarding sexual freedom and pleasure seemed impossible to follow; he repeatedly pursued younger men who used him for his fame and money, or heterosexual men whose love remained unrequited. His self-loathing over his "hideous" appearance and incessant bouts of illness fueled Strachey's private torments regarding his sexual identity. Nevertheless, scholars continue to read Strachey's homosexuality, more so than any of his publications, as "a weapon of twentieth-century revolt."[45]

Disregarding the personal struggles of individual men such as Strachey, certain literary critics have perpetuated this notion of homosexuality as formative of modernity itself. In his now classic 1978 essay "Eros and Idiom" George Steiner defined homosexuality as a deliberate "creative" rejection of conventional realism, a strategy of opposition, and the artist's most emphatic stance against philistinism.[46] Similar to Michael Holroyd and Bertrand Russell, Steiner sees this search for a "genuine extra-territoriality," or a "posture genuinely offensive," as self-conscious and always transgressive. George Piggford also recently applauded Strachey's writing and personal styles as deliberate "camp" parodies of the dominant culture.[47] Although Strachey's homosexuality did involve the breaking of laws and moral codes, the degree of "choice" is questionable, as is the subversiveness of his theory of love, which was based on racial, class, and gender hierarchies. Also, Steiner insists that in the twentieth century the homosexual artist remained the only outsider, the "grand refuser" of bourgeois values.[48] More recent critics such as David Eberly and Christopher Reed echo Steiner's analysis, reading Strachey's idiosyncratic posture and dress as the "embodiment of a visibly effeminate man whose mannerisms came to encode homosexual recognition in a hostile society." Strachey, the occasional cross-dresser and bedridden neurasthenic, transgressed patriarchy's ultimate prohibition: the feminized man.[49]

In her examination of Bloomsbury's sexual politics, Linda Hutcheon also argues that homosexuality was a deliberate form of anti-Victorian revolt. Yet, she seems to contradict this claim when she writes, "given the restrictive social code, one was a rebel, a challenge to society by one's very existence as a homosexual"—an existence that may not have involved any exercise of choice at all.[50] However, Bloomsbury's enemies did perceive the members' homosexuality as a choice and attacked their art and their sexual mores as inseparable entities. Roy Campbell, for example, condemned the members as "sexless folk whose sexes interact" and part of "the literary androgynous riff-raff."[51] In *The Apes of God*, Wyndham Lewis satirized Strachey as Matthew Plunkett, a homosexual feasting on "Eminent Victorian giants," trying to be "normal" by seducing the boyish Betty Bligh (Dora Carrington). In the 1954 introduction to the novel, Lewis recalled the "wave of male perversion among the young" in the 1920s, of which Bloomsbury was a part, and Lewis condemned male inversion as a "nasty pathological oddity."[52] D. H. Lawrence declared the men of Bloomsbury to be like "beetles . . . horrible and unclean . . . thinking of them sends me mad with misery and hostility and rage."[53]

Was Strachey's homosexuality simply motivated by a desire to shock? Hutcheon points out that none of the writers of Bloomsbury, who talked incessantly in private about semen and buggery, made sex the focus of their publications. Unlike D. H. Lawrence and Radclyffe Hall, whose works were banned, Forster, Woolf, and Strachey used their lives as "subtle vehicles" of rebellion. Forster deeply regretted the impact of social convention on individual consciousness, which delayed the publication of *Maurice* until 1971; before his death, he noted in his diary, "I should have been a more famous writer if I had written or rather published more, but sex prevented the latter."[54] Aware of his friend's homosexual novel, Strachey secretly ridiculed the project as well as its author. Writing to his brother James, Strachey called Forster "a mediocre man . . . he will come to no good and in the meantime he's treated rudely by waiters."[55]

Though he mocked Forster's literary efforts, Strachey, too, found that the unpublished page afforded more freedom to write about sex and male desire. Curiously, he disliked novels that dealt openly with sex, describing them as "so self-conscious and tentative and nervous and ignorant,"[56] and he understood David Garnett's reluctance to battle the censors and become "a test case of bawd."[57] More disturbing is the way in which Strachey used hints of homosexuality to attack his male subjects for publication, for example, referring to General Gordon's fondness for the boys of Khartoum and Prince Albert's distaste for the queen's amorous advances. But in his private essays and stories for the Cambridge Apostles and the Bloomsbury Group, Strachey's stories of all-male love are reverential and stress the intellectual and spiritual superiority of these relations. When Keynes suggested that their notion of the Higher Sodomy seemed to "wrap them [the younger Apostles] in our own filth packet,"[58] Strachey was quick to reply that they "may be sinning," but at least they did so "in the company of Shakespeare and Greece."[59] It was this association of male love with high culture that rescued Strachey from the restrictive atmosphere of 69 Lancaster Gate, and from the phenomenal realm outside Cambridge and Bloomsbury that defined his feelings as "unnatural."

In her Memoir Club essay for Bloomsbury, Virginia Woolf also made this connection between male homosexuality and liberation—her own. Her introduction to her brother Adrian's Cambridge friends, Strachey, Leonard Woolf, and G. E. Moore, enveloped her in a new circle, in which men "never seemed to notice how we were dressed or if we were nice looking or not. All this seemed to have no meaning in their world." Instead, she and her sister Vanessa discussed with these young men "the abstract"—Truth, Beauty, Reality, Art, and even Plato. Very soon she realized "the truth" about her brother's friends:

> I knew theoretically from books, much more than I knew practically from life. I knew there were buggers in Plato's Greece; I suspected it was not a question one could just ask—that there were buggers in Trinity College, Cambridge. But it never occurred to me that there were buggers even now in the Stephens' sitting room at Gordon Square.[60]

Once Strachey uttered the sacred word "semen" in her presence, Virginia Stephen realized that "with that one word, all barriers of reticence and reserve went down." The newly formed Bloomsbury Group now "discussed copulation with the same excitement and openness that we had discussed the nature of good." The young men enjoyed shocking their new female acquaintances with stories of Apostolic affairs, and Virginia and Vanessa "listened with rapt interest to the ups and downs of their chequered histories. There was nothing one could not say at 46 Gordon Square." Not only in their personal relations but in their writing and art, the Bloomsbury members tried to be as unlike their "repellent Victorian ancestors" as possible.[61]

However, the Apostles did little to welcome these women to their own sacred terrain at Cambridge. During Virginia Stephen's visit to the sitting room of some Apostles in 1909, she was greeted with silence: "We had nothing to say to each other, and I was conscious that not only my remarks but my presence was criticized. They wished for truth and doubted if I could speak it."[62] Cambridge would always stand as a barrier between the men and women of Bloomsbury. Long after graduation, into their old age, the Apostles returned for weekend retreats, to meet and help elect new members to their Society, and to read essays on the joys of the Higher Sodomy. Virginia Woolf, eventually tired of this "bugger revolution" that allowed for discussion of only male Love and not sapphism, voiced her resentment against this bastion of male privilege, not only in *A Room of One's Own,* but much earlier in her letters to Strachey. She found it difficult to write to him when he was at Cambridge—"that detestable place."

Despite the tensions that clearly existed in his relations with Woolf and the other women of Bloomsbury, Strachey's feminism, as with his homosexuality, has earned him the label of modernist. Carolyn Heilbrun applauds the Strachey and Stephen siblings for their efforts to detach themselves from the "masculine orgy" of their fathers' generation. Not only were such women as Vanessa Bell and Virginia Woolf considered the intellectual equals of their male friends, but Bloomsbury allowed "the feminine force" to dominate the group. Quentin Bell's unbiased picture of Bloomsbury as a "moral adventure" and feminist utopia in which women were on a completely equal footing with men continues to intrigue feminist scholars such as Jan Marsh, who sees gender as irrelevant to Bloomsbury.[63]

In opposition to this view, Jane Marcus offers a scathing portrait of Strachey and his male colleagues as the "new bullies" of Virginia Woolf's generation. Part of an "intellectual aristocracy," these men asserted a "homosexual hegemony over British culture." The ideology of male superiority and valorization of homosexual over heterosexual love, the study of Greek, and the secret codes of the Apostles resulted, according to Marcus, in a subtle yet still dangerous form of woman hating. Armed with class and cultural power, these men left Cambridge and found key positions in education, government, and publishing and as writers.[64] Thinking of the Apostles, their privileges and power, triggered Woolf's urge to "vomit a green vomit." Woolf expressed her disillusionment with her male colleagues, who merely paid lip service to feminism and liberation, in *Three Guineas*. Woolf called upon working-class men, not the men of Strachey's class, to be the allies of women in their struggle against patriarchy. The tradition of same-sex bonding and fraternity among the middle and upper classes excluded all women and working men from the "means of production of culture in politics, law, literature, and life."[65]

Since Marcus, other feminist scholars have begun to question the gender politics and sexual radicalism of modernism. The modernist's questioning of authority and the shift from outsider to insider was gender based, with, as Woolf realized, women largely absent from the transition. Bonnie Kime Scott, for example, describes modernism as a "masculine frenzy" in which male writers and artists, unconsciously or deliberately, used conventional inscriptions of sexuality and gender.[66] The phallocentric language and images of the vorticists and the orientalism of the Bloomsbury artists all relied on Victorian definitions of femininity and masculinity. Within these modernist groups, despite the presence of "strong women," men reigned, reaped the glory, and shunned "bold feminine modernity."[67] Meanwhile, the mental health and the personal relationships of women received more attention than their work. Scott blames historians of modernism for concentrating on small sets of male participants, while paying lip service to the writings of Virginia Woolf.

In an attempt to correct this marginalization of women from historical and literary accounts of modernism, critic Suzette Henke offers such subcategories as "early male modernism," "masculinist modernism," and "bold feminine modernity," the last category being negatively received by male writers. Henke suggests that "a different dimension of modernism," or "an alternative to the Pound era," can be found in the works of Woolf, H. D., Djuna Barnes, Gertrude Stein, and other women writers. Nevertheless, modernism remained an exclusively male club, motivated by a "phallocentric project."[68]

Such modernists as Wyndham Lewis and Ezra Pound, founders of the short-lived vorticist movement, seemed obsessed with virility, "hard, precise images," and a poetic language "as much like granite as it can be."[69] Suffragettes and aesthetes proved favorite targets of ridicule in the vorticists' journal, *Blast*. These men equated modernity with masculinity, originality with the phallus, and the mind with an "upspurt of sperm."[70] The mission of modernism, according to its male leaders, was to "drive any new idea into the great passive vulva of London."[71] Meanwhile, rival D. H. Lawrence advocated England's salvation through a "true phallic marriage" in which woman yielded "some sort of precedence to man." Lawrence especially disliked the members of the Bloomsbury Group who seemed to reject "the essential blood contact between man and woman."[72] Ignoring Strachey's very phallic description of the biographer's art (penetrating his subjects, falling upon their flanks), Bloomsbury, to Lawrence's dismay, seemed to seize upon the images of androgyny and bisexuality instead.

The most critical revision of modernism has come from Sandra Gilbert and Susan Gubar. Their three-volume study, *No Man's Land: The Place of the Woman Writer in the Twentieth Century*, examines the ongoing battle of the sexes from the Victorian era to the present and the impact of this sexual struggle on literature. Gilbert and Gubar argue that the modernist exhortation to "make it new" was *not* a gender-free statement. Lawrence, Pound, Eliot, and Joyce, for example, were driven by sexual anxieties, a fear of emasculation, and a desire to reestablish sex polarity. The rise of the female imagination, Gilbert and Gubar add, was the central problem for the twentieth-century male imagination. In short, the rise of the New Woman was not matched by the coming of a New Man but was instead identified with a crisis of masculinity.[73] Male intellectuals' hostility toward what they perceived as threatening female autonomy triggered the modernist reaction against literary women.

Gilbert and Gubar, similar to Henke and Scott, virtually ignore Strachey in their examinations of the "male club" of modernism. They return to Bloomsbury primarily to discuss one such dreaded autonomous woman, Virginia Woolf, and her relations with male modernists outside of the group. Woolf's literary reactions against T. S. Eliot and Joyce provide valuable insight into her texts, but her long-standing friendship and professional rivalry with Strachey are equally revealing of what Gilbert and Gubar call Woolf's "flight from patriarchy."[74] On the other hand, Heilbrun's equation of Strachey's homosexuality with his modernist attitude is *too* simplistic. Heilbrun assumes that Strachey's homosexuality made him more sympathetic toward women, more eager to break free of Victorian gender roles and sexual polarization. Indeed, critics such as Lawrence sneered at the men of Bloomsbury, especially the invalidish Strachey with his shrill voice and coterie of strong women. Yet, these rivals shared more with Strachey than they dared to realize. Strachey, too, was driven by sexual anxieties, by a conflict between his homosexuality and his urge to be "manly," and by his hostility toward the very women he regarded as his colleagues. Ultimately, very little difference exists between the "openly misogynistic writers" and the "quasi-feminists"—both felt threatened by female competition.[75]

Male and female modernists did work together, embarking on joint literary projects as friends, co-editors, readers, and revisers of one another's work. However, a kind of "scribbling rivalry" developed among mutually admiring pairs, and the male praises of women's writings were especially problematic.[76] Referring to the cases of Hemingway and Stein, D. H. Lawrence and Katherine Mansfield, Robert Graves and Laura Riding, Gilbert and Gubar need to add Strachey and Woolf to their discussion. The Bloomsbury motto of friendship without jealousy broke down as soon as Woolf and Strachey became published authors. Strachey's letters to other friends frequently criticized Woolf's works as incoherent, without substance, and difficult to read, yet to her face he praised the novelist. Even his praises undermined her texts and confidence; Strachey told Woolf that to write like her "would be to write like Virginia"—a phrase that Woolf interpreted as "a fatal event, it seems."[77] Or, Strachey simply used the tactic of silence. When he said nothing in response to *Jacob's Room,* Woolf seemed disappointed, noting in her diary, at least "when Lytton picks holes, I get back into my working fighting mood."[78] Meanwhile, Woolf relished Strachey's literary decline in the years that followed his successful *Eminent Victorians.* She regarded his writing as a "supremely skillful rendering of the old tune," but not "first rate." Strachey, she believed, was too concerned with plot and suffered from "a failure of vitality."[79] She finally confronted Strachey with her criticisms of *Elizabeth and Essex,* and again in her diary, she wrote:

> I had no longer anything to envy him for; and how dashing off
> Orlando I had done better than he had done; and how for the first
> time I think, he thought of me, as a writer, with some envy.[80]

Recording these anxieties and reservations, Strachey and Woolf waged private literary combat against each other. Perhaps the anger of the male intellectual was motivated by a feeling of abandonment; the female muse had become self-willing and self-willed.[81]

Gilbert and Gubar suggest that Woolf wrote *Orlando* as a response to Joyce's "he-goat" vision of male mastery.[82] Heilbrun adds that Strachey's biographies shared with Woolf's an understanding of "the androgynous mind."[83] However, given the aforementioned diary entry, and that both *Elizabeth and Essex* and *Orlando* were written during the same period (1928), it seems that Woolf and Strachey were engaged in more of a professional rivalry than a friendly feminist collaboration. Both writers claimed to alter the method and content of biography. But whereas Strachey was more concerned with debunking and shrinking heroes, Woolf was concerned with restoring women to the historical record and undermining biography's patriarchal bias.

In a letter to Vita Sackville-West (the model for Orlando), Woolf promised to "revolutionise biography in a night," not only competing with Strachey in this category, but also attacking the limits of his own literary revolution.[84] In *Orlando* Woolf tried to write a revisionary biography in which costume, not anatomy, is destiny; Orlando has a wardrobe of male and female selves and fulfills Woolf's fantasy of gender fluidity.[85] In Strachey's account, however, anatomy (female anatomy, that is) is perversion. Regarding Elizabeth I, Strachey hinted at a special cause for her neurotic condition: "Her sexual organisation was seriously warped." A physical malformation as well as a "deeply seated repugnance to the crucial act of intercourse" marked the queen with "a certain grotesque intensity."[86] Strachey's attempts to understand Elizabeth's "virginity complex" resulted, in Woolf's view, in a poor book unworthy of its author. Trying to explain his failure, she and Strachey both blamed his poor health and the suffocating praise of Carrington and Strachey's young men.[87]

Despite Virginia Woolf's criticisms, some scholars persist in reading Strachey's biographies as proof of his feminism. Hoberman positions Strachey's imaginative biographies against Leslie Stephen's "masculine grasp of facts." Critiquing the Victorian cult of masculinity, Strachey looked at ambitious women who challenged male-conceived heroism and feminine submission. Strachey's homosexuality and the influence of his politically active sisters, Hoberman adds, enabled him to see beyond the narrow confines of "masculinity" and "femininity."[88] Similar to Heilbrun, Hoberman regards Strachey as the champion of women who violate socially defined roles and are excluded from the legitimate exercise of power. However, even Hoberman cannot ignore the biographer's obsession with the women's repressed sexuality and his need to explain their successes and failures in terms of this repression. Elizabeth's indecisiveness in political matters is really a symptom of repressed desire; when she executes Essex she "overthrows manhood" and protects her virginity for good. Alice Fox suggests that Virginia Woolf disliked *Elizabeth and Essex,* not because of its mediocre writing, but because of its antifeminism.[89] Perhaps Woolf also recognized in the biography of Elizabeth's freakish "virginity complex" Strachey's parody of her own sexual history.

Strachey and Woolf engaged in another rivalry—not just the writing of modern biography, but the creation of the androgyne. A literary and sexual interest in androgyny was central to the Bloomsbury rebellion. The new "modern I," which recognized a multiplicity of selves, was not simply male or female but embraced a mixture of maleness and femaleness, uniting to explore a range of sexual and literary possibilities. Strachey, who in a poem declared of his own heart, "I do not know your sex,"[90] celebrated such "feminine virtues" as the "writing of good letters," and his biographical interest in powerful women has been read as his support and identification with the "feminine force."[91] Barbara Fassler discusses the revolutionary implications of Strachey's works, citing his attacks on paternalistic religion, militarism, and sexual polarization. He seemed to understand the need for a balance of the masculine and feminine to prevent the horrors of empire and war.[92] Nightingale's sweetness mitigated her indomitable will, while Essex's flowing hair and jeweled ears drew attention away from the codpiece that proclaimed an astonishing virility. Such was Strachey's definition of androgyny, which Fassler and Heilbrun have accepted without even asking if or how Strachey's biographies challenged the Victorian sexual/gender order. Orlando's fragmented, two-sexed self was offered as proof of Woolf's claim that "everyone is partly male and partly female."[93] Yet, even Woolf defined androgyny as a fusion, a heterosexual wedding of the masculine and feminine. Neither she nor Strachey questioned the definitions of those terms handed down to them by the Victorians.

Within avant-garde circles, it became a form of radical chic to present oneself as an androgyne. A man who spent much of his time in an interior space, who devoted himself to the cultivation of style, and who was a passive, languid lover of fashion and ornamentation was not necessarily homosexual but was certainly not "manly." After Wilde's trials for sodomy, any male who deliberately fashioned himself as a dandy or androgyne in essence declared himself to be unmanly, and it was from Wilde that Strachey learned the style and performance of gender ambiguity. Henry Lamb, Duncan Grant, and Dora Carrington all painted Strachey's portrait to emphasize his androgynous qualities; the reclining figure at home, frail, with a book in his hands, created an image of the ivory-tower effeminate male, the antithesis of Victorian virility.

Heilbrun interprets and applauds Strachey's behavior as the transcendence of self, of sex. As the living example of androgyny and forerunner of the sexual revolution of the 1960s, Bloomsbury, according to Heilbrun, led a movement away from the prison of gender toward a world in which individual roles and the modes of personal behavior could be freely chosen.[94] However, the association between androgyny and counterculture has come under fire from other feminist critics who define androgyny as a conservative, misogynistic ideal strongly tied to the classical and patriarchal order. Catherine Stimpson, for example, sees Bloomsbury's androgyny as inseparable from its class snobbery and intellectual elitism.[95] In addition, Elaine Showalter refutes the vision of Bloomsbury as a gender-relaxed utopia. In particular, she rejects Virginia Woolf as a positive role model for women authors and blames the myth of androgyny for Woolf's failure to confront her own painful femaleness.[96]

The irony of androgyny is that although the concept manifests sexual and political anarchy, it still assumes the old polarization and hence undercuts the very sense of independence and selfhood it is meant to encourage. As a "sexist myth," the wholeness of androgyny has been the privilege of the masculine, while the feminine remains defined as immanence, close to nature, lacking the "hole" of man.[97] Furthermore, although such "feminized males" as Strachey represented the "decadence" of modern life, they were not always in sympathy with the aims of feminism. In fact, most male modernists used androgyny as a parody; cross-dressing at parties was a temporary release but also a joke used to seek the applause of friends. The androgynous performance ultimately reinscribed the very gender hierarchies that were allegedly being called into question.[98]

What these critics ignore, however, are the limits of androgyny for men, especially the male homosexual. The feminized male had more at risk in fin de siècle England than the masculinized female.[99] Although moralists and social Darwinists called the New Woman who rode bicycles and wore split skirts a "freak of nature," these masculinized women were not the targets of a legal system that cast suspicion on any effeminate male. When a man took on the "feminine style," he was hailed either as subversive or pathological, and though the androgynous image seemed liberating for him, he risked being associated with a condition of sexual marginality and discrimination.[100]

In Strachey's case, the adherence to a transcendental ideal that denied the body and sex, that stressed the spiritual and not the physical, proved just as, if not more so, confining as it did for Woolf. Adorning his bedroom fireplace was Boris Anrep's mosaic of a reclining hermaphrodite—testimony, according to Holroyd, of Strachey's longing to change his sex. However, Strachey did not really want to change sexes, to become a woman; he instead longed to embody both sexes within him. Perhaps Showalter's criticism of Woolf's androgyny applies to Strachey's as well. Strachey used androgyny to avoid the athletic requirements and compulsory heterosexuality of bourgeois masculinity, but also to escape what he considered "the constraints of a body associated with base appetites of the flesh, putrefaction, and decay."[101] Since Strachey's body was one frequently racked with poor health, his wardrobe changes allowed him to express what he considered his feminine side (his frailty and dependence on others) without completely renouncing his claim to manliness. In his writings, Strachey's male characters tend to own this power of both sexes. When the women do, they appear as grotesque anomalies, while men such as Essex remain beautiful and heroic: "The flaunting man of fashion whose codpiece proclaimed an astonishing virility, was he not also with his flowing hair and jewelled ears, effeminate?"[102]

Strachey's friends read his androgynous performances in different ways. David Garnett believed Strachey's yellow waistcoats and velvet coats created a clever deception, making Strachey appear silly and harmless, until he used his scathing wit to attack: "some people will believe you are a butterfly and some will see your anxious face and lean hands and a quivering sting and believe you to be a wasp."[103] Still, certain members of his circle did not applaud his attempts at cross-dressing, though done in private. After a party in which Strachey, in feminine attire, flirted with the artist Mark Gertler (who was in love with Dora Carrington), he wrote to Clive Bell describing Gertler's hostile rejection:

> I daresay I am exceptionally foolish and at moments I admit that I feel profoundly ashamed of myself. For a middle-aged literary man, with beard and eyeglasses, to be gallivanting in pink satin shoes and sprigged muslim![104]

When twenty-eight-year-old Virginia Stephen donned male attire as part of the Dreadnought Hoax, she was trying, according to Phyllis Rose, to escape and ridicule paternal authority. Dressed in a caftan, turban, mustache, and beard, and with a blackened face, she boarded the British man-of-war as the emperor of Abyssinia. The imposture was discovered, and the press was not so shocked that she had undergone a race change, but that she had impersonated the opposite sex.[105] Her life would be a series of such rebellions against her sex— earning her own money, marrying outside her class, rejecting motherhood. Strachey also transcended the limitations of his sex but faced less censure than his female colleagues. When Strachey privately wore Ottoline's clothes, he tried to bridge the sexes but still retained his claim to patriarchy. Curiously, he was critical, as he notes in many of his letters to his sister Dorothy, of other writers who were too "flamboyant" in their dress and mannerisms.

Other male modernists dressed flamboyantly (T. S. Eliot, for example, wore face powder), but they saw this act of cross-dressing as parodic submission. Through a paradoxical yielding to sexual disorder, these men hoped to gain the sexual energy needed for ascendancy.[106] Marjorie Garber's interpretation of male appropriation of female costume and makeup is less critical than Gilbert and Gubar's. Transvestism, she argues, empowers men *and* women, creating an "intermediate zone" of liminality and change where they can deconstruct the binary of gender norms, even for a brief moment.[107]

Strachey and Woolf both entered this intermediate zone of gender ambiguity through another strategy—illness. However, mental and physical illness seemed to offer Strachey more of an escape than it did for Woolf. Many of Strachey's ailments, according to his doctors, had no physiological source. While several of their Bloomsbury colleagues, including James and Alix Strachey, Adrian Stephen, and Katherine Cox, underwent and studied psychoanalysis, Strachey and

Woolf avoided Freudian diagnosis. Woolf's battles with mental illness neither empowered her nor freed her from conventional restraints, as some studies on female hysteria suggest.[108] In fact, Virginia's dependence on Leonard, his insistence on her infertility, and the restrictive rest cures made Virginia a prisoner of her health. The "best of these illnesses," Virginia wrote in her diary, "is that they loosen the earth about the roots. They make changes. People express their affection."[109] Strachey apparently agreed with this aspect of illness. When he retreated to his bed, usually after a disastrous or unrequited love affair, he received constant attention and nursing from his sisters and female colleagues. Woolf secretly suspected that Lytton exaggerated his age and poor health to arouse the pity of young men.[110] Nevertheless, Ottoline Morrell treated him like a little boy, Carrington concocted cures, and his sisters set aside their professional work to tend to Lytton's health.

Diagnosed in 1900 as a neurasthenic by the family physician, Roland Brinton, Strachey continued to follow the doctor's order of bed rest well into middle age. Toril Moi sees hysteria as an inefficient revolt by women, a declaration of defeat, but was this the case for men?[111] The male neurasthenic appeared effeminate, bound to the private space of the home, and a professional failure. At public school and university, no one could believe that the frail stooped figure of Lytton was the son of a general. Neurasthenia characteristically incapacitated victims between the ages of twenty and fifty, a period of productivity for most men, when they were likeliest to exhaust their nerve force in hard professional effort.[112] After leaving Cambridge, Strachey worked as a freelance journalist for the *Spectator;* he had not yet found his "calling," and though he longed to write a great novel, he knew not how to begin. Writing from his sickbed to his brother James, Strachey exclaimed:

> I suppose I shall go on muddling and recovering through all eternity. I've been doing it now for these years. Perhaps in the end my health'll permanently collapse. . . . I wish I could lie down and be quiet for years and years and then wake up and find myself famous.[113]

Possibly, Strachey's illnesses allowed escape from professional activity and Lady Strachey's control. Such nervous ailments in men were not only a sign of effeminacy but, as in the case of hysterical daughters, a rebellion against parental expectations. During the years between his successful reign at Cambridge and his career as a bestselling author, Strachey repeatedly railed against the stifling atmosphere of his home; he felt adrift, with a "blank" future ahead of him and a series of disastrous love affairs. He filled his days treating a variety of ailments, from headache to indigestion to "nerves," and reproaching himself for failing at love and work. Being bedridden and homebound had certain advantages, though. In a letter to Duncan Grant, Strachey wrote:

> Here I am at last, utterly silent, by my gas fire, at ten, with nothing to hope for, and nothing to look back upon but the broodings of the day and a few faces and a few aborted tears. . . . Oh, how glad I am that I'm not a man!

Strachey seemed almost relieved that his illnesses allowed him to be passive: "Don't you see, a woman need only say yes or no."[114] This freedom from masculinity did have its drawbacks. A few months later, Strachey again wrote to Grant of his wish for "a room of one's own with a real fire and books and tea and company and no dinner bells and distractions and a little time for doing something."[115] At twenty-nine he had not yet achieved financial independence, and though the private sphere offered him shelter from failure in the public world, this shelter had become a prison. Three years later he still struggled with the decision to leave home, the very thought of which gave Strachey "the shivers."[116]

By 1925 Strachey finally considered psychoanalysis as a cure, conceding that some of his symptoms were perhaps psychological. Though he never did "wrestle" with a doctor on a sofa, as his sister-in-law Alix teased, he did read about analysis on his own.[117] Virginia Woolf stood alone in her hostility to the idea of being analyzed. James Strachey wondered why Leonard did not "persuade" her to see a psychoanalyst about her "mental breakdowns," but Alix believed that Virginia's imagination, fantasies, and "madness" were interwoven—that "if you stopped the madness you might have stopped the creativeness too. . . . It may be preferable to be mad and be creative than to be treated by analysis and become ordinary."[118] Strachey's primary objection to psychoanalysis was the costly "cures" for homosexuality promoted by doctors and undergone by some of his younger Cambridge friends.

Strachey came to realize that neither illness nor androgynous poses offered him much freedom in his repressive culture. Androgyny remained an ideal, not a possible reality. In his unfinished play, "The Power of Love: An Interlude," the goddess Diana teaches the lesson that sex change is beyond the power of even the gods. "There is a limit," Diana declares, "so Fate has willed, whatever their bidding—he shall be forever he, and she be she."[119] Strachey could worship the hermaphrodite and play at cross-dressing, but he tended to remind himself, and his readers, of the dangers of crossing boundaries. In *Elizabeth and Essex,* Strachey lovingly describes the Elizabethans' fondness for effeminate costume before he concludes with a warning:

> And the curious society which loved such fantasies and delicacies—how readily would it turn and rend a random victim with hideous cruelty! A change of fortune—a spy's word—and those same ears might be sliced off, to the laughter of the crowd, in the pillory.[120]

For the effeminate man of the Elizabethan or Edwardian era, experimentation and public display could lead to the questioning of his sexuality, blackmail, and even criminal prosecution under the law.

It is interesting that while Strachey admired men who show a "certain strain of femininity," he was less generous toward women who show a strain of masculinity. Although it is Strachey's studies of best-loved British women that have earned him the reputation as a feminist biographer, a renewed examination of these portraits suggests a very different interpretation. Heilbrun insists that "if one looks at Strachey's works in the light of androgyny, one begins to see in it revolutionary implications."[121] Strachey, she argues, shared with his subjects Nightingale and Elizabeth I "a mixed nature"; he "understood that women may be remarkably effective in 'men's' jobs, that the world might profit from the leadership of gifted women who need not sacrifice sexuality, of gifted men who need not sacrifice impulses to gentleness."[122] Heilbrun's critique of Strachey's use of androgyny overlooks too eagerly his literary treatment of women.

The women whose lives Strachey documented seemed to challenge conventional gender norms and the limited sphere of female action, but did Strachey view their lives as androgynous texts? Strachey actually used his authority as their biographer to strip them of their political and sexual powers and restore the gender boundaries they disrupted. In writing the biographies of powerful women, Strachey regretted that "it's very difficult to penetrate the various veils of discretion."[123] Nevertheless, Florence Nightingale and Queens Victoria and Elizabeth I all fell victim to Strachey's penchant for satire, exposure, and ridicule. In each literary portrait, he expressed his intention to unveil the mysteries behind the public images of Britain's heroines; he wanted to destroy the myths that other writers and the women themselves created for posterity. The legend of Nightingale, for example, the "lady with the lamp," the saintly self-sacrificing angel of mercy, was, Strachey reveals, "something else." Beneath the starched uniform moved an authoritarian with "an indomitable will."[124] Strachey also peered under Victoria's folds of black velvet, muslin streamers, and heavy pearls to uncover a "menace," while Elizabeth's huge hoop, stiff ruff, swollen sleeves, and powdered pearls disguised, not a lionhearted queen, but a hysteric. The biographer ensured his readers that these women wanted him to "look below the robes," to discover the source of the "discordance" between the flesh and the "image of regality."[125] Each unveiling revealed dark secrets of sexual obsessions and fears, and internal battles between the women's masculine and feminine "elements."

To all of his female subjects Strachey attributed similar motives, natures, complexes, and methods. Each succeeded in her mission, "not by gentle sweetness and womanly self-abnegation," but by "strict method, by stern discipline, by rigid attention to detail, by ceaseless labor and by fixed determination."[126] At times, he sympathized with the lack of opportunities and support for women in the public sphere of professional work and politics. Strachey's feminist leanings suggest the influence of his sisters, who, similar to Nightingale, "repressed the passional nature" to "form a true and rich life." Compared to the mission of a female reformer, what was "a desirable young man?" he asked. "Dust and ashes! What was there desirable in such a thing as that?"[127]

The powerful women of Strachey's biographies also display monstrous and "uncivilised" characteristics. When Nightingale "tasted the joys of power," she resembled "those Eastern Emperors whose autocratic rule was based upon invisibility." Her "tentacles" reached the India Office and succeeded in establishing a hold "even upon slippery high places." The reformer became a ravenous tigress with grasping claws as she "gnashed her teeth against the intolerable futility of mankind." She also had the "deadly and unsparing precision of a machine gun."[128] The queen under whose reign Nightingale served shared her animalistic tendencies. Victoria, the "fiery steed," would open her mouth "as wide as it can go, showing not very pretty gums." Eating as heartily as she laughed, the monarch "gobbled" incessantly.[129] While

Victoria the girl queen gradually transformed into the matriarch in mourning, Elizabeth became more "grotesque" as she aged. Strachey paints Elizabeth as "an old creature, fantastically dressed, still tall though bent, with hair dyed red above a pale visage, long blackening teeth," and with "fierce, terrifying eyes, in whose dark blue depths something frantic lurked—something almost maniacal." In short, Elizabeth, who swore and spat, "was no woman."[130] Rushing into the queen's bedroom, the handsome courtier, the Earl of Essex, discovered a different Elizabeth, "unpainted, without her wig, her grey hair hanging in wisps about her face, and her eyes starting from her head."[131] Stripped of her robes and mask, the real Elizabeth appeared horrific to the young earl, and to Strachey's readers.

In addition to these undressings, Strachey further demystified his female subjects by either depriving them of their sexual power or exaggerating their libidinal appetites. With their intact, iron-clad hymens, Florence Nightingale and Queen Elizabeth were rendered as harmless as the maternally fertile Victoria. Elizabeth's repression of her "passional nature," Strachey explained, was facilitated by a physical deformity—"she had a membrana on her."[132] When the women expressed desire, it assumed the form of "lasciviousness" and a quest to dominate; it was desire "strong in nothing but perversity."[133] Regarding the relations between Nightingale and the cabinet minister Sidney Herbert, Strachey noted that "the roles were reversed." The qualities of pliancy and sympathy fell to the man, those of command and initiative to the woman. Nightingale "took hold of him, shaped him, absorbed him, dominated him through and through," and Herbert "did not resist—he did not wish to resist."[134] The same relations existed between Elizabeth and Essex: "Fate had reversed the roles and the natural master was a servant." Elizabeth's "mixed elements" of a "woman's evasiveness" and "male courage, male energy" did not signify a triumph of androgyny but rather a "grotesque anomaly."[135] Resorting to Victorian definitions of appropriate masculine and feminine behavior, Strachey perceived Elizabeth's examples of the former as dangerous to her male subjects. Her need to wrestle and master men, to hold them at her mercy, and to order their executions was an abuse of male "vigour and pertinacity." Strachey revealed his own fear of the powerful woman, as he suggested that, in killing those she loved, Elizabeth "was overthrowing manhood."[136] The final victory, however, belonged to the biographer. Strachey concluded his portraits with parting glances of senile, feeble, grandmotherly women with "the sting . . . taken out."[137]

At times in Strachey's biographies of these women, it seems that he is writing his own life. However, he does not embrace, as Heilbrun insists, the kindred feminine spirit he shares with them; in fact, Strachey sees this feminine side of them (and of himself) as the source of their weakness and failure. It was Victoria's "misfortune" that the "mental atmosphere" of her adolescence "was almost entirely feminine." Similar to young Strachey, Victoria lacked the presence of a father or older brother "to break in upon the gentle monotony of the daily round with impetuosity, with rudeness"; the princess "was never called by a voice that was loud and growling; never felt as a matter of course, a hard rough cheek on her own soft one; never climbed a wall with a boy." Instead, Victoria, as with Strachey, "had lived so closely and so long" with her mother "that she had become a part almost of her existence."[138] Such an upbringing, Strachey suggests, made the queen too passive and weak, less than human, so that when her sexuality was finally allowed an object, it overwhelmed her. Strachey shared with Victoria (or his version of Victoria) a need to submit to dominant men but also passivity when confronted with desire.

Similar to Victoria, Elizabeth was overwhelmed by lust but rarely allowed to indulge in it. Though a virgin and old, she had "an amorousness so irrepressible as to be always obvious and sometimes scandalous. She was filled with delicious agitation by the glorious figures of men."[139] Strachey wrote *Elizabeth and Essex* during his troubled relationship with the much younger Roger Senhouse, who served as the model for Essex. Essex is really the ideal that Strachey longed for since Cambridge: an attractive youth who enjoyed "all the sports of manhood" but who loved reading, too, and whose health fluctuated from "vigorous vitality" to weakness.[140] After reading the biography, Keynes wrote to Strachey, "You seem, on the whole, to imagine yourself as Elizabeth, but I see that it is Essex whom you have got up as yourself. But I expect you have managed to get the best of both worlds."[141] Overall, Strachey sympathized most with the aging Elizabeth, her longing to be flattered, "her lasciviousness that could hardly be defined," but she had to remind herself repeatedly that she "was something more." What was it? Was she a man? Though the presence of young men made her forget this part of her makeup, she was able to conquer "woman's inward passion" with the "enthralling force" of her intellect.[142]

In creating an androgynous Elizabeth, Strachey defined the queen's male half as the source of her intelligence and reason and her female half as the source of both passion and illness. In looking for the cause of his own poor health, Strachey diagnosed Elizabeth, whose physical being and her mind were dominated by "complicated contrasts." All of Strachey's symptoms became Elizabeth's: rheumatism racked her tall and bony frame, intolerable headaches laid her prone in agony, and a hideous ulcer poisoned her existence for years. In addition to the serious illnesses, a long succession of minor maladies, "a host of morbid symptoms," held Elizabeth's contemporaries "in alarmed suspense" and probably were to blame for her "deep-seated repugnance to the crucial act of intercourse."[143] Bowing to Freud, Strachey concluded that these symptoms were of a hysterical origin: "That iron structure was a prey to nerves," but, in Elizabeth's case, there was a special cause for her neurotic condition—"her sexual organisation was seriously warped." Perhaps a physical malformation or a psychological obsession inspired her fear of sex. Strachey understood such anxiety, for he had internalized self-loathing, a revulsion for the physical act of sex, and at times regarded his homosexuality as a disease. He, similar to Elizabeth, was "malformed."[144]

Strachey dedicated *Elizabeth and Essex* to his brother and sister-in-law, James and Alix Strachey, both trained in Freudian analysis. Whereas English critics and historians disparaged the text, Freud saw it as Strachey's greatest work. Strachey had both dabbled in and ridiculed psychoanalysis for years. Evidence of Freud's and James's influence on Strachey is apparent in several of his earlier works. Strachey's 1914 short story "According to Freud" utilizes *The Psychopathology of Every Day Life,* translated for English readers that same year, to discuss the impossibility of accidents, the unconscious self, and the sexual symbolism of fountain pens. *Eminent Victorians* addressed the existence of dual personalities, and *Queen Victoria* exposed the monarch's Oedipal complex. Strachey's casual use of Freud can be seen in such sweeping and unsubstantiated diagnoses, as in the case of Victoria—"a martyr to anal eroticism."[145] This use of Freud is what Martin Kallich sees as distinctly "modern" about Strachey's writing.[146] Although Strachey never explicitly acknowledged his indebtedness to Freud, he did refer to the "modern psychology" that "give[s] him confidence" to interpret the lives of his subjects.[147] The connection between Bloomsbury and psychoanalysis had been established, not only with James Strachey as Freud's student and translator, but also with Adrian and Karin (née Costello) Stephen becoming analysts in 1920. By 1924 psychoanalysis had become a central issue in England, as evidenced by the debate on Freud in *The Nation*. James and Alix Strachey provided Lytton with an informal education in Freudianism while he researched *Elizabeth and Essex*. For example, they advised him on the condition of vaginismus, what they described as an involuntary convulsion or constriction of the vagina that made penile penetration impossible.[148] Strachey added his own touch to this condition; in his biography, Elizabeth's vaginismus became a hysterical condition, not a physiological one.

Strachey had no correspondence with Freud, but Freud wrote to the biographer in 1928 to applaud *Elizabeth and Essex* and his earlier publications. The letter reveals Freud's praise for Strachey (and himself) as well as a shared desire to penetrate the mysteries of the virgin queen:

> This time you have moved me more deeply, for you yourself have reached greater depths. . . . As a historian, then, you show that you are steeped in the spirit of psychoanalysis . . . you have known how to trace back her [Elizabeth's] character to the impressions of her childhood. You have touched upon her most hidden motives with equal boldness and discretion. . . . My opinion is that it was Elizabeth—the childless woman—who suggested to Shakespeare the character of his Lady Macbeth.[149]

Freud and Strachey both used psychoanalysis to reveal secrets, neuroses, and sexual fears. By retelling Elizabeth's and other women's stories, they disarmed them of their sexual powers and made them less fearsome.

Although both Freud and Strachey acknowledged female sexual desires (such recognition can be interpreted as modern), they interpreted these desires as an expression of male identification, a desire for penetration, or a sickness. According to Freudian psychology, femininity is failed masculinity, and a "truly feminine" woman lacks an active libido.[150] For Strachey, Victoria's sexuality is especially problematic. Her upbringing in a wholly "feminine atmosphere" left her with an Oedipal complex, searching for a father figure who would dominate her. With Albert, she became "all breathless attention and eager obedience" to "her beloved lord and master";[151] for Disraeli, "she would do anything," and at last she is mastered by her servant John Brown, whom she allowed to take liberties with her which would have been unthinkable from anybody else. To bully the Queen, to order her about, to reprimand her . . . when she received such treatment from John Brown she positively seemed to enjoy it.[152]

However, contradicting this "dominant motif" and her passive sexuality was Victoria's need to force others to submit, and this love of power turned the woman into a rigid "stunted person."[153]

The female subjects of Strachey's biographies represent composites. The sensuality of Lady Ottoline and Vanessa Bell, the intellect of Virginia Woolf, the overbearing will of Lady Strachey, and the reformist zeal of the Strachey sisters all surfaced in the literary portraits of women rulers and public servants. Ironically, he published the bulk of his writings while he lived with Dora Carrington, whose domesticity freed him to attack his female subjects. It was as though he had reclaimed his masculinity that had withered during a lifetime of dependency and illness. As Susan Suleiman observes, "male writers have needed the loving support of their muses, mistresses, or mothers in order to put them aside, deny them, reject them, idealize them, or kill them in their writing."[154] By rewriting the lives of famous women, telling their secrets, and revealing their "true inner selves," Strachey (in the tradition of Victorian social scientific epistemology) tore away the aura of mystery surrounding them. Their unveiling was his triumph; he had, at last, succeeded in discovering what was "hidden in them."

For the most part, Strachey's attempts at unveiling his female subjects contrast with Virginia Woolf's process of recostuming hers. Woolf's attitude toward her androgynous characters is often playful and sympathetic, whereas Strachey mainly has contempt for the "objects" of his studies. In *Orlando,* Woolf suggests that not biology but clothing is destiny:

> Though different though the sexes are, they intermix. In every human being a vacillation from one sex to the other takes place, and often it is only the clothes that keep the male or female likeness, while underneath, the sex is the very opposite of what it is above.[155]

Orlando's cross-dressing allows him/her the pleasures of both sexes and the love of both sexes equally. Woolf envisioned Orlando as fantasy—a rejection of traditional biography that depicted stable identities which can be objectified and judged. Yet, in her fictional biography and elsewhere, even Woolf falls into the same trap as Strachey: she conceptualizes androgyny as a marriage of masculine and feminine traits, traditionally defined as innately different. Hence, when Orlando awakes as a woman, "his form combined in one the strength of a man and a woman's grace."[156] Just as Strachey imagined androgyny as men and women climbing walls together, Woolf envisioned the couple in the taxi cab in *A Room of One's Own*. Woolf insisted that "some collaboration has to take place in the mind between the man and the woman before the act of creation can be accomplished. Some marriage of opposites has to be consummated."[157] Woolf's reliance on a paradigm of heterosexist language undermines her claim in *Orlando* that sex and identity are separate and is further proof of the insufficiency of androgyny to transcend gender.[158]

Where Woolf finally parted company with Strachey was in their conception of history. Woolf recognized what Strachey needed to ignore, that history is a series of costume changes. In her final novel *Between the Acts,* published posthumously, Woolf stages a conversation that she quite possibly could have had with Strachey. Talking to Isa and the homosexual character William Dodge, Lucy Swithin declares, "The Victorians . . . I don't believe that there ever were such people. Only you and me and William dressed differently." In response, Dodge assumes, "You don't believe in history."[159] Woolf had at last come to terms with the Victorians, despite her youthful loathing and rebellion, whereas Strachey died with his illusions of generational and ideological differences in tact. Strachey not only believed in history's discontinuity but remained dependent on it. He ridiculed the past and its heroes and used his modernist posturing to distance himself from the Victorians. For Strachey, the Victorian Age would always be "a singular epoch." In his preface to *Eminent Victorians,* Strachey stated that the history of the Victorian Age will never be written for "we know too much about it."[160] Strachey could not distance himself from that past, and at times he found comfort and solace in traditional values regarding gender, class, and race. In the end, what he wrote was not the history of the nineteenth century but a myth of the Victorians. According to Strachey, "that was enough . . . the myth was there—obvious, portentous, impalpable; and so it remained to the last."[161]

Yet, as Virginia Woolf finally regretted, Strachey's picture of the Victorians was *not* enough, nor did his version of modernism succeed in creating a new and alternative way of looking at gender, sex, and history. The costume of modernism did not destroy the gender codes or the affiliation with the paternal tradition that her Bloomsbury colleague upheld. Even Strachey's homosexuality, which Woolf once applauded, now seemed to her another form of exclusion, as misogyny and patriarchy, so evident in his writings, remained the weapons of male revolt. Still, Woolf mourned the loss of Strachey years after his death. In a letter to his sister Pernel, Woolf acknowledged their common background, ambitions, and also their tensions, and despite fighting "like cats and dogs," they would always be "of one flesh." Despite their secret rivalry, she acknowledged how vital their sex war was to her career as a writer. "I wake in the night—with the sense of being in an empty hall—Lytton dead—what is the point of it—Life—when I am not working suddenly becomes thin, indifferent, Lytton is dead."[162]

Conclusion

Although he devoted his career to chronicling the lives of others, Lytton Strachey had no intention of writing his own life's history. That story, he said, he would leave to others to tell. Perhaps that is why he was so adamant about saving every written record of his history, whether "ideas for a play," "scribblings," or correspondence, and urged his friends to do the same. Instead of using the telephone, he insisted on mail correspondence and requested friends to save and return his letters. He seemed to be preparing for the day when "some impartial biographer would write a documented essay on our [Bloomsbury's] relations." After all, he reasoned, "it would really be a most instructive and entertaining study."[1]

Since the 1960s interest in the Bloomsbury Group has burgeoned into an industry in historical and literary studies, yet few scholars have achieved the impartiality that Strachey had hoped for, or claimed to hope for, in a biographer. Strachey himself did not approach his subjects with objectivity, though he said he did otherwise. Edmund Wilson's obituary for Strachey in 1932 explained that Strachey's "chief mission . . . was to take down once and for all the pretension of the Victorian Age to moral superiority," but Strachey's irony was so acid, it dehumanized his subjects.[2] Reviewing the first edition of Michael Holroyd's biography of Strachey, Margaret Cruikshank attacked what she perceived as Holroyd's homophobia. In her review Cruikshank raised the question, If a biography is unsympathetic toward its subject, should it even be attempted? Looking to Strachey for an answer, Cruikshank answered in the affirmative.[3] For Strachey, so critical of his own physical and intellectual flaws, an unsympathetic portrait was far better than oblivion, of becoming passé.

Such a fate appears unlikely for the Bloomsbury Group. What makes Strachey and his colleagues of such continuing interest to us? Janet Malcolm suggests that the Bloomsbury members were not "really so fascinating," but that they wrote so well and so incessantly about themselves and one another.[4] Also, the offspring of Bloomsbury, such as Quentin Bell and Angelica Garnett (Vanessa Bell's children), continued to write about their parents' artistic accomplishments and unconventional living arrangements. Bloomsbury's letters, journals, essays, poetry, and fiction reveal an inner life created for public consumption. Strachey relished the fact that the recipients of his letters found them "so exquisite," and though he feared in 1908, in the early days of the Bloomsbury gatherings, that "my story is now quite unfit for publication," he still demanded that these letters be saved for future use.[5]

Interest in the Bloomsbury Group has been cyclical. The 1930s' generation regarded the group as too apolitical, and literary critics waged a campaign against the writings of the living and dead members. Unlike Bloomsbury's emphasis on aesthetic emotions and personal relations, writers such as George Orwell, Aldous Huxley, and Christopher Isherwood were interested in political engagement, social realism, and collectivism. By the 1960s, however, group members stood as symbols of sexual revolution. Historian Piers Brendon notes that Strachey, "with his pacifism, his homosexuality, and his bohemianism, made him a patron saint of the flower power generation."[6] Strachey's behavior, similar to Wilde's, had led to a collapse between the categories of homosexual and bohemian, which perhaps explains why the surviving members of Bloomsbury now so reluctantly accepted the label of sexual rebels. Approached with offers by independent filmmakers such as Ken Russell, James Strachey, Frances Partridge, and David Garnett feared that their private lives would be exposed to a prurient public. The members of the group did not want their hard-earned respectability to be destroyed with publicized proof of homosexual indiscretions. In 1903 Strachey had wondered "when publication [of our letters] comes will our readers really be up to it? . . . Will they think us affected and vulgar and indecent and self-conscious and horribly young?"[7] The executors of Strachey's estate, upon reading drafts of Holroyd's biography in 1966, now worried that such a project would "probably be a ghostly caricature . . . likely to cause injury to several and cause a witch hunt which may do great harm."[8]

After vetoing Ken Russell's film, the surviving Bloomsbury members decided to take charge of the publications of their memoirs and biographies and hence create their own image for public consumption. A more relaxed sexual atmosphere and changes in British law (the Sexual Offenses Act of 1967 decriminalized homosexual unions between consenting adults) finally paved the way for the publication of Forster's novel *Maurice,* and of biographies of Keynes, Dickinson, and Strachey that acknowledged the centrality of homosexuality in their lives. Holroyd's research on Strachey impelled Carrington's friends to reread her letters as well. David Garnett published excerpts from her diaries, her brother Noel produced a book on her painting, and Carrington's art at last received public exhibition. Meanwhile, Virginia Woolf became an icon for the women's movement, and Quentin Bell's biography of his aunt restored her to an ascendant position within British modernism. Not to be outdone, Leonard Woolf began publishing his multivolume autobiography, using his Hogarth Press to commemorate the Bloomsbury spirit of rebellion.

Bloomsbury's rejection of convention became a model for the 1960s' own liberation and generational conflict. This is how Bloomsbury's survivors hoped to be perceived as they edited the essays they had once shared with one another years before. Most of these essays were the product of the Memoir Club, inaugurated by the group on March 4, 1920, and which continued to meet until 1954. Each member was required to present a personal and "frank" recollection. Strachey read his "69 Lancaster Gate," Keynes presented "My Early Beliefs," and Virginia Woolf reminisced in "Sex Talk in Bloomsbury." The essays, now made available to larger audiences, addressed the role that Bloomsbury played in freeing their generation from their parents' strict codes of sexual and moral conduct. As Woolf proclaimed, "we were all easy and gifted and friendly . . . having the capacity for enjoying ourselves thus." She also wondered, "could our fathers?"[9] Woolf's other memoir, "Old Bloomsbury," shared with Strachey's "Lancaster Gate" an indictment of "the suffocating closeness" of their childhood homes, crammed with heavy furniture and too many people. They relished the freedom they found in the Gordon Square residence of the Stephen siblings and believed that as a new group, "we were full of experiments and reforms—we were going to paint; to write; to have coffee after dinner instead of tea at nine. . . . Everything was going to be new; everything was going to be different."[10]

Almost thirty years later, Bloomsbury still stands as a symbol of sexual anarchy. Thousands of visitors have made pilgrimages to the Charleston Farmhouse where Vanessa Bell and Duncan Grant once lived, loved, and worked, and by 1995, Bloomsbury's sexuality had even infiltrated popular culture. Michael Holroyd revised his two-volume biography of Strachey into one neat and more manageable edition. Able to include specific details and names of those now dead, Holroyd replaced his literary criticisms of Strachey's writings with more sections devoted to his sexual and emotional relationships. Also, Bloomsbury at last made its way to the screen, in Christopher Hampton's film *Carrington* (1995). Based on Holroyd's book, the film shrouds the story of Dora Carrington's life in the shadow of Strachey's and a series of male lovers. Hampton has merely accepted the assumption made by Carrington's Bloomsbury colleagues, who claimed that her life was worthy of such attention because of her relationship with Strachey. Carrington's life, according to David Garnett, did not truly begin until 1915 when she earned admittance into the group and Strachey's affections.[11] Bloomsbury has been transformed in these latest efforts and made more accessible for public enjoyment. In place of Carrington's painting of Strachey on the frontispiece of Holroyd's biography is the movie still of actress Emma Thompson and actor Jonathan Pryce. This odd couple has assumed mythic proportions—symbolizing both sexual emancipation and the purest form of love. (As the film caption notes, "She had many lovers but only one love.")

Another theory for Bloomsbury's allure comes from Angeline Goreau. In her review of Holroyd's 1995 "new biography" of Strachey, she suggests that the group represents "an extended dysfunctional family whose emotional turmoil mirrors our own preoccupation with damaged lives."[12] During the 1960s, the great interest in Bloomsbury lay in the frank disclosure of taboo material, but in the 1990s, Bloomsbury became a cautionary tale rather than an exemplary one. Despite the wild parties and sex talk, most of Bloomsbury's experiments, especially in bisexuality, resulted in despair, jealousy, illegitimate births, and angry children.[13] Or, perhaps this renewed interest in Bloomsbury is a backlash against the moral and political conservativism of the 1980s and early 1990s and cries from British and American politicians and social critics for the renewal of Victorian values of industriousness, sobriety, respectability, and individualism. The Bloomsbury myth both reinforces this image of the Victorians and offers an outlet or escape from it, in 1918 or today.

Yet Strachey's debunking of the Victorians and his credo of sexual liberation have not always been championed by scholars. Historian Gertrude Himmelfarb, in her 1968 review of the first edition of Holroyd's biography of Strachey, deliberately conflated Bloomsbury and homosexuality and pointed to Strachey's "venomous" assault on beloved Victorian icons as evidence of the homosexual "personality." Calling Strachey's writing "tirelessly fey in rhetoric" she tried to discredit Bloomsbury's rebellion by tainting the group's leader as "destructive of authority, suspicious of morality."[14] Since 1968 Himmelfarb's prolific defenses of Victorian liberalism and bourgeois culture have helped to resurrect an image of his ancestors that Strachey worked so hard to undermine. As Richard Altick notes, Victorians today are not recalled in "Stracheyesque" terms but are praised for their political and artistic contributions, and it is *Eminent Victorians,* not the Victorian mode of civilization, that has been discredited by historians.[15] Strachey unwittingly started the Victorian industry, but contemporary scholars, collectors of Victorian memorabilia, and the media have turned their backs on his virulent anti-Victorianism in favor of a nostalgia for the past.

Lytton Strachey may have deliberately falsified certain historical facts to attack his subjects, but it is his sexuality, not his biographies, that continues to intrigue Bloomsbury fans and scholars. James Strachey believed that Lytton's Cambridge years had an important effect on the subsequent mental life in England, especially on the attitude of ordinary people to sex.[16] In fact, during those years (1902-1908) Strachey's numerous essays on sex, especially all-male love, were directed to a very selective audience, the Apostles. His compositions remained unpublished until thirty years after his death, and his campaign for toleration for homosexuality was aimed at the already enlightened. Among those outside of Cambridge, Strachey's ideas aroused loathing and hostility or simply indifference. Responding to Leonard Woolf's charge that, similar to Socrates, he had corrupted the youth of Cambridge, Strachey pointed out that "it is after all rather an important difference that I haven't been condemned to death. And shall I ever be? Won't the whole world be converted first?"[17]

Strachey did little to carry his crusade outside the walls of Cambridge, however, ridiculing the efforts of sex reformer Edward Carpenter and the writings of Forster. In fact, he wanted to preserve the distinction between the real and the phenomenal, the lower and higher forms of love. The type of love he preached was at odds with what he saw as the spread of sodomy "of such a dreadful sort!" in England, in which "little boys of 13 are what the British public love."[18] Strachey feared that outside the protective atmosphere of Cambridge, relations between men, whether physical or spiritual, could not help but become corrupt. At one point he longed to save Duncan Grant from "the phenomenal world [that] stands there gaping to swallow him up. . . . I want him in the Society, on the hearthrug, in our own wonderful, exciting, intimate, eminent world."[19] Such statements reflect Strachey's own insecurities about that phenomenal world which competed with his idealized version of male Love and threatened to make even the Higher Sodomy appear perverse to outside observers.

The most common charge directed against the Apostles and Bloomsbury by their critics involved the social elitism of both groups. The members belonged to a leisured class that lived for years on unearned incomes, and though they considered themselves "outsiders," they exercised considerable influence in publishing, journalism, art galleries, and universities. Wyndham Lewis parodied Bloomsbury as "a select and snobbish club" that "aped" the artist's life but produced only bad art and literature.[20] In response to D. H. Lawrence's barrage of insults regarding the Apostles' lack of virility, Keynes assumed the writer was simply jealous and overwhelmed by Cambridge: "It was obviously a civilization, and not less obviously uncomfortable and unattainable for him."[21] However, critics came from within the privileged bastion of Cambridge as well. Rupert Brooke, as previously discussed, frequently complained about "the subtle degradation of the collective atmosphere of the people in those regions—people I find pleasant and remarkable as individuals." After enlisting for military service, he asked a friend to "spit at Bloomsbury from me."[22] Critics from the 1930s to the 1950s carried on Brooke's mission of "spitting" at Bloomsbury. Husband and wife team F. R. and Q. D. Leavis used their quarterly *Scrutiny* to destroy the Bloomsbury mystique. The Leavises especially disliked Woolf's feminism and Strachey's "cheap manner" of writing. Bloomsbury's greatest fault, according to these critics, was its lack of moral seriousness.[23]

Such accusations of Bloomsbury's disconnectedness from larger political and social causes were unfounded. Despite his virulent denunciations of the group, D. H. Lawrence received the group's written support during the obscenity trial for his novel *The Rainbow,* as did Radclyffe Hall for *The Well of Loneliness.* Strachey saw these crusades not as endorsements of the works themselves (which he found mediocre) but for the larger fight against censorship; it was censorship, after all, that forced him to rely on the method of "indirect attack" in his own writings. Strachey and his colleagues were linked to other radical trends in British culture, such as psychoanalysis, suffrage, sexology, and pacifism, all very unpopular and controversial crusades before 1918. Though these movements gained respectability and acceptance after World War I, there was still no place for the homosexual in British society. Still a legal, medical, and moral threat, Strachey found a protective atmosphere within Bloomsbury, while many of his Brothers, including Keynes (once his fellow priest in the Cambridge campaign to convert all to the Higher Sodomy), married in their middle age.

As a sexual movement, Bloomsbury revealed the paradoxes of modernism. Memoirs of Bloomsbury members recounting their youthful days all attest to the relaxed atmosphere in which they talked ceaselessly about sex and experimented with homosexuality, bisexuality, and extramarital sexual relations. They considered this new sexual openness as indicative of a break with their repressive past. However, as Steven Marcus, Michel Foucault, Peter Gay, and countless other Victorian scholars have argued, the Victorians were far from silent on the subject of sex, and not necessarily prudish.[24] The Victorians, in fact, seemed obsessed with bodily fluids, genitalia, and the discussion of desire—absent in bourgeois women yet rampant among men, foreigners, and the working classes. The "discursive explosion" in sexuality permeated medicine, politics, religion, art, and literature. Bloomsbury simply continued a tradition that sanctioned male license yet now allowed for more sexual freedom for upper-middle-class women as well.

When Strachey wrote about eminent Victorians, he did not deny them their sexuality. He transformed Victorian leaders into lascivious women with Oedipal complexes, husbands into latent homosexuals, and schoolmasters and military heroes into pederasts who, similar to General Gordon, lured "susceptible and serious youths" with their devotion "to the Greeks." Strachey had learned from the Victorians how to use charges of perversity to blacken and damage reputations. His depictions of women especially borrowed from the Victorian literary tradition of the monstrous woman whose sexuality destroys men, but in analyzing the virginity complex of Elizabeth, he turned the nineteenth-century cult of virgin worship on its head. Elizabeth's virginity made her not a heroine but a grossly malformed woman.

While Strachey struggled to reconcile two poles of masculinity—the bourgeois man of action and the effeminate homosexual—he continued to dichotomize women, even those of Bloomsbury. His letters to his Cambridge Brothers revealed a view of Virginia and Vanessa Stephen as incomplete women: Vanessa so fertile yet without her sister's intelligence; Virginia, so brilliant, yet sadly barren. The few women in Bloomsbury, despite their individual artistic and intellectual achievements, accepted the men's criticisms and contributed to a discourse of sex that focused on male sexuality and male fluids. In the early days of Bloomsbury, Vanessa and Virginia Stephen expressed gratitude that Strachey, by uttering the word "semen," allowed them at last to discuss buggery, but the discussions about sex tended to be about only male homosexuality, never sapphism, nor heterosexual sex. Strachey even defined the mission of the biographer in deliberately phallic terms: "fall[ing] upon the flank," the biographer, in short, penetrates his subject "with a careful curiosity—a power belonging solely to the male body/intellectual."[25]

How do we explain, then, women's attraction to Strachey? In his "oriental" gowns and confined periodically to the sickbed, Strachey appeared weak and sexually safe to the Stephen sisters, who had been stymied by a patriarchal household. And Carrington, so insecure about her potential as an artist, found a new career caring for the domestic needs of Strachey. At times, however, those close to Bloomsbury began to criticize the male domination of the group. Isabel Fry, for example, accused Gordon Square of being "nothing better than a male brothel" for Strachey and his "bugger" friends, and as she aged and achieved her own fame as a writer, Virginia Woolf found herself avoiding Strachey's company, due to his insistence on male superiority.[26] She, too, began to use the term "bugger" as a way to deride Strachey's "revolution" in sexual mores. What she finally recognized was that misogyny was the constant of both literary traditions, whether Victorian or modern.

Strachey, despite his modernist posturing, seemed to take greater comfort in playing the role of Victorian patriarch in his relations with women. While Roger Fry hinted that Carrington would never be a successful artist, Woolf believed that it was Carrington, not Strachey, who was truly "modern." In her diary she criticized Strachey's failures:

"never an Omega, never a Post-Impressionist movement . . . and his way of life, insofar as it is unconventional, is so by the desire and determination of Carrington."[27] Even Carrington at times tired of darning socks while the men discussed Einstein's theory of relativity. Anger and self-reproach occasionally underscored the pride she took in her devotion to Strachey. Writing to Alix Strachey, who had married Lytton's younger brother, James, Carrington wondered why they didn't both become "Sapphos" instead. "We might have had such a happy life without these Strachey's."[28] Her frustrations over "too much frying and not much sleep" compelled her to ask Virginia Woolf, "How can I do woodblocks when for the last month . . . I've been a ministering angel, hewer of wood, and drawer of water."[29]

Keynes asserted that the young men of Cambridge who went on to form the core of Bloomsbury "repudiated entirely customary morals, conventions, and traditional wisdom," but not all beliefs, especially those concerning women's inferiority, were rejected.[30] Indeed, the Apostolic view of women seemed much harsher than that of the Victorians. Eschewing religion and God, the Apostles therefore denied women even the moral and spiritual superiority the Victorians allotted them. Women's bodies were, according to Strachey, "great pots" for children, and sometimes even receptacles for the men's own sexual release. Describing to his homosexual lover David Garnett his heterosexual affair with Vanessa Bell, Duncan Grant wrote, "I copulated on Sunday with her with great satisfaction to myself physically. It is a convenient way, the females, of letting off one's spunk and comfortable. Also the pleasure it gives is reassuring."[31] Strachey, however, never understood Grant's lapses in his homosexuality and insisted that lust for women, similar to blacks (putting the two types of phenomenal inferiors in the same category), was "different . . . more foul."[32]

Strachey's view of male homosexuality as the dominant and purer form of sexuality was in part a defense mechanism, since the law certainly did not agree with his opinion. In 1914 he wondered:

> how many people . . . are lying in gaol at this moment in England because their pricks have become stiff on unconventional occasions? I shudder to imagine . . . . What is there in this ridiculous white secretion that pulls down the corners of English men's mouths?[33]

Years later, while on vacation with Sebastian Sprott, he played piquet and at intervals read the trial of Leopold and Loeb. Not only in England did "unnatural secretions" lead to charges of criminality.[34] Strachey's letters since his university days frequently made passing references to the suspicions of outsiders, the arrests of schoolmasters, the trial of Oscar Wilde, and the need for caution. Among his friends he adopted the "effeminate" dress that, since Wilde's trial, signified homosexuality, but in public, Strachey appeared an ordinary (though very thin and tall) gentleman in tweed.

These costume changes, which Virginia Woolf came to see as irrelevant markers of Victorianism and modernism, did in fact have great personal and historical meaning. For Woolf, the modernist in dandy's clothes was just as much a misogynist as the Victorian in the sober tweed suit. But, when Strachey announced in letters to friends and family that he was wearing tweed, shooting at stags, and saluting his father's portrait, it is not clear if he was conforming to the Victorian cult of masculinity or parodying it. In other words, was he resisting identification with "queerness," or was the wearing of tweeds for him just as subversive as his donning of bright cloaks, velvet suits, and earrings? Though he felt that his brothers, "beard and all," who served the empire, were complete strangers to him, Strachey also knew how and when to play "milord anglaise, with smart clothes and notebook."[35] Strachey had learned from Wilde a style of rebellion now associated with inversion after 1895, but the invert disguised in the clothes of a "manly man" also indicates how easily the norms of bourgeois masculinity could be appropriated or discarded.

Although Strachey could play with his wardrobe, there were still some limits to his public rebellion. While the New Woman of the postwar era achieved the freedom to display heterosexual affection in public, such liberties did not exist for the homosexual. Aware of this disparity, Strachey angrily wrote to Leonard Woolf about the privileges allotted to "normal" couples:

> I must say I am sometimes a little annoyed at their affectionateness. Wouldn't you be? Two people loving each other so much—there's something devilishly selfish about it. Couples in the road with their silly arms round their stupid waists irritate me. . . . I want to shake them.[36]

Forbidden by law and social custom to express homosexual affection in public, Strachey could at least find a temporary release from phenomenal restrictions and his own inhibitions in his private writings.

The previous chapters attest to Strachey's difficulties in expressing desire, his unsuccessful affairs, and the guilt he experienced, since even the readings of Plato could not counteract his society's dictums against all-male love. Forging a homosexual identity was central to Strachey's self-fashioning, but it was a process laden with anguish and insecurity. What models had he to choose from? For fellow Cambridge Brother Leonard Woolf, the Higher Sodomy was entertaining, a sign of exclusivity, and a passing phase before entering the phenomenal state of marriage, but for Strachey it signified all-male desire and a permanent identity. If he looked to sexology to justify the Higher Sodomy, Strachey saw only the image of the invert, as defined by Karl Ulrichs and Magnus Hirschfeld in Germany, and by Havelock Ellis and Edward Carpenter in England. Was he part of an "intermediate sex"? Since he longed to change his sex, this liminal state should have pleased Strachey, but this new category also implied deviance and congenital abnormality. Was he a man with a woman's soul trapped in his body, a soul that was expressed, according to Ellis, by the invert's passion for music and Shakespeare and an inability to whistle?[37] One of Strachey's mentors at Cambridge, Goldsworthy Lowes Dickinson, tried to appreciate the woman's soul that he believed occupied his body and hence promised him "a more romantic and passionate life than others." However, accepting this theory compelled Dickinson to also accept the notion that such a life was "in most cases an unhealthy, unbalanced, perhaps ultimately insane one."[38]

An alternative discourse posited homosexuality as the highest, most perfect stage of gender differentiation and therefore appealed to the Higher Sodomite. According to this model, the male-identified man expressed a heightened form of masculinity; he was the purest "manly" representation of his sex. The male homosexual would have most in common with the heterosexual man who shared his delight in male companionship and disdain for women. Both "types" of men acted as the protectors of bastions of patriarchy, male dominance, and male separatism. Similar to the heterosexual male, the homosexual saw the exclusion of women from his intimate life as virilizing.[39]

As Elaine Showalter argues, misogyny did not originate with homosexual men, but it did nurture their wish to idealize relationships between men as more spiritual, intellectual, and pure than heterosexual love. Late Victorian defenders of the gender differentiation model included Wilde, who argued that women's bodies were unaesthetic. Women's need to produce children deprived them of a more transcendent and nonpurposeful love. During the 1890s, Charles Kains-Jackson's journal *The Artist* also promoted the "new chivalry" that exalted the youthful masculine ideal.[40] The lives and performances of feminized/aesthetic men such as Wilde and Strachey and the texts they produced can be seen as an expression of their alienation from dominant social structures. This "counterdiscourse" of symbolic resistance to bourgeois masculinity was not only connected to elite homosexual subcultures but defined against an aggressive contempt for women.[41]

While the rationalization of homosexual desire as aesthetic experience had as its subtext an escalating contempt for women, it also led to self-contempt for men such as Strachey who feared sullying the ideal with sexual acts.[42] The physical and profane aspects of homosexual desire, implied by Ellis's or Wilde's models, disturbed Strachey, who so often was unable to follow his own advice to "fuck and bugger to his heart's content." In his search for a model of behavior, Strachey experimented with androgyny, using his body, voice, and clothes to blur gender distinctions. Yet, as Showalter points out, and as Strachey discovered, androgyny poses a trap for those who use it. Androgyny both denies the body its existence and magnifies the individual's insecurities about his or her sexuality.[43]

Strachey did use his homosexuality as part of his modernist posturing. He transformed his sexuality into something much greater— making it something separate from himself and symbolic of a larger cultural rebellion. Holroyd faults Strachey for his "exaggerated self-preoccupation," suggesting that Strachey's homosexuality and "his passion for the applause of others" were somehow linked and ultimately acted as the limiting factor in his creative output.[44] Literary critic Geoffrey Grigson likewise blames the "essentially coarse style" of *Eminent Victorians* and *Queen Victoria* on Strachey's "nasty homosexuality." Grigson accuses Strachey of being spiteful and ungenerous toward "those who [did] not share his condition."[45] Exploiting sexual ambiguity, Strachey presented himself as an acolyte of the perverse.[46] When he did use his effeminate posturing to entertain friends or shock the war tribunal, he was pronounced "the incarnation of modern irreverence . . . the Mephistopheles of that mysterious satanic world of Bloomsbury."[47]

At times Strachey believed that being homosexual made him unlike and superior to the Victorians. His "Greek soul" also came equipped with higher critical powers that he applied to battling his Victorian nemesis. To do this, Strachey first had to create a myth of the Victorians of repression and hypocrisy, which historians have only recently begun to deconstruct. In his own version of *Eminent Victorians,* A. N. Wilson argues that popular attitudes toward the Victorian age have been strongly shaped by the savage satirical portraits drawn by Strachey, Woolf, and their peers. Sanctimonious imperialists or ridiculous prudes—what we are left with is a caricature of the Victorians.[48]

In his preface to *Eminent Victorians,* Strachey shared his insight on the writing of biography. "Human beings," he wrote, "are too important to be treated as mere symptoms of the past. They have a value which is independent of any temporal processes, which is eternal and must be felt for its own sake."[49] Such advice poses a challenge for the analysis of Strachey's own life and work, since he pitted himself so vehemently against the Victorians and proclaimed as his mission the destruction of their legacy. Strachey posed as the literary champion of truth, destroying icons, removing masks, and exposing his subjects to ridicule. In his efforts to destroy what he called the "glass case age" of the Victorians, Strachey created a trap for himself. In striving to be "modern," he incessantly looked to the past—to the Greeks for validation of homosexual love and male superiority and to the Victorians for a literary formula. Working against his will to modernity was the comfort Strachey found in his ancestors' traditions of privilege, authority, and gender and class exclusivity. Repulsed by, yet also attracted to, the eminent Victorians, Strachey existed, as his colleague Gerald Brenan noted, on the borderline of these two movements.

Returning to the question of why Bloomsbury continues to intrigue us, Strachey would answer, quite simply, that their stories are instructive and entertaining. Strachey's life, rather than his writings, has survived the passage of time. This fame would please him since it is based on an interest in the personal (exposing the private desires, ambition, weaknesses of public figures) that he initiated with *Eminent Victorians.* He believed that "we are all cupboards—with obvious outsides which may be either beautiful or ugly, simple or elaborate, interesting or unamusing—but with insides mysteriously the same—the abodes of darkness, terror, and skeletons," and it was this "mysterious inside" that he explored in his writing and self-fashioning.[50] Furthermore, Strachey's life *was* his greatest work of art. As he pointed out, even a biography tells its readers as much about the character of the writer and the times the biographer lives in as it does about the subject. If we read Strachey as a text, we see several chapters: a man at odds with his culture, unmanly, neurasthenic, and effeminate; a sexual rebel parodying bourgeois masculinity; and a respectable author, sexual imperialist, and patriarch. In a diary entry, Strachey warned the "inquisitive reader" who dared to "peep between the covers" that he or she "will find anything but myself, who perhaps after all does not exist but in my own phantasy."[51] Indeed, this fantasy of Strachey's true self remained divided between the modern and the "glass case age."

Notes

Introduction

1. Lytton Strachey to "Topsey" Lucas, letter dated October 30, 1927, British Museum MSS ADD 53788 (hereafter referred to as BM MSS).
2. Lytton Strachey to "Topsey" Lucas, letter dated November 1, 1927, BM MSS ADD 53788. In his letter, Strachey wrote, with some envy, "There are so many modern writers I can't see the point of, whom so many other people like very much, that it looks to me as if there were certain qualities I'm impervious to."
3. Malcolm Bradbury, "London 1890-1920," in Malcolm Bradbury and James McFarlane, eds., *Modernism 1890-1930* (Harmondsworth, Middlesex, England: Penguin, 1976), pp. 178-179.
4. Lawrence B. Gamache, "Toward a Definition of Modernism," in Lawrence B. Gamache and Ian S. MacNiven, eds., *The Modernists: Studies in a Literary Phenomenon, Essays in Honor of Harry T. Moore* (London: Associated University Press, Inc., 1987), pp. 32-45.
5. Noel Annan, *Our Age: The Generation That Made Post-War Britain* (London: Fontana, 1990), p. 73. Also see Paul Fussell's *The Great War and Modern Memory* (London: Oxford University Press, 1975) and Paul Levy's edited collection of Strachey's essays, *Lytton Strachey: The Really Interesting Question and Other Papers* (London: Weidenfeld and Nicolson, 1971).
6. Michael Holroyd, "On the Border-Line Between the New and the Old: Bloomsbury, Biography, and Gerald Brenan," in Joe Law and Linda K. Hughes, eds., *Biographical Passages: Essays in Victorian and Modernist Biography* (Columbia: University of Missouri Press, 2000), pp. 42-43.
7. Carolyn Heilbrun, *Toward a Recognition of Androgyny* (New York: Alfred A. Knopf, 1973).
8. Edmund Wilson, cited in Holroyd, "On the Border-Line Between the New and the Old," p. 40.
9. See Christopher Reed's discussion of Bloomsbury in "Making History: The Bloomsbury Group's Construction of Aesthetic and Sexual Identity, " *Journal of Homosexuality,* 27.1-2(1994):189-224. See also his "Bloomsbury Bashing: Homophobia and the Politics of Criticism in the Eighties," *Genders,* 11(1991):58-80. George Piggford discusses Strachey as camp artist and writer in "Camp Sites: Forster and the Biographies of Queer Bloomsbury," in Robert K. Martin and George Piggford, eds., *Queer Forster* (Chicago: Chicago University Press, 1997), pp. 89-112.
10. The most recent book to emulate Heilbrun's view of Bloomsbury is by Jan Marsh, *Bloomsbury Women: Distinct Figures in Life and Art* (New York: Henry Holt and Co., 1996). Her analysis is in sharp contrast to the anti-Strachey position led by Jane Marcus in *Virginia Woolf and the Languages of Patriarchy* (Bloomington:

Indiana University Press, 1987).

11. Marsh, *Bloomsbury Women*, p. 30.

12. Lytton Strachey, "Will It Come Right in the End?" Apostle paper delivered in 1908, BM MSS, unbound.

13. Lytton Strachey, cited in Michael Holroyd, *Lytton Strachey: A Biography* (Harmondsworth, Middlesex: Penguin, 1987), p. 312. Strachey referred to the Victorians enclosed in glass after reading the life of fellow Apostle Henry Sidgwick.

14. See Rita Felski's discussion of Victorian gender codes and how fin de siècle modernists attempted to subvert Victorian ideology in *The Gender of Modernity* (Cambridge, MA: Harvard University Press, 1995), p. 18.

15. Mary Poovey, *Uneven Developments: The Ideological Work of Gender in Mid-Victorian England* (Chicago: University of Chicago Press, 1988). See Chapter 1.

16. Michael Holroyd, *Lytton Strachey: A Critical Biography* (London: William Heinemann, Ltd., 1967-1968).

17. Julian Symons, "Ham Spray Revisited: Second Thoughts on Lytton Strachey and His Style," *Times Literary Supplement* (August 26, 1994):4-5. Symons reviews Michael Holroyd's 1995 revised biography of Strachey.

18. Lytton Strachey to Lady Ottoline Morrell, letter dated October 31, 1916, cited in Holroyd, *Lytton Strachey: A Biography*, p. 310.

19. Heilbrun, *Toward a Recognition of Androgyny*, p. 118.

20. Quentin Bell, "Bloomsbury and the Arts in the Early Twentieth Century," *Leeds Art Calendar*, 55(1964):18-28.

21. Lytton Strachey to Clive Bell, letter dated October 21, 1909, cited in Holroyd, *Lytton Strachey: A Biography*, p. 454.

22. Lytton Strachey to Duncan Grant, letter dated August 23, 1909, BM MSS ADD 57932.

23. Critics' reviews cited in David Gadd, *The Loving Friends: A Portrait of Bloomsbury* (London: Hogarth Press, 1974), p. 143.

24. Ibid., p. 144.

25. Strachey referred to sex as "the very interesting question" in an untitled Apostle essay delivered to the Society in 1911, BM MSS, unbound.

26. Strachey uses both phrases, "explorer of the past" and "modern inquirer," in his preface to *Eminent Victorians* (London: The Knickerbocker Press, 1918).

27. Gerald Brenan's comment about Strachey's work, cited in Holroyd, "On the Border-Line Between the New and the Old," p. 29.

28. Lytton Strachey to Leonard Woolf, letter dated January 7, 1902, in which Strachey speaks of his "disease" that prevents him from loving women as he "ought." Also cited in Holroyd, *Lytton Strachey: A Biography*, p. 194.

29. Eve Kosofsky Sedgwick, *Between Men: English Literature and Male Homosexual Desire* (New York: Columbia University Press, 1985).

30. See Ed Cohen, *Talk on the Wilde Side: Toward a Genealogy of a Discourse on Male Sexualities* (New York: Routledge, 1992) and Alan Sinfield, *The Wilde Century: Effeminacy, Oscar Wilde and the Queer Moment* (New York: Columbia University Press, 1994). Cohen notes that some two decades after Wilde's trial, Forster's Maurice could claim "I am an unspeakable of the Oscar Wilde sort," thus demonstrating the ways in which Wilde had been made to carry the burdens of transgression against which normative masculinity was now defined (p. 100).

31. For the link between Greek studies and homosexuality, see Richard Jenkyns, *The Victorians and Ancient Greece* (Cambridge, MA: Harvard University Press, 1981); Frank Turner, *The Greek Heritage in Victorian Britain* (New Haven, CT: Yale University Press, 1987), and Linda Dowling, *Hellenism and Homosexuality in Victorian England* (Ithaca, NY: Cornell University Press, 1994). The most thorough treatment of the Apostles and Hellenism to date appears in Paul Levy's study of G.E. Moore, while Richard Deacon's study of the Apostles lacks analysis and is laden with homophobia. Richard Lubenow's recent study of the Apostles does not even address the topic of sexuality—a strange omission since this topic dominated the weekly meetings of the Brothers. All of these are discussed in Chapter 1.

32. Jeffrey Weeks, *Sex, Politics and Society: The Regulation of Sexuality Since 1900* (London: Longman, 1981). According to Weeks, the process of labeling gives homosexuals a subculture with its own language, gestures, and meeting places. Whether the men call themselves or are called "inverts" or "Higher Sodomites," they have achieved a form of unity and resistance.

33. Ed Cohen, "Writing Gone Wilde: Homoerotic Desire in the Closet of Representation," in Regina Gagnier, ed., *Critical Essays on Oscar Wilde* (New York: G. K. Hall & Co., 1991), p. 71.

34. For a discussion of the changing meaning of effeminacy since the Wilde trials and the British public's new fear of the effeminate aesthete, see Joseph Bristow's introductory chapter to *Effeminate England: Homoerotic Writing After 1885* (New York: Columbia University Press, 1995).

35. For a discussion of the "queer" image, see Alan Sinfield's *The Wilde Century*, especially pp. 188-126.

36. Richard Dellamora, *Apocalyptic Overtures: Sexual Politics and the Sense of an Ending* (New Brunswick, NJ: Rutgers University Press, 1994), p. 63.

37. Strachey's leading role in the Apostles and Bloomsbury and the spirit of free inquiry among the members of both groups are discussed by Leonard Woolf in *Sowing: An Autobiography of the Years 1880-1904* (London: Hogarth Press, 1960). Excerpts are found in S.P. Rosenbaum, ed., *The Bloomsbury Group: A Collection of Memoirs, Commentary, and Criticism* (Toronto: University of Toronto Press, 1975), pp. 92-109.

38. Barbara Fassler, "Theories of Homosexuality As Sources of Bloomsbury's Androgyny," *Signs* (Winter 1979):237-251.

39. For a discussion of these male modernists, see Sandra Gilbert and Susan Gubar, *No Man's Land: The Place of the Woman Writer in the Twentieth Century,* Volume I: *The War of the Words* (New Haven, CT: Yale University Press, 1988).

40. See Gilbert and Gubar, *No Man's Land,* Volumes I through III, and Bonnie Kime Scott, ed., *The Gender of Modernism* (Bloomington: Indiana University Press, 1990).

41. Marjorie Garber argues in *Vested Interests: Cross-Dressing and Cultural Anxiety* (New York: Routledge, 1992) that although "bohemian" subcultures, such as the Cambridge Apostles and Bloomsbury Group, constitute a community outside of class, they create a male monopoly on intellect and imagination.

42. Robert Elbaz, *The Changing Nature of the Self: A Critical Study of the Autobiographical Discourse* (Iowa City: University of Iowa Press, 1987), p. 155.

43. Stephen Greenblatt, *Renaissance Self-Fashioning: From More to Shakespeare* (Chicago: University of Chicago Press, 1980), p. 3.

44. See Michael Adams, *The Great Adventure: Male Desire and the Coming of World War I* (Bloomington: Indiana University Press, 1990); Robert Wohl, *The Generation of 1914* (Cambridge, MA: Harvard University Press, 1979); and Jerrold Seigel, *Bohemian Paris: The Culture of Politics and the Boundaries of Bourgeois Life, 1830-1930* (New York: Viking, 1986) for discussions of the sense of alienation and identity crisis experienced by young men across Europe at the fin de siècle.

45. Rita Felski makes a similar claim about the gender politics of modernism in her introduction to *The Gender of Modernity*.

46. For a discussion of the fin de siècle discourse of "race suicide" and the image of the homosexual, see Elaine Showalter, *Sexual Anarchy: Gender and Culture at the Fin de Siècle* (New York: Viking, 1990).

47. Marianne DeKoven, *Rich and Strange: Gender, History, Modernism* (Princeton, NJ: Princeton University Press, 1991), p. 20.

48. Judith Butler, *Gender Trouble: Feminism and the Subversion of Identity* (New York: Routledge, 1990), p. 140.

49. Sinfield, *The Wilde Century*, p. 142.

50. For a discussion of Forster's *Maurice*, see Bristow, *Effeminate England*, p. 81.

51. Perry Meisel, *The Myth of the Modern: A Study of British Literature and Criticism After 1850* (New Haven, CT: Yale University Press, 1987).

52. For a discussion of Bloomsbury's attitudes toward politics, see Paul Levy's commentaries in *Lytton Strachey: The Really Interesting Question,* and Strachey's statement as a conscientious objector is reprinted in Michael Holroyd, ed., *Lytton Strachey by Himself: A Self-Portrait* (London: Vintage, 1994), p. 136.

53. See Elaine Showalter's *Sexual Anarchy: Gender and Culture at the Fin de Siècle* (New York: Viking, 1990) for a discussion of the New Woman, decadence, homosexuality, and other forms of "anarchy" at the fin de siècle.

Chapter 1

1. Lytton Strachey to John Maynard Keynes, letter dated April 8, 1906, King's College, Cambridge MSS, Keynes Papers, Volume II (hereafter referred to as Keynes Papers).

2. Strachey refers to the "New Style of Love" in a letter to Keynes, dated April 15, 1905, Keynes Papers, Volume II.

3. Leonard Woolf describing the atmosphere at Cambridge in *Sowing: An Autobiography of the Years 1880 to 1904* (London: Hogarth Press, 1960), p. 171.

4. Lytton Strachey to Leonard Woolf, describing the "truths" that he discovered as an Apostle, January 19, 1906, Berg Collection, Strachey-Woolf Letters, 112 A.L.S., New York Public Library (hereafter referred to as Berg).

5. Bertrand Russell, "Portraits from Memory: Keynes and Strachey," reprinted in S.P. Rosenbaum, ed., *The Bloomsbury Group: A Collection of Memoirs, Commentary, and Criticism* (Toronto: University of Toronto Press, 1975), p. 403.

6. Noel Annan, *Our Age: The Generation That Made Post-War Britain* (London: Fontana, 1990), p. 134.

7. Paul Levy, *G.E. Moore and the Cambridge Apostles* (London: Papermac, 1989), p. 227.

8. See Keynes's discussion of the Apostles as "immoralists" in "My Early Beliefs," his 1938 essay for the Bloomsbury Memoir Club, cited in Robert Skidelsky, *John Maynard Keynes,* Volume 1: *Hopes Betrayed, 1883-1920* (London: Macmillan 1983), p. 143.

9. Strachey refers to homosexuality as "unnatural passions" in "Maxims and Reflections," n.d., British Museum MSS, unbound (hereafter referred to as BM MSS).

10. Richard Deacon, *The Cambridge Apostles* (New York: Farrar, Straus and Giroux, 1985). See Chapters 15 and 16 for details of the espionage among the Brothers.

11. Michael Holroyd, *Lytton Strachey: A Biography* (Harmondsworth, Middlesex: Penguin Books, 1987), pp. 182-183.

12. G. Lowes Dickinson's description of the Society's atmosphere, in Dennis Proctor, ed., *The Autobiography of G. Lowes Dickinson* (London: Duckworth, 1973), p. 68.

13. Lytton Strachey to his mother, cited in Holroyd, *Lytton Strachey: A Biography,* p. 105.

14. Deacon, *The Cambridge Apostles,* p. 56.

15. Deacon's attempt to identify Strachey as the corrupter of the Society has recently been challenged by the most recent study of the Society that completely refuses to address the sexuality of its members. W.C. Lubenow ignores the dominating role that the Higher Sodomy played in Apostolic discussions and minimalizes Strachey's influence by reducing his homosexuality to an expression of "aspects of his personality, his wit, and dramatic power." See W.C. Lubenow, *The Cambridge Apostles, 1820-1914: Liberalism, Imagination, and Friendship in British Intellectual and Professional Life* (Cambridge: Cambridge University Press, 1998), p. 412.

16. Levy, *G.E. Moore and the Cambridge Apostles,* p. 65.

17. This revolt against bourgeois Christianity is the theme of several of Strachey's essays delivered before the Society, including "Will It Come Right in the End?", 1908, and "Is Death Desirable?", n.d., BM MSS, unbound.

18. Deacon, *The Cambridge Apostles,* p. 6.

19. Levy, *G.E. Moore and the Cambridge Apostles,* pp. 71-74.

20. Richard Dellamora, *Masculine Desire: The Sexual Politics of Victorian Aestheticism* (Chapel Hill, NC: 1999), p. 16.

21. Eve K. Sedgwick, *Between Men: English Literature and Male Homosocial Desire* (New York: Columbia University Press, 1985).

22. Ibid.

23. See Jeffrey Richards, "'Passing the Love of Women': Manly Love and Victorian Society," in J. A. Mangan and James Walvin, eds., *Manliness and Morality: Middle-Class Masculinity in Britain and America, 1800-1940* (Manchester, England: Manchester University Press, 1987), pp. 93-100.

24. John Boswell, *Same-Sex Unions in Premodern Europe* (New York: Villard Books, 1994), p. 21. See Chapter 3 for a discussion of same-sex unions in the Greco-Roman world.

25. Ibid. See Chapter 3 for a discussion of the ancient Greek model of friendship.

26. Linda Dowling, *Hellenism and Homosexuality in Victorian Oxford* (Ithaca, NY: Cornell University Press, 1994), p. 80.

27. Richard Jenkyns, *The Victorians and Ancient Greece* (Cambridge, MA: Harvard University Press, 1980), p. 293.

28. Dickinson's discussion of all-male love in an unmailed letter to Ferdinand Schiller, quoted in Proctor, *The Autobiography of G. Lowes Dickinson,* pp. 10-11.

29. Sebastian Sprott to Lytton Strachey, in reference to an unnamed work on sexology, August 27, 1922, Strachey Papers, BM MSS ADD 60699.

30. Lytton Strachey, diary entry for November 13, 1896, reprinted in Michael Holroyd, ed., *Lytton Strachey by Himself: A Self-Portrait* (London: Vintage, 1994), p. 86.

31. Lytton Strachey to J.T. Sheppard, letter dated September 27, 1903, King's College, Cambridge MSS, unbound letters (hereafter referred to as King's MSS).

32. A series of letters between Strachey and Keynes dated April 1907 discussed the rumors of the Apostles' homosexuality and their need for more caution in sending letters. Keynes Papers, Volume III.

33. James Eli Adams, *Dandies and Desert Saints: Styles of Victorian Masculinity* (Ithaca, NY: Cornell University Press, 1995), p. 207.

34. Lytton Strachey, "Menage a Trois," written about 1904, cited in S.P. Rosenbaum, ed., *Victorian Bloomsbury: The Early Literary History of the Bloomsbury Group* (London: Macmillan, 1987), p. 270.

35. Lytton to James Strachey, letter dated November 26, 1908, BM MSS ADD 60707.

36. Lytton to James Strachey, letter dated November 6, 1909, BM MSS ADD 60708.

37. Lytton Strachey, "The Fruit of the Tree," June 1901, BM MSS, unbound.

38. Lytton Strachey, "The Resignation," n.d., BM MSS, unbound.

39. Lytton Strachey, "Diary of an Athenian 400 B.C." n.d., BM MSS, unbound. In this story, Strachey defends the purity of "the Love of Souls" yet admits that others may see him as unclean. "Remember that the thing itself may not be bad, though some make a bad use of it."

40. Levy, *G.E. Moore and the Cambridge Apostles,* p. 106.

41. Ibid., p. 105.

42. Ibid.

43. Goldworthy Lowes Dickinson, *The Greek View of Life* (Ann Arbor: University of Michigan Press, 1958), p. 175.

44. Proctor, *Autobiography of G. Lowes Dickinson,* p. 90.

45. Ibid., p. 91.

46. Goldworthy Lowes Dickinson, "Body and Soul: A Dialogue," in Ibid., pp. 273-283.

47. Charles Hession, *John Maynard Keynes: A Personal Biography of the Man Who Revolutionized Capitalism and the Way We Live* (New York: Macmillan, 1984), pp. 40-41.

48. Strachey refers to his "unnatural passions" and "unnatural affections" in "Maxims and Reflections," n.d., BM MSS, unbound.

49. Levy, *G.E. Moore and the Cambridge Apostles,* p. 141.

50. Ibid., p. 142.

51. Lytton Strachey to G.E. Moore, letter dated October 11, 1903, Cambridge University Library MSS, unbound. Strachey declared, "I date from Oct. 1903 the beginning of the Age of Reason."

52. J.M. Keynes cited in Hession, *Keynes: A Personal Biography,* pp. 44-45.

53. G.E. Moore, Apostle paper, quoted in Levy, *G.E. Moore and the Cambridge Apostles,* pp. 141-143.

54. For a more detailed account of the Moore-Ainsworth relationship, see Ibid., pp. 212-214.

55. Ibid.

56. Ainsworth to Lytton Strachey, letter dated November 23, 1903, BM MSS ADD 60655, Volume 1.

57. Russell's discussion of homosexuality in the Society is included in Levy, *G.E. Moore and the Cambridge Apostles,* pp. 238-239.

58. Russell's letters to Lady Ottoline Morrell, quoted in Rosenbaum, *Victorian Bloomsbury,* p. 210.

59. Lytton Strachey, diary entry for August 6, 1905, reprinted in Holroyd, *Lytton Strachey by Himself,* pp. 116-117.

60. Ralph Hawtrey's comment about the Society, as told by Harry Norton to Strachey, letter dated July 25, 1906, BM MSS ADD 60682.

61. Skidelsky, *John Maynard Keynes,* Volume 1, p. 120.

62. Leonard Woolf to Strachey, letter dated November 12, 1905, Leonard Woolf Papers; University of Sussex Special Collections (hereafter referred to as Woolf Papers); Virginia Woolf describing the Apostles in her Memoir Club essay "Old Bloomsbury," 1922, reprinted in Jeanne Schulkind, ed., *Moments of Being* (London: Grafton Books, 1989), p. 208.

63. Leonard Woolf to Strachey, letter dated October 14, 1906, Woolf Papers.

64. Lytton Strachey to Walter Lamb, letter dated March 23, 1907, BM MSS ADD 60675.

65. L. Woolf, *Sowing,* p. 172.

66. Strachey-Woolf Letters, 1906-1909, Berg.

67. Strachey to Leonard Woolf, letter dated May 27, 1909, Berg.

68. J.T. Sheppard to Lytton Strachey, letter dated March 29, 1903, BM MSS ADD 60697.

69. Lytton Strachey, untitled poem, in a letter to J.T. Sheppard, November 18, 1902, King's MSS, unbound.

70. J.T. Sheppard to Lytton Strachey, letter dated July 3, 1903, BM MSS ADD 60697.

71. J.T. Sheppard to Lytton Strachey, letter dated January 11, 1902, BM MSS ADD 60697.

72. J.T. Sheppard to Lytton Strachey, letter dated June 10, 1903, BM MSS ADD 60697.

73. Lytton Strachey to J.T. Sheppard, letter dated October 11, 1903, King's MSS, unbound.

74. J.T. Sheppard to Lytton Strachey, letter dated ?, 1906, BM MSS ADD 60698.

75. Lytton Strachey, "Iphigenia in Tauris," 1903, Strachey Papers, BM MSS, unbound.

76. J.T. Sheppard to Strachey, letter dated June 10, 1903, BM MSS ADD 60697.

77. Lytton Strachey to Leonard Woolf, letter dated November 30, 1904, Woolf Papers.

78. Lytton Strachey describing the Hobhouse "affair" to Leonard Woolf, letter dated November 30, 1904, cited in Holroyd, *Lytton Strachey: A Biography,* p. 246.

79. Lytton Strachey, "The Two Triumphs," a poem to Arthur Hobhouse, dated March 10, 1905, BM MSS ADD 60694.

80. Lytton Strachey to Walter Lamb, letter dated March 23, 1907, BM MSS ADD 60675.

81. Lytton Strachey to Duncan Grant, letter dated January 25, 1906, BM MSS ADD 57932.

82. Lytton Strachey to J.M. Keynes, letter dated August 3, 1905, Keynes Papers, Volume I.

83. Lytton Strachey to J.M. Keynes, letter dated October 11, 1905, Keynes Papers, Volume I.

84. Strachey, as quoted in Holroyd, *Lytton Strachey: A Biography*, p. 292.

85. Lytton Strachey's description of the artist in a letter to James Strachey, cited in Ibid., p. 451.

86. J.M. Keynes to Lytton Strachey, letter dated October 18, 1905, Keynes Papers, Volume I.

87. Lytton Strachey, "Should We Have Elected Conybeare?", Apostle essay, dated November 14, 1903, BM MSS unbound.

88. Leonard Woolf to Lytton Strachey, letter dated June 21, 1906, Woolf Papers.

89. Strachey, as quoted in Holroyd, *Lytton Strachey: A Biography*, p. 237.

90. Lytton Strachey to Duncan Grant, echoing Wilde's "the love that dare not speak its name," in a letter dated September 5, 1905, BM MSS ADD 57932.

91. Alan Bray, *Homosexuality in Renaissance England* (London: Gay Men's Press, 1982), p. 86.

92. MacCarthy, as quoted in Lubenow, *The Cambridge Apostles,* 1820-1914, p. 78.

93. James Strachey, untitled essay written for the Society, 1909, BM MSS, uncataloged.

94. Lytton Strachey to J.T. Sheppard, letter dated ?, 1903, King's MSS, unbound.

95. Lytton Strachey, "The Two Triumphs."

96. Lytton Strachey, "The Haschish," unpublished poem, dated September 1908, BM MSS ADD 60694.

97. Lytton Strachey, "Shall We Take the Pledge?", Apostle essay, dated February 2, 1905, BM MSS, uncataloged.

98. Lytton Strachey, "The Crow," unpublished poem, ?, 1905, BM MSS uncataloged.

99. Lytton Strachey to Duncan Grant, letter dated November 23, 1907, BM MSS ADD 57932.

100. Lytton Strachey to J.M. Keynes, letter dated January 14, 1906, Keynes Papers, Volume II.

101. Arthur Hobhouse to Lytton Strachey, letter dated April 29, 1906, BM MSS ADD 60670.

102. Holroyd, *Lytton Strachey: A Biography*, p. 237.

103. Lytton Strachey to J.M. Keynes, letter dated December 3, 1905, Keynes Papers, Volume I.

104. J.M. Keynes to Lytton Strachey, letter dated March 11, 1906, Keynes Papers, Volume II.

105. J.M. Keynes to Lytton Strachey, letter dated January 22, 1906, Keynes Papers, Volume II.

106. Lytton Strachey to J.M. Keynes, letter dated January 23, 1906, Keynes Papers, Volume II.

107. Lytton Strachey to J.M. Keynes, letter dated October 13, 1905, Keynes Papers, Volume I.

108. Lytton Strachey to J.M. Keynes, letter dated February 14, 1906, Keynes Papers, Volume II.

109. Duncan Grant to Lytton Strachey, letter dated October 11, 1905, BM MSS ADD 57933.

110. Lytton Strachey to Duncan Grant, letter dated October 11, 1905, BM MSS ADD 57932.

111. Lytton Strachey to Duncan Grant, letter dated November 7, 1907, BM MSS ADD 57932.

112. Duncan Grant to Lytton Strachey, letter dated May 5, 1909, BM MSS ADD 57933.

113. J.M. Keynes to Lytton Strachey, letter dated January 1, 1906, Keynes Papers, Volume II.

114. J.M. Keynes to Lytton Strachey, letter dated January 31, 1907, Keynes Papers, Volume III.

115. Lytton to James Strachey, letter dated July 15, 1908, BM MSS ADD 60707.

116. James to Lytton Strachey, letter dated November 2, 1908, BM MSS ADD 60707.

117. Carolyn Heilbrun, *Toward a Recognition of Androgyny* (New York: Alfred A. Knopf, 1973), p. 123.

118. Barbara Fassler, "Theories of Homosexuality As Sources of Bloomsbury's Androgyny," *Signs* (Winter 1979):249.

119. Lytton Strachey to Duncan Grant, letter dated May 4, 1909, BM MSS ADD 57932.

120. Lytton Strachey to Duncan Grant, letter dated July 3, 1908, BM MSS ADD 57932.

121. Skidelsky, *John Maynard Keynes,* p. 196.

122. Quoted in Ibid., p. 201.

123. Duncan Grant to James Strachey, letter dated April 22, 1909, BM MSS ADD 60668.

124. Quoted in Skidelsky, *John Maynard Keynes,* p. 202.

125. Holroyd, *Lytton Strachey: A Biography,* p. 451.

126. Ibid., p. 451.

127. Lady Ottoline Morrell's memoirs, cited in Ibid., p. 453.

128. Ibid., p. 453.

129. Lytton Strachey to Lady Ottoline Morrell, letter dated January 25, 1912, cited in Ibid., p. 453.

130. Henry Lamb to Lytton Strachey, letter dated November 24, 1911, BM MSS ADD 60673.

131. Lytton Strachey to Henry Lamb, letter dated February 19, 1912, cited in Holroyd, *Lytton Strachey: A Biography,* p. 486.

132. Lady Ottoline's diary, cited in Ibid., p. 497.

133. Henry Lamb to Lytton Strachey, letter dated August 20, 1912, BM MSS ADD 60673.

134. Lytton Strachey, untitled Apostle essay, dated May 20, 1911, BM MSS, uncataloged. Paul Levy titled the essay "The Really Interesting Question."

135. Ibid.

136. Holroyd, *Lytton Strachey: A Biography*, p. 521.

137. Lytton Strachey to J.M. Keynes, letter dated November 4, 1905, Keynes Papers, Volume I.

138. Lytton Strachey, "Maxims and Reflections," n.d., BM MSS, unbound.

139. Lytton Strachey to Ralph Partridge, letter dated January 1920, BM MSS ADD 62891.

140. See Holroyd, *Lytton Strachey: A Biography*, pp. 789-790, for excerpts from Strachey's and Partridge's letters to each other.

141. Lytton Strachey to Dora Carrington, letter dated May 21, 1921, BM MSS, no. 62892.

142. Quoted in Holroyd, *Lytton Strachey: A Biography*, p. 888.

143. See Ibid., pp. 940-945, for excerpts of letters between Strachey and Senhouse.

144. Lytton Strachey to Roger Senhouse, letter dated February 1930, cited in Ibid., p. 941.

145. Roger Senhouse to Strachey, letter dated April 1920, cited in Ibid., p. 945.

146. In his diary entry for September 5, 1931, Strachey writes (unconvincingly) about his feelings for Senhouse: "I hardly feel as if I could now be shattered by him as I was during the 'black period.' . . . No! I am really calm—that dreadful abysmal sensation in the pit of the stomach is absent. What a relief. . . . The inexpressible charm of his presence, the sweetness of his temper, his beautiful affectionateness— why should these things make it difficult for me . . . ?" The diary has been reprinted and titled "A Fortnight in France," in Michael Holroyd, ed., *Lytton Strachey by Himself: A Self-Portrait* (London: Vintage, 1994), pp. 161-184.

147. Ibid., pp. 176-177.

148. Ibid., p. 180.

149. Lytton Strachey to Duncan Grant, letter dated September 7, 1908, BM MSS ADD 57932. He asked, "Why are all women hollow, hollow?"

150. J.M. Keynes to Strachey, letter dated April 10, 1907, Keynes Papers, Volume 3; Strachey to Leonard Woolf, November 16, 1907, Berg.

151. Dickinson's reaction to Carpenter's writings is quoted in Annan, *Our Age*, p. 146.

152. Strachey to his sister Philippa, letter dated ?, 1924, BM MSS ADD 60721.

153. Strachey refers to "Oscar's trials" in a letter to Carrington, dated September 5, 1921, BM MSS ADD 62893."It's very interesting and depressing. One of the surprising features is that he very nearly got off. If he had, what would have happened, I wonder? I fancy the history of English culture might have been quite different, if a juryman's stupidity had chanced to take another turn."

154. Lytton Strachey to J.M. Keynes, letter dated ?, 1908, Keynes Papers, Volume 3.

155. Keynes to Strachey, letter dated April 10, 1907, Keynes Papers, Volume 3.

156. J.M. Keynes responds to Lawrence's criticisms in "My Early Beliefs," in S.P. Rosenbaum, ed., *The Bloomsbury Group: A Collection of Memoirs, Commentary and Criticism* (Toronto: University of Toronto Press, 1975), p. 49.

157. Bertrand Russell, quoted in Ibid., p. 49.

158. See D.H. Lawrence's "A Propos" to *Lady Chatterly's Lover* for his discussion of the phallic regeneration of England through sexual "blood contact" between men and women.

159. Lytton Strachey to David Garnett, letter dated November 11, 1915, Raymond H. Taylor Collection, Department of Rare Books and Special Collections, Princeton University Library (hereafter referred to as Taylor Collection).

160. Lytton Strachey to David Garnett, letter dated October 23, 1928, Taylor Collection.

161. Strachey's doubts about Brooke's membership are in letters from June 1907 though February 1908, Berg.

162. Forster's reaction to Strachey is quoted in Rosenbaum, *Victorian Bloomsbury*, p. 242.

163. Rita Felski, *The Gender of Modernity* (Cambridge, MA: Harvard University Press, 1995), p. 106.

164. Jenkyns, *The Victorians and Ancient Greece*, p. 282. Jenkyns argues that upper-class university-educated Victorian men saw in Plato an "intellectual sympathy and moral good."

165. Peter Gay, *The Bourgeois Experience: Victoria to Freud,* Volume II: *The Tender Passion* (New York: Oxford University Press, 1986), p. 237.

166. J.M. Keynes, "My Early Beliefs," in Rosenbaum, *The Bloomsbury Group,* p. 63.

167. J.M. Keynes to Duncan Grant, letter dated February 11, 1909, BM MSS ADD 58120.

168. Lytton Strachey to Leonard Woolf, letter dated February 19, 1909, Woolf Papers.

169. Lytton Strachey to Leonard Woolf, letter dated April 1905, Woolf Papers.

170. Quoted in Irving Singer, *The Nature of Love,* Volume I: *Plato to Luther* (Chicago: University of Chicago Press, 1984), pp. 6-7. Singer defines idealization as the bestowal of traits and value upon an individual that he or she in reality does not possess.

171. Lytton Strachey to J.M. Keynes, letter dated November 27, 1905, Keynes Papers, Volume I.

Chapter 2

1. Lytton Strachey to John Maynard Keynes, letter dated July 1, 1906, King's College, Cambridge University MSS, Volume III (hereafter referred to as Keynes Papers).

2. See Chapter 4 of Lytton Strachey, *Eminent Victorians* (London: The Knickerbocker Press, 1918/London: The Folio Press, 1967), on the fall of General Gordon for Strachey's critique of British imperialism. The 1967 revised edition is cited in the following pages.

3. See Eric J. Leed, *The Mind of the Traveler: From Gilgamesh to Global Tourism* (New York: Basic Books, 1991), for an examination of travelers' motives across the ages.

4. Jeffrey Weeks, *Coming Out: Homosexual Politics in Britain, from the Nineteenth Century to the Present* (London: Quartet Books, 1983), p. 43.

5. Edward Said, *Orientalism* (New York: Vintage Books, 1979), p. 190. "Oriental sex," Said adds, became a standard commodity, a part of mass culture, and readers and writers could experience it without even traveling to the Orient.

6. Robert Aldrich, *The Seduction of the Mediterranean: Writing, Art, and Homosexual Fantasy* (New York: Routledge, 1993), p. 167.

7. Douglas A. Lorimer, *Colour, Class, and the Victorians: English Attitudes to the Negro in the Mid-Nineteenth Century* (New York: Holmes and Meier, 1978), pp. 131, 100.

8. Said, *Orientalism,* p. 190.

9. I am using Steven Maynard's phrase to denote the imaginative and literal, often sexual, exploration of the city that was the privilege of bourgeois men. See Maynard's "Through a Hole in the Lavatory Wall: Homosexual Subcultures, Police Surveillance and the Dialectics of Discovery, Toronto 1890-1930," *Journal of the History of Sexuality,* 5(2)(October 1994): 207-242.

10. See Jonathan Dollimore's account of Wilde and Gide in Algiers, in *Sexual Dissidence: Augustine to Wilde, Freud to Foucault* (Oxford: Clarendon Press, 1991), and *The Memoirs of John Addington Symonds,* Phyllis Grosskurth, ed., (London: Hutchinson, 1984), in which Symonds discusses his love for working-class youths.

11. Stephen Adams, cited in Parminder Kaur Bakshi, *Distant Desire: Homoerotic Codes and the Subversion of the English Novel in E.M. Forster's Fiction* (New York: Peter Lang, 1996), p. 68.

12. Ed Cohen, *Talk on the Wilde Side: Toward a Genealogy of Discourses on Male Sexualities* (New York: Routledge, 1993), p. 145.

13. Richard Sennett, *Authority* (London: Secker, 1980), pp. 33-34.

14. Peter Stallybrass and Allon White (photographer), *The Politics and Poetics of Transgression* (London: Methuen, 1986), pp. 201-202. They argue that the discovery of pleasure and desire within the realm of the "low other" is not a transgressive act and does not erase but reaffirms boundaries. The surveyor of the other defines himself through the exclusion of the designated low.

15. Michael Roper and John Tosh, eds., *Manful Assertions: Masculinities in Britain Since 1800* (London: Routledge, 1991), Introduction, p. 15.

16. See Kaja Silverman's discussion of T. E. Lawrence in *Male Subjectivity at the Margins* (New York: Routledge, 1992), pp. 299-318.

17. Lytton Strachey, "The Mask of Gold," poem dated March 9, 1905, British Museum MSS, unbound (hereafter referred to as BM MSS).

18. Strachey usually referred to his homosexuality as a higher expression of love, but his repeated failures to find his ideal compelled him to sometimes criticize his own desires as "unnatural."

19. Strachey's introduction to his Liverpool Diary, March 3, 1898, reprinted in Michael Holroyd, ed., *Lytton Strachey by Himself: A Self-Portrait* (London: Vintage, 1994), p. 92.

20. Lytton Strachey, "69 Lancaster Gate," reprinted in Ibid., pp. 16-28.

21. Strachey, "Lancaster Gate," in Ibid., pp. 26-27.

22. Lady Jane Strachey, *Nursery Lyrics* (1903), BM MSS ADD 60648.

23. Lady Jane Strachey, unpublished diary, dated 1899, BM MSS ADD 60639.

24. For a discussion of the creation of imperial manhood in the nursery and at public school, see John M. MacKenzie, ed., *Imperialism and Popular Culture* (Manchester, England: Manchester University Press, 1986), and J.A. Mangan, ed., *"Benefits*

Bestowed"?: Education and British Imperialism (Manchester, England: Manchester University Press, 1988).

25. Philip Dodd, "Englishness and the National Culture," in Robert Colls and Philip Dodd, eds., *Englishness: Politics and Culture 1880-1920* (London: Croom Helm 1986), p. 3.

26. Mangan, *"Benefits Bestowed,"* pp. 5-8.

27. Lytton Strachey, diary for December 1892 through May 1893, reprinted in Holroyd, *Lytton Strachey by Himself,* pp. 39-81.

28. Lytton Strachey, "An Adventure in the Night," 1893, BM MSS, unbound.

29. Satya P. Mohanty, "Drawing the Color Line: Kipling and the Culture of Colonial Rule," in Dominick LaCapra, ed., *The Bounds of Race: Perspectives on Hegemony and Resistance* (Ithaca, NY: Cornell University Press, 1991), pp. 311-343.

30. Lytton Strachey, "Shall We Be Missionaries," Apostle essay, dated 1902 BM MSS, unbound.

31. Lytton Strachey, "Warren Hastings," Cambridge thesis, dated September 26, 1901, BM MSS unbound.

32. Lytton Strachey to Bernard Swithinbank, unpublished letter, dated September 20, 1908, King's College, Cambridge MSS, unbound (hereafter referred to as King's MSS). Much to his dismay, Strachey failed to dissuade Swithinbank from moving to Burma.

33. Michael Holroyd, *Lytton Strachey: A Biography* (Harmondsworth, Middlesex: Penguin Books, 1987), pp. 174-175.

34. Lytton Strachey to Duncan Grant, letter dated February 5, 1906, BM MSS ADD 57932.

35. Lytton Strachey to Bernard Swithinbank, letter dated September 21, 1908, King's MSS unbound.

36. Ibid.

37. Ibid.

38. Lytton Strachey, "Shall We Go the Whole Hog?" Apostle essay, dated 1902(?), BM MSS, unbound.

39. Bakshi, *Distant Desire,* p. 72.

40. Ronald Hyam, *Empire and Sexuality: The British Experience* (Manchester, England: Manchester University Press, 1990), p. 25.

41. Leonard Woolf to Lytton Strachey, letter dated April 16, 1905, Leonard Woolf Papers, University of Sussex Special Collections (hereafter referred to as Woolf Papers).

42. Ibid.

43. Oliver Strachey's description of the life of a civil servant in India, letter to Pernel Strachey, dated ?, 1899, BM MSS ADD 60723.

44. Oliver Strachey to Lytton Strachey, letter dated August 3, 1906, BM MSS ADD 60724.

45. Robin W. Winks and James Rush, eds., *Asia in Western Fiction* (Honolulu: University of Hawaii Press, 1990), p. 67.

46. Strachey to Virginia Woolf, letter dated February 6, 1922, reprinted in James Strachey and Leonard Woolf, eds., *Virginia Woolf and Lytton Strachey: Letters* (New York: Harcourt, Brace and Co., 1956), p. 137.

47. P.J. Rich, *Chains of Empire: English Public Schools, Masonic Cabalism, Historical Causality, and Imperial Clubdom* (London: Regency Press, 1991), p. 160.

48. Strachey, "A Fortnight in France," diary for September 1931, reprinted in Holroyd, *Lytton Strachey by Himself*, p. 186.

49. Sir Richard Burton, *The Erotic Traveler*, Edward Leigh, ed. (New York: Putnam 1966), pp. 51-52.

50. Leonard Woolf to Lytton Strachey, letters for 1904 through 1911, Woolf Papers.

51. Winks and Rush, *Asia in Western Fiction*, p. 39.

52. Duncan Grant to Lytton Strachey, letter dated April 15, 1910, BM MSS ADD 57933.

53. Marjorie Strachey to Lytton Strachey, postcard, dated ?, 1903, BM MSS ADD 60723.

54. Lytton Strachey to J.M. Keynes, letter dated December 31, 1905, King's College, Cambridge, Keynes Papers, MSS Volume I (hereafter referred to as Keynes Papers).

55. Lytton Strachey to J.M. Keynes, letter dated April 12, 1923, Keynes Papers, Volume V.

56. Lytton Strachey to Leonard Woolf, letter dated April 23, 1913, Woolf Papers.

57. I am borrowing Kaja Silverman's term, from *Male Subjectivity at the Margins*.

58. Marjorie Garber, "The Chic of Araby: Transvestism, Transsexualism, and the Erotics of Cultural Appropriation," in Julia Epstein and Kristina Straub, eds., *Body Guards: The Cultural Politics of Gender Ambiguity* (New York: Routledge, 1991), pp. 223-247.

59. Lytton Strachey, "An Arabian Night," n.d., BM MSS, unbound.

60. Paul Levy, ed., *Lytton Strachey: The Really Interesting Question and Other Papers* (London: Weidenfeld and Nicolson, 1971), p. 156.

61. Lytton Strachey, "A Curious Manuscript Discovered in Morocco," n.d., BM MSS, unbound.

62. Lytton Strachey, "The Intermediaries, or Marriage a la Mode," n.d., BM MSS, unbound.

63. H. Rider Haggard, *She: A History of Adventure* (Mattituck, NY: Amereon House, 1982), p. 49.

64. Lytton Strachey to Clive Bell, letter dated May 21, 1909, BM MSS ADD 71104.

65. Lytton Strachey, "A Son of Heaven," originally written in 1913, BM MSS, unbound.

66. For an account of the Dreadnought Hoax, see Sandra Gilbert and Susan Gubar, *No Man's Land: The Place of the Woman Writer in the Twentieth Century*, Volume II: *Sexchanges* (New Haven, CT: Yale University Press, 1989), p. 324.

67. See George Piggford, "Camp Sites: Forster and the Biographies of Queer Bloomsbury," in Robert K. Martin and George Piggford, eds., *Queer Forster* (Chicago: Chicago University Press, 1997), pp. 89-112.

68. Lytton Strachey, "The End of General Gordon," *Eminent Victorians* (London: The Folio Press, 1967), p. 212.

69. Ibid., p. 246.

70. Grosskurth, *The Memoirs of John Addington Symonds*, p. 272.

71. Vanessa Bell to Lytton Strachey, describing her own visit to Italy, letter dated April 16, 1909, BM MSS ADD 60641.

72. Duncan Grant to Lytton Strachey, letter dated March 26, 1913, BM MSS ADD 57933.

73. Aldrich, *The Seduction of the Mediterranean,* p. 99.

74. Richard Dellamora, "E.M. Forster at the End," in Peter F. Murphy, ed., *Fictions of Masculinity: Crossing Cultures, Crossing Sexualities* (New York: New York University Press, 1994), pp. 279-280.

75. Lytton Strachey to Dora Carrington, citing Forster's description of Italy's "amusements," letter dated May ?, 1919, BM MSS ADD 62889.

76. Lytton Strachey to Lady Ottoline Morrell, letter dated March 26, 1913, cited in Holroyd, *Lytton Strachey: A Biography,* p. 531.

77. Strachey's letter to Lady Ottoline Morrell, dated March 24, 1913, cited in Ibid., pp. 530, 533.

78. Strachey to Lady Ottoline Morrell, letter dated April 17, 1913, cited in Ibid.

79. Holroyd, *Lytton Strachey: A Biography,* p. 847.

80. Lytton Strachey to Ralph Partridge, letter dated June 1922, cited in Ibid., p. 847.

81. Lytton Strachey to David Garnett, letter dated December 21, 1926, cited in Ibid., p. 917.

82. Strachey's and Senhouse's discussion of their relationship is related in letters, quoted in Ibid., p. 941. Looking back on their previous romance, Strachey told Senhouse, "I don't see why you should be afraid of being in a false position so long as I am under no misapprehension about your feelings. I can't believe that there's the slightest danger of my supposing (or expecting) your affection to be love." Letter dated March 23, 1927, Berg Collection, New York Public Library (hereafter referred to as Berg).

83. Lytton Strachey to Duncan Grant, letter dated August 1, 1909, BM MSS ADD 57932.

84. Lytton to James Strachey, 1909, quoted in Holroyd, *Lytton Strachey: A Biography,* p. 421.

85. Lytton to James Strachey, letter dated August ?, 1909, BM MSS ADD 60707.

86. This is Kaja Silverman's argument in the case of T.E. Lawrence, in *Male Subjectivity at the Margins.*

87. See Dollimore's *Sexual Dissidence,* in which he discusses difference as the basis of desire in the cases of Gide and Wilde, who traveled to Algiers in search of sexual release among the young male prostitutes.

88. Stallybrass and White, *The Politics and Poetics of Transgression,* p. 126. These literary critics note that the central feature of the urban geography of the bourgeois imaginary was the other—the working or poor man.

89. Ibid.

90. Lytton Strachey, diary for 1898, Liverpool, reprinted in Holroyd, *Lytton Strachey by Himself,* p. 93.

91. Judith R. Walkowitz, *City of Dreadful Delight: Narratives of Sexual Danger in Late-Victorian London* (Chicago: University of Chicago Press, 1992). See Chapter 1, "Urban Spectatorship."

92. Ibid., p. 20; here she is citing the work of Stallybrass and White on the city as the locus of fear, desire, and disgust.

93. Robert Skidelsky quotes the letters between Lytton and his brother James in which they discuss Keynes's practice of tabulating his exploits. See *John Maynard Keynes,* Volume I: *Hopes Betrayed, 1883-1920* (London: Macmillan, 1983), p. 204.

94. Strachey's Liverpool diary, reprinted in Holroyd, *Lytton Strachey by Himself,* p. 92.

95. Lady Ottoline Morrell, diary, quoted in Holroyd, *Lytton Strachey: A Biography,* p. 453.

96. Ibid., p. 529.

97. Max Beerbohm, quoted in Ibid., pp. 481-482.

98. Strachey, quoted in Ibid., p. 459.

99. Henry Lamb to Lytton Strachey, letter dated January 10, 1915, BM MSS ADD 60694.

100. Lytton Strachey to Lady Ottoline Morrell, cited in Holroyd, *Lytton Strachey: A Biography,* p. 629.

101. Lytton Strachey to Vanessa Bell, letter dated July 1, 1916, Raymond H. Taylor Collection, Department of Rare Books and Special Collections, Princeton University Library (hereafter referred to as Taylor Collection).

102. Lytton Strachey, "Scribblings," n.d. (probably 1914), BM MSS, unbound.

103. Lytton Strachey to James Strachey, letter dated July 15, 1915, BM MSS ADD 60710.

104. J.M. Keynes to Lytton Strachey, letter dated September 17, 1910, Keynes Papers, Volume III; Duncan Grant to Lytton Strachey, letter dated February 27, 1908, BM MSS ADD 57933.

105. Holroyd, *Lytton Strachey: A Biography,* p. 579.

106. Peter Bailey, "Will the Real Bill Banks Please Stand Up?": Towards a Role Analysis of Mid-Victorian Working-Class Respectability, *Journal of Social History,* 12(3):1979, p. 343.

107. Letters between Lytton Strachey and Ted Rousell, July and August, 1917, BM MSS ADD 60694.

108. Forster records Strachey's reaction in his 1960 "Terminal Note" to *Maurice* (New York: W.W. Norton and Company, Inc., 1971), p. 252.

109. Lytton Strachey to Henry Lamb, letter dated February 20, 1914, BM MSS ADD 60675.

110. Lytton Strachey to Virginia Woolf, untitled poem, included in a letter dated April 15, 1916, cited in Woolf and Strachey, *Letters,* pp. 77-79.

111. Lytton Strachey to J.M. Keynes, letter dated September 24, 1914, Keynes Papers, Volume V. He told Keynes that he was knitting a muffler in navy blue "for the neck of one of our sailor lads. I don't know which, but I have my visions."

112. Lytton Strachey to Vanessa Bell, letter dated July 1, 1916, Taylor Collection.

113. Lytton Strachey, "Monday June 26 1916," reprinted in Holroyd, *Lytton Strachey by Himself,* pp. 141-158.

114. Ibid., p. 143.

115. Ibid.

116. Ibid., p. 147.

117. Ibid., p. 149.

118. Ibid., p. 155.

119. Ibid., p. 154.

120. Walter Lamb to Lytton Strachey, letter dated January 23, 1910, BM MSS ADD 60675.

121. Lytton Strachey to Duncan Grant, letter dated June 25, 1907, BM MSS ADD 57932.

122. Lytton Strachey's untitled poem to Duncan Grant, August 25, 1908, BM MSS ADD 57932.

123. Lytton Strachey to Duncan Grant, letter dated June 25, 1907, BM MSS ADD 57932.

124. Lytton to James Strachey, letter dated December 9, 1908, BM MSS ADD 60707.

125. Lytton Strachey to Dora Carrington, letter dated September 3, 1916, BM MSS ADD 62888.

126. Lytton Strachey to J.M. Keynes, letter dated February 1, 1916, Keynes Papers, Volume V.

127. For a discussion of the passage of the Labouchere Amendment, see Jeffrey Weeks, *Coming Out,* pp. 11-22.

128. Lytton Strachey to J.M. Keynes, letter dated September 17, 1907, Keynes Papers, Volume IV.

129. Weeks, *Coming Out,* p. 133.

130. Richard Ellmann, *Oscar Wilde* (New York: Alfred A. Knopf, 1988) p. 389; Weeks, *Coming Out,* p. 40.

131. Lytton Strachey to Roger Senhouse, letter dated December 10, 1926, Berg, ALS 366.

132. For a discussion of Carpenter, see Weeks, *Coming Out,* pp. 68-83.

133. Eve K. Sedgwick, *Epistemology of the Closet* (Berkeley: University of California Press, 1990), p. 175.

134. Lytton Strachey, "The Springalt Page," 1921(?), BM MSS, unbound.

135. Quoted in Carrington's poem to Strachey, August 18, 1916, BM MSS ADD 62888.

136. Lytton Strachey, "Ascensions," poem dated 1905(?), BM MSS, unbound.

137. There were a few "scares" in which rumors circulated about the Apostles' use of Greek studies to conceal homosexual behavior, hence Keynes's warnings to Strachey to use caution in their correspondence. Seth Koven refers to the impact of the Wilde trials, which led to a backlash against all forms of homoeroticism that in the Victorian era would have been acceptable. See Koven, "From Rough Lads to Hooligans: Boy Life, National Culture, and Social Reform," in Andrew Parker et al., eds., *Nationalisms and Sexualities* (New York: Routledge, 1992), p. 375.

138. Dollimore, *Sexual Dissidence,* pp. 338-339.

139. Strachey's introduction to George H. Rylands' *Words and Poetry,* p. 40.

140. Lytton Strachey, "Liverpool Diary," dated March 20, 1898, reprinted in Holroyd, *Lytton Strachey by Himself,* p. 104.

141. Forster's 1961 "Terminal Note" to *Maurice,* p. 254.

Chapter 3

1. Gerald Shove to Lytton Strachey, n.d., British Museum MSS ADD 60697 (hereafter referred to as BM MSS).

2. Carolyn Heilbrun, *Toward a Recognition of Androgyny* (New York: Alfred A. Knopf, 1973), p. 115.

3. Lytton Strachey, "69 Lancaster Gate," essay delivered before the Blooms-bury Memoir Club, June 1922; reprinted in Michael Holroyd, ed., *Lytton Strachey by Himself: A Self-Portrait* (London: Vintage, 1994), p. 25.

4. Ibid., p. 25.

5. Ibid., p. 20.

6. Lady Jane Strachey, diary entry for March 22, 1886, MSS ADD 60718.

7. Lytton Strachey to Lady Jane Strachey, letter written on his thirty-sixth birthday, cited in Michael Holroyd, *Lytton Strachey: A Biography* (Harmondsworth, Middlesex: Penguin, 1987), p. 631.

8. Lady Strachey to Philippa Strachey, letter dated March 8, 1900, MSS ADD 60718.

9. Strachey, "69 Lancaster Gate," in Holroyd, *Lytton Strachey by Himself*, p. 28.

10. Lytton Strachey, "Songs of Animals, Fishes, and Birds," 1887, MSS, unbound.

11. Lytton to James Strachey, letter dated January 2, 1913, MSS ADD 60709.

12. Lytton Strachey to Lady Strachey, postcard dated December 31, 1917, India Office Library MSS Eur F127/341.

13. J.M. Keynes to Duncan Grant, letter dated October 1, 1910, BM MSS ADD 58120.

14. Lytton Strachey to J.M. Keynes, cited in Holroyd, *Lytton Strachey: A Biography*, p. 39.

15. Lytton Strachey, "Something Wrong," 1902(?), BM MSS, unbound.

16. Lytton Strachey, *A Son of Heaven,* an original play, dated 1913, BM MSS, unbound.

17. Lady Strachey to Lytton, cited in Michael Holroyd, *Lytton Strachey: The New Biography* (New York: Farrar, Straus, and Giroux, 1994), p. 441.

18. Philippa to Lytton Strachey, letter dated ?, 1892 , BM MSS ADD 60727, and Marjorie to Lytton Strachey, letter dated ?, 1890, BM MSS ADD 60722.

19. Lytton to Philippa Strachey, letter dated April 23, 1906, BM MSS ADD 60720.

20. Marjorie to James Strachey, letter dated March 14, 1911, BM MSS ADD 60722.

21. Lytton to Philippa Strachey, letter dated September 1, 1906, BM MSS ADD 60720.

22. Lytton to Philippa Strachey, letter dated September 4, 1911, BM MSS ADD 60720.

23. Philippa to Lytton Strachey, letter dated February 28, 1895, BM MSS ADD 60727.

24. Philippa to Lytton Strachey, letter dated February 25, 1919, BM MSS ADD 60728.

25. Philippa to Lytton Strachey, letter dated February 25, 1919, BM MSS ADD 60728.

26. Lytton to Philippa Strachey, letter dated ?, 1919, BM MSS ADD 60721.

27. Steven Mintz, *A Prison of Expectations: The Family in Victorian Culture* (New York: New York University Press, 1983), pp. 148-151.

28. Philippa to Lytton Strachey, letter dated November 6, 1895, BM MSS ADD 60727.

29. Lytton Strachey, "69 Lancaster Gate," in Holroyd, *Lytton Strachey by Himself*, pp. 26-27.

30. See the letters between Lytton Strachey and Dorothy Bussy, Raymond H. Taylor Collection, Department of Rare Books and Special Collections, Princeton University Library.

31. Pernel to Lytton Strachey, letter dated October 19, 1922, BM MSS ADD 60725.

32. Lytton Strachey to J.M. Keynes, letter dated December 8, 1906, King's College, Cambridge MSS, Keynes Papers, Volume II (hereafter referred to as Keynes Papers).

33. René Girard, cited in Eve Kosofsky Sedgwick, *Between Men: English Literature and Male Homosocial Desire* (New York: Columbia University Press, 1985), pp. 21-22.

34. Leonard Woolf to Lytton Strachey, letter dated July 30, 1905, Leonard Woolf Papers, University of Sussex Special Collections (hereafter referred to as Woolf Papers).

35. Sir Osbert Sitwell, a press clipping in which he describes the Strachey sisters, BM MSS ADD 60654.

36. Pernel to Lytton Strachey, letter dated February 1, 1904, BM MSS ADD 60725.

37. Pernel to Lytton Strachey, letter dated December 9, 1900, BM MSS ADD 60725.

38. Lytton Strachey to Duncan Grant, letter dated February 20, 1907, BM MSS ADD 57932.

39. Lytton Strachey to Duncan Grant, letter dated May 22, 1907, BM MSS ADD 57932.

40. Lytton Strachey to Duncan Grant, letter dated May 22, 1907, BM MSS ADD 57932.

41. Lytton to James Strachey, letter dated May 19, 1907, BM MSS ADD 60706.

42. Bernard Swithinbank to Lytton Strachey, letter dated February 22, 1907, BM MSS ADD 60731.

43. For a history of women at Cambridge, see Rita McWilliams-Tullberg, *Women at Cambridge: A Men's University—Though of a Mixed Type* (London: Victor Gallancz Ltd., 1975).

44. J.M. Keynes to Duncan Grant, letter dated February 16, 1909, BM MSS ADD 58120.

45. Lytton Strachey to Duncan Grant, letter dated September 7, 1908, BM MSS ADD 57932.

46. Walter Ong, cited in Sandra Gilbert and Susan Gubar, *No Man's Land: The Place of the Woman Writer in the Twentieth Century*, Volume I: *The War of the Words* (New Haven, CT: Yale University Press, 1988), p. 243.

47. Lytton Strachey, notebook entry, n.d., BM MSS, unbound.

48. Lytton Strachey, "Does Absence Make the Heart Grow Fonder?" Apostle paper delivered to the Society on November 19, 1904, BM MSS, unbound.

49. Lytton Strachey, "Should We Have Elected Conybeare?" Apostle paper delivered to the Society on November 14, 1903, BM MSS, unbound.

50. Dadie Rylands to Lytton Strachey, letter dated March 3, 1925, BM MSS ADD 60695.

51. Lytton Strachey to Duncan Grant, letter dated February 25, 1906, BM MSS ADD 57932.

52. Ibid.

53. Lytton Strachey, "Curious Manuscript Discovered in Morocco and Now Printed for the First Time," n.d., BM MSS, unbound.

54. Lytton Strachey to Duncan Grant, letter dated March 11, 1906, BM MSS ADD 57932.

55. James to Lytton Strachey, letter dated May 4, 1910, BM MSS ADD 60708.

56. J.M. Keynes to Lytton Strachey, letter dated January 10, 1906, Keynes Papers, Volume II.

57. Lytton Strachey to J.M. Keynes, letter dated January 24, 1906, Keynes Papers, Volume II.

58. J.M. Keynes to Lytton Strachey, letter dated August 20, 1905, Keynes Papers, Volume I.

59. Lytton Strachey to J.M. Keynes, letter dated September 7, 1905, Keynes Papers, Volume I.

60. Ibid.

61. J.M. Keynes to Duncan Grant, letter dated August 8, 1908, BM MSS ADD 58120.

62. Lytton Strachey to Duncan Grant, letter dated February 5, 1906, BM MSS ADD 57932.

63. Walter Lamb to Lytton Strachey, letter dated February 23, 1907, BM MSS ADD 60675.

64. Lytton Strachey, "Shall We Take the Pledge?" Apostle paper, delivered to the Society on December 2, 1905, BM MSS, unbound.

65. Lytton Strachey to Leonard Woolf, letter dated July 1902, Woolf Papers.

66. Ibid.

67. Lytton Strachey to Duncan Grant, letter dated March 11, 1906, BM MSS ADD 57932.

68. Lytton Strachey to Duncan Grant, letter dated February 6, 1906, BM MSS ADD 57932.

69. Leonard Woolf to Lytton Strachey, letter dated May 19, 1907, Woolf Papers.

70. James Strachey to Duncan Grant, letter dated September 1, 1908, BM MSS ADD 60713.

71. James Strachey to Duncan Grant, letter dated April 16, 1909, BM MSS ADD 60713.

72. For a discussion of the James Strachey–Rupert Brooke "affair," see Murray H. Sherman, "Lytton and James Strachey: Biography and Psychoanalysis," in Norman Kiell, ed., *Blood Brothers: Siblings As Writers* (New York: International Universities Press, 1984), pp. 329-364.

73. J.M. Keynes to Duncan Grant, letter dated April 17, 1913, BM MSS ADD 58120.

74. Lytton Strachey to Virginia Stephen, letter dated August 24, 1908, reprinted in Leonard Woolf and James Strachey, eds., *Virginia Woolf and Lytton Strachey: Letters* (New York: Harcourt, Brace and Co., 1956), p. 14.

75. Lytton Strachey to Virginia Stephen, letter dated September 27, 1908, in Ibid., p. 17.

76. Lytton Strachey to Virginia Stephen, letter dated November 8, 1912, in Ibid., p. 54.

77. Lytton to James Strachey, letter dated March 9, 1909, BM MSS ADD 60707.

78. Leonard Woolf to Lytton Strachey, letter dated February 1, 1909, Woolf Papers.

79. Ibid.

80. Lytton Strachey to Leonard Woolf, letter dated February 19, 1909, Leonard Woolf Papers.

81. Ibid.

82. Lytton Strachey to Virginia Stephen, letter dated February 17, 1909, in Woolf and Strachey, *Letters,* p. 38.

83. Virginia Woolf, diary entry for December 14, 1929, reprinted in Anne Olivier Bell, ed., *The Diary of Virginia Woolf,* Volume III (London: Harcourt Brace Jovanovich, 1977), pp. 272-273.

84. Virginia Woolf, diary entry for November 28, 1929, reprinted in Leonard Woolf, ed., *A Writer's Diary: Being Extracts from the Diary of Virginia Woolf* (London: Hogarth Press, 1954), p. 138.

85. Virginia Woolf made this reference to Strachey in a letter to Molly MacCarthy, dated March 1912, cited in Nigel Nicolson and Joanne Trautmann, eds., *The Letters of Virginia Woolf,* Volume I (New York: Harcourt Brace Jovanovich, 1975), p. 492.

86. Clive Bell to Lytton Strachey, letter dated August 9, 1908, BM MSS ADD 60655.

87. Lytton Strachey to Virginia Woolf, letter dated February 25, 1916, regarding *The Voyage Out,* in Woolf and Strachey, *Letters,* p. 73.

88. Virginia Stephen to Lytton Strachey, letter dated November 20, 1908, in Ibid., p. 22.

89. Virginia Stephen to Lytton Strachey, letter dated January 28, 1909, in Ibid., p. 32.

90. Virginia Woolf to Lytton Strachey, letter dated May 21, 1912, in Ibid., p. 48.

91. Lytton Strachey to J.M. Keynes, letter dated January 30, 1907, Keynes Papers, Volume III.

92. Lytton Strachey to Leonard Woolf, letter dated February 19, 1909, Woolf Papers.

93. Vanessa Bell to Lytton Strachey, letter dated August 27, 1908, BM MSS ADD 60655.

94. Lytton to James Strachey, letter dated May 30, 1914, BM MSS ADD 60710.

95. Lytton Strachey to Clive Bell, letter dated October 25, 1915, King's College, Cambridge MSS, unbound (hereafter referred to as King's MSS).

96. Lytton Strachey, "Monday June 26 1916," reprinted in Holroyd, *Lytton Strachey by Himself,* p. 142.

97. Ibid., p. 144.

98. Ibid., p. 149.

99. Lytton to James Strachey, describing Lady Ottoline, letter dated November 18, 1910, BM MSS ADD 60708.

100. Lytton Strachey to Duncan Grant, letter dated April 6, 1910, BM MSS ADD 57932.

101. Holroyd, *Lytton Strachey: A Biography*, p. 453. This is Henry Lamb's account.

102. Henry Lamb to Lytton Strachey, describing Lady Ottoline's concern for Strachey, letter dated April 22, 1911, BM MSS ADD 60673.

103. Holroyd, *Lytton Strachey: A Biography*, p. 497.

104. Ibid.

105. Lady Ottoline's descriptions of Strachey, in Ibid., pp. 443-455.

106. Ibid., p. 454.

107. Ibid., p. 463.

108. Lytton to James Strachey, letter dated November 5, 1909, BM MSS ADD 60708.

109. Lytton to James Strachey, letter dated October 2, 1912, BM MSS ADD 60709.

110. Lytton to James Strachey, letter dated October 2, 1912, BM MSS ADD 60709.

111. Dora Carrington to Noel Carrington, letter dated December 27, 1916, cited in Holroyd, *Lytton Strachey: A Biography*, p. 637.

112. Maureen Connett, "Carrington," *Bedfordshire Magazine*, 21(Autumn 1987):71.

113. For details of their nighttime encounter, see Holroyd, *Lytton Strachey: A Biography*, p. 634.

114. Ibid.

115. Dora Carrington to Philippa Strachey, letter dated February 1932, BM MSS, unbound.

116. See the chapter on Bloomsbury in Heilbrun, *Toward a Recognition of Androgyny*.

117. Dora Carrington to Lytton Strachey, letter dated June 4, 1916, BM MSS ADD 62888.

118. Lytton Strachey to Dora Carrington, letter dated June ?, 1916, BM MSS ADD 62888.

119. Lytton Strachey to Clive and Vanessa Bell, letter dated November 6, 1917, BM MSS ADD 71104.

120. Lytton Strachey to Virginia Woolf, letter dated December 21, 1917, in Woolf and Strachey, *Letters*, p. 89.

121. Carrington described the sex act in these terms in a letter, dated April 16, 1915, to Mark Gertler, who was actively seeking to bed her at the time. Cited in Noel Carrington, ed., *Carrington: Letters and Extracts from Her Diaries* (London: Cape, 1970), p. 17.

122. Dora Carrington, diary entry, cited in Holroyd, *Lytton Strachey: A Biography*, p. 683.

123. Lytton Strachey to Dora Carrington, letter dated March 23, 1917, BM MSS ADD 62888.

124. Dora Carrington to Lytton Strachey, letter dated July 5, 1918, BM MSS ADD 62889.

125. Dora Carrington to Lytton Strachey, letter dated August 18, 1916, BM MSS ADD 62888.

126. Dora Carrington to Lytton Strachey, letter dated May 14, 1921, cited in Gretchen Gerzina, *Carrington: A Life* (New York: W.W. Norton and Co., 1989), pp. 167-168.

127. Dora Carrington, "Her Book," unpublished diary, 1932, BM MSS, unbound.

128. Dora Carrington to Alix Strachey, letter dated April 15, 1921, BM MSS ADD 65158.

129. James Doggart to Lytton Strachey, letter dated December 30, 1921, BM MSS ADD 60665.

130. Lytton Strachey to Dora Carrington, letter dated September 27, 1919, BM MSS ADD 62891.

131. Lytton Strachey to Dora Carrington, letter dated August 25, 1929, BM MSS ADD 62895.

132. Dora Carrington, "Her Book," unpublished diary, 1928-1932, BM MSS, unbound.

133. Dora Carrington to Lytton Strachey, letter dated May ?, 1921, BM MSS ADD 62892.

134. Lytton Strachey to Dora Carrington, letter dated May 15, 1921, BM MSS ADD 62892.

135. Ralph Partridge to Lytton Strachey, letter dated May 17, 1921, BM MSS ADD 60690.

136. Dora Carrington to Lytton Strachey, letter dated February 14, 1922, BM MSS ADD 62893.

137. Dora Carrington to Lytton Strachey, letter dated ?, 1922, BM MSS, unsorted letters.

138. Cited in Gerzina, *Carrington: A Life,* p. 187.

139. Lytton Strachey to Dora Carrington, letter dated ?, 1922—"Yes, indeed, our triangular life is a happy one. May it long last!"—BM MSS, uncataloged letter.

140. Carrington to Frances Marshall, letter dated ?, 1926, cited in Carrington, *Carrington: Letters and Extracts,* pp. 332-333.

141. Lytton Strachey to Dora Carrington, letter dated April 17, 1930, BM MSS ADD 62895.

142. Dora Carrington to Lytton Strachey, letter dated May 27, 1919, BM MSS ADD 62890.

143. Dora Carrington to Lytton Strachey, letter dated June 26, 1919, BM MSS ADD 62890.

144. Lytton Strachey to Dora Carrington, letter dated June ?, 1919, BM MSS ADD 62890.

145. Gerzina, *Carrington: A Life,* p. 304.

146. Dora Carrington to Lytton Strachey, letter dated November 4, 1929, BM MSS ADD 62895.

147. Dora Carrington to Lytton Strachey, letter dated July 21, 1920, BM MSS ADD 62892.

148. Lytton Strachey to Dora Carrington, letter dated July 22, 1919, BM MSS ADD 62890.

149. Dora Carrington to Lytton Strachey, letter dated September 9, 1919, BM MSS ADD 62891.

150. Dora Carrington to Lytton Strachey, letter dated May 2, 1921, BM MSS ADD 62892.

151. Virginia Woolf, diary entry for March 17, 1932, cited in Gerzina, *Carrington: A Life,* p. xxiv.

152. Connett, "Carrington," pp. 69-74.

153. Final entry in Carrington's diary, "Her Book," BM MSS, unbound.

154. Ruth Brandon, *The New Women and the Old Men: Love, Sex, and the Woman Question* (New York: W.W. Norton and Co., 1990), p. 251.

155. See Holroyd, *Lytton Strachey: A Biography,* pp. 635-644, for a discussion of Carrington's sexuality.

156. Ibid., p. 870.

157. Brandon, *New Women and Old Men,* p. 261.

158. Elaine Showalter, *A Literature of Their Own: British Women Novelists from Bronte to Lessing* (Princeton, NJ: Princeton University Press, 1977), p. 273.

159. Gerzina, *Carrington: A Life,* pp. 68-69.

160. Gilbert and Gubar, *No Man's Land,* Volume I.

161. Virginia Woolf describes Strachey's "invalidish" and "old maid" mannerisms in a diary entry for November 15, 1919, reprinted in Bell, *The Diary of Virginia Woolf,* Volume I, pp. 311-312.

162. Lytton Strachey to J.T. Sheppard, letter dated April 7, 1903, King's MSS, unbound.

Chapter 4

1. Leonard Woolf, quoted in Richard Shone, *Bloomsbury Portraits* (Oxford: Phaidon, 1976), p. 137.

2. For a discussion of British modernism, see Norman F. Cantor, *Twentieth Century Culture: Modernism to Deconstruction* (New York: Peter Lang, 1988); Hugh Kenner, *A Sinking Island: The Modern British Writers* (New York: Alfred A. Knopf, 1988); Charles Harrison, *English Art and Modernism 1900-1939* (Bloomington: Indiana University Press, 1981); Michael H. Levenson, *A Genealogy of Modernism* (Cambridge: Cambridge University Press, 1984).

3. See Rita Felski's discussion of Stallybrass and the problematic term "modern," in *The Gender of Modernity* (Cambridge, MA: Harvard University Press, 1995), Introduction.

4. See the introduction to Ulysses D'Aquila, *Bloomsbury and Modernism* (New York: Peter Lang, 1989).

5. Wyndham Lewis, quoted in Levenson, *Genealogy of Modernism,* p. 76.

6. Virginia Woolf's now famous comment that "on or about December 1910 human character changed" first appeared in her 1924 essay, "Mr. Bennett and Mrs. Brown," reprinted in Virginia Woolf, *Collected Essays,* Volume I (London: Hogarth Press, 1966), p. 320. For a larger discussion of the meaning of her statement, see Peter Stansky, *On or About December 1910: Early Bloomsbury and Its Intimate World* (Cambridge, MA: Harvard University Press, 1996).

7. Lytton Strachey to J.M. Keynes, cited in Michael Holroyd, *Lytton Strachey: A Biography* (Harmondsworth, Middlesex: Penguin, 1987), p. 312.

8. Perry Meisel, *The Myth of the Modern: A Study in British Literature and Criticism After 1850* (New Haven, CT: Yale University Press, 1987); D'Aquila, *Bloomsbury and Modernism.*

9. Virginia Woolf, cited in John Halperin, *"Eminent Victorians* and History," *Virginia Quarterly Review,* 56(3)(Summer 1980):436.

10. Roger Fry, cited in D'Aquila, *Bloomsbury and Modernism,* p. 4.

11. Mortimer's review, cited in Michael Holroyd, *Lytton Strachey: The New Biography* (New York: Farrar, Straus and Giroux, 1994), p. 605.

12. Edward Said, *The Word, the Text, and the Critic* (Cambridge, MA: Harvard University Press, 1983), pp. 19-20.

13. Virginia Woolf, quoted in Charles Hession, *John Maynard Keynes: A Personal Biography of the Man Who Revolutionized Capitalism and the Way We Live* (New York: Macmillan, 1984), p. 97.

14. Ibid., p. 103.

15. Wyndham Lewis, cited in Dennis Brown, *The Modernist Self in Twentieth Century English Literature: A Study in Self-Fragmentation* (New York: St. Martin's Press, 1989), p. 6.

16. Ibid., p. 99.

17. Ibid., p. 74.

18. Virginia Woolf to Lytton Strachey, letter dated October 4, 1908, cited in Nigel Nicolson and Joanne Trautmann, eds., *The Letters of Virginia Woolf,* Volume I, *1888-1912* (London: Harcourt Brace Jovanovich, 1977), p. 369.

19. Lytton Strachey, *Eminent Victorians* (London: The Folio Press, 1967), preface, p. 22.

20. Ibid., pp. 21-22.

21. Lytton Strachey to J.T. Sheppard, letter dated March 17, 1906, King's College, Cambridge MSS, unbound (hereafter referred to as King's MSS).

22. Strachey, *Eminent Victorians,* p. 22.

23. Henry Lamb to Lytton Strachey, upon reading a draft of *Eminent Victorians,* letter dated October 10, 1915, British Museum MSS ADD 60674 (hereafter referred to as BM MSS).

24. Lytton Strachey to Virginia Woolf, letter dated November 8, 1912, reprinted in Leonard Woolf and James Strachey, eds., *Virginia Woolf and Lytton Strachey: Letters* (New York: Harcourt Brace and Co., 1956), p. 54.

25. Strachey wrote in *Eminent Victorians* that Arnold's legs were too short for his body. When questioned about this, he replied that "if they weren't, they ought to have been." Cited in John Halperin, *"Eminent Victorians* and History," *Virginia Quarterly Review,* 56(3)(Summer 1980):442.

26. Richard Altick, *Lives and Letters: A History of Literary Biography in England and America* (New York: Alfred A. Knopf, 1965), p. 281. See Chapter 9, "The Stracheyan Revolution."

27. Ibid., p. 290. The term "new biography" was first used by Virginia Woolf in her 1927 review of Harold Nicolson's *Some People.* She credited Strachey's *Eminent Victorians* as the first example of the new biography.

28. Virginia Woolf on the "new biography," cited in Ruth Hoberman, *Modernizing Lives: Experiments in English Biography 1918-1939* (Carbondale: Southern Illinois University Press, 1987), p. 199.

29. Strachey's essay on Gibbon and the art of history writing, cited in Hoberman, *Modernizing Lives,* p. 41.

30. Ibid., p. 35.

31. Paul Fussell, *The Great War and Modern Memory* (London: Oxford University Press, 1975), p. 35.

32. David Garnett, cited in Hoberman, *Modernizing Lives,* p. 35.

33. Lytton Strachey to Virginia Woolf, letter dated November 8, 1912, in Strachey and Woolf, *Letters*, p. 54.

34. Fussell, *The Great War*, p. 3.

35. Ibid., p. 188.

36. Rupert Brooke refers to Strachey and the other Higher Sodomites in his war poem "Peace" (1914): "leave behind a world grown old and cold and weary / leave the sick hearts that honour could not move / and half-men, and their dirty songs and dreary / and all the little emptiness of love." Reprinted in Geoffrey Keynes, ed., *The Poetical Works of Rupert Brooke* (London: Faber and Faber, 1977), p. 19.

37. Lytton Strachey, "Sennacherib and Rupert Brooke," Apostle essay, 1915, BM MSS, unbound; also reprinted in Paul Levy, ed., *Lytton Strachey: The Really Interesting Question and Other Papers* (London: Weidenfeld and Nicolson, 1971), pp. 42-44.

38. Lytton Strachey in his statement before the Hampstead Advisory Committee, March 7, 1916, reprinted in Michael Holroyd, ed., *Lytton Strachey by Himself: A Self-Portrait* (London: Vintage, 1994), p. 138.

39. Lytton to James Strachey, cited in David Gadd, *The Loving Friends: A Portrait of Bloomsbury* (London: Hogarth Press, 1974), p. 104.

40. Levy, *Lytton Strachey: The Really Interesting Question*, p. 14.

41. Holroyd, *Lytton Strachey: A Biography*, p. 571.

42. Strachey's confrontation with the war committee and his subsequent physical examinations are discussed in Ibid., p. 571.

43. Cyril Connolly, cited in Holroyd, *Lytton Strachey: A Biography*, pp. 731-732.

44. Strachey to Mary Hutchinson, quoted in Noel Annan, *Our Age: The Generation That Made Post-War Britain* (London: Fontana, 1990), p. 115.

45. Holroyd, *Lytton Strachey by Himself*, p. 110.

46. George Steiner, "Eros and Idiom," in *On Difficulty and Other Essays* (New York: Oxford University Press, 1978), p. 117.

47. George Piggford, "Camp Sites: Forster and the Biographies of Queer Bloomsbury," in Robert K. Martin and George Piggford, eds., *Queer Forster* (Chicago: Chicago University Press, 1997), pp. 89-112.

48. Steiner, "Eros and Idiom," p. 118.

49. David Eberly and Christopher Reed, cited in Stephen Barber, "Lip-Reading: Woolf's Secret Encounters," in Eve Kosofsky Sedgwick, ed., *Novel Gazing: Queer Readings in Fiction* (London: Duke University Press, 1997), p. 415.

50. Linda Hutcheon, "Revolt and the Ideal in Bloomsbury," *English Studies in Canada,* 1(Spring 1979):78-93.

51. Campbell, cited in Ibid., p. 78.

52. Lewis, cited in Ibid., p. 79.

53. D.H. Lawrence, letter to David Garnett, dated April 19, 1915, cited in S.P. Rosenbaum, ed., *The Bloomsbury Group: A Collection of Memoirs, Commentary, and Criticism* (Toronto: University of Toronto Press, 1975), p. 369.

54. E.M. Forster, cited in Hutcheon, "Revolt and the Ideal," p. 92.

55. Lytton to James Strachey, letter dated February 5, 1914, BM MSS ADD 60709.

56. Lytton Strachey to Clive Bell, letter dated August 10, 1918, BM MSS ADD 71104.

57. David Garnett to Lytton Strachey, letter dated June 16, 1925, BM MSS ADD 60667.

58. Keynes to Strachey, cited in Robert Skidelsky, *John Maynard Keynes,* Volume I: *Hopes Betrayed, 1883-1920* (London: Macmillan, 1983), p. 164.

59. Lytton Strachey, "Diary of an Athenian, 400 B.C.," 1900, reprinted in Levy, *The Really Interesting Question,* p. 141.

60. Virginia Woolf, "Old Bloomsbury," reprinted in Jeanne Schulkind, ed., *Moments of Being* (London: Grafton Books, 1989), p. 211.

61. Ibid., pp. 211-213.

62. Ibid., pp. 212-213.

63. Carolyn Heilbrun cites Quentin Bell in *Toward a Recognition of Androgyny* (New York: Alfred A. Knopf, 1973), p. 127; Jan Marsh, *Bloomsbury Women: Distinct Figures in Life and Art* (New York: Henry Holt and Co., 1996), p. 6.

64. Jane Marcus, "Liberty, Sorority, Misogyny," in Carolyn Heilbrun and Margaret Higonnet, eds., *The Representation of Women in Fiction* (Baltimore, MD: Johns Hopkins University Press, 1983), p. 61.

65. Ibid., p. 68.

66. Bonnie Kime Scott, ed., *The Gender of Modernism: A Critical Anthology* (Bloomington: Indiana University Press, 1990). See Scott's introduction.

67. Ibid.

68. Suzette Henke, "(En)Gendering Modernism: Virginia Woolf and Djuna Barnes," in Kevin Dettmar, ed., *Rereading the New: A Backward Glance at Modernism* (Ann Arbor: University of Michigan Press, 1992), p. 325.

69. Ibid., p. 326.

70. Sandra Gilbert and Susan Gubar, *No Man's Land: The Place of the Woman Writer in the Twentieth Century,* Volume II: *Sexchanges* (New Haven, CT: Yale University Press, 1989), p. xi.

71. Ibid., p. xi. Ezra Pound's statement of the phallic mission of modernism.

72. D.H. Lawrence, "A Propos" to *Lady Chatterley's Lover* (New York: Bantam Books, 1983), p. 352; and Scott's introduction to Lawrence in *The Gender of Modernism,* p. 219. For a discussion of Lawrence's and Strachey's mutual aversion, see Holroyd, *Lytton Strachey: A Biography,* pp. 606-610. Lawrence also tried to rescue David Garnett from what he called the "beetles"—Duncan Grant, Strachey, and Keynes (the homosexual members of the group).

73. Gilbert and Gubar, *No Man's Land,* Volume I: *The War of the Words* (1988), p. 156.

74. Ibid., p. 344.

75. Ibid., p. 149.

76. Ibid., p. 149.

77. Anne Olivier Bell, ed., *The Diary of Virginia Woolf,* Volume 3, *1925-1930* (London: Harcourt Brace Jovanovich, 1980), diary entry for June 15, 1929, p. 231.

78. Virginia Woolf, diary entry for October 14, 1922, reprinted in Bell, *The Diary of Virginia Woolf,* Volume 2, p. 207.

79. Bell, *The Diary of Virginia Woolf,* Volume 1, entry for January 24, 1919, pp. 235-236.

80. Bell, *The Diary of Virginia Woolf,* Volume 3, entry for June 15, 1929, p. 234.

81. Gilbert and Gubar, *No Man's Land,* Volume I, p. 161.

82. Ibid., Volume II, p. 344.

83. Heilbrun, *Toward a Recognition of Androgyny*, p. 149.

84. Virginia Woolf to Vita Sackville-West, describing her new type of biography, letter dated October 9, 1927, in Nicolson and Trautmann, *Letters*, Volume III, p. 429.

85. See Gilbert and Gubar's discussion of *Orlando* in *No Man's Land*, Volume II, Chapter 4, "Cross-Dressing and Redressing: Transvestism As Metaphor," pp. 334-335.

86. Lytton Strachey, *Elizabeth and Essex: A Tragic History* (London: Chatto and Windus, 1928), pp. 24-26.

87. Bell, *The Diary of Virginia Woolf*, Volume 3, entry for November 28, 1928, p. 208.

88. Hoberman, *Modernizing Lives*, p. 53.

89. Alice Fox, cited in Ibid., p. 183.

90. Lytton Strachey, "To The Unknown," poem dated February 16, 1918, BM MSS ADD 71104.

91. Strachey's essay on "Walpole's Letters" in *The Athenaeum*, August 15, 1919, states that "the really essential element in the letter writer's make-up is a certain strain of femininity," BM MSS, unbound.

92. Barbara Fassler, "Theories of Homosexuality As Sources of Bloomsbury's Androgyny," *Signs*, 5(2)(1979):237-251.

93. Virginia Woolf, *A Room of One's Own* (London: Harcourt Brace Jovanovich, 1929), p. 104.

94. Heilbrun, *Toward a Recognition of Androgyny*, p. 123.

95. Catherine Stimpson, "The Androgyne and the Homosexual," in *The Androgyny Papers*, a special issue of *Women's Studies*, 2(2)(1974):239.

96. Elaine Showalter, *A Literature of Their Own: British Women Novelists from Bronte to Lessing* (Princeton, NJ: Princeton University Press, 1977), p. 150.

97. Cynthia Secor, "Androgyny: An Early Reappraisal," *The Androgyny Papers*, a special issue of *Women's Studies*, 2(2)(1974):163.

98. Felski, *The Gender of Modernity*, p. 92.

99. The Criminal Law Amendment Act punished acts of "gross indecency" committed by men in public or private. Women were excluded from this law.

100. See Felski's discussion of the limits of androgyny, *The Gender of Modernity*, pp. 91, 104.

101. Ibid., p. 109.

102. Lytton Strachey, *Elizabeth and Essex*, pp. 9-10.

103. David Garnett to Lytton Strachey, letter dated March 18, 1916, BM MSS ADD 60667.

104. Lytton Strachey to Clive Bell, letter dated February 18, 1918, BM MSS ADD 71104.

105. Phyllis Rose, cited in Gilbert and Gubar, *No Man's Land*, Volume II, p. 324.

106. Ibid., p. 334.

107. Marjorie Garber, "The Chic of Araby: Transvestism, Transsexualism, and the Erotics of Cultural Appropriation," in Julia Epstein and Kristina Straub, eds., *Body Guards: The Cultural Politics of Gender Ambiguity* (New York: Routledge, 1991), p. 239.

108. See Elaine Showalter's criticisms of feminist scholars who argue that hysteria was a self-conscious choice, a rebellion against conventional femininity, in her

introduction to *The Female Malady: Women, Madness, and English Culture, 1830-1980* (New York: Penguin, 1987).

109. Bell, *The Diary of Virginia Woolf,* Volume 3, entry for November 27, 1925, p. 47.

110. Ibid., entry for June 16, 1925, p. 31.

111. Toril Moi, "Representations of Patriarchy: Sexuality and Epistemology in Freud's Dora," in *In Dora's Case: Freud-Hysteria-Feminism* (New York: Columbia University Press, 1985), p. 192.

112. For a discussion of male neurasthenia, see Janet Oppenheim, *"Shattered Nerves": Doctors, Patients, and Depression in Victorian England* (Oxford: Oxford University Press, 1991).

113. Lytton to James Strachey, letter dated March 9, 1909, BM MSS ADD 60707.

114. Lytton Strachey to Duncan Grant, letter dated November 4, 1908, BM MSS ADD 57932.

115. Lytton Strachey to Duncan Grant, letter dated August 23, 1909, BM MSS ADD 57932.

116. Lytton to James Strachey, letter dated October 2, 1912, BM MSS ADD 60709.

117. Alix Strachey to her husband, James, discussing Lytton's attitude toward psychoanalysis, letter dated February 9, 1925, reprinted in Perry Meisel and Walter Kendrick, eds., *Bloomsbury/Freud: The Letters of James and Alix Strachey, 1924-1925* (London: Chatto and Windus, 1986), pp. 198-199.

118. Alix to James Strachey, letter reprinted in Ibid., p. 309.

119. Lytton Strachey, "The Power of Love: An Interlude," unfinished play, n.d., BM MSS, unbound.

120. Lytton Strachey, *Elizabeth and Essex,* pp. 9-10.

121. Heilbrun, *Toward a Recognition of Androgyny,* p. 136.

122. Ibid., p. 151.

123. Lytton Strachey to Clive Bell, letter dated December 28, 1918, BM MSS ADD 71104.

124. Lytton Strachey, *Eminent Victorians,* p. 139.

125. Lytton Strachey, *Elizabeth and Essex,* p. 11.

126. Strachey's description of Florence Nightingale in *Eminent Victorians,* p. 139.

127. Ibid., p. 127.

128. Ibid., pp. 163-165.

129. Lytton Strachey, *Queen Victoria* (New York: Harcourt, Brace and Company, 1921), p. 91.

130. Lytton Strachey, descriptions of Elizabeth in *Elizabeth and Essex,* pp. 17, 27.

131. Ibid., p. 216.

132. Ibid., p. 23.

133. Ibid., p. 128.

134. Lytton Strachey, *Eminent Victorians,* p. 151.

135. Lytton Strachey, *Elizabeth and Essex,* p. 13.

136. Ibid., p. 263.

137. Strachey's description of Nightingale in her old age in *Eminent Victorians,* p. 172.

138. Lytton Strachey, *Queen Victoria,* p. 291.

139. Lytton Strachey, *Elizabeth and Essex,* pp. 22-23.

140. Strachey's description of Essex in *Elizabeth and Essex,* p. 4.

141. J.M. Keynes to Lytton Strachey, letter dated December 3, 1928, King's College, Cambridge MSS, Keynes Papers, Volume V.

142. Lytton Strachey, *Elizabeth and Essex,* p. 26.

143. Ibid., the descriptions of Elizabeth's ailments are on pp. 19-20, 24.

144. Ibid., p. 20.

145. Lytton to James Strachey, letter dated January 24, 1920, BM MSS ADD 60712.

146. Martin Kallich, *The Psychological Milieu of Lytton Strachey* (New York: Bookman Associates, 1961), p. 131.

147. Ibid., pp. 42-43.

148. Meisel and Kendrick, *Bloomsbury/Freud,* p. 309.

149. Freud to Strachey, letter dated December 25, 1928, reprinted in Meisel and Kendrick, *Bloomsbury/Freud,* pp. 332-333. (Copyright 1967 A.W. Freud et al., by arrangement with Paterson Marsh Agency, London.)

150. Moi, "Representation of Patriarchy," pp. 191-192.

151. Lytton Strachey, *Queen Victoria,* p. 252.

152. Ibid., p. 371.

153. Ibid.

154. Susan Suleiman, cited in Mark Spilka, *Hemingway's Quarrel with Androgyny* (Lincoln, NE: University of Nebraska Press, 1990), p. 1.

155. Virginia Woolf, *Orlando: A Biography* (New York: Harcourt, Brace and Co., 1928), p. 189.

156. Ibid., p. 138.

157. Virginia Woolf, *A Room of One's Own,* p. 104.

158. JoAnne Blum, *Transcending Gender: The Male/Female Double in Women's Fiction* (Ann Arbor, MI: UMA Research Press, 1988), p. 26.

159. Virginia Woolf, *Between the Acts* (London: Harcourt, Brace and Co., 1941), p. 175.

160. Strachey, *Eminent Victorians,* preface, p. 21.

161. Ibid., p. 165.

162. Virginia Woolf to Pernel Strachey, letter dated December 30, 1931, BM MSS ADD 60734.

Conclusion

1. Lytton Strachey to James Strachey, letter dated January 16, 1914, British Museum MSS ADD 60710 (hereafter referred to as BM MSS).

2. Edmund Wilson's obituary of Strachey is quoted in Julian Symons's review of *Lytton Strachey: A Biography,* by Michael Holroyd, *Times Literary Supplement* (August 26, 1994):4-5.

3. Margaret Cruikshank, "Buggery in Bloomsbury," *Gay Literature* 5(1976):22-24. Also, Strachey once told G.M. Trevelyan that in writing biography, "you must choose people whom you did not much like in order to satirize them—like the Victorians"; letter dated August 1928, BM MSS ADD 60732.

4. Janet Malcolm, "A House of One's Own," *The New Yorker* (June 5, 1995):64.

5. Lytton Strachey to Clive Bell, letter dated June 12, 1908, BM MSS ADD 71104.

6. Piers Brendon, cited in Michael Holroyd, "On the Border-Line Between the New and the Old: Bloomsbury, Biography, and Gerald Brenan," in Joe Law and Linda K. Hughes, eds., *Biographical Passages: Essays in Victorian and Modernist Biography* (Columbia: University of Missouri Press, 2000), p. 40.

7. Lytton Strachey to Saxon Sydney Turner, letter dated August 2, 1903, BM MSS, unbound.

8. After reading drafts of Holroyd's biography of Strachey, David Garnett urged James Strachey to put a stop to the book; letter dated June 29, 1966, BM MSS, unbound. In 1968 Noel Carrington wrote to Alix Strachey after hearing of Russell's plans to make a film of Holroyd's book and called on other living Bloomsbury members to stop the project; letter dated November 17, 1968, BM MSS, unbound. Eventually Holroyd had to agree to certain revisions and omissions and promised to state "categorically" that Lytton was never impotent nor did he have a mother-fixation; Holroyd to James Strachey, letter dated February 16, 1967, BM MSS, unbound.

9. Virginia Woolf, describing "A Bloomsbury Party," cited in S.P. Rosenbaum, ed., *The Bloomsbury Group: A Collection of Memoirs, Commentary, and Criticism* (Toronto: University of Toronto Press, 1975), p. 23.

10. Virginia Woolf, "Old Bloomsbury," cited in Malcolm, "A House of One's Own," p. 58.

11. David Garnett's claim about Carrington's "significance" is quoted in Frances Spalding, "Painting Out Carrington," *The New Yorker* (December 18, 1995):71.

12. Angeline Goreau, review of Michael Holroyd's *Lytton Strachey: A Biography, New York Times Book Review* (June 11, 1995):7.

13. See Angelica Garnett's scathing portrait of Bloomsbury in *Deceived with Kindness: A Bloomsbury Childhood* (London, New York: Harcourt Brace Jovanovich, 1984), which is discussed in Malcolm, "A House of One's Own," pp. 58-79.

14. Gertrude Himmelfarb, cited in Regina Marler, *Bloomsbury Pie: The Making of the Bloomsbury Boom* (New York: Henry Holt and Company, 1997), pp. 90-91.

15. Richard D. Altick, "Eminent Victorianism: What Lytton Strachey Hath Wrought," *The American Scholar,* 64(1)(Winter 1995):81-89.

16. Michael Holroyd records his discussions with James Strachey regarding the impact of Lytton on British society in the preface to the revised edition of *Lytton Strachey: A Biography* (Harmondsworth, Middlesex: Penguin, 1987).

17. Lytton Strachey to Leonard Woolf, letter dated July 18, 1906, Berg Collection, Strachey-Woolf Letters, 112 A.L.S., New York Public Library (hereafter referred to as Berg).

18. Strachey to Leonard Woolf, letter dated June 20, 1907, Berg.

19. Strachey to Leonard Woolf, letter dated February 2, 1906, Berg.

20. Wyndham Lewis, *The Apes of God,* cited in Rosenbaum, *The Bloomsbury Group,* pp. 332-334.

21. Keynes's response to Lewis is cited in Rosenbaum, *The Bloomsbury Group,* p. 390.

22. Rupert Brooke's criticism of Bloomsbury is cited in Ibid., p. 330.

23. Excerpts from the Leavises' attacks on Bloomsbury are cited in Ibid., pp. 387-402.

24. See Michel Foucault, *The History of Sexuality,* Volume I (New York: Vintage Books, 1980), and Peter Gay, *The Bourgeois Experience: Victoria to Freud,* Volume II: *The Tender Passion* (New York: Oxford University Press, 1986).

25. See Strachey's preface to *Eminent Victorians* (London: The Folio Press, 1967).

26. Isabel Fry to Virginia Woolf, letter dated February 22, 1914; Woolf declared that by 1925 "the pale star of the Bugger has been in the ascendant too long." Cited in Anne Olivier Bell, ed., *The Diary of Virginia Woolf,* Volume III (London: Harcourt Brace Jovanovich, 1977), diary entry for April 19, 1925, p. 10.

27. Virginia Woolf, cited in Jan Marsh, *Bloomsbury Women: Distinct Figures in Life and Art* (New York: Henry Holt and Co., 1996), p. 102.

28. Dora Carrington to Alix Strachey, letter dated October 9, 1920, BM MSS ADD 65158.

29. Dora Carrington to Virginia Woolf, letter quoted in Spalding, "Painting Out Carrington," p. 74.

30. J.M. Keynes, "My Early Beliefs," Memoir Club essay, reprinted in Rosenbaum, *The Bloomsbury Group,* p. 61.

31. Duncan Grant's diary entry for 1918, quoted in Malcolm, "A House of One's Own," p. 70.

32. Lytton Strachey to Leonard Woolf, letter dated June 26, 1906, Berg.

33. Lytton Strachey to James Strachey, letter dated March 26, 1914, BM MSS ADD 60710.

34. Lytton's March 1925 vacation with Sprott is described in his letter to Carrington dated March 30, 1925, BM MSS ADD 62894.

35. Lytton Strachey to Dorothy Bussy, letter dated August 23, 1931, Raymond H. Taylor Collection, Princeton University.

36. Lytton Strachey to Leonard Woolf, quoted in Geoffrey Grigson's review of Holroyd's *Lytton Strachey: A Biography, The Listener* (October 12, 1967):473.

37. See Havelock Ellis, *Studies in the Psychopathology of Sex,* Volume I on inversion (New York: Random House, 1903).

38. G.L. Dickinson in an unmailed letter addressed to Ferdinand Schiller, quoted in Dennis Proctor, ed., *The Autobiography of G. Lowes Dickinson* (London: Duckworth, 1973), pp. 10-11.

39. See Elaine Showalter, *Sexual Anarchy: Gender and Culture at the Fin de Siècle* (New York: Viking, 1990), Chapter 9, for a discussion of the gender differentiation model as an alternative to sexology's "invert."

40. Ibid., p. 174.

41. Rita Felski, *The Gender of Modernity* (Cambridge, MA: Harvard University Press, 1995), p. 93.

42. Showalter, *Sexual Anarchy,* p. 176.

43. Elaine Showalter, *A Literature of Their Own: British Women Novelists from Bronte to Lessing* (Princeton, NJ: Princeton University Press, 1977), See Chapter 10, "Virginia Woolf and the Flight into Androgyny."

44. Holroyd, quoted in Cruikshank, "Buggery in Bloomsbury," p. 23.

45. Grigson's review of *Lytton Strachey: A Biography,* p. 473.

46. Judith Butler, cited in Felski, *The Gender of Modernity,* pp. 204-205.

47. F.L. Lucas's obituary for Strachey, "An Artist in History," *The Observer* (January 24, 1932), BM MSS, unbound.

48. Introduction to A.N. Wilson, *Eminent Victorians* (New York: W. W. Norton, 1990).

49. Strachey, preface to *Eminent Victorians,* p. 22.

50. Lytton Strachey to J.T. Sheppard, letter dated September 26, 1902, King's College, Cambridge MSS, unbound.

51. Diary entry for August 3, 1898, reprinted in Michael Holroyd, ed., *Lytton Strachey by Himself: A Self-Portrait* (London: Vintage, 1994), pp. 91-92.

Index

*For Product Safety Concerns and Information please contact
our EU representative GPSR@taylorandfrancis.com Taylor & Francis
Verlag GmbH, Kaufingerstraße 24, 80331 München, Germany*

T - #0130 - 270225 - C0 - 212/152/11 - PB - 9781560233596 - Gloss Lamination